Just a Little Lie

An Alison Kaine Mystery

Kate Allen

New Victoria Publishers

Published by New Victoria Publishers, Inc., a feminist literary and cultural organization, PO Box 27, Norwich, VT 05055-0027

Cover Photo by Judy Sanchez

printed and bound in Canada
1 2   3 4 5   2003   2002   2001   2000 1999

Library of Congress Cataloging-in-Publication Data

Allen, Kate, 1957-
    Just a little lie : an Alison Kaine mystery / by Kate Allen.
        p.   cm.
    ISBN 0-934678-94-4
    I. Title.
    PS3551.L3956J87   1998
    813' .54--dc21   98-27388
                                                                    CIP

I'd like to thank all the women who have gone out of their way to write to me, speak to me and send e-mail. Writing is rather like performing for an audience that is never seen and it is always wonderful to get encouragement from a fan. Thank you. And, as always, a special thanks to the Free Range Chicken Society.

KATE ALLEN has three other books in the Alison Kaine Mystery series:
Tell Me What You Like
Give My Secrets Back
Takes One To Know One

and one mystery featuring phone psychic Marta Goicochea
I Knew You Would Call

Kate is currently working on a mystery about vampires, dykes and cats. To see work in progress or to order her serialization, Gratuitous Sex, visit her web site at **www.users.uswest.net/~kateallen**
or email her at **kateallen@uswest.net**

All of Kate Allen's books, plus many other mysteries, adventure stories, romances and humor are available from:
New Victoria Publishers
PO Box 27
Norwich, VT 05055
800-326-5297
email: **newvic@aol.com**
website: **www.opendoor.com/NewVic/**

or find them at your favorite independent bookstore

Chapter One

Alison Kaine recognized the women as soon as she pulled into the United pickup lane. Five of them this trip—two from California, one from Alabama, and one from Phoenix if she remembered correctly the information her girlfriend, Stacy, had given her. The fifth was from Somewhere On the East Coast, which was the way that people in Denver liked to refer to any city with toll roads and skyscrapers, as if the power of naming was so strong they could make any place past Montana disappear just by withholding it. Westerners were like that.

The two Alison had pegged as the California girls both had an end-of-the-summer tan and blonde hair that had been helped along by the sun or by somebody good enough to make it look as if it had. Alison took an anxious little glance in the vanity mirror. No tan or charming sprinkling of freckles there. Except for skiers nobody had a tan yet in Denver. It had been an unusually long and overcast winter, which had been hard for a population used to a few sunny days a week no matter how deep the snow on the ground. Even now, a lovely spring day in April, Alison knew that snow was still never far from the fickle mind of the weather goddess. She had lived in Denver all her life and had spent a good many Aprils and Mays shaking snow off her blossoming lilacs.

She sighed over her pale, indoor skin but cheered up when she checked out her new, butch haircut. She also liked the look of the silver earcuff that Stacy had given her for her thirty-sixth birthday. She looked just fine, she told herself sternly, and she didn't need to let any surfer girls make her feel inferior before they even said a word. There was plenty of time for them to make her feel inferior later. Everybody's got baggage; part of Alison's was the occasional attack of insecurity.

She sat for a moment behind the wheel of the van, waiting for first contact and then finally realized that even though she had picked them right out of the crowd and they had presumably picked each other out of the crowd, none of them had picked her out of the crowd, even though there was a card with the Wildfire logo stuck up in the corner of the windshield.

She opened the driver's door and stepped out, ignoring some idiot in a

Honda who wanted to jockey a few feet closer to the United sign and thought the whole world should get out of his way so he could do it. She stood for a moment, just testing to see if the leather gaydar was going to kick in without a signal and then pulled her heavy leather jacket after her, slipping her arms into the sleeves with the ease of long practice.

Ding-ding-ding-ding! All four heads snapped to full attention, eyes bright, chins up. The response couldn't have been better. Alison felt as if she'd slapped the blue and red bubble gum machine from her patrol car on top of her head and let it rip. She knew it was childish, but she couldn't help but get a little chuckle out of the way leatherwomen were able to turn the blinders on. You weren't anybody unless you had the jacket.

There was a lot of baggage (the Samsonite kind, not the emotional kind) which was not a surprise. This was her fifth run to the airport today and every one of the women headed for Wildfire, the Denver leatherwomen's conference, had arrived with luggage in both hands and a stack on the sidewalk.

At dinner the night before with Stacy and Stacy's best friend, Liz, Alison had tried to blame the femmes, but Stacy had hooted that one down. "Excuse me? I don't think so, girlfriend! It's those butch women who are bringing a different pair of boots for every event and bullwhips and chain mail besides! I can pack for a whole weekend in an overnight bag and make a flogger out of an old bicycle tire and some duct tape when I get there if I have to!"

This was a lie of such O.J. Simpson proportions—except for the part about the flogger—that Alison and Liz had just given one another a quick look agreeing on silence and gone back to eating sushi. Stacy required more bearers for a week in San Francisco than Fanny Bullock Workman had taken to the Himalayas. She needed a separate bag on wheels just for her heels.

Stacy, however, had twisted herself into such a knot over the conference that she was ticking like a time bomb and neither Alison nor Liz wanted to be within sight when she went off. Stacy on a tear was like one of Macy's balloons springing a leak, breaking its rope and ripping down Park Avenue at full, unfettered speed, mowing down the little people, tearing chunks out of cars and buildings without a backward glance. They had both seen it before and thought it would be really nice if someone else—preferably someone from out of town with whom they did not want to be buddies—got a chance to see it this time. Liz, who was the world's highest recognized authority on Stacy tears, had been trying for a week to set her off on strangers like dynamite in front of a forest fire. Her preferred target would have been Alison's best friend, Michelle, but since Michelle loathed Liz she had not been able to arrange an innocent meeting.

Butch and femme aside, the travelers were going to have to squeeze to get everything in, even though the van, borrowed from Stacy's femme friend Beth, who used it for transporting her Irish wolfhounds, was good-sized.

Alison gave a brief group greeting… "Here for Wildfire? Glad to see you!" …and then went around to open the double doors at the back of the van. She was all too aware of the eyes on her back, sizing her up, making predictions, creating fantasies. She was a tall, butch dyke, which meant that she was used to a quick once-over from other tall, butch dykes. That had happened all her life, and even more so in the past three years since she had been dating Stacy. Stacy liked butch women and what Stacy liked Stacy pretty much got, so Alison had bowed before her desire. Not that it had been a stretch—Alison, in her olive drab, flannel plaid and Birkenstocks had been a butch explosion waiting to happen. Just add water. Or, in this case, just add Stacy.

So, silly girl that she was, Alison had thought she would be totally prepared for the butch women flying into Denver for the four days of Wildfire. She thought they'd look at one another with quick glances calculating weight and height to the centimeter, play a little bone crunch while shaking hands, make a few macho job and hobby references, and then go their separate ways like dogs who have done a little obligatory growling and sniffing.

But she'd based that plan on the real world and just one day of doing airport pickup—and that was before the conference even started—had taught her a few things, the main one being that they weren't in the real world anymore. In the real world one couldn't go wrong with a friendly offer to help carry baggage. But, as Alison had discovered the day before, in the leather world there were a hundred different ways one could offend with that same offer and she had already been on the wrong side of every one of them. There had been butch gals who had been ticked that she had even asked and femme gals who had been ticked that she hadn't asked quickly enough. There had been women traveling with slaves who felt her offer out of line, femmes who had thought she was insinuating they were weak and incapable, and women who did need help but thought she should have been a bit more circumspect asking. Alison was a very bright woman; she didn't need to be taught the same lesson more than a couple of times. Less if there was beating involved.

"Welcome to Denver," she said, giving the four of them her biggest Mile High smile. "My back is bothering me, so I'm going to ask everyone to take care of their own luggage." She put her hand on her hip and stood, still smiling, by the door while the four of them sorted everything out among themselves. It was the coward's way out and she knew it and didn't care. She simply didn't have the energy to negotiate every little thing and besides, her back did hurt. For that matter, so did her hips and her right arm and both hands, which were swollen as well, all effects of her chronic fibromyalgia syndrome, which she found so boring and annoying she could barely stand to think of it, let alone discuss it with anyone else. She was already going to have to do ice packs and extra meds tonight; she didn't need to see who could piss higher on the tree before they even left the airport.

There was about five minutes of milling around. Some of the women loaded their own bags and some women helped or were helped. There was some commenting on the storage space, which smelled of wolfhound even though Alison had vacuumed and put a sheet down. But finally everyone was buckled in and Alison went back to lock the doors, congratulating herself. She hadn't been scolded even once. She wondered for a moment where the fifth passenger was, but she wasn't going to wait.

"Wildfire?" asked a new voice literally at her elbow. Alison was confused a moment, until she realized the woman speaking, a butch type wearing glasses, was in a wheelchair. Her skin was that color Americans call black, though it was closer really to a deep brown with an almost golden glow. Her hair was at that point where black and grey are struggling for dominance and cut close to her head. She was wearing a very old, very weathered leather jacket over her jeans and in her lap was a tank of oxygen, attached to a tube, which was clipped beneath her nose.

"Yeah," Alison answered, trying to think quickly. Stacy hadn't said anything about a wheelchair pickup. There had been only one wheelchair pre-registration and since Beth herself had been scheduled for that pickup she hadn't shown Alison how it was done. Oh, dear, she was going to be ignorant and possibly offensive.

The woman must have sensed her panic.

"Oh, this is just a ride," she said, waving back toward the miles of corridors. Denver International Airport was bigger than a lot of towns in Colorado. "I just can't walk that far. Not unless I stay in a motel on the way!" She stood slowly and turned to the attendant, a woman wearing a United uniform, holding a five-dollar tip in her hand as she gave up the chair.

"I'm Bernie. From Phoenix. Sorry I'm late." The woman offered Alison a frail hand. The skin on it and her forearms was puppy-ear soft and loose, as if she had recently lost a lot of weight. Despite this she gave the old butch squeeze. "I think they're bringing the baggage. Oh, here it is."

Another tip and Bernie climbed into the van with a hand from one of the California girls while Alison stacked her bags in the back most seat. The wolfhound area was full with the grate pulled across it. There was room for one woman beside the luggage and one beside Alison. The other three squeezed together in the middle.

"Ah am so excited to be he-ya!" One of the blonde girls Alison had pegged as Californian claimed the front passenger seat, although the moment she opened her mouth it was obvious that she was actually the Alabama passenger. There I go again with stereotypes, thought Alison, who scolded herself every chance she got. There were many—it was a full time job. "I missed Powersurge last year. Did any of you all go to Powersurge last ye-ah?" She twisted around in the seat, waiting for an answer.

Powersurge, which Alison had not attended last year, though Stacy and

Liz had been twice, was kind of the mother of lesbian leather conferences. Oh, it had been done before and it had been done sooner and it had even been done in Denver, but nobody had done it quite like the girls in Seattle, who three times running had produced an event that really had it all. Powersurge had play space and dress up dinners and workshops and dungeon space and vendors and if the Denver girls had been smart, thought Alison, looking in the side mirror while the rest of them told stories, they would have just been content to go to Seattle every two years and say thank-you nicely to the women who produced it. But could dykes ever, ever pass up an opportunity for controversy? No, of course they couldn't, and that was the reason Alison was driving back from D.I.A. for the fifteenth time in two days and Stacy had her knickers in a twist.

At the last Powersurge there had been a big old hassle, meetings, boycotting and the whole nine yards over the issue of transsexuals and who really was a woman and who wasn't and so who should be allowed to attend and who shouldn't. Alison, who had heard all about it second hand, had never quite identified all the factions. It was all very confusing. What she did know was that a direct consequence of that brouhaha had been the formation of several splinter groups which had agreed to produce a rotating leatherwomen's conference in their home towns on the years there was no Powersurge. And that was why Stacy and Liz with about fifteen other local leatherwomen formed the Wildfire Committee and got involved right up to their eyeballs. Which was, of course, the reason Alison was driving Beth's van and also the reason Stacy had been strung tighter than catgut for about three weeks.

There was just so much that could go wrong when you packed two hundred leatherwomen into the same space for four days, and for Stacy, who could make a great big deal out of almost anything, this had been just too much fuel for the imagination. Usually Stacy's imagination was a big plus, but for the past twenty-one days it had been turned only toward catastrophe. There had been no sex and Alison had pretty much resigned herself to the fact that everyone was going to get laid this weekend but her. Stacy had been way too occupied with predicting disasters—the work crews weren't going to show, the caterers were going to cancel, there were going to be knock-down drag-out fights and, most important of all, some empty-headed femme was going to look prettier than she did—to even think about doing the nasty herself. Alison had tried to initiate over the weekend—nothing elaborate, just a little McSex before *The X-Files*—but the whole mission had been aborted when Stacy sat bolt upright in the middle of foreplay, exclaiming, "Toilet paper! Are they supposed to supply toilet paper, or are we?"

The 'they' of Stacy's question were the two delightful gay boys from whom the Wildfire group was renting the three-story Victorian mansion they called Tara in which the conference—dungeons, workshops, leather mall and all—was being held. Tara was a prize. From the Seattle gals the Wildfire collective knew it was hard to find a place for this type of event. Well, what was hard was not so much finding someone who would rent to them, but someone who would rent to them a second time.

But the gay boys, friends of Stacy's cleaning faggot, Lawrence, had been thrilled to rent the house for four days. They had started the renovation of Tara by transforming the servants' quarters on the third floor into a lovely little apartment in which they were now residing themselves, but had agreed to stay with friends during the conference, which was not too much to ask considering the price they were charging. They were fine with anything the leatherwomen did as long as it stayed behind closed doors and no lube got on the wallpaper. What the neighbors thought was not an issue. The area of town in which the Tara was located was not a nice one. The only place you'd really want to go was the Mercury Cafe or Muddy's bar. The boys were hoping that one day soon it would become a nice area, reclaimed by renovation and gay money, but they were the first kids on the block to have sunk any money, and in general, nice tenants who wouldn't tear down the chandeliers were a way down the road.

"I was at Powersurge last year," volunteered the other blonde behind Alison. She was a handsome, sturdy butch whom Alison had sized up in that brief moment of touching hands as being both a little shorter and weighing a little less than Alison. Her name, Alison recalled from the intros, was Pat. Or at least that was the name she was using this weekend. Alison had met a lot of women in the past two days and she hadn't heard so many made-up names since she'd been kicked off womyn's land. The difference was that rather than being called Star and Bear the leatherwomen were called things like Master Mad Dog and Leatherbaby. "It was fabulous! The whole—"

"I guess you were at Powersurge! Why don't you just tell everyone what you were doing at Powersurge? And you don't even have the common courtesy to keep it at Powersurge! Do you think I can ever go back there? You've destroyed it for me! I can never go again! But do you have the decency to at least stay away from this conference, just so I can have some place I can go without seeing you and her? Oh, no, of course not! That would involve morals, wouldn't it? That would involve some show of decency and conscience, and we all know you don't have those things, don't we?"

The outburst from the rear seat was so ugly and unexpected that Alison, jerking as if she'd been sprayed with vomit, almost drove right through the lowered arm of the airport parking tollbooth. She hit the brake just in time. She glanced in her mirror. The woman who had saturated the car with anger was a mildly pretty femme of about Alison's height, though she was so thin that the words 'eating disorder' sprung to mind immediately. She was obviously aware that her thick, chestnut hair was her crowning glory, for it was twisted up in an elaborate knot that would have been more suitable for a cocktail party than a plane ride. Her outfit, short skirt and high heels, was a bit much for five in the afternoon too. Alison guessed that she and both blondes were early thirty-somethings, which she felt was old enough to know better than to cause public scenes. They obviously knew one another, so were probably the two from California.

The femme was saying, "Don't you blame me! If you'd been taking care of me the way our contract agreed you were going to take care of me, I wouldn't have had to look somewhere else! Why the hell was I there alone anyway? I'm not going to stay locked up in my room the rest of my life because you might see me at the store!"

The butch Pat turned savagely in her seat. "Get over it! You didn't get what you wanted for the first time in your whole life! It was bound to happen sometime—it was better that it happened now than when you're sixty! You might have died of shock! At least now you can get a lot of professional help and maybe get a life! Or if you don't want to do that, there's probably a whole lot of sick puppies this weekend you can lie to and manipulate!"

"Lie! Lie!? Okay, let's talk about lying! Let's talk about contract violation! Do you think anybody's going to play with you this weekend? I don't think so! Not when I tell everybody how you trashed our contract! Not if I have to stand right next to you and tell every woman who smiles in your direction! Not if—"

"Knock it off!" Alison spoke in her sternest voice. There wasn't a whole lot more she could do. Rattled at the tollbooth, she'd accidentally entered the middle lane of I-70 and her chances of cutting to the breakdown lane within the next couple of minutes were slim. She was going to have to work her way over as carefully as if she were playing Frogger.

"You fucking, lying bitch!"

Alison's stern tone might as well have been shouted out the window for all the notice that the two women took. Furious, the femme reached up over the seat and grabbed a handful of the butch's hair. She jerked her head forward and then back, banging it against the window. "You fucking, lying bitch!"

Oh, this was great. They were going to go right off the road and up in flames because of some ex-lovers' quarrel. Alison did a quick lane change, cutting a little too close in front of an RV, whose driver let her know with a blast on the horn. A quick glance to the mirror showed the femme's elbow planted firmly in the neck of the woman with the oxygen tank, Bernie.

"Knock it off!" she shouted again, starting to pull onto the shoulder. "We're going to be in an accident if you don't knock it off!"

The woman who from elimination must be the East Coast dyke, sat beside Pat with a frozen look on her face as if she'd attended too may bad family dinners as a child, but Bernie grabbed the femme's tightly clasped fist. She pulled back on her thumb and a second later the femme flew back against her seat shrieking as the black woman's hand grazed her nose on the way.

"Don't you treat her like that!" Pat made a sudden change of alliance from the window seat. "Don't you hit her! I'll knock the shit out of you if you hit her! I've knocked the shit out of women who looked at her wrong—don't think I won't do it!" She started to climb right over the petrified woman in between.

"Knock it off!" said Alison for the third time. She cut the engine." You either stop it right now or you're walking to town!"

She would have liked to think that it was her I-mean-business voice and bearing that switched Pat's channel, but she knew in her heart it was not. These two were way too involved with one another to even hear outside interference.

"Oh, Baby! What'd she do to you?" Pat pulled a black bandanna from her back pocket and held it up to the femme's nose. "Oh, Baby, you know I can't bear to see you hurt!"

"Assholes!" said Bernie, but the two were not listening.

Tenderly, as if she had a broken leg instead of a fat lip, Pat crawled right over the top of the others into the back seat and cradled her ex-girlfriend in her arms. Bernie rebuckled her seatbelt as she and the woman with the frozen smile resettled themselves.

The Alabama woman gave Alison a look that was all too readable. These people are crazy. Let's get where we're going and let's get there quick. Alison started the engine.

Chapter Two

"So that was bad enough," Alison said to Liz, "but do you know what they did then?"

"Could have been anything with this crowd," Liz replied in a distracted voice. "They could have set one another on fire in a suicide pact. I am noticing a great deal of blurred boundaries." The observation was acute, but her voice didn't hold that oh-so-gleeful tone into which it usually slipped during a good gossip. Like Stacy, Liz had been preoccupied with the conference for several weeks, though unlike Stacy, her attitude had been that everything and everyone was going to turn out just fine, so why fuss?

Still, though she may have achieved her own personal nirvana, Liz was not immune to the tizzies of Mistress Anastasia, which was why she was carrying Stacy's briefcase and only half listening to Alison as they hurried up the street. They had pulled up to the Detour, the bar where the first night Meet and Beat was being held, at almost the same instant—Liz on an errand of retrieval connected with registration and Alison coming from home, where she'd gone for a two-hour nap after her last run. The parking lot was full and both had been forced to park on the street two blocks away.

"Worse," Alison replied, hurrying a little to keep up. She knew that the last thing Liz wanted to do at this moment was listen to her story, but she figured that, with Stacy topping the registration, Liz distracted was about the best she was going to get. "No, they climbed into the back and fucked like walruses the whole rest of the way." Alison had seen a bit of walrus foreplay at Seaworld a couple of summers before, and it had left quite an impression. "And I don't mean a little discreet petting either—I mean screaming and bucking and lube flying!"

"You should have done something about that," Liz replied, which was the last thing Alison wanted to hear. She knew she should have done something about it! That was the point of the story!

"Duh!" she replied. "Except what? I didn't have a fire hose with me." She had been hoping Liz would be a bit more sympathetic to her plight. First of all, how was she supposed to know what was okay and what wasn't? From Stacy's conference stories she knew that public sex was not at all unheard of, though she had always imagined an audience being much more pleasant than the stony, pissed off silence in which she and the other three passengers had sat on the forty-five minute ride.

Liz didn't answer. She had come to a halt and was looking intently up the street toward the bar, shading her eyes with one hand.

"Oh, man," she said. "Is that what I think it is?"

Alison looked. In front of the door marched a tight little circle of women carrying signs.

"Oh, honestly," said Liz. "This is so irritating."

"Who are they?" asked Alison, squinting and trying to read the signs. Liz's far-sightedness was the stuff of legends.

"Oh, it's the Vanilla Sex Nazis," replied Liz in a disgusted tone.

"Are you sure?" Alison, who really did not like unpleasantness of any kind, was not surprised to feel herself getting an upset stomach. She knew that there was a large group of women within the lesbian community who wanted to make sure the right to choose didn't extend to the leathergirls. How could she not know? She had been snubbed and called names before. But a protest at the door was not something she had anticipated, and it was not something good. With her FMS flaring it had become important lately to remain on an even keel whenever possible. That meant no picketing, please.

"I recognize some of them from that SEPS group in Michigan," Liz answered. "Unless they're cloning themselves. That would be like them."

Indeed, there was a kind of sameness to the women marching in rank. It was not in their size or color or how they dressed, but more in the tight little expressions of disapproval they wore. Alison watched in dismay as they confronted a group of leatherwomen headed for the door. She had heard stories from both Stacy and Liz about the women who had called themselves SEPS (an acronym Stacy swore stood for Sisters Endlessly Persecuting Sisters) at Michigan several years before. Their title had become a kind of generic word within the leather community to refer to all the woman whose main hobby, instead of sewing or softball or cat shows, was confronting leatherwomen.

"Guess what," said Alison after a moment of staring. "It gets better. Look at the woman with the blue sign."

Now both of them were shading their eyes. They put their hands down at the same moment and looked at one another with identical looks of dismay. There was no doubt about it. One of the main protesters was Liz's ex-lover, Carla.

Carla had been one of those dates who in the end had turned out just not to be worth the six months of hot sex. But then, isn't hindsight always twenty-twenty? Two years ago none of them would have predicted that Carla would go from a leather jacket and consensual kinky sex straight to the ranks of abused victims. The rapidity with which she had made this switch had set so many heads spinning in Denver that a few were still reeling from the shock. It had been a relief to them all when Carla stopped stalking Liz at leather events and finally—probably a new girlfriend, everyone said—dropped out of sight.

Grimly, they girded their loins and walked forward. As soon as they were within shouting distance, the taunts began.

"You should be ashamed," shouted a woman holding a sign with the circular slogan 'Women against violence against women.' "S/m promotes violence against women!"

"Fuck you," said Liz. "I'll do whatever I want in my own bedroom." Alison couldn't think of anything more original, so she kept her mouth shut. She was looking at Carla who was holding a sign that read, 'Victim of ritual s/m abuse.' Carla was not looking back at Alison. She was not looking at any of them.

Another couple, two women obviously doing the daddy/boy thing had come up behind them and were now being included in the taunting.

"Men rape and abuse women! Why do you want to identify with them?"

"Be proud to be women! Be proud to be lesbians!"

Suddenly, the younger of the daddy/boy duo threw herself right down on the ground in front of the line of protesters.

"Ooooh," she howled in a disgraced voice. "I am bad! I am worthless! I am the scum of the earth!" She writhed on her back like a puppy showing submissiveness. "Punish me! Please punish me, Mistresses Separatist!"

The leatherwomen burst into laughter. Alison laughed so hard she snorted like a pig. The protesters lost it totally, jerking back as if they had been splashed with filth. The daddy/boy jumped up off the sidewalk and pranced, pleased with herself.

"Now, there's a good dog," said Liz. "I wish I had a biscuit." They took advantage of the protesters' momentary distraction to push through the bar door.

Even though they had come early, the bar was already crowded and there were few tables to be had. The best one was being borne down upon by group traveling in pack formation. The Queen Bee was a tall woman Alison guessed to be in her forties. Her face was pale and gaunt, framed with long dark hair. About her swarmed five or six younger women, deferring to her as if to royalty. She was holding the handle of a chain leash which was attached to a collar around the neck of a nearly nude woman following behind her. Alison remembered bringing the whole bunch of them in from the airport the day before. Even then the woman with the leash hadn't been wearing much.

Liz tossed the briefcase over three heads and onto the table. "Claimed," she said sweetly to the woman who was obviously the head handmaiden. She was one of those big old butch girls who were the lead dog for a reason. Always ready for a fight to the death.

"Get your ass—" began the woman.

"Oh, let's not talk about my ass," interrupted Liz in a seductive tone. "Let's talk about yours. I'd love to give you a good beating if you could take it. Meet me tonight at the dungeon?"

That took the air out of her, and without a lead the rest of the team got tangled in the traces. They milled about, making a few threatening noises, and then suddenly at some command from the Queen Bee regrouped and changed direction.

"Looking to get your butt kicked this weekend?" asked Alison, dropping into the chair across from Liz.

"Oh, you'd defend me," Liz answered. "And I do so enjoy twisting Queen Livia's tail. It's so rare anyone does it."

"I hope that protesting thing isn't going to be a problem," Alison said, looking over her shoulder at the front wall, which had a bank of windows. "What is with Carla, anyway? Did you do something to her that I don't know about?"

"No," said Liz. "You know the whole story. Carla decided that she couldn't have sex any more…"

"And you dumped her," filled in Alison.

"Hardly a dump!" Liz protested. "We weren't really girlfriends…"

"She thought you were girlfriends," said Alison.

"Well, we weren't! We were just fuck buddies!"

"You were girlfriends," said Alison. "You made us go on double dates with you. That's the deciding line—you don't force your friends to double date with your fuck buddies."

"May I tell this story?" asked Liz. "Okay, maybe she thought we were girl-friends. Maybe we were girlfriends. But I didn't want to do the celibate girl-friend thing. Support, lavish with attention and let sleep in my bed without sex—that spells 'cat' to me. And I already had a cat. So, I dumped her. If you can call it that. But I was honorable about it! You know I was!"

Alison had to acknowledge this. Liz had been honorable—far more honorable, in fact, than she herself would have been in the same circumstances. Liz had been up front with Carla, had tried to salvage the friendship, and when that had failed had even paid for Carla, who was as yet so young that her jobs skills were mostly knowing how to run a cash register, to go into therapy. All this while Carla was trashing the s/m community in general and Liz in particular.

"You were honorable," admitted Alison. "If it had been me, I would have just killed her and left her body in an alley." She waved down a waitress and looked out the window. The SEPS, Carla right in the lead, had regrouped and were trying to deter another group of leatherwomen from entering the bar. "Shame! Shame!" could be heard. They were going to have to work on their strategy—across the room Alison could see the young woman who had hor-rified the protesters telling the story to friends with sweeping hand gestures.

You could bet they'd all be out there rolling on the ground in a minute.

"I should have," Liz admitted. "Maybe it's not too late." She stood, picking up the briefcase. "Well, I'm supposed to go and work the registration table. I think the work exchange person didn't show."

"That would certainly vindicate Stacy," Alison replied. There had been an ongoing argument about work exchange from the day the Denver girls had committed to the event. Stacy, who had eventually been voted down, had been vehemently opposed to any work exchange whatsoever. If they couldn't pay the eighty dollars, then she didn't want them there, with the exception of Denver women whose trustworthiness could be vouched for. "If you see Salad, would you head her this way? She's supposed to drive the next shift, but I don't want to give up the table."

Liz nodded. Alison watched her slow progress to the registration table, and then watched Stacy's equally slow progress back toward her. She had almost reached Alison when a big, butch gal stepped into her path.

"Mistress Anastasia!" The name was long and drawn out—Alison hadn't heard such a squeal since the last time she saw k.d. lang live and the dykes in the cheap seats had gone crazy. She would not have guessed the big butch woman in the leather jacket could make such a sound. But then, life was full of surprises, wasn't it? She had the feeling this weekend was going to offer enough surprises to last for six months. Make that a year, she amended mentally as she watched the big woman pick Stacy up and lift her high in the air as if they were part of the Olympic ice hockey team.

Stacy responded graciously, posing with her hands on the woman's shoulders and one leg raised in the back as if she were a fifties film starlet getting ready to exchange a chaste kiss before the wedding. Only her outfit was in contrast to this little display of coyness—like the butch, she was totally leathered from top to bottom. A small herd of bovines had given their lives for fashion here.

The butch began to bring Stacy down a little too fast—Stacy was a big, tall woman—and Alison sprang to her feet, just in case Stacy landed on her two-inch heels with a crash and needed an arm. But the bigger woman set Stacy down as gently as if she were a little china doll. She and Alison shared a butch-bonding glance—Alison's acknowledging what a good job the other woman had done showing off her sweetheart and returning her without harm, and the other woman nodding thanks for spotting.

There was some kind of commotion outside and suddenly the flow of women heading up to the bar and registration table reversed itself, catching the big butch woman in an eddy. She waved as she was swept out the open door.

Alison, by hooking one leg around their table and holding tightly to Stacy's arm, managed to save them from a similar fate. She was not going to lose their table. There were only chairs for about half of the women crowding the two rooms of the Detour and she intended to hog hers all night. Let somebody younger perch on the windowsill. They would have to kill her to get her chair.

Hastily, as if her thoughts could be heard, she amended this ultimatum. Because, frankly, some of the women she had seen looked like they might not only enjoy a little death scene, but might then like to sit around and suck on the bones later. Okay, okay—she knew that almost everyone was just accessorizing, but she had never seen so much metal outside a hardware store in her life! Chains wound up like epaulets were fixed to the shoulders of leather jackets with big heavy clamps for what use Alison, who was a light player, did not care to speculate. Chains were draped to form harnesses and halters and belts—one woman was even wearing some kind of collar made out of barbed wire (being hugged gingerly). An electromagnet would have lifted nine tenths of the clientele to the ceiling.

Stacy sank back down in her chair, fluffing her skirt (as much as leather can be fluffed, which with Stacy was actually quite a bit) and crossing her legs daintily. This was another reason they needed to keep the chairs—Stacy's high heels were causing a ripple in the butch girls reaching clear into the other room, but they were made to be looked at, not walked in. Only Alison knew that Stacy's black leather medical bag, which was probably tucked behind the registration table, carried not only the array of toys about which half the girls at the bar were fantasizing, but Stacy's sneakers and glasses as well. "Heels and contact lenses all weekend," Stacy always said, "is way too heavy bottoming for me."

"That gal at the bar thinks you're flipping for her," Alison said, nudging Stacy with her elbow. With a jerk of her head, she motioned toward a compact Latina in a leather biker's cap who was sitting at the bar, gazing at Stacy with a hungry look.

"Oh, let her dream," Stacy replied. She took a compact and lipstick from her purse—a black beaded clutch that was a completely separate entity from her toy bag—and retouched her lips with as much care as if she had been selected for a *Girlfriends* cover. You could tell Stacy was trolling when she started doing her make-up in public. All around them, heat started rising off the same women who had been covertly looking at Stacy's high heels. It made Alison nervous. She was beginning to feel like sitting next to Stacy was like sitting next to the keg at a frat party—an innocent bystander might get hurt in the fray.

"Where'd Liz go?" she asked, because Liz had disappeared and she thought there might be safety in numbers. It was not that Alison thought anyone was doing anything unwanted or uninvited, really. But, then, who could tell? Right at that very moment, across the room, there were two women cutting the sleeves of a third's T-shirt as she screamed and struggled and swore, and nobody was paying a bit of attention, figuring they were just exhibitionists. Alison stared just a bit too long, and was caught by the woman struggling, who gave her a reassuring little wink.

"I think she's fucking in the bathroom," said Stacy, rolling her lips slowly and sensuously together. She snapped her compact closed, and Alison felt the same little shiver when she heard that noise as she did at the snap of a latex glove.

"Based on what?"

"Based on that I don't see her. My experience with Liz at a leather event is that if you don't see her, she's fucking in the bathroom. More than ten minutes and it's somebody's car."

Alison wondered if she wasn't just a bit out of her depth, and if this were perhaps, after all, an experience better lived vicariously. She looked out across the sea of leather and chrome. There must have been over a hundred women in the room, and judging from the squeals and hugs and thrown kisses, Stacy knew them all. Alison examined a nasty little feeling in the pit of her stomach. Was she jealous? Because, if she were, then she definitely would have been better off staying home and helping Michelle hook up running water to the garage. Alison and Stacy had been monogamous during the three years they had dated, and that had worked out fine. But Stacy had been getting a little edgy lately. Alison was not a heavy player. Stacy knew that, and was willing to make some concessions so that her main squeeze could get what she wanted. Another girlfriend in town, no. Been there, done that, got the T-shirt. Alison was just too damn old for nonmonogamous relationships right on her own doorstep. In her opinion, they took too much energy. She was no longer capable of staying up till two in the morning twice a week to sort things out and make sure everyone was 'getting what they needed.'

But she didn't care if Stacy had done a scene or two while she had been at Powersurge. A nameless stranger whom Alison would never meet seemed safe. If details were presented right, with no hints of a cozy breakfast the next morning, Alison was even able to get turned on listening to snippets of these adventures.

Wildfire, however, was close to home and experimental. It was Stacy who had suggested a little latitude, and a few ground rules too, which had all boiled down to being attentive to one another and having sex exclusively with each other no matter what else was going on.

This had seemed doable to Alison back in the days when registrations were just starting to trickle in. Now faced with all these big butch types, she was wondering how many of these women had Stacy played with? A question, she decided after a moment's deliberation, better not asked.

"I don't think I dressed right," she said to Stacy with just the slightest hint of a whine. She was wearing jeans and a tight, black T-shirt, which had looked good at home but now seemed a little boring. With her eyes she followed two women with identical facial tattoos.

"You should have worn your cop uniform," said Stacy, I-told-you-so lacing her voice. "Everybody loves a girl in uniform. You'd have women all over you." Then, realizing that there was some actual anxiety going on, she changed tack and leaned across the table to pat Alison's hand. "Baby," she said, "accessories aren't everything. Anybody can go to Home Depot, but most women here are wishing they were as hot in their gear as you are in your jeans."

Alison squeezed her hand and smiled. Every once in a while—like for the past few weeks—she would forget why it was that she dated Stacy and how sweet she could be when not in high tizzification. It was always good to get a reminder.

There was another little commotion by the door. A small woman dressed in kind of grunge/slut femme outfit spotted an old friend and leapt right up into her arms, her legs around her waist so that everyone in the room and a couple of innocent patrons who'd just come in for a drink could see she was wearing nothing beneath her long black skirt. The girls liked that. There were whistles and calls.

"Where's Dana?" asked Alison. Dana, a Seattle friend who was staying with Stacy, had come in on one of the early morning flights when Beth was driving.

"Over there," said Stacy, tilting her glass to indicate the other side of the room, past the woman who was giving the peep show. Alison caught Dana's eye and waved her over. She noticed Stacy looking thoughtfully at Dana's feet as she carefully picked her way through the crowd. Stacy felt it was the height of poor manners for any other femme to wear higher heels than hers, and was totally capable of sawing an inch off Dana's spikes once they got home.

"Hi," said Dana, when she finally reached the table. Like Stacy, Dana who had red, red hair and I-sunburn-easily skin, was dressed to the nines in high femme-fatale style. She looked great, and her little half smile told them she realized it. That was good. Alison, Stacy and Liz had met Dana two years before when she had flown to Denver, expecting to spend time with an old lover who had turned out to be dead. With no money and locked into her plane ticket, Dana had spent the week in the apartment of her dead lover, Tam, and had been instrumental in helping Alison find Tam's killer. It had taken Dana a long time to get over Tam's death, and even longer to get over the emotional abuse that had surrounded the relationship. Over the winter both Stacy and Alison had received long distance phone calls frightening in their loneliness and despair. It was a relief to see Dana looking as if she was no longer sleeping each night with Tam's memory.

Dana was still standing without a word. Belatedly, and only clued in by a raised eyebrow from Stacy, Alison realized Dana was waiting for her to offer her seat. She jumped to her feet. Dana thanked her with a dazzling smile, and leaned over the table with an air indicating there was gossip to be had.

"This person over here," she said, indicating with a lifted eyebrow so subtle that it could have been overlooked completely, "is transsexual. Pre-op. Do you have the dick-in-the-drawer rule?"

She was referring to the famous rule published in the Powersurge flyers each year, which simply stated that if you could not slam your dick in a drawer and walk away from it, you could not attend a dungeon. What with the really butch girls who were pre-op female-to-male, and the really femme girls who were pre-op male-to-female and all their lovers and supporters, controversy reigned.

"Well, we ended up agreeing to be the Open-to-Transsexuals conference," Stacy said. "The Atlanta gang is going to do a local conference in two years and they're going to be really strict women-born-women-and-still-women. It seemed like a fair way to do it. We told everybody about it in the information packets."

Recognizing Dana's obvious disappointment in this vein of gossip being closed so sensibly she said, as way of compensation, "Liz and I were thrown out of the Dykes With Dicks workshop last year. We were disrespectful. Everybody else was really serious and we laughed." She paused for a moment, waving to someone across the room and then added, "We were thrown out of a lot of workshops last year."

Alison knew from previous nostalgic conversations about the good old days, that Liz and Stacy had also been thrown out of two hotels and a Phranc concert as well..

"Well…" said Dana, looking around for a new victim.

"Who's that woman over here that looks like a zombie?" asked Alison, crouching down by the table. It was not ideal. Hopefully one of the others would want to mingle, and she could claim a chair again. She nodded toward the woman who had vied for the table with Liz. "She looks like she's been dead a week." It was not kind, but there was a hint of truth to it. The Queen Bee was standing next to a wall while her court buzzed around her with an indignant hum, presumably trying to pressure some of the little people out of their table. She was still holding the leash. The woman in the collar, which was pretty much the biggest thing she was wearing, was kneeling at her feet. Alison hoped they didn't get raided.

"Oooh, that's Livia!" Dana, rather than Stacy, jumped in to answer this one. They both crossed their fingers in front of them as if to ward off a vampire. "Major headtripping. And a lot of bleed-through—you know, blurring the boundaries. Lots of money, lots of power plays. Stay away from that one." Alison watched the woman peel a fifty off a huge wad of bills and hand it to the Lead Dog, who dutifully headed toward the bar.

"There's another one to stay away from," said Stacy, flicking her fingers briefly toward a woman wearing chaps and a tight Harley T-shirt. So far, Stacy was the unchallenged Queen of Gossip.

"Mmm," agreed Dana, who was now scanning the room as if it were a salad bar, wondering just exactly what she could fit on her plate and rejecting immediately the iceberg lettuce.

"Very unsafe top, doesn't know what she's doing, doesn't know when to stop. Also has terrible table manners, so don't let her tie you up or take you out to lunch." The woman in chaps cruised their table, oblivious to the fact that Stacy had just cut her to pieces and tossed her into the trash.

A tall butch pushed her way past the table, smiling at Stacy and Dana. She was so handsome that even Alison, who generally noticed other butches only when they were squeezing her hand, felt a little flutter.

"Zoriah," said Dana, without being asked. "She's married and she's faithful. Isn't it sad? Sometimes I have to go home and cry about it at night."

The squatting was getting to be too much on her thighs, so Alison stood. She surveyed the room as Dana and Stacy continued the dueling gossips scene. The woman whose shirt had been cut off was now having a beer with the woman who'd done the cutting. The grunge femme was sitting on the lap of her friend, facing her. Somebody was packing. A couple of the bodybuilder butch girls had slipped off their jackets and were doing the butch thing—flexing pecs and deltoids as if they were competing for Mr. Universe. Over in the corner, a couple of vanilla gals who had obviously just wandered in to have a few after work and ended up being trapped, were holding their glasses tightly, sitting still as rabbits, as if any sudden movement might draw unwanted attention. One was darting her eyes toward the door—she was going to make a break for it as soon as there was an opening—but the other was licking her lips like a poor kid in a candy shop as she looked at Dana. She caught Alison's eye and flushed, then pretended to be looking out the window.

"So, then she said..." Stacy and Dana were really on a roll. The bar was now so crowded that there was very little room to maneuver and Alison knew she was going to need to visit the little butches' room soon. She tried to plan her strategy. If there was just an opening into which she could merge, she probably would be carried back by momentum. She took a deep breath, knowing she was going to have to create a space, and hoping this would not offend the honor of some top-and-only-top gal to the point where gauntlets would have to be thrown down.

There had been quite a bit of chatter—hell, lets just call it what it was—there had been total bedlam since she had arrived. The women in line to register in the poolroom had changed a dozen times, but the line had never gotten any shorter. Women were three deep at the bar, and all around them were little scenes of greeting—'Haven't seen you since Michigan,' 'Are you going to MSIL?', 'Read your story in *On Our Backs*.' As well as chatting and cruising and greeting long lost friends, a good number of women had pulled out their conference schedules and were deciding which events they just had to attend.

Beth had lobbied for registration totally separate from the first event, partly because anyone who had asked for last minute community housing had to bring her luggage to the bar while she got an address and keys. Stacy had rallied the rest of the committee to vote her down by saying, "Fuck them, they should have gotten it together earlier so they could get their information in the mail like everybody else!"

Alison was just getting ready to cut in front of a woman wearing a leather vest and dog collar when suddenly she caught sight of a lovely femme weaving her way through the crowd. She was a tall woman, although not so tall that Alison began looking for the signs—Adam's apple, large hands and feet—of transgender. But taller than Alison to begin with, and pushed up two inches by spike heels that would be sending Stacy into a spasm of jealousy. She had blonde hair done up in a twist and was wearing not leather, but a cream colored dress that had obviously come from a vintage store—lots of old lace and sashes and that blocky fifties style which only looks good on a certain build. It looked good on her. Alison felt her mouth going dry as she watched her approach. This was how she had reacted to Stacy the first time she had seen her, decked to the nines. Alison was a sucker for femme drag. It wasn't something she discussed with everybody—her best friend and neighbor, Michelle, would have had something to say about every article of clothing that turned Alison on. High-heeled shoes—oppressive, bad for the feet and back, made running and escape impossible, just one step up from foot binding. Stockings—what was the point? They didn't keep you warm; they snagged every time, just another manipulation to keep women consuming. Lingerie—invented by men and pornographers. Alison knew the whole spiel, and even agreed with some of it in theory. But what could she say? It was like being tied up and fucked in the ass—if that's what you liked, that's what you liked, and you might as well come right out and say it. She loved femme dykes. She loved the trappings. This woman was fishing with the right bait.

She passed Alison no more than a foot away. As she came directly opposite, she turned her head just a little and gave Alison a quick up and down look, a Hmm-do-I-want-to-have-you-for-my-dinner? look. She was flagging on the left with three of the daintiest leather and chrome bracelets Alison had ever seen. She lifted that hand to brush back a strand of blonde hair, as if to make sure that, if Alison decided she did want to be a main dish on this plate, she knew what she was getting into. She went right up to the bar—suddenly there was an opening where there had been four women the moment before—and said, "A white Russian, please."

"Who is that?" asked Stacy, her whisper doing little to disguise just how ticked she was to be wearing not just the second but the third highest heels in the room.

"Oh, her?" Dana stirred the little cocktail straw in Alison's diet soda—she apparently thought it went with the chair—and smiled at her. Because of the angle at which she was sitting, Stacy had missed the look the woman had given Alison. Dana had not. "She's our mystery girl this weekend. I've seen her around, but nobody seems to know anything about her—not where she came from or where she's been. I've heard some rumors about her, but nothing first hand. Nothing solid. She flags top, but she hasn't played with anyone I know."

"What's her name?" asked Stacy, which was convenient for Alison, who was beginning to have more positive thoughts about playing with other people this weekend.

"Chili Dog," Dana replied. Both Alison and Stacy turned toward her with absolutely horrified looks, and she laughed so hard over her own wit tears came to her eyes. Dana had a fabulous laugh, very warm and infectious, so that in a moment Stacy and Alison were also laughing over the idea of such a beautiful, put-together femme calling herself Chili Dog.

Stacy gently dabbed at her eyes with a lace handkerchief from her dainty clutch, disturbing neither contacts nor eye make-up.

"Oh, and look, Scar's here." Dana flicked her fingers over Alison's shoulder. Alison turned her head. Scar could have been a huge butch girl with a shaved head, a blonde femme who should have asked her friends' opinion before going out in the outfit she was wearing, or a smaller butch in military uniform.

"She might be here, but she's not doing work exchange," said Stacy, pleased as could be. "At least I pushed that through!" To Alison she said, "I'm going to make you a cheat sheet of who to avoid, but until I do, stay away from Scar."

An angry voice cut across the roomful of conversation, a voice Alison had heard once before. "What the hell was that? I can't believe you did that! What, you're just going to get up in my face with every fucked up, weenie-bait bottom you meet? You are not going to disrespect me like this! It's not happening!"

Stacy and Dana both sat up with startled expressions and turned toward the sound, old gossip forgotten in the face of hot new action.

"You tell me you love me, you can't live without me, you'd rather die than live without me! You'd rather kill me and kill yourself both if you can't have me! Tell me you love me not more than an hour ago and then you're already here passing it out to any sorry-ass, ugly bitch who walks by!"

"Oh, that's those two crazy women I brought in from the airport." Alison leaned forward to take in the whole scene.

"Oh, god, Tricia Newman," said Dana. "Queen of the bleed-through. I have never been to a leather event where she wasn't causing a scene." She did not sound at all displeased. Altercations were good if you weren't involved. It was kind of like watching Jerry Springer.

Stacy, however, looked supremely irritated that someone had gotten through the oh-so-rigorous screening of having eighty dollars just to cause a commotion at her event.

"Well, if the femme is Tricia and the butch is Pat, that just makes them a couple of Pattys," said Alison, watching to see if chairs or shoes were going to start flying, as they so often did on Jerry Springer. She had been watching a lot of trash talk shows in the middle of the night when she couldn't sleep.

Not more than five feet away from them, Butch Patty had Femme Patty backed up against the wall by the door, shaking her finger in her face. They weren't exactly shouting and they weren't exactly brawling, but you could tell it was coming. "They did this same shit in the van on the way in from the airport—I thought we were going to go right off the road. I'm not kid—"

"Oh, I see, it's okay for you to have your little chippy? When we're together! When we're under contract together and that's okay? You just fuck who you want and shame me in front of my friends, the ones to tell me because you're such a fucking liar! But I'm not supposed to talk to anybody else even though we're not even together anymore? What do you want me to do—do you want me just to go to one of those cybergenics places and have myself froze and then you could just keep me in your freezer—make sure nobody else ever touched me but you wouldn't have to touch me either?" Femme Patty pushed away from the wall. The sudden movement changed a shaken finger into a rap on the nose.

"Hey, none of that in here!" This was from a woman who must have been the sorry-ass, ugly, weenie-bait bottom bitch whose proximity had started this round of the Patty show. She looked just like anybody else to Alison. "Don't you hit her!" She shot out a hand, grasping Butch Patty's fingers in a fist. She was the bigger of the two and the surprised grimace on Butch Patty's face told the audience she was the stronger also.

In Alison's eyes the weenie-bait butch was being really restrained and reasonable. She herself would have knocked the Pattys' heads together, but then, she'd been there for Act One.

Femme Patty, however, reacted as if the woman had come in swinging a mace. "Don't you treat her like that!" she said, changing alliances so totally free of embarrassment that Alison almost admired it. Well, not admired exactly. What she felt was the same 'Well, look at that' feeling she got when she read about people who made their living sticking nails up their nose or eating light bulbs. You acknowledged it if forced, and then walked away really fast. Femme Patty brought up a hand tipped with long, red claws, obviously ready to match action to words on the spot. "Don't you touch her! I'll take your eyes out if you touch her!" The weenie-bait butch threw up her other hand and took a wicked swipe on the sleeve of her leather jacket.

"Can you say 'sociopath'?" Dana asked, and leaned across the table, totally content to take it all in as if it were part of the entertainment.

Stacy was not.

"Not at my party!" she announced loudly, obviously ready to jump right into the fray and take a few heads off.

Alison almost let her. A blow up and screaming match would have done Stacy a world of good. More importantly, it would have done Alison and Liz a world of good.

Unfortunately, paycheck or not, Alison was a cop and a woman of honor, and this obviously seemed like a situation calling for defusion, rather than confrontation. Confrontation, she feared, was going to light a fuse none of them might have any power to put out at all.

"Bunny," she said in a soothing voice, laying her hand on Stacy's arm, "I wonder if that's—"

"Don't you call me 'Bunny'! I'm not your 'Bunny'!" In a nanosecond Stacy had gone from an irritated patron to almost pure berserker. Alison was not sure if her head was going to blow up or just start spinning around like a top.

"You're my bad-ass bunny," she soothed, standing with the same caution one might use in approaching an unknown Rottweiler. "You're the baddest bunny I know—and the prettiest, too." A compliment was never a bad idea under any circumstance. "But I just wonder if—"

Stacy was beyond being reasoned with. She jerked her arm away and began pushing her way through the crowd, which had started to circle up at the sound of raised voice. They were sitting inside the innermost circle—it was only going to take a few shoves for Stacy to reach the brouhaha. Alison threw up her hands, hoping it did not turn into the kind of situation where she was required to get gallant and come to the aid of the lady. She didn't feel she showed well in those circumstances. Her strengths lay more in the being complimentary and giving good presents area.

By the time Stacy reached the door the weenie-bait butch had faded as far as possible into the background. The Pattys were doing just fine without her. They had gone back into mutual attack mode without so much as missing a beat.

"I am not under contract to you any more!" Butch Patty was screaming into Femme Patty's face. "Get that out of your head! You ended that contract the minute you stopped taking care of me! I didn't end that contract—you ended that contract!"

"I don't think so! I don't think so! What does it say on this paper, then?" Reaching into her bodice, she whipped out a folded sheet of typing paper. Alison was fascinated—it was certainly the best improvisational theater she had ever seen. "Slave on the run!" Femme Patty shouted, holding the paper above her head. Her hand was shaking with rage. "Slave on the run!" She looked out into what had become an audience. "You don't want to get involved in this! You don't want to have anything at all to do with this woman—she's contracted to me until the millennium and I have the paperwork to prove it!"

"This stops here." Alison was really sorry to see Stacy step in at this point. So, judging from the collective sigh she heard around her, was the rest of the audience. Everybody wanted to see the papers and find out how the story ended, although Alison, at least, suspected it was going to be a serial. "We are not going to have this kind of drama here." Stacy had chosen to play her role contained and regal. It looked great, but Alison could have told her it wasn't going to work. The Pattys rolled right over the top of her like a steamroller.

"You can take that and wipe your butt with it!" Butch Patty made a grab for the paper, almost knocking Stacy off balance. Alison sighed, knowing that the gallant part was coming. She looked around the room, trying to spot Flame, the Denver woman who was acting as bouncer. She would handle this so much better. But though almost every face in the room was now turned toward the door, Alison didn't see her, which meant she wasn't there. Flame was six feet four inches and had a mane of curly red hair with a life of its own—she was impossible to miss.

"Slave on the run!" Femme Patty shouted.

"Sanctuary!" Butch Patty shouted back, clutching at Stacy. She must have identified her as management from her nametag. "Amnesty!"

The front door of the bar suddenly flew open, hitting Femme Patty in the ass. She staggered forward, falling into Stacy and taking her to the floor. A small crowd of leatherwomen pushed into the room, followed by angry shouts from the picket line. The first two women through the door went right down into the dog pile, but the four or five behind them managed to stay on their feet. They were all talking at once and they were angry. That much Alison could tell from their faces, because she couldn't understand a word they were saying. There was too much going on. Around the place where the women had fallen others were trying to assist—some offering a hand and others trying to restrain the Pattys, who had taken the opportunity to trade a few blows in the confusion. Alison was relieved to see Dana, who had somehow managed to get right up next to the fray, pulling Stacy to her feet. This was the kind of situation where people were trampled. Stacy popped up like they were Explosion teammates, rather than two girls in heels.

The door flew open again, but this time women were going out. There was scattered roaring among the first rank and several women who appeared to be uninvolved bystanders, including one of the waitresses, were sucked out into the street with them. Alison could no longer see Stacy and her heart sank. She had either gone down or out the door. Alison didn't know which she should hope for.

"What the hell is going on?" yelled Liz to Alison from across the top of the crowd. She was standing on the registration table. Liz was as capable a woman as you could find and that included knowing when it was time to get up on a table.

"I don't know." Alison had been pushed clear to the other side of the door, over by the front windows. There was such a commotion she was not sure Liz had heard her answer, even though she had shouted. Whatever had happened outside, it had pissed off everybody. Some of the women from that first push were still inside and they were all talking at once to the crowd around them in hard, angry voices. For some reason some of the women in the bar seemed to be disrobing. Alison could not see Stacy or Dana at all. She turned to the window.

The picketers were still out in full force, though they were no longer carrying signs. Surely, however, they were not the reason for the retreat? They had been annoying when she and Liz had entered, but that was all. Even if the SEPS had linked arms there hadn't really been enough of them to keep a determined group from coming or going.

As Alison watched, she saw Carla on the front line, shouting something she couldn't hear through the glass. What the hell did she have in her hands? Whatever it was, she held it up high above her head, shaking it like a trophy and doing a little victory dance. What was it?

Oh, dear. Alison took another look, and then looked back into the women by the door. Oh, Jesus, no wonder they were so pissed! What Carla was holding was the same thing Alison had gotten her eight-year-old nephew for his birthday. A Supersoaker. And, judging from the sound of the crowd, it wasn't filled with water, either. Now that she knew what to look for, Alison could see swaths of lavender paint decorating jackets and hair. Leather was expensive. Alison's own jacket had cost over a hundred dollars, and it was modest compared to some of these gals' outfits. No wonder, also, that the women who were the maddest were taking their leather off before mounting a defense. Heads were going to roll. If Carla had any sense she'd run just like a little bunny while she had the chance. It was obvious that there was going to be a rumble.

Alison turned to Liz and waved. "Do you see Stacy?" she shouted. Oh, god, she hoped Stacy wasn't going to get caught in the middle of anything. Stacy was her own darling goddess, but she had a hot temper, and was totally capable of stripping right down to her earrings and French cut panties, smacking a few heads and ending up in the pokey bottoming for someone named Big Mama.

Liz did not even try to answer. She was kneeling on the table, talking to the women in front of her. There was a little ripple in the crowd, a switch from attention being focused on the door to attention being focused on Liz. Hands were raised. Liz threw herself down upon them as if into Tribe 8 mosh pit. Carefully, she was passed over to Alison above the women's heads. Alison snagged her and held her for a moment on her hip—there wasn't room for her to stand on the floor. Liz shook herself loose to balance with one foot on the windowsill and the other on Alison's knee.

"Oh, man, what a bunch of assholes!" she said, her face pressed to the glass. "There's going to be a fucking riot!"

"Yeah, with my girlfriend right in the heart of it! Do you see either of them?"

"Dana got pushed back in the poolroom. She's okay. Stacy's probably right on the front line gearing up to tear someone's heart out with her bare hands. At least, we better hope it's her bare hands. Then maybe she'll only be charged with manslaughter."

Oh, god. Alison's heart sank. How many of the women inside the bar were wearing knives as props? It could really get ugly, and if it got ugly, the leatherwomen were certainly not going to be cut any slack when the cops arrived.

Suddenly, the sound from the street burst into the bar. The front door must have been reopened. The SEPS were catcalling. "You're a disgrace to all lesbians! You're worse than men—they can't help it, but you choose to be this way!" Carla was not the only one with a booby-trapped squirt gun. A number of them, leaking lavender, orange and raspberry were leveled at the door, at the leather dykes stripped to different degrees starting to pour out. Some still had their jackets on—no one was going to make them take them off for nothing. Others were sacrificing T-shirts, and still others were totally bare to the waist, taking it on the breasts.

Liz had been right, there was Stacy in the middle of the fray, looking so angry that she might just chew the head off anyone who got in her way. To Alison's great relief, she had not stripped totally, just her jacket and shoes. She must have gotten paint on her skirt as she went out the first time, and figured it lost to the cause. She came boiling out through the fire of paint right at the head of the crowd, her hands in front of her face, straight for Carla, whom she hated with a vengeance for the way she had treated Liz—a best friend thing.

East Colfax Avenue had seen it all. People didn't stop for a little thing like a brawl. The paint guns, however, were a twist with enough innovation to start drawing a crowd. Several totally innocent bystanders—young men and women in punk gear who were just trying to go to McDonald's—had been caught by crossfire and it was obvious to Alison that they were going to join the fray any moment. Between them and the furious leatherwomen it looked as if the SEPS were going to get the shit kicked out of them.

Except for the three or four days just before her period, Alison did not believe in violence. No matter the evidence to the contrary and Saddam Hussein aside, a large part of her believed the same thing it had believed in the seventies—that almost every conflict could be resolved by talking over good food. No matter how many times in her years as a cop she had been forced to knock heads in self-defense, she did not believe that knocking heads was good.

But what could she do, caught in the crush by the window, aside from hoping Stacy didn't actually tear Carla limb from limb and put the whole conference on the front page of the *National Enquirer*? And, she could not help thinking, the women with the squirt guns had really brought this on themselves. She was reminded of a conversation she had overheard at Michigan around 1990 when s/m wars were going strong. "They brought in leaflets that trashed us, they sent out letters that trashed us, they lied about us to the producers and then they were upset because we were angry. It was like they thought they were some kind of exterminators and we were roaches—it never occurred to them that the roaches might get their feelings hurt!"

The women with the paint guns, however, had not made the mistake of thinking the roaches might not fight back. As they held the crowd back with well placed streams of paint—they were now aiming for faces, which was much more debilitating than shots to the body—several of them picked up the whistles from around their necks and began blowing.

Immediately a blue, open bed Chevy pickup truck whipped around the corner and stopped in the right traffic lane. The SEPS had practiced—Alison had to give them credit. While the women closest to the truck hastily climbed into the bed, the front row covered their retreat without faltering. The women in the truck then laid down a line of fire as soon as they were standing. The woman sitting in the passenger seat of the cab had, for some reason, a bandanna over her face and a floppy hat like a western stick-up artist. She also had her own paint gun catching Stacy on the side of the head just as she reached Carla. Stacy let out a howl, but stubbornly kept her hand clenched in Carla's hair. Carla drove the barrel of her Supersoaker into Stacy's gut. As Stacy doubled over Carla gave her a hard shove which sent her to the pavement, then turned and sprinted to the truck where she was pulled aboard by a dozen anxious hands. A moment later the driver hit the gas and swerved out into traffic.

Alison closed her eyes. The truck looked awfully damn familiar. Hadn't she seen it parked behind the house a time or two when Michelle had guests? And was it more than coincidence that all the paint was the same color as the decorative shingles on the front of her own house, which Michelle had redone in shades of sherbet just a month before? If Michelle was involved, she didn't want to know.

Chapter Three

"This is the line we, as the Wildfire Committee, have decided to take if there is any more separatist confrontation or attack this weekend." Liz stood on the front steps of Tara to speak to the seven women whom Alison had just delivered from the guest hotel. It was Alison's fourth loop from hotel to Tara and Liz had caught each group before going inside, saying the same thing over and over. "We are now on private property and the men who own it have agreed to press trespassing charges if our space is violated again. We are not fighting, we are not engaging. We are calling the police. Anybody who needs to leave before the police arrive for personal reasons will be given a chance to do so, although I want everyone to know that I'm a lawyer and we are not breaking any Colorado laws as long as no money is exchanged for sex acts, and nobody is supposed to do that anyway. If anything happens and you choose to stay you're choosing to accept the fact that there are going to be cops here, probably men, for as long it takes to have these women removed. We expect total cooperation from anyone who stays—no dirty looks, no remarks, nothing. If you don't like the police, then don't stay. If you think you can't keep from mixing it up with these crazy women, then don't stay. We've taken some precautions to try to keep strangers from approaching too close, which makes it important to have your nametags on all the time. We know the names of some of the women who were using the paint guns last night and plan on bringing a civil suit against them for property damage—also, one women had to go to the hospital because she got paint in her eyes. She's okay. If you or your clothing was damaged and you're interested in joining the suit you need to talk to me so we can start documenting evidence. We're sorry it happened, we don't know where the leak was and if it's any consolation I didn't want to spend my weekend this way either."

There were a couple of questions, but Alison had heard the answers already, so she went inside to get a bagel. She also needed to find Salad to give her the van keys, since it was her turn to drive and Alison's turn to mingle. There was supposed to be a work exchange person to spell them further, but she hadn't shown up.

The separatist action the night before had done exactly what it had been meant to do—cause such a disturbance in the conference-goers that the planned event—a goods-and-services auction—had been sucked down the drain. A good half of the women at the bar had been marked with paint. A lucky few had only been spattered with a handful of drops which could be wiped off quickly before they dried. A large group, however, had entire outfits ruined, and were now also sporting punk hair in a variety of colors they probably wouldn't have chosen themselves. Worse, several women who had been hit in the face required medical attention. While Stacy had not been one of these, Liz had spent almost an hour carefully using Q-tips and cotton balls to remove lime green paint from her face, ears and hair. This had taken place at Stacy's home, for the owners of the bar had apologetically but firmly refused to let anyone who had been painted re-enter. Alison could see their point—they had just redecorated as well as having no idea, when saying yes to the event, that there was going to be trouble. The waitress who had been caught in the fray had an ugly orange streak in her hair, a bad bruise on her elbow and had been in tears.

Well, how could they have known? thought Alison. The Wildfire group themselves had no idea there was going to be trouble. Liz's comment about not knowing the leak had been meant merely to pacify and cover ass. It was true they hadn't advertised in the local lesbian papers, but neither had they tried to keep the event a secret. They had a web site, for crying out loud!

So, the auction had been scrapped as women, many complaining loudly, had gone back to their homes or hotel rooms or the emergency room. It had been Salad's turn to drive the van, but there had been such a crowd all wanting to leave at the same time that Alison and a couple other locals took women in their cars while Salad took shifts to the main hotel. The out-of-town women who were staying in community housing mostly got rides with their hostesses. Or hosts, depending on how you were bending your gender.

There had been a lot of bitching and moaning, a good deal of it directed toward the Wildfire group, which Alison resented on Stacy and Liz's behalf. How could they have anticipated something like this? From the conversation in the van that morning Alison knew that some women had arranged quick private parties, but she guessed that an equal number had gone home and gone to bed early, as she had herself the moment she was through driving. Everyone had been looking forward to the auction and mingling; it was hard to switch horses in mid-stream, particularly if yours had been shot out from beneath you. Alison had slept fitfully.

As often is the case, though, things seemed much better in the light of day. Everyone who climbed into the shuttle had been cheerful and optimistic and had listened to Liz's little speech the same polite way you listen to the stewardess when she's standing right next you in the aisle. You have no intention of ever actually using that bottom seat as a flotation device, but it doesn't hurt to at least pretend you're paying attention.

Inside the stately old home women were mingling at a frantic pace. There was a lot of the same delighted squealing of the previous night as old friends came together, but there was also an undertone of let-me-check-my-datebook energy as people set up playdates. One night had already been blown and everybody had come to party.

Alison threaded her way through the crowd carefully, turning her head from side to side to check out the cool costumes. Mostly variations of what she'd seen the night before at the bar, but with more nudity because they were on private property. There were several women wearing nothing but leather harnesses with their jeans and quite a few femmes wearing little wisps of nothing over nothing at all. In opposite corners of the vendors' room stood the two Pattys, both flirting loudly and gaily with other women while taking quick glances over their shoulders. Didn't have to call the Psychic Friends' Network to figure out what was going to happen there. Alison herself had gone army—camouflage pants, matching cute cap, combat boots, and a tight olive drab T-shirt. This outfit had been shopped for and put together by Stacy when Alison had put her foot down and said no way and for the last time, she was not going to wear her police uniform! She was drawing appreciative looks.

Vying for a spot at the brunch buffet, Alison brushed up against the woman with the oxygen tank from the shuttle ride with the Pattys the day before, but she couldn't come up with a name .

"Hey!" she said, trying to turn and be friendly without losing her place by the table. "How do you like Denver? Just one big old brawl after another, huh?"

The woman who was doing some heavy cream cheese and bagel action herself, laughed. "Okay, you've impressed me. It's a happening kind of place," she said. "But enough!"

Alison picked up a cluster of purple grapes and put them on her plate. There was a great spread—two huge platters of bagels—half a dozen kinds—with a whole produce section of fruits and vegetables arranged so artfully around them that Alison actually hesitated before taking a banana. Oh, well, she decided, not all beautiful things were meant to last.

"Did you hook up with your housing hostess?" she asked. Damn it, why could she remember every single little thing about this woman, including where she was from, but not her name? She did a quick scan of her front torso, looking for the name badge everyone was supposed to be wearing around their necks. Nope—oh, there it was, tied by the elastic to the right-hand belt loop of the woman's jeans.

"Well, not exactly. I mean, I got the keys, but didn't actually meet my hostess. And my name is Bernie."

"Pretty obvious, huh?" Alison asked with chagrin.

"Painfully," replied Bernie in a cheerful voice, slapping a couple of cucumber slices on top of her cream cheese. "But then, I have the advantage." She pointed to Alison's name tag, which was hanging down right in the middle of her olive drab T-shirt, good girl that she was.

"It does look pretty nerdy, doesn't it?" asked Alison. A quick glance around told her none of the other butches were conforming. "I think I'm going to steal your idea."

"Well," laughed Bernie, "I always was kind of a trend-setter." She wiggled the tips of her fingers in a little wave and trundled away.

Alison looked around for a place to sit down. Most of the chairs she could see were already taken. As she looked, however, a woman who had been sitting on a built-in bench on the first landing of the epic staircase stood up. Quickly Alison ran up the eight stairs and sat down, just beating a daddy/boy couple who both glared at her. She pretended not to notice. Perfect place to sit and be an audience.

"Hi."

Alison turned to look at the woman who sat down beside her. She seemed familiar, but that was kind of a given, wasn't it? Two hundred women in a fairly small space—it was kind of like living on Gilligan's Island. You saw a lot of the Professor and Mary Ann.

It seemed to her, however, that there was a special reason for noticing this women. It wasn't her dress or her looks, which might have stood out in Lakewood but weren't pushing any kind of extreme with this crowd. She was a couple of inches shorter than Alison and about the same weight, but she carried it differently. She was dressed in some kind of military dress uniform which had been made for someone larger and altered inexpertly. Her head was dwarfed by the large flat topped hat which presumably went with the uniform, giving the whole outfit a dressing-up-in-Daddy's-clothes kind of look, which probably would have really pissed her off had she but known. She would have done better to dress like Alison. They made camouflage in small sizes. Or maybe she was into the not-quite-getting-it-look. Who knew? She'd had bad acne as a teenager—there were faint scars still on her cheeks. She had the kind of face which lends itself well to being a dyke; if she'd been straight she would have been thought homely, but she'd be kind of a cute little butch in an intense kind of way if she lost the hat. She had startlingly pretty eyes, bright blue, and a faint scar on the right side of her face, cutting across the outer tip of her eyebrow and disappearing beneath her hair. Alison wondered if she was on the Stay-Away-From cheat sheet Stacy had given her, but she could hardly get it out and look.

"Hi," she said again. Alison waited with interest to see what was going to happen next. She herself was not interested in butch-on-butch energy, but that was just a personal thing. She hated raisins with a passion, but it didn't mean that the whole world had to go without raisins. Although she'd had her share of androgynous lovers when she was younger, she'd never, since becoming butch-identified, been hit on by another butch and she was curious to see how it was done. She wondered if the woman had been attracted because they were both wearing military garb. "Are you really a cop?" the woman asked.

Alison wasn't sure if she'd misread the signs or if this was just a lead in. Either way, it was a road down which she did not plan to travel. There were way too many points at which it could be unpleasant, the least of which being a little leather outing at 400 Police Plaza which might very well screw up her disability pay. If that was the way she decided to go. Her rheumatologist had told her to think about it if things didn't start getting better within the next year. She was currently taking what Stacy believed was a little leave of absence to think things over. The thinking things over part was true. Except that Stacy thought she was wondering whether she wanted to be a cop her whole life, while Alison was wondering if, with her FMS, she *could* be a cop her whole life. She hadn't told Stacy about it because that would mean telling Stacy about the battle she'd been fighting alone for a year and how was she going to do that? She didn't even know what to say in explanation, let alone how she wanted to be treated.

"No," she said, and in case that wasn't clear enough, "Are you really a Marine?" It came out sounding exactly like what it was, a very defensive lie. She tried to soften it with a little laugh, which lay awkwardly against it like a piece of eyelet lace tacked to a leather jacket.

"No, really," the woman persisted. "My name is Scar, by the way." She offered a hand. Someone, thought Alison, had at one time taught her lovely manners. Her handshake was all a handshake should be—firm without power play, ten seconds and no more. She leaned in close but not too close and scooted back out of Alison's personal space the moment she let go.

"Really," she persisted, trying to skewer Alison with a piercing look. "Somebody—one of the women working here—told me you're a local cop."

G-hey! thought Alison grimly. G-hey! was Salad's girlfriend and she had the habit of just blurting whatever came into her mind without stopping to consider that some of the information she carried in her head was really not hers to give. Alison thought about burning her house to the ground. She or Flame, the bouncer, had to be the leak. But Flame had never expressed any interest in anything about her—Alison was not sure if she even knew her name. Stacy and Liz, for all the bad behavior and duplicity of which they were capable, knew how paranoid she could be about being outed as a cop.

"No," she said, looking for a graceful opening and simultaneously wishing she could remember what Stacy or Dana had said about this woman in last night's gossip session. She looked down the stairs, but before she could make a graceful escape both the hall and stairs were suddenly crowded with thrillseekers all trying to go downstairs at the same time. The ten o'clock workshops must have just let out. Even if she jumped up right that second she was going to end up trapped not more than two feet away from Scar. Alison had a sneaking suspicion Scar was not the kind of person afraid to make a public scene. Until the crowd dispersed it seemed there were only two choices: Scar wondering quietly if she was a cop or everyone within hearing distance wondering if she was a cop.

"Do you think we should police our own community?" Scar had obviously made up her mind. Either Alison was a cop, in which case she was going to hear the story, or she wasn't a cop, in which case she was going to hear the story anyway. "I mean, if we find out something really bad? I don't know what to do about it. I think I should talk to you."

This piqued Alison's curiosity. Because, come on, it had to be really bad if one of these gals was thinking of talking to the police. All around them were women with shaved heads and beards, women with scarification and enough piercings to make going through a metal detector a major ordeal. Women hunched beneath the weight of their toy bags and not afraid to use them, either. Women into beating, caning, cutting, suffocation, fire, fisting, cocksucking, bondage, struggle, simulated rape and Daddy scenes, and that was just what Alison had seen personally. Unless Scar was here by accident— and that was going to take a major suspension of disbelief—these were her people. Coming to a leather convention and complaining about how nasty things were was kind of like going to Michigan and pissing and moaning because of all those women with their shirts off—although Alison seemed to remember that someone had actually written to LC and done that last year. So what could this woman have seen to freak her out, a dead body? Alison hoped not—Stacy would be bound to get pissy and blame her.

"I really can't help you," she said firmly. Or, as firmly as she got when not on duty, which meant she was open to all kinds of bargaining and manipulation. She knew this about herself and so added quickly, "I've got to go. My girlfriend wants me…" she trailed off, trying to think of something urgent. Actually, the task probably didn't matter. It was probably enough to establish there was both a girlfriend and a commitment.

No, it wasn't. Scar plowed forward. "I can't just pretend I didn't hear it. I can't pretend I don't know. I have to tell someone! But I don't want to screw anyone here if I can help it." She looked off into space when she said this, forming her face into a posture so noble and selfless that it made Alison wonder if screwing someone here was exactly what she had in mind. "I'm not even sure it's a police thing. I guess it would depend on the statute of limitations. Maybe it's a lawyer thing. But something should be done."

Dammit! thought Alison crossly. Why was she always getting sucked into these things? Was there a sign on her forehead that glowed, like Dorothy's kiss from Glenda the Good Witch of the North? By visualizing Stacy at the height of a tear, Alison summoned up a firm wall of resolve. "I think that if you have a problem you should go to one of the women who organized the event. They're the ones with the red name tags." Stacy wasn't going to like that, but at least Alison wouldn't get blamed and sometimes that was as good as it got.

"But most cops can be so close-minded," Scar continued, obviously not hearing. "They see leather, they see whips and they don't look much beyond that. I thought it would be so much better if one of our own—"

"Okay," said Alison, giving in and abandoning the denial without apology or explanation. "What did you see?" Obviously she did have a sign on her forehead. Listening, however, was all she was going to do. Oh, and passing it on to Stacy or Liz if she thought it was warranted. Liz, probably. At the moment it was better to send anything unpleasant through a messenger.

"It wasn't so much what I saw as what I heard." She leaned close and confidential, whispering like she was Mata Hari, glancing quickly from side to side to make sure she wasn't overheard. "I had a playdate. Through the personals. It worked out fine—we both wanted to do it again. She's letting me stay with her—boy, did that help the money situation… I don't know how I was going to pay for a hotel and the conference." Here Scar looked cross, her tone conveying the opinion this should have been handled better. "…they couldn't find community housing for me. So that was great. But afterwards, when we went to the Meet and Beat—"

The traffic in the hall had changed. The women leaving workshops had pushed their way to the kitchen or porch, but a whole new crowd, on their way to workshops, had started up the stairs, the overflow eddying around the bench where they sat.

Scar looked at her watch. "Oh, damn," she said. "I've got to lead a workshop. I can't talk now. I'm out at noon. I'll find you then." Before Alison could protest or talk about priorities Scar was gone, swirled up the stairs by the current.

Christ! thought Alison irritably. One minute the woman was forcing a dreadful confession on her and the next minute she had someplace to go. She must not watch enough TV—if she did she'd have known that this was the point at which she'd turn up murdered before she could point the finger. Was there really a problem, or was she just another dyke with a drama? Maybe Stacy would know.

Alison looked out over the thinning crowd into the kitchen. Standing by the buffet was the love of her life, talking to a big, butch girl wearing a black Jane's Addiction T-shirt with a pack of cigarettes rolled up in the left sleeve, black jeans and Doc Martens. It was the woman who had lifted Stacy high in the air the night before. Stacy was laughing and tossing her head in a way that made both her curls and her earrings dance. Gone was the irritation that had ruled for three weeks. You never would have guessed this was a woman who had threatened to burn the catering place to the ground if they backed out.

Alison was struck with a flash of jealousy so hot she was surprised it didn't leap right out of her mouth and cut the other woman down like a laser. Dammit, she'd been on the wrong end of that bad mood too many times to count in the past month and now here was Stacy exchanging honey-eyed words with some out-of-towner! It was so unfair! She was not quite sure how she got across the hall, but in less than a minute she was there by Stacy's side.

"Hello," Alison said, first to Stacy and then to the other woman. Alison took Stacy's hand, realizing just a moment too late it was a mistake. Stacy, who didn't mind a slight sprinkling of jealousy like jimmies on a soft cone, would not put up with being treated like a possession or accessory. She liked the idea that women were willing to come to blows over her, but always made it quite clear that in the end she would do exactly as she pleased. Alison dropped her hand hastily, but she could tell from the way that Stacy turned her head away stiffly, the damage was already done. She stood awkwardly, hands by her sides, while Stacy finished chatting up the butch girl, who it turned out she knew from Powersurge. Her tone was light and polite and everything she said perfectly acceptable to say in front of the girlfriend, but beneath it rode a line of irritation so strong Alison knew she was not only going to get her head bitten off, but chewed into tiny little pieces as well. Damn it all, why hadn't she listened to Liz and aimed Stacy at Michelle?

Tentatively, she tried moving away in an Oh-I-just-have-something-to-do way, but Stacy responded as quickly as a motion sensor. Her hand shot out and clasped Alison's in a manner which probably looked lovely and sensitive to onlookers, but was in reality as binding as a handcuff. "What exactly was that?" Stacy asked. "You know how I feel about being grabbed! You might as well have come up and pissed on me to mark your territory! I will not be bullied, Alison! I won't be bullied and I won't have any rumors spread that I will be bullied!"

If they had been in private Alison might have just lain down and taken it. She was wrong and she knew she was wrong, she knew better than to grab at Stacy because she was feeling insecure. Stacy was nobody's piece of jewelry to be worn on the arm and she had often mentioned how she hated possessive butches like Beth's girlfriend, whose idea of the perfect femme was one who would nod and look pretty and not say a word to anyone else.

But they weren't in private, they were in public, and for all Stacy's hissed whisper Alison knew everyone around her was listening, which embarrassed her and made acquiescence impossible. She might let Stacy tie her up and fuck her in the ass, but she was damned if she was going to be called pussy-whupped outside a scene.

"I didn't think…" she began, not at all sure of what she didn't think, but knowing it didn't matter, because Stacy was sure to cut her off anyway.

"You sure as hell didn't!" cut in Stacy, true to form. "You take my hand because you're hot for me or because you want to help me or tell me how you feel, but don't you dare take my hand to drive someone away from me! You might as well put a big sign on me that says, 'I don't trust my girlfriend!' as do that! How do you think that makes me feel?"

"Look," said Alison in a low voice, as if a low voice was going to signal Stacy that this really wasn't the time and place. Yeah, right. "I didn't mean to grab you. Not like that. I just looked across the room and you looked so pretty…" With Stacy, it was never a mistake to work a compliment into the apology right away. "And I was upset about what this woman was telling me…"

The big butch gal had wandered back into the kitchen and was picking at grapes from the breakfast table while rather obviously listening to every word being said with some amusement. There was nothing Alison hated more than an audience and no audience she hated more than a room full of butches. She had not felt this embarrassed over a scolding since sixth grade, when her mother had read her the riot act in front of her tomboy softball team. With unusual grace for twelve-year-olds, the other girls—eighty per-cent of whom had later turned out to be dykes—had wordlessly agreed to pretend it had never happened, but Alison had still burned the rest of the season, imagining knowing looks and whispers. She had stayed home for the last two games, feigning illness.

"I have worked my butt off on this convention and the last thing I need…" Stacy was working herself up to full tear mode, her voice growing louder with each word. The room was emptying rapidly. A few of the butches shot sympathetic looks toward Alison as they retreated, carrying plates loaded with fruit and bagels on which they had not had the time to spread cream cheese. The big butch girl gave Alison a wink, which infuriated her so that she cut Stacy off in midsentence.

"Stop it! Stop it right now! I am not going to have a fight with you in front of all these people. It's not happening!"

"Oh, right, you can grab me in front of all these people…"

Alison held up her hand and walked through the nearest door, which happened to be the one that led to the back yard.

The grounds of the mansion, Tara, had probably not been left com-pletely intact—those Victorians had liked to surround themselves with a lot of space and since there was no income tax they had been able to afford it. But a huge hunk behind the house, easily the size of three lots, remained, as did a dry marble fountain, several stone benches, a lovely little gazebo and a ton of perennial shrubs. If Alison had not been in a state of upset and offended butch dignity, she might have been able to imagine the way it had once looked—regal and beautiful. It must have been a riot of color in the summer.

There was no one else in the yard except for a very large woman wear-ing a black skirt and corset who was wandering along the back fence, looking at the shrubs and showing no sign of wanting company. Alison was more than grateful. She didn't want to talk to anyone at the moment—not shop, not Stacy, not even How-about-them-Silver Bullets? What she wanted to do was go home and sulk and she'd do it in a moment if she could just find Salad and get her to take over the van. Failing that, she wanted to go straight out to the van and start driving, perhaps grazing Stacy's little red Miata on the way out.

The yard—or perhaps she should say estate—was entirely enclosed by a six foot privacy fence. The really good kind, with two layers. No looking through the cracks here. It wasn't at all Victorian, but at least it kept the winos from sleeping in the fountain. Alison followed the fence around to the front, where she found a gate. Locked with a padlock.

"Dammit to fuck!" No way was she going back through that house for at least another five minutes, which would, hopefully, give Stacy time to work the head off her tear. Probably she was ripping the hearts out of strangers even now. It would be a bad day for the lesbian community if Stacy ever got it into her head to carry an automatic weapon.

There was a stone bench near the gate, canopied by a lattice overgrown with wild roses, just starting to green. Alison sank down upon it and rested her back against the wall. She was just going to sit there and drink the can of Diet Pepsi she had in her daypack and think only about things calm and beautiful. Maybe eat a snack. When she got upset she couldn't sleep, and when she couldn't sleep her hands swelled up and when her hands swelled up her face swelled up and—well, it just went on from there. But here in the garden it was lovely and peaceful and there was no Stacy and—

"You shouldn't be here! What gave you the right to crash into my life like this!"

Alison jumped. The words were hissed in a sibilant whisper, but so close Alison could hear the fury clearly. She looked around scanning the bushes and shrubs before she realized it was coming from a window three feet above her head. Oh, god, she thought, I'm in hell! The Pattys must have taken it into the bathroom, which of all places, she thought, really should be sacred. A bad bathroom experience could make you neurotic forever.

"This is ridiculous! You act as if I did something to hurt you! I didn't do a thing to hurt you! I loved you!" The second voice was also a whisper, as if the speaker didn't want to be overheard. That wasn't like the Pattys, thought Alison. Usually they preferred an audience. How long was this going to go on? Was it worth gathering her things and looking, probably futilely, for another private spot? Two minutes of the Pattys, dreadful as they were, was much better than facing Stacy while she was still on boil. It would be like riding the Mind Eraser at Elitche's—not a personal choice, but endurable with closed eyes and clenched teeth.

"You didn't love me! If you'd loved me you would have left me alone! Let me be a child. You would have let me grow up! What you did was use me! You used me and you taught me that being a lesbian was bad!"

"What are you talking about, baby? I don't think being a lesbian is bad! How could I teach you something that I don't believe myself?"

"You do believe it! All that lying and denial and sneaking around…"

"I couldn't help that! Who was going to understand? Don't blame me for the way that society looks at people like us! I can't help it if there wasn't a place for our love! The best thing that I could do was create a place for it! Don't blame me if it wasn't perfect—I did the best I could. And you wanted it! I would have gone away at any point if you'd said the word. You never said it! You hung onto to me like I was your salvation!"

"Because you groomed me for it! I would have had to have been Superwoman to push you away! I was so young. You were my teacher—my salvation; why couldn't you have been content to just leave it at that? What you did was like incest; there could never be any balance of power!"

Okay, this had gone on too long whoever it was. It was making Alison very uncomfortable. Watching Ricki Lake, where people told their sordid stories to the world willingly was one thing, listening to a two-woman show which could have been planned for sweeps week—Did Someone Tell You It Was Bad To Be a Lesbian and Now You Want To Confront That Person?—was a bit too much. Alison stuffed her unopened Diet Pepsi and bag of crackers and cheese back into her pack and left with a huff she hoped the women inside could hear—not that it would make a difference. They were way too into their own show to care about the audience.

As she headed for the back door, Alison flushed with the shame of publicly airing her own dirty laundry. She and Stacy had sounded just like the dueling Pattys—a couple of assholes that thought the world wanted to listen to their petty personal problems. Alison's mother had raised her to believe that only trashy people quarreled in public, and though she had thrown a lot of her mother's advice and modeling right in the trash heap along with those silly Kotex belts, this particular adage was one she had taken to heart. There was no way on God's green earth she was going to put up with another public harangue, even if it meant avoiding Stacy the whole rest of the weekend. She was willing to walk away as many times as it took.

She glanced about cautiously before stepping inside the door. Stacy was neither in the kitchen nor in the part of the hall Alison could see from the back steps. The kitchen traffic had adjusted itself to normal—a few women fixing bagels, a few leaning against the counters and talking. A couple was obviously waiting to use the bathroom, hanging out by the closed door as if somebody was going to cut them off if they weren't vigilant.

"Hello, coward!" hissed a voice close to Alison's ear. She jumped and landed awkwardly. Liz watched with evil satisfaction.

"Jesus, Liz, I think I sprained my ankle!"

"It serves you right! What's the big idea, detonating the bomb and then running off to leave the rest of us to take the blast!"

Alison was quite selfishly cheered to hear that Stacy had scattered her Staciness over the crowd. "Did she get you?" she asked, rotating her ankle to see if it had that six weeks in ice packs feel.

"She got me, she got Beth, she got Salad, she got several people just minding their own business on the porch and then I believe that she went on to get some guy sleeping on the sidewalk, who practically had a heart attack. Oh, and if it's any consolation, she also got that big butch girl she'd been flirting with."

It was consolation. "Did she get G-Hey!?" she asked, hopefully. That would make it perfect.

"No. But I don't think she's over it yet, so there's still hope. Why don't you like G-Hey!?"

"Because she doesn't think about anything she says. She just blurts everything out. Where's Stacy now?" Alison stretched her neck around the corner like a cautious cat.

"That would be called *honesty,* Alison. And God only knows where the Evil Bitch went. I think she might have gone to get Pepsi and cigarettes. Or maybe a gun."

"I gotta go now," said Alison. "Do me a favor and give these to Salad." She pushed the keys into Liz's hand and moved off quickly before she could protest. She held herself back from an outright run, because that would look so undignified, but she moved through the house at a pretty good clip, making it clear to the front steps before getting caught.

"Pardon me."

Alison did not look up. She probably wouldn't have stopped at all if the woman hadn't stepped right in her path and put her hand on her arm.

"I have to go right now," she said between clenched teeth. If she stayed out of Stacy's sight for a couple of hours there was every reason to believe Stacy would get over her tantrum without feeling the need to ream her out completely. It was no time for small talk.

"I have a message for you," the woman persisted. "I'll be in terrible trouble if I don't deliver it. I don't know what she'll do; I'd probably have to find someplace else to sleep tonight."

"I don't care," said Alison, pushing around her and taking the steps two at a time. It was difficult to push Alison to rudeness, but it had been a hell of a morning. Her car was parked up the street and she made for it with such determined focus that she didn't realize the woman had trailed along behind her.

"It's important," she said plaintively when Alison stopped to look for her keys.

Alison was startled and jumped, which did not make her disposed to grant a favor. On the other hand, they were out of Stacy's sight.

"What?" she asked in a guarded voice, keys at the ready in case it got weird.

The woman was a bit shorter than Alison and though she had a beautifully shaped mouth and long, silky eyelashes, the thing that drew your eye was her shaved head. After a moment one could notice several piercings and cat's eye glasses with purple rims, but for the first few moments it was the head.

"What?" Alison asked again, trying not to speak to the top of the woman's head. It wasn't as if she had never seen a lesbian with a shaved head before. Of course she had. Who hadn't? She had even seen some on whom it looked good. That hadn't happened here. This had been a very bad choice, making the woman's head appear a couple of times too small for her body, so that she looked like a kinky version of those Bo-Bo the Clown dolls— punch it in the head and it would always come back to standing.

"Please," said the woman, "you've got to help us! Dana said you helped her. She said maybe you could help us, too!"

Alison silently cursed Dana. She might saw an inch off her high heels herself.

"This can't go on! It's killing her! I've been watching her and it's eating her up inch by inch! It can't be allowed to go on—it's like allowing someone to stand at the base of the Statue of Liberty and just file away and file away until it falls over!"

Alison regarded her with a raised eyebrow and some amazement. The last time she had seen this kind of zeal it had ended badly with a death and a funeral pyre. There was, however, a certain cautious attraction to a person in this state—it raised Alison's curiosity and at the same time made her question her own day-to-day life, where there was happiness and contentment but very rarely zeal.

"Look," she said, jiggling the keys in one hand, "I have no idea what you're talking about. I don't even know your name."

"I don't have a name this weekend. I'm Livia's Best Boy this weekend." She said it proudly, obviously expecting Alison to understand and be impressed.

Alison shook her head. Okay, so she was a dummy and a novice and just couldn't pretend to be anything else.

"Livia's Best Boy?" The woman raised an eyebrow as if she thought Alison just hadn't heard the first time. When Alison shook her head a second time she paused for a long moment, as if trying to marshal an explanation for something so very basic that she never had needed to explain it before. Shoes or something.

"This weekend," she said slowly, enunciating every word clearly and a little loudly, "I'm taking care of Livia's needs. She chose me to do that. There was a long list of people who wanted to do it, but she chose me." For a moment she lost that air of speaking to Forrest Gump and wriggled with pure delight. "Of course, I've been waiting. I've been to a lot of events with her group. I've really learned a lot about being a submissive. It's hard work trying to anticipate all of someone's needs. You don't realize what hard work it is until you try it." She cocked the other eyebrow as if inviting comment.

"It comes naturally to me," said Alison dryly, thinking of the many needs of the lovely Stacy. Even as they spoke she was probably failing her in some way of which she was not aware.

"Everybody thinks it's no big deal," Best Boy complained. "Like it's just running a bunch of errands or something. But that's not it at all. It's hard! It's like giving your soul for the entire weekend, like putting it in her hands without expecting anything back. That's the key, not expecting anything, just letting the fact that you've done well be your only reward."

It was a fairly interesting conversation and one Alison would certainly carry back to Stacy and Liz to hear their views. Maybe only Liz. She didn't want to put any new ideas in the head of Mistress Anastasia. Mistress Anastasia had enough ideas of her own. But right now she wanted to know what this woman's desperate problem was.

"So who's Livia?" she asked. The name sounded familiar, but Stacy and Dana had pointed out half a dozen women the night before.

"You don't…she's like…I can't believe—" Best Boy lapsed into an amazed silence, as if Alison hadn't been able to name the president. "She's only like the woman who runs the leather camp at Michigan. That's all! She's like, like Sappho or something! Like everyone wants to sit at her feet just so they can learn from her! Like everyone wants to stay in her hotel suite and be invited to her parties! And she's so generous with her money! I waited three years for this, just to be allowed to sleep at her feet!"

Hmm, thought Alison, not liking Livia already.

"And she wants what with me?" she asked.

"I'm only authorized to bring you to her," said Best Boy regretfully. "I wish I could tell you. I wish I knew myself. I'd tell you, even if I was punished for it! Because I know she's going to play it down. I know she's going to be brave and act like it's not important. She's like that. You have to keep that in mind when you talk to her. She won't tell you how bad it's been, but I know. I've seen."

Alison felt as if she were speaking to someone who had just found Jesus, and that alone was enough to make her wary. Zealots could be interesting for a moment or two, but ultimately she was not comfortable around them. Mainstream Americans were not really taught to worship anyone, aside from film stars and certain members of foreign royalty. That was the reason it made everyone so nervous when fundamentalist groups holed up in Waco or Coeur d'Alene. It was not so much the stockpiled guns but the fact that the converts had lost the middle class barometer, which warned nice people when they were getting that look in their eyes.

"I just don't think..." Alison started. She had no idea what this woman, Livia, was really like, but seeing her through the burning eye of Best Boy had pushed the warning button. "I really doubt I can help in any way. I don't feel that well and besides, my girlfriend is looking for me."

"She'll pay you money," blurted Best Boy. "She'll pay you well. She's generous with her money." She reached into a pouch that hung around her neck and extracted five bills. She extended them. "That's just for listening," she said.

Alison looked at the money. Five hundred dollars. Money had been tight while she wasn't working. Five hundred dollars could pay her part of the mortgage this month, her part of the shingles that had been damaged last year by the hail. Five hundred dollars could pay for new brakes or clear up her VISA bill. She thought, with shame, of the closed look on the face of the waitress last weekend when she had come back with the refused card on her tray and of the casual way Stacy had paid. Not trying to make her feel embarrassed, but she had nevertheless been embarrassed. Five hundred dollars... She turned her head, afraid her need was so great it floated above her head in a bubble, the way a roast chicken would float above Garfield's head in a cartoon.

"She gave me money for a cab," Best Boy said. "I've got it waiting down the street."

Chapter Four

They didn't take the cab, because there was no way Alison was going to be stuck in a hotel with people she didn't know. Call it control issues, call it whatever you damn wanted to call it, but uh-uh, no fucking way. She was taking her own car. Maybe Best Boy had money for cab fare, but she didn't. And in Denver, you could usually find a place to park, even downtown. The hotel, in fact, had a private garage run by a nice young man dressed in uniform, who promised to bring her car right up to the front if she called ahead.

"Thank you so much," said Best Boy in the elevator. "You don't know how much this means to me. I really want to do a good job this weekend. As good as Livia deserves."

Alison said nothing, wishing the money was in her wallet and she was out the door. She did not have a good feeling about this. She hated it when she was driven by money. She had always scorned people who kissed ass to inherit or keep a job. It was easy to be scornful when you had a steady paycheck.

The room to which Best Boy led them was not an actual suite, but the middle of three adjoining rooms, all doors open. In the room to the right there was some kind of whipping and fire scene going on. In the room to the left several women were lying on one of the queen-sized beds in bathrobes watching *Deep Space Nine* on the TV. Or at least Alison thought it was, although the holographic doctor from the other show seemed to be visiting the station. It was always a problem for her when the characters crossed shows.

The middle room was the lounge. There were several trays of meat, cheese and veggies out on the bureau and bottles of alcohol and mixers on the desk. Their very size told Alison they had not come from the tiny hotel refrigerator at ten bucks a pop. The chairs from all three rooms had been pulled in to form a circle and in the most comfortable sat the woman with Morticia Adams hair who had tried to bully Liz out of the table the night before. Her Lead Dog was brushing her hair with long, careful strokes. Like it was going to make a difference.

"Oh, shit," thought Alison. Had to be someone Stacy didn't like, just to make things more interesting. Because if Liz was openly antagonistic, it was a sure thing Stacy didn't like her. Alison almost turned and left right then, but for the thought of the five hundred dollars just for listening.

"Here she is, my mistress," said Best Boy. She stood in front of Livia with her hands clasped in front of her and her head bowed, not meeting her eyes, her tone subdued. Alison had to admit that she was pretty good.

Livia held out a hand, into which Best Boy placed the taxi money, the five hundred dollars and the key card. Sitting beside her on an empty chair was a bowl full of chocolates. She picked up one and fed it to Best Boy with the tips of her fingers, then picked up another and fed it to the woman who was crouched beside her on the floor, wearing nothing but a collar and a leash. "There, my pet," she said to her. She took the leather handle of the leash and placed it between the woman's teeth. "Take care of yourself for a little while. Don't let anyone touch you." She made a dismissing motion and everyone in the whole room rose and headed for one of the adjoining doors, except for the pet, who went into a corner and curled up on a blanket. With a start Alison realized that, in one way or another, this woman was topping everybody here. Nice gig if you could get it.

Livia waited until the doors were closed before acknowledging Alison.

"I'll want you to sign a contract," she said, picking up a briefcase that sat beside her on the floor. She opened it and slid a typed paper across the table.

Alison picked it up, more because she was curious than because she had any intention of signing anything. She tried to keep a poker face, but could feel her eyebrows rising as she read. First off, she was to agree that she would not share any information revealed in the investigation with anyone. She would neither talk nor write about it. Second, Livia would have the final say about any action taken. She would discuss her plans with Livia, inform her immediately of any new information, consult with her before she did anything. The police were not to be called under any circumstances, nor the organizers of the event.

Alison knew a bottoming contract when she saw one. "I'm not signing up to bottom for you," she said, trying to keep her voice civil as she slid the contract back across the table. No way was she signing that. Discretion was one thing, but what if she found out Livia or one of her girls was a murderer or something? "I'm here to maybe take an investigating job. You tell me what the problem is and maybe I'll decide to help you." She did not mention the five hundred dollars just for listening. Already she knew that Livia was not the kind of woman to whom you admitted any vulnerability.

"Everyone who works for me bottoms for me," Livia stated flatly, giving Alison the alpha dog stare which she had become far too used to in the last couple of years.

"Then get somebody else to do it," Alison replied, standing. She was glad she had insisted on bringing her own car, and at least it would be a story for Stacy.

"Someone is blackmailing me," Livia said. "I want you to find out who it is and I want you to stop her."

Alison turned and cocked an eye toward the contract.

"Oh. A test." Livia smiled the kind of mirthless little smile one seldom sees outside of German POW movies. "I wouldn't have wanted someone I could control that easily. Bottoms…" she laughed disparaging and brushed her hands together as if she were wiping away something nasty.

Alison wandered over to the bureau where she began making herself a sandwich with Swiss cheese and cucumbers. There could be a couple of things going on here. Either Livia really had wanted her to sign the contract or this was plan two and Livia was already playing games. Either choice left a nasty little taste in Alison's mouth. She hadn't liked the disparaging remark about bottoms, either, which was something Stacy never would have said. She had taught Alison to respect bottoms. 'After all, it doesn't happen with-out them.' It sounded like bleed-through to Alison.

"Why don't you get somebody in your own town to do it?" she asked, opening the refrigerator to see if there was any mayonnaise. "You need some-body local for blackmail." She didn't say, you need the police, because she had no idea what the local police were like where Livia lived and if they would have either the desire or manpower to investigate the complaint of a leather lesbian. Besides, Livia probably didn't want to expose her dirty little secrets to strangers. That was the whole point about blackmail. That was why it worked.

"She's here," said Livia. "Whoever it is, she's here at the conference. It should be simple enough for you to find out who it is. You have had some experience, haven't you? That little femme thing—what was her name? The redhead." That would be Dana. "She told my boy you had helped her." She gave another little wave, putting femmes on the same page as bottoms.

This also did not go over at all well with Alison, who adored femmes.

"Something about a murder?" Livia queried, her eyes gleaming. Alison realized the tone. Hiring someone who had touched a lesbian murder was obviously Livia's version of driving over to Boulder and chipping off a piece of the house where JonBenet was murdered. Well, if that was her game then the price had just gone up.

"Five hundred dollars just for talking to you, another thousand if I take the case, whether I find out who it is or not. And I do things my own way."

She had half hoped the excessive fee too as the belligerence would make Livia wave her away, but she was disappointed. Livia merely reached into her pocket and pulled out a wad, peeling off ten more hundreds, which she placed on the table beside the others. Alison looked at the money and sighed. She had trapped herself with her own cleverness. She took her sandwich and went back to the table. She didn't clean up after herself. She figured Livia had a crew to do that.

"What does she want from you and what is she threatening to tell?" she asked. She didn't have her notebook with her, so she pulled the contract across the table and flipped it over.

"I don't know either of those things," Livia said. "I only know that it's someone here." She opened her briefcase again, this time pulling out a fat manila envelope padded with bubble wrap. She started to hand it to Alison and then hesitated, pulling it back toward herself. Livia, Alison thought resignedly, was always on stage. This was going to be like being prop girl for Barbra Streisand.

"But it is confidential," Livia said firmly. "I have to insist on that. If I wanted everyone to know then I wouldn't be hiring you."

Alison nodded. That seemed reasonable. She waited for the envelope and after a moment Livia released it.

Inside were half a dozen sheets of plain white typing paper, each sealed in its own ziplock bag. Across the top of each paper were typed two or at the most three sentences, beneath which was attached a photograph. Alison glanced through the papers, which appeared to be arranged in chronological order. The top page read merely, 'I know where you live.' The snapshot was of Livia, dressed in a grey power suit, in front of an apartment building. Her pumps were grey, as were her hose, and her hair was twisted up in a chignon which did not flatter. The name of the building, the Longfellow Arms, was clear as was the fact Livia had a set of keys in the hand reaching for the door. Either a telephoto lens or really, really close, thought Alison.

She picked up the second picture. A variation on the theme. This time the photo was of Livia bending down to unlock the door of a little black Mercedes Benz and the caption read, 'And I know what you drive.' This time it was the license plate that showed clearly.

The third page was different in that it had two photos and two captions. The first photo was once again Livia, this time stepping through the glass doors of a large brick building. She held a briefcase in one hand. Her skin looked a little blotchy, as if perhaps she was trying a new kind of make-up and hadn't quite got the hang. The caption beneath this photo read, 'And I know where you work.'

The second photo on the page also had Livia as its theme, but in a much different setting. It was immediately evident to Alison that it had been taken by not just a different camera, but a different person altogether. It had also been taken outside, but not in the city. There were three women in it. One was a lovely, big, butch woman with dark, spiked hair and sunglasses, standing in front of a grey tent. She was wearing black pants with a matching body harness and held her arms in a body builder's stance that made the muscles in her chest and shoulders stand out. Automatically Alison put her at about her own height—maybe a couple of inches taller—and maybe fifty pounds heavier with the weight distributed pretty evenly all over. She had a dragon claw tattoo on her right shoulder.

In the corner of the photo and obviously not its focus, was Livia with long dark hair pulled back in a ponytail, sitting in a lawn chair. She was fully clothed, right down to a black baseball cap. At her feet, however, knelt a woman who was partially if not totally nude. Alison couldn't say for sure about shoes and socks, because her feet were beneath her, but everything else was showing, including a line of stripes down her back and buttocks. It was unclear what she was doing—perhaps attempting to kiss Livia's foot. She might also have just been sitting or being praised after a heavy scene. Livia had one booted foot up on her shoulder. She was holding a bullwhip that draped across the woman's back.

Alison looked at the photo and then up at Livia. Even if the photographer hadn't aimed at her, there wasn't any question that it was her. She had a self-satisfied look on her face, which Alison had already seen once or twice just in the ten minutes since they'd met. The caption under this photo read, 'But, do THEY know what you do?'

On the next page was a lone photograph of what appeared to be the front of a large brick building. Over the bank of glass doors was a large rectangular sign reading Michigan Mercy Medical. There was no caption. Alison was confused for a moment, until she realized that it went with the photo of Livia from the previous page. The photographer had taken one photo of Livia close up and then another just to show that she really did know where Livia worked.

"So who have you pissed off?" she asked Livia. Besides me, she added mentally.

"There are always people who are jealous." Livia raised a hand dismissively. "Always. It's been a problem before. I have money and I have influence and I use it as I see fit. If I were to give you a list of little girls who've gone away with their noses out of joint you'd need a computer to handle it. It wasn't any of them. They couldn't seize the power. That was the problem to begin with."

"Well, it would be a good idea to have a list anyway," Alison replied, working hard to sound civil. What an asshole! Why was she always ending up working for people like this? Just for once, why couldn't somebody really, really nice be in trouble and want to give her a thousand dollars?

"We'd have to start with your girlfriend, then." Livia's answer was short and she probably thought it was emotionless too. But Alison could hear the underlying purr of satisfaction. The money and the words between them had meant nothing—Livia was still going to play games.

"And do you want me to talk to her or do you want me to talk to you?" Alison tried to keep her own voice from giving away the annoyance she felt. It was better than working at McDonald's, just remember! She had no fear at all that Stacy was the blackmailer. If Stacy had a problem with people, they knew it. None of this skulking around.

"Oh, please!" Livia held up a hand as if to brush off something totally ridiculous. "I wouldn't even have even mentioned it except that I found it amusing. You have to understand, the world of s/m is a lot like the food chain. Some of these little tops from the sticks who've gobbled up a guppy or two think that puts them at the top of the chain. They're always surprised when they meet someone big enough to flip them over."

Great, now Livia was comparing Stacy to plankton. She'd love that.

"Sometimes, though, I'll bet one of those skinny little moray eels you haven't been watching reaches up and bites you right on the butt," Alison couldn't help saying. Deadpan, of course.

Livia curled up the corners of her mouth into the kind of utterly humorless smile Data's evil twin, Lore, got before doing something horrible like killing his own father or trying to ally with the Borg. Alison was a little frightened by the way this comparison had popped into her mind. Maybe Stacy had been more successful with the *Star Trek* thing than either of them had realized.

"And there are bottom feeders also." Another little smile. Oh, Livia'd made a joke. It made Alison a tiny bit more willing to like her. Say a milliwatt. "But do go ahead and talk to your little femme girlfriend; I'd love to hear if she has any insight at all into why she did what she did."

Yeah, right, thought Alison. She was going to go get Stacy all pissed off over past injustices and then run back and dissect her id with Livia. That would be the day.

"What is it you do here?" Alison asked, pointing at the hospital picture.

"I'm a...doctor. A lung specialist."

Alison had listened to a whole lot of people lie. She had been told the outrageous lie and the outright lie and the half truth and the lie of omission; the lie to keep the cops off the block, the lie to cover something serious, the lie of embarrassment and the lie to protect a loved one. She couldn't always tell if someone was lying; in her experience anyone who could was just another kind of sociopath. It took one to know one. Still, she was instantly alert to the half beat in which Livia had faltered. She's a nurse, she thought in disgust, and she doesn't want to tell me, because she thinks it's not high enough up the food chain.

"Okay," Alison said, "I might as well talk to your..." what did she call them? Groupies? "—people while I'm here."

"There's no need to do that." Livia answered so quickly she must have been anticipating the question. "I know my own people. They're above suspicion. I wouldn't have them near me if they weren't."

"Okay," said Alison, who was starting to lose her temper. "Let me see if I have this straight. You want me to find someone who's blackmailing you for no reason, but you don't want to tell me who might want to and you don't want me to ask any questions. Is that it?"

"That's absolutely it," Livia confirmed. She leaned back, smiling, and at that moment Alison knew this was really much less about blackmail than it was about being center stage. Livia, she imagined, had been playing the lead in her own little show for years. But it must have been like twenty years in *The King and I*—no matter the success, one began to yearn for something different. So she was creating a new role. Livia the oppressed, refusing to bow beneath pressure. Livia the clever, who had the money to hire a minion she would manage with the same skill she managed the rest of her staff. Livia the martyred, possibly, and Livia the vindictive most certainly. Also, but this probably wasn't going to be played for the general public, Livia the paranoid, who didn't want her hired gun to find out anything about her unless she said it herself. It'd be interesting to cut the inner circle away from the herd and see what they had to say.

"What's she asked for?" Alison asked, turning the last bag over to see if there was something she had missed. "Does she want money?"

"If that's what she wants she hasn't asked for it." Livia's voice carried a hint of irritation, which was strange. She wanted to be hit on for money? "This was in my registration packet." She reached into the briefcase again and pulled out the familiar red program. Alison had one just like it somewhere. It told the rules and the workshops and the good places to eat and when the shuttles were running and half a dozen other things anyone planning on leaving the dungeons needed to know.

"Mmm, I don't know how to tell you this, but we all got one of these."

"I know that! Look at the back!"

Alison flipped the flier over. Though she had seen most of the material before it had gone to the printers, she had given her own registration packet only the most cursory of glances. The back of the flier, she saw, was like a personals page. Okay, now she remembered Stacy talking about this. Here's what the deal was. If you pre-registered and paid a couple of extra bucks you could have a personal in both the program and the advance flier. That way attendees could meet up for pre-conference parties or arrange playdates ahead on the phone or computer. It had seemed like a good idea at the time.

"This!" Livia said, stabbing her finger toward the page. There in the middle, surrounded by a border of stars, was a huge ad in bold face, circled with a black marker:

LOVE TO PLAY? LOVE TO PARTY? FOOD, FEMMES AND FROLIC— EVERYONE WELCOME! LIVIA'S PLACE AT THE CONFERENCE HOTEL, FRIDAY NIGHT—AFTER THE FEAST UNTIL SUNRISE. CHECK MESSAGE BOARD FOR ADDRESS. FEMME TOPS ESPECIALLY WELCOME.

"I take it you didn't put this in here?" Alison had to bite her lip and think again about minimum wage jobs to keep from laughing. Okay, blackmail and extortion were both terrible habits which she absolutely could not condone, but still. Whoever was doing this really had Livia's number. Maybe that was why Livia would have preferred money—after all, you can pay money and be done with it. Judging from the look on her face there was nothing she would like less than hosting a party open to the common folk.

"This was inside it," she said, tossing a piece of paper onto the table.

"I like Chivas Regal," it read. "I like roast beef and Swiss cheese and sourdough bread and chocolate. A party puts me in a charitable mood and drives the price way down."

Alison picked it up by the corners and thought about fingerprints. She noticed that this note had been printed on a different printer, inkjet as opposed to dot matrix.

"So you're partying tonight and there's going to be chocolate and roast beef?"

Livia shuddered. "And the masses as well. What else can I do?"

"You could call her bluff," said Alison. "Do you think you'd really get fired based on this?" She pointed to the photo.

"Yes," said Livia shortly, "I do. I'm sure of it."

"Well, then," said Alison, "I guess I'll see you tonight." She reached for the packet of photos.

Livia's reach was quicker. "You don't need that," she said.

"I do if I'm going to find that woman in the photo," Alison said. "Don't you think that's a pretty obvious place to start?"

Livia considered this for so long Alison made herself a second sandwich. Better than being an unaccredited actor on the Livia show. Finally Livia took the one photo out of its ziplock, ripped off the part that showed her and handed it to Alison.

"What about…" Alison began, gesturing to the nude woman Livia held between forefinger and thumb.

"That's fuckbaby," Livia said, gesturing to the corner. "She hasn't been anywhere without me in five years. She doesn't know anything." She stood. Livia had spoken. They were through talking.

Alison turned toward the door, but Livia called her back. She'd bet that was a habit of Livia's—dismiss her servants and then call them back for one last word, just to show who was boss. "What's your phone number?" she asked, "In case I need to check on things?"

If Alison had been thinking she wouldn't have done what she did, which was to open her checkbook to the back, rip out a deposit slip printed with her phone number and address and hand it to Livia. But it was something she did with her friends, and besides, just then she glanced over in the corner where the woman Livia called fuckbaby was curled up and saw that she was watching them quietly from beneath one slitted lid just as her cat, KP, did. It made her want to leave the room quickly and so she did. She was careful not to let the door hit her on the butt on the way out.

Chapter Five

Even though she hadn't called ahead the nice boy downstairs had Alison's car up front in a matter of minutes. She wished she had the money to tip but she only had hundreds and she wasn't that impressed.

She sat out front for a good ten minutes, trying to decide what to do. Home was the most inviting. She could go home, take a five or six hour nap and blow off everybody. It wasn't as if she could make Stacy much madder than she already was and what, really, was the point of playing detective for Livia? Livia had paid her that money the same way another woman might buy a piece of garden sculpture from a famous artist whose work she didn't particularly like. It was a show of wealth and power and not much more. It was like that episode of *The Next Generation* where a private collector who specialized in the one-of-a-kind had held Data captive. Again Alison was a little bothered by being able to pull up a *Star Trek* analogy. But the analogy worked. All she was to Livia was the only android in Star Fleet or the last quagga. Livia had Her Boy, Her Pet and now Her Private Detective. She didn't expect Alison to really find out anything. If she had, she would have given her something to go on. She would have let her speak to the women in the next room. She would have made more of the money being contingent on a solution.

But… Alison sighed. Why, oh why was she cursed with the Puritan work ethic, the sense that there was always that big account book in the sky wherein was recorded laziness, sloth, cheating, dishonesty? She could no more take Livia's money without at least trying than she could be happy getting a check for not being a police officer. And that meant back to Tara because the only people she was going to find at home were Janka and baby Sammy and they didn't know a thing about Livia.

Stacy was practically waiting at the curb when Alison pulled in. Even from a distance, Alison could see that Evil Stacy was gone. The vile aura, which had surrounded her for days, had disappeared. She was greeting the women returning from their hotels sweetly, asking how the conference was going for them, listening and nodding her head so gravely you got the idea she was going to run right inside and fix the play space or buy strawberry cream cheese herself.

"I'm sorry I yelled at you," she said as soon as Alison was within earshot.

"I'm sorry you yelled at me, too," said Alison. "We sounded just like the Pattys and I hate that. It made me feel stupid. It embarrassed me in front of the other butches." She was usually very gracious about accepting Stacy's apologies without scolding, but she felt strongly about this.

Stacy reacted as she always did to criticism—defensively. "I'm Italian," she said. "We're passionate. You take everything too seriously—sometimes I'm just blowing off steam."

"Lots of times you're just blowing off," Alison replied, wondering if this was going to lead right back to fighting, but willing to risk it. "And the only time you're ever Italian is when you've just," she wanted to say 'acted like an asshole' but thought it wouldn't be taken well, so said instead, "overreacted. The Italian defamation league is going to get down on you if you don't stop it."

Stacy got kind of a sour look on her face and Alison held her breath, wondering if she was going to blow again. Then Stacy gave a great big sigh. "I'm sorry. I was just in a tizzy and it blew right at that moment. I had to apologize to about twenty people."

This was good. If Stacy had apologized to pretty much the whole conference, then Alison's name as a bad girlfriend was clear.

"So what's the penalty?" Stacy asked. Important blow-ups, of course, were to be discussed, but little things were settled by penalty which Alison tended to pay quite a bit more than Stacy. She thought for a moment. They were not the fighting and fucking type, or at least Alison wasn't and Stacy knew better than to suggest it, for she had learned it was apt to lead to a fight much more volatile than the first. Instead Stacy became affectionate, tolerant and a good listener when she was sorry. Which, Alison figured, made it the perfect time to tell her about taking the job for Livia.

"Do you have a list of everybody who's here?" she asked. "That's what I want."

"Well, I have the name tag list. It doesn't have everybody's real name. Salad has that one on her computer." Stacy was puzzled, but game. Paying a penalty was ever so much nicer than dealing with the sulks and nobody sulked like Alison.

"Let's go some place more private and sit down for a few minutes," Alison suggested.

They found an empty workshop room and gossiped for a few minutes. Stacy told Alison that there had been a Patty exchange in the fisting workshop and Alison told Stacy about the scene she had overheard in the bathroom. The SEPS had not shown up and Stacy thought that Dana had her sights on Liz, although Dana was so wound up it was hard to tell for sure. She might be scatter-shooting.

"I got a job!" Alison finally said, with a lot more enthusiasm than she actually felt. "I got hired to do some sleuthing!" She felt it prudent to work 'sleuthing' into the conversation as soon and frequently as possible. Stacy, a voracious reader of mysteries, was much more likely to respond favorably if she could be made to feel the game was afoot.

"Oh?" Stacy, even in reconciliatory mode, was ever alert to the possibility of being set up.

"I got hired by somebody out of town to find a blackmailer," Alison explained, toying with the possibility of pretending she just didn't remember Stacy and Livia had bad blood between them. Well, it was worth a try. "Someone named Livia? Kind of an asshole?"

"Oh, god!" Stacy put her hand over her face. "Say it ain't so, Joe! What a horrible woman! And you promised—no dead bodies! No dead bodies at the conference! You promised!"

"And I have kept my promise," Alison replied a bit tartly. "It's not murder, it's blackmail. That's why I want the list. I want you to tell me everything about everybody."

It was a good approach, buoyed up by the fact Stacy was not yet in the clear about the fight.

"Okay, okay," she said, somewhat less than graciously. "But I'm not going anywhere with that woman, so don't even suggest it."

"Okay," said Alison, pretending to make a note. "Look, I'll tell you what. Get it out and pick out everybody you know is in Livia's private party first."

Stacy pulled a piece of folded paper out of her purse and smoothed it out on the shaky card table that, with about ten folding chairs, composed the entire furnishings of the room. "Okay, Yesman—she's been Livia's loyal follower forever. Longer than anyone else I know. Never has gotten the boot and has been with her through a couple of dynasties. The name says it all—you know? Everyone should have a name like that—it would just make things easier." She scanned the sheet for a moment and then added, "And Livia's would be 'Asshole.'"

"What would mine be?" asked Alison, hoping for Hardbody or Irresistible.

"Yours would be Stacy's," Stacy replied, still engrossed in the list. "Actually, Livia is pretty good. At least she knows how deadly she is. It would have to be Caligula to be clearer. Oh, here's someone you might want to talk to. She was in with the Livia crowd last year, but she's not any more and I've heard she's bitter. Look," she said, turning around. "Let's make a chart." She pulled a second piece of paper from her purse, glanced at the writing on the front, which looked to Alison like a shopping list, decided it could be sacrificed and turned it over.

"Don't be getting all Kinsey Millhone on me," Alison warned. It was a sore spot.

"You could learn a thing or two from Kinsey if you'd just let yourself," said Stacy absently. She had already warmed to the task; names and lines were flowing beneath her pen as if she were a cartographer. "Okay, here's loathsome Livia, Queen of the Mindfuckers." As she spoke she was circling Livia's name with a circle of lines like the rays of a child's sun. "And here's the most recent court. Now, Yesman is part of the Seattle crowd—I know that because she was driving a van at Powersurge and they only let their own people drive. Jean Verene I know from MISL a couple of years ago and she used to be with Master Mad Dog when she was Madam Mad Dog. Mad Dog and Jean Verene are both from Portland, so it's a good bet that Dana might know a little bit more about them, because the Portland girls and the Seattle girls tend to party together. This woman here," she tapped her pencil on the list, "I think maybe she's connected to those two Pattys. I think I saw that Butch Patty with her at the last Powersurge and I saw Femme Patty having some kind of ugly little exchange with her in the leather mall this morning. This name—Best Boy? Livia usually has a Best Boy with her. Do you know if she does this year?"

"Yeah," Alison replied. "Purple glasses. Pretty eyes. Kind of a bad shaved head thing going."

"Okay, I know just who you're talking about. She's been with the Livia court for a couple of years, too. I can't remember what she used to be called. What she is this weekend is kind of like being Livia's personal secretary. They don't have sex and probably never have. Livia will probably top her in one scene this weekend if she's really good—maybe she'll let the rest of the private party gang bang her when she's done. Then everyone will go home happy."

Liz wandered into the room, obviously looking for Stacy. "Are we made up?" she asked.

"Yes," said Stacy. "Do I have to make a separate apology to you?"

"That depends," she said, sitting down beside Stacy and looking at the chart. "Did you get a present?" she asked Alison.

"She's making me share confidential information and I'm buying her dinner too," Stacy answered. Alison was warmed. Stacy knew she was broke. This was Stacy's way of making sure she could be included in dinner without embarrassment.

"Then I should at least get a pack of cigarettes," said Liz, leaning over the chart and pointing to a name. "This woman used to be lovers with Dana's ex, Tam. Of course, I don't know what you're doing, so I don't know if you want dead people on your chart."

"Dead people are good," said Stacy. "Because that gives her one degree of separation from both Dana and Livia, because I know that Dana said Tam was in Livia's court for at least a season."

"You're putting Dana on the chart?" asked Alison, somewhat taken aback.

"Oh, you have no killer instinct," scoffed Stacy. "You don't think anyone you like could be a blackmailer."

"You're a real pussy," agreed Liz. "Who's being blackmailed and where's my cigarettes?"

"I don't have any cigarettes," said Stacy. "I'm not getting you any cigarettes. That was a disgusting thing we all did and we're not going there again."

"What about a chocolate bar?" Liz asked, hopefully.

"I don't have chocolate either, unless you want one of those Dicks on a Stick that they're selling down in the mall."

"I can't," said Liz regretfully. "Maybe if somebody made me suck one as part of a scene, but I can't just chomp one down like a Krackle Bar. And I don't want it bad enough to let either of you top me." She turned to Alison. "I know a secret that makes Michelle look bad."

Michelle Martin was Alison's best friend of over two decades and the year before they, along with Janka Weaversong, Michelle's partner, had purchased a house together over in the Platte Park area. Michelle disapproved heartily of Alison's involvement with Stacy and the leather scene. Because Alison wouldn't let her be too awful to Stacy, Michelle and Liz were open antagonists.

"Do tell," said Alison distractedly, still looking at Stacy who was writing as fast as Data.

"Persimmon is in Boulder," Liz announced.

"What?!" From the grin on Liz's face, Alison knew that she could not have come up with a better response if it had been staged. "Oh, goddammit!"

Persimmon was a New Mexico dyke Michelle and Alison had met while on their ill-fated trip to womyn's land the year before. Sammy had been only a few months old at the time and colicky. Janka had been cross and worn down, and Michelle had used this as an excuse to have an intense affair with Persimmon, which had come perilously close to upsetting all of their lives. She had regained her senses only at the very last moment. Alison had thanked the goddess and put that little chapter behind her. Persimmon in Boulder was most upsetting.

"Yep!" said Liz, who seemed annoyingly pleased at introducing something which threatened to be a major problem into Alison's holodeck. "Salad told me. She said she's taking a couple of classes and doing a little wage work before going back down to Mariposa for the summer."

"Oh, I could just kill her!" said Alison. All thoughts of Livia flew out of her head before her distress, like snow before the wind.

"Oh, Alison," said Stacy in an attempt to comfort, "it doesn't mean they picked up where they left off. Maybe Michelle doesn't even know Persimmon's up here."

"She knows," said Alison grimly. Persimmon in town explained a lot of things. Well, there was nothing that she could do about it now. Maybe she'd twist Michelle's head off when she went home.

"Are you going to tell Janka?" Liz asked, hopefully. She rather liked Janka and would have loved to introduce her to kink and then get in Michelle's face about it. "Can I? I could send her one of those letters that you make from words cut out of the newspaper? I've always wanted to and the ink jet printer has made it obsolete."

"You're a twisted sister," said Alison.

"And your point would be?"

"My point would be that I don't know anything to tell Janka, even if I was going to tell her, which I wouldn't do even if I did know something. And anything that happens to Michelle and Janka is going to affect me, too, so just turn your wretched energy toward good instead of evil and help Stacy and me here. If you do I'll get you cigarettes and a candy bar both."

"You won't be getting any cigarettes," Stacy corrected. She was circling and slashing furiously with her felt-tipped pen. "If I'm not smoking, then nobody's smoking. You can get her one of those horrible Seven-Eleven hot-dogs that she eats when nobody's looking."

Liz moved up to look over her shoulder, then picking up the list from the table, she said, "Let me look at that. Now, what is it we're doing and who's being blackmailed?"

"We're writing down everything we know about everybody here and how they connect to one another," said Alison, staring mesmerized at the amazing amount of information taking shape beneath Stacy's lovely hands. "Livia is being blackmailed and she's hired me to find out who's doing it." She looked up at Liz. "It's a secret, by the way." She had no qualms about telling either Liz or Stacy, who she figured were part of the Alison Kaine agency simply by extension, as were Michelle and Janka and occasionally her father and partner, Robert. Stacy and Liz were both good at keeping secrets, as long as you made it really clear they were secrets. "Incidentally, it isn't you, is it?"

"No, but only because I didn't think of it."

Alison pulled the envelope out of her daypack, looking over her shoulder at the door. "That's locked, isn't it?" she asked Liz. "I mean, the woman is paying me fifteen hundred dollars for some privacy. Can you imagine? Why do you suppose she was willing to pay me so much?"

"Well, for one thing," said Liz, "she probably didn't earn it. She probably robbed a corpse or killed her own mother."

"Let me ask you," said Stacy, "Did you resist her to begin with?"

"Yeah, kind of," said Alison, not knowing if this was good or bad. "I wouldn't sign a bottoming contract."

"That explains it then. She paid you that much because she wanted to prove you had a price. I've seen her do that before—lay out big sums of money or bribes in front of women who didn't want to play by her rules. She's obsessed with money, and she thinks everybody else is, too. When she runs into someone she can't buy it's really upsetting to her—it's like fucking with the natural order of her universe."

"Well, she bought me," said Alison frankly. "I didn't like her, but you really seem to hate her. What's that about?"

Liz and Stacy looked at one another.

"Gee, where shall we start?" asked Liz. "She's a mindfucker and I am not into mindfucking. And neither are half of the women she's doing it to, but they're either too inexperienced to know what's going on or too inexperienced to know it's not just part of the job."

"She likes inexperience," said Stacy, picking up the pen again. "Is Clarinda connected with Dragonslayer?" she asked Liz. "I saw them talking today, but I couldn't tell if it was because they knew one another or because they just wanted to know one another."

"I don't know who Dragonslayer is," said Liz.

"Oh, yeah, sure you do. She's the big butch with the facial tattoo and the shaved head."

"Well, that narrows it down to about fifty."

"And a nose ring?"

"Okay, that eliminates one."

"And she's got a string of barbed wire tattooed around both arms? She auctioned off a caning the last time we were at Michigan."

"Oh, okay," said Liz. "I know who you're talking about. Her name used to be Suzy."

The tattoos had made Alison think of the photo Livia had given her of Falcon. She pulled it from between the pages of her datebook. "Do you know her?"

"Nope," said Stacy immediately.

"You hardly even looked," Alison protested.

"Someone like her, I'd remember." Stacy loved big old butch girls.

Liz took a moment longer with the photo.

"I don't know who she is," she said finally, "but I do know that the photo is more than four years old."

"Because?"

"Well, look at where this tent is." She pointed. "I know it's Livia's; she goes for grey and I've never seen another one like it."

"Money can't buy you love," said Stacy, "but it can buy you some cool camping equipment." Stacy was an enthusiastic camper, which just went to show one should never trust stereotypes. She had some pretty cool camping equipment herself.

"It's on a hill," Liz went on, ignoring the ever-present Stacy commentary. "I even know where that hill is; it's up above the acoustic stage. That was where the leather camp was after they blocked us out of main camping. But it was only there for a year, or maybe two. Then four years ago they moved down to the Twilight Zone, which is all flat camping."

"So you were there the year this was taken?" Alison asked.

"Well, I think so," said Liz slowly, still looking at the photo. "I think we both were." She glanced at Stacy. "We didn't camp in the leather camp, though. We camped over in Solanes Ferns."

"How come?"

"Oh, it's too noisy in the leather camp," said Stacy . "There are scenes going on twenty-four hours a day. I can't sleep if I camp there. Plus, I just can't stand that awful Livia and she runs the whole show there."

"Yeah," agreed Liz. "If you camp there you're kind of automatically part of the gang that money can buy and I didn't spend four years in law school to be topped financially by a—" She looked at Stacy again. "What is it that she says she does?"

"Well, that depends on who you talk to," Stacy replied. "I've heard people say she's an investigative reporter. Supposedly she specializes in serial killers."

"Yeah, I've heard that one. I've also heard that she's a court psychologist. You know, she tells the jury whether the defendants were crazy or not when they committed the crime. It's always this big mystery. Livia can't tell because she's so important that word might get out!"

"They're a theme," Liz suggested. "I personally believe that she works some shit job at Burger King and lives in her car so she can save up all her money to buy innocents at Michigan."

"What is there to buy?" Alison asked, puzzled. "You mean like she gives people money to bottom for her?"

"Too upfront," said Stacy. "What she does is supply food for anybody who camps there."

"But there's food at the festival."

"Well, yeah. But she comes in with a truckload of groceries—coffee, cigarettes, beer, meat, Twinkies. You can get a real powerful craving for junk food after five days of pasta and tabouli."

"And she's got the best camping equipment," put in Liz. "Like really good carts to haul stuff in. And she throws a big before and after festival party, you know, she rents a suite at a local hotel and if you're invited she picks up the bill."

"So you don't like her because she's ostentatious, possibly a liar and fucks with people's heads." Alison ticked the list off on her fingers.

"Yeah, plus she insulted Stacy. Boy, this photo really reminds me of someone." Liz held the photo at arm's length, as if this was going to jog her memory.

"Yeah, she pissed the hell out of me," Stacy confirmed. Alison did not bother to ask why—she knew that was a story which would come without urging. Stacy held onto a grudge forever. "Liz and I were hanging out at the leather camp and there were these women trying to put up a tent that was just like mine and so I went over to help them and here comes Livia saying, 'Oh, god, you're never going to get anything done right with a femme helping! If that's not the blind leading the blind!'"

Alison winced, glad she had not been around to see the tizzy that must have followed. "So what did you do?" she asked politely, as Stacy was obviously dying to tell. That something had been done was a given.

"Oh, she went off into a tailspin," cut in Liz. "She told Livia she was topping the tent scene and chased everybody off, including the women who owned the tent, and then Stacy put up the whole damn tent by herself." Liz started to laugh and took a moment to contain herself. "Then she waited until Livia was at the showers and dropped her tent, and cut the bungee cords in all her poles so that when she tried to put it back up the poles came apart and she was standing there looking like an idiot. Well, not her exactly, but a couple of the women she had bottoming for her."

"Pissed me off," said Stacy shortly.

"It was in the rain, too," Liz added.

"She's lucky she didn't get her head put on a stake," said Stacy, baring her teeth in a horrible grimace. "That's what I did to my last lover. That's why you haven't met her," she added to Alison.

This was something best left alone, but Alison could not resist picking it like a scab. She asked in a voice meant to sound casual, "What did your last lover do?"

"Pissed me off," Stacy said again. "Slept with my neighbor. You'll recognize it if it happens. You'll feel a searing pain and then you'll start floating down a long white corridor with all the voices of your dear departed calling to you."

"Do you have any photos from the festival that year?" asked Alison hastily. Stacy's talk of unfaithful lovers was making her nervous.

Stacy shook her head.

"You know what?" said Liz, tapping the photo. "I think the reason this woman seems familiar is because of this tattoo." She held the photo out toward Stacy, pointing at the shoulder. "Isn't that one of Ariadne's tattoos?"

Stacy looked again. "Maybe. It does look like a dragon's claw, and she was pretty heavy into dragons for a while. Didn't do anything else."

"Is she here?" Alison asked.

"Nah, she got religion a couple of years ago. Something weird—a cult thing I heard. They worshipped watermelons or something. Never seen her since that summer. Who's next on the list?"

"Well, what's the deal with this woman called fuckbaby? Is that a creepy name or what?"

"Coulda been worse," said Stacy cheerfully. "Knowing Livia I'm surprised she doesn't call her Slit or Gash. Livia's had fuckbaby, gee, forever." She looked over at Liz. "Has there ever been a pre-fuckbaby era?"

"One year," said Liz. "Because, don't you remember all the rumors the year she first brought her? Like that she was her patient from the mental hospital? Or that she was…well, she couldn't have been one of the victims of the serial killers, could she? Maybe she was somebody that Livia found hiding under a bed at the scene of the crime or something gruesome like that. All kinds of rumors. That's why Livia got her—she's a conversation piece. I've never heard her say a word. According to the Livia gossip she's been in the scene for five or six years."

"Oh," scoffed Stacy, "I'll bet she isn't Livia's live-in at all. She's probably some wealthy doctor who gets off on doing the total bottom thing a couple of weeks a year." She looked at her watch. "We should go find Dana. We told her we'd all go out together to the Merc," she explained to Alison.

Alison was still looking at the chart. "What's different about Salad's list and this list?" she asked, wondering if there was any point in pursuing the other.

"Oh, Salad has real names on her list. We had to do that for registration. Real names and driver's licenses. A couple of sixteen-year-olds showed up at Powersurge last year—not a good situation." The three of them looked at one another. They all knew what she was talking about.

"But we can let you look at it." Failing to make Alison into Kinsey Millhone, Stacy was becoming Kinsey herself. Alison could see that if she wasn't careful, soon she'd be pushed to the sidekick role.

"Hmmph." Liz cleared her throat. They both looked at her, suspecting a lawyer sidebar. There was a special 'Hmmph' that preceded lawyer sidebars and they were both pretty good at recognizing it. "Not to be a drag or anything—" Liz began.

"Cut to the chase," advised Stacy. "What is it that we're doing that you disapprove of?"

"Well, isn't there a little confidentiality issue here?"

"Are you going to use this information for evil?" Stacy asked Alison.

"Nope," Alison replied.

"Then that takes care of that. Let's go find Dana."

On the way out of the room Stacy squeezed Alison's ass and whispered, "Your name should really be Hot Stuff, honey."

"Oh," said Alison, "I didn't think you even noticed that I was pouting."

"It's my job to notice, oh Light of my Life."

Dana was not in the kitchen, so they split up. Alison went into the dining room first, which was empty except for a woman shackled to the fireplace. She was dressed completely in leather, including gloves and a hood over her head. Beside her, fastened to the wall with a thumbtack, which would upset the gay boys, was a sign that read, "Scare me. I'll fight you like the dickens, but that's the way I like it. My safeword is Harmony." Behind the hood could be heard a steady stream of cursing and threats… "You're going to hear from my lawyers you fucking asshole shithead bitches! I'm getting out of here and…" But Alison did not hear the word Harmony so she shrugged and left the room. She liked to play 'No, no, don't, don't' herself sometimes.

She went out onto the porch which was one of those lovely old affairs and practically ran into Scar, whom she had totally forgotten in the Livia excitement. She was standing over on the side where the porch was shaded by a giant oak. All the gals in full leather had congregated there in the shade, while the ones who were wearing little slips of nothing were laughing and smoking on the south side. Inadvertently this had created one camp that was pretty much butch and one that was pretty much femme.

Scar was standing by the rail working out with a pair of nunchuks. She was pretty good, but no one was really paying attention. In fact, the impression Alison got was of deliberately turned backs. The conversations around her were just so animated, the interest in books and newspapers just so very intense. Scar looked like the third grader nobody likes, playing by herself on the playground, trying to pretend it's by choice. She had lost the uniform jacket and hat. Her dark hair, Alison noticed, was thin and patchy in a couple of places.

"Hey," said Alison, slouching onto the rail beside her. "Let's talk." Liz could find Dana—she wanted to get Scar's story over and done with. She didn't want to be stalked the rest of the weekend.

Scar looked pitifully glad to see her, though her tone when Alison answered was firm and casual. Hey, Alison could take this conversation or leave it; she wasn't waiting for handouts.

"I heard something upsetting," Scar said in a stage whisper, which Alison could not help but feel was meant to carry. Scar struck her as the kind of person who is always on stage, always in the midst of a crisis. The kind that would create a crisis if need be. Her next sentence did nothing to belie this impression. Scar was trying to tell the story with the proper amount of dignity and horror, but she could not keep a certain amount of relish out of her voice. She gave her head a tiny swing from left to right, looking to see if anyone was noticing her importance. "I had a playdate before the conference began and something horrible came up. Something unethical, you know, a story involving somebody that was underage." Alison remembered the conversation she had overheard from the bathroom. Had one of those women been Scar's playdate?

"Why haven't you told the Wildfire people?" Alison asked reasonably. "That's why they're here. They're monitoring the dungeons and the play space. They don't want anything unethical or dangerous going on."

Scar blew her lips out with a quick puff—a stage gesture of impatience. "I told you before that won't work." She looked Alison slowly up and down, another stage gesture. Weighing what she saw. Deciding if this was a Cop Who Could Be Trusted. "Look," she said, after just the right pause. Her timing was good—you had to give her that. "I am not a perfect person. I admit that. Some years ago I did some stupid things. I was young, I was stupid, I was going through some really hard times without a lot of support. My parents don't approve of me being a dyke, let alone a leather dyke. They were trying to have me committed. Not a new story, is it?"

Alison shook her head. Scar was right; parents and husbands had been using mental hospitals to control nonconforming women for years.

"So they did a lot of shitty things to try and make it look like I couldn't take care of myself. They emptied out my bank account, they got me thrown out of my apartment—anyway, I was freaking out. And I did some things I shouldn't have done. Five years ago. Five years. And let me tell you, people here won't let me forget it." She made a rueful, bemused little gesture, and once again beneath the leatherwoman trappings, Alison saw the nice, polite girl her mother had raised, dressed in a plaid school skirt with her feet crossed at the ankles. "So that's why I haven't talked about this stuff to the Wildfire mistress…" That had to be Stacy. "…because she is one of those women who will never, never forget."

To her surprise—she had rather made up her mind to dislike this woman—Alison felt a little twinge of sympathy. Dykes did have long and often unforgiving memories. But cleaning out her bank account? How could that be? Scar was at least as old as she was—surely she didn't have an account with her parents' name on it.

"So, are you going to listen to me, or should I just go fuck myself? I've decided not to go to the police. The other police, I mean. I couldn't do that to everyone here." Damn, she had gone back into being noble, which was much harder to take than honest and vulnerable. "It's you or nobody, and I guess I could live with nobody. It's not as if it's my story and, in all fairness, she says she doesn't want to do anything, but she's over the edge." The 'she' was so heavily shrouded with secrecy that Alison was surprised that Scar hadn't gotten all Poe and called her Mme. P. "Though I don't know if she's really in a place where she should make that choice. It seems to me she's really afraid and that her life could even be threatened if she did anything." She shook her head ruefully and held up her hands in a little shrugging, take-your-choice gesture—honest as the day is long, officer, I just want to do what's right.

"Come sit in my car with me," Alison said, making up her mind. No matter the holes she saw in the story even before she heard it, she could not just blow off Scar without at least listening. That honor thing again.

Scar looked doubtful, giving another one of those almost imperceptible glances up and down the porch. Checking the audience. Alison checked as well. Nobody with their hand obviously to their ear. Maybe one or two not quite so engrossed in their conversations as they were pretending to be.

"Free our sisters!" The cry, probably meant to be loud and rallying, instead sounded a little ragged. All the same, everyone turned to look at the little band standing resolutely on the lawn. There was a collective sigh of resignation. No Supersoakers today, but still the same grim looks of determination. Alison recognized a few of the women from the night before. No Michelle. Thank god for small favors.

"Shuttle's leaving," she called to anyone who might like to evacuate. "Going to the hotel and the Merc." Defuse, defuse, defuse. She saw Carla in the crowd and felt equally torn between guilt—she had meant to reach out to Carla, who had obviously been suffering personal problems when she left the leather community, but never had gotten to it—and a desire to thump her on the head.

A couple of women picked up their bags and newspapers and made for the van, again talking to one another in that totally engrossed, we're-ignoring-you manner. Another few stood up and went for their own cars. Everybody else just stared blandly. Last night, when everybody had been kind of high on confrontation, it had been kind of fun—at least before the squirt guns had come out. Now they were over it. Now it was boring. Alison had to admire the way the leatherwomen closed ranks and stuck to the game plan. The femmes sitting on the front steps drew their skirts aside as if they were touching something nasty when the little band hesitantly broached the stairs, and went on talking about going back to school and new purses.

One of the SEPS, Alison noticed with some trepidation, was carrying a pair of bolt cutters. She wondered, as the SEPS pushed their way through the front door, pushing even though no one was trying to hold them back, if she should go follow. Wildfire had decided on no reaction, no confrontation. Stacy, however, wasn't going to stand still if they started trashing Tara. But Flame was inside and if anyone could handle a disarming, it would be her. You don't have to be super cop all the time, Alison scolded herself.

She turned back toward Scar who had taken advantage of the vacated porch chairs to sit down. "So, you coming along?"

A cheer floated out through the French doors, followed by the sound of laughter and general commotion. Alison turned to look again. The head SEP, waving the bolt cutters in triumph, charged through the door and onto the porch, followed by her little band, sticking so closely there was some stumbling. Alison realized that in the middle of the cluster was the woman who had been chained to the fireplace. The long chain had been cut, but her hands were still shackled behind her.

"Free our sisters!" bellowed the head woman again. She was stocky with gingery hair and large breasts. If nothing else, Alison almost had to admire her resolve. The attendants were all looking pretty spooked, clinging to each other in a way probably meant to represent solidarity, but in reality looking like a good healthy fear of getting the shit kicked out of them. Which might still happen, Alison thought. Wildfire had laid down the law of no confrontation, but that was going to go only so far with some of the leather-women. Their normal state was confrontation, and it was taking a lot of will power and whispered encouragement from neighbors to remain passive.

"Free our sisters!" shouted the head honcho again, like she was stuck in some feedback loop. She was about Alison's age, one of the seventies dykes who had stayed with the flannel shirts and bowl haircut. Or maybe someone who had just come out. Those women who shot into the lesbian community after being married to a man for twenty years could become real gong bangers. She raised the bolt cutter, nosing it between the hands of the woman in the hood. Everybody held their breath, hoping this wasn't going to turn into an ambulance scene. But, no, the chain popped without a second of resistance leaving fingers intact. One of the attendants rushed forward and pulled the hood off the woman's head.

Alison didn't know the woman beneath the mask. Delicate features, long dark hair. Probably femme, really pretty. She looked around, confused, trying to figure out what was going on. Up to this point, Alison thought, she might have believed the commotion part of some wild scene.

"Oh, shit," she said finally, looking at the fearful, triumphant faces of the women surrounding her, "I thought I was going to get fucked." She pulled herself from the huddle and launched herself directly at Scar, sitting by the rail. A look of intimacy passed between them, for just long enough that Alison wondered if this was Scar's playdate. Perching on Scar's knee she pouted, "Daddy, I've been a really bad girl. Don't you think you should spank me?"

Alison hadn't heard such a great whoop of laughter since she had last seen Paula Poundstone. She herself laughed until tears rolled down her eyes, clutching her sides helplessly as she gasped for air. The SEPS stood together for a moment, looking around them with confused faces which gradually all turned a shade of red. Alison heard Carla hiss to one of the others, "I told you that wasn't going to work!" Alison almost felt sorry for them.

"Look this way, ladies!" Liz's voice sounded behind Alison, and of course she looked that way. Everybody did. Liz was holding a whirring video camera up to her right eye.

"Say hello to the judge, ladies!" Liz commanded brightly. She must have had the camera in her car, Alison thought. She knew that Liz, being the only one of them with a camera, was supposed to be in charge of shooting the Fantasy performances later that night. "Let's put some names on these trespassers, shall we, audience? Local girls, anybody?"

"Carla Carter!" sang out someone in the back. "She lives over on Vine Street and works in the dairy department at Rainbow Grocery!" Rainbow Grocery, a Capitol Hill institution originally owned by the Moonies, had actually been Wild Oats for over ten years, but all the locals knew what she meant. "She used to be in the leather scene herself!"

"Paulette Huin!" called Stacy's friend, Beth. "She lives over in Platt Park and she works for the John Elway dealership. She says she's a dyke, but everybody knows she sleeps with her ex-husband every couple of months."

Carla had merely looked resigned and annoyed when her name had been mentioned, as if expecting something of the sort, but the woman Alison supposed to be Paulette Huin looked completely amazed and taken aback.

"I can't remember her name, but the woman in the Cris Williamson T-shirt owes my girlfriend money," volunteered a butch Alison did not know. "She borrowed two hundred dollars and then decided she didn't have to pay it back because it would be perpetuating violence against women. I don't know where she lives, but I'm going to follow her when she leaves because we're looking to serve small claims papers on her."

"I did not!" The woman in the Cris Williamson T-shirt was even more taken aback than Paulette Huin. Nobody, however, was listening. They were getting into this.

"Red there is Jenine Dykeflower," called someone else, referring, Alison supposed, to the woman with the bolt cutters. "She lives in Capitol Hill, too, and she doesn't pay income tax because she thinks it contributes to the male war machine. She's using her lover's dead mother's social security number."

Up to this point Alison had wondered if there wasn't a little creativity being used in the identifications. Carla's she knew was true, but she thought the woman who had made the claim about the SEPS in the Cris Williamson T-shirt was an out-of-towner. This last accusation, however, was such a dyky thing to do, up to and including telling people what she was doing, that Alison, and judging from the silence everyone else in the crowd, believed it completely. Nobody could top it. Even Liz couldn't think of anything cheerful and annoying to say. She walked in close with the camera, swinging it to catch the protesters' faces, and then walked back inside the mansion, clicking it off. As if cued, the leather dykes began to buzz with very intense, very interesting conversations. Slowly, like a soft ice cream cone losing its structural integrity, the group began to melt off the porch.

Alison looked around the porch. To her annoyance, Scar had disappeared in the confusion, as had the woman who had been wearing the leather hood. Fine, let her keep her big secret. Alison hadn't wanted to hear it to begin with. She walked inside and joined Liz, who was huddling with Stacy and Dana.

"I bet we don't see them again," said Liz in a very self-satisfied voice. "Sometimes that old fishbowl effect really comes in handy. I'm starving—let's go eat!"

Chapter Six

As always, the Mercury Cafe was hopping and as always, the clientele was mixed and interesting. There were some guys in suits with their briefcases open on the table between them—probably feds from one of the downtown buildings. There were two families, one with two mommies, a toddler and baby who had obviously been adopted from overseas, and another with parents who just as obviously aspired to a no interference kind of discipline, for their children were running laps around the pool tables, all three carrying honey bottles like weapons. Luckily, the parents were just getting their check, so it seemed safe to sit down at a back table beneath the neon tiger. Service at the Merc was never speedy—it was not a good place to go if you had a plane to catch—but Alison was willing to bet that this little family had inspired record time from kitchen to table.

Their original dinner group had grown to include not only Dana but also Beth and her girlfriend, whose name Alison couldn't remember because she didn't like her. That power of naming thing again. Beth's girlfriend was the kind of butch who was always trying to piss higher on the pole than the other butches. Didn't matter if she'd won last night, she still wanted to do it every single time. It involved a whole lot of posturing and attempts to keep the conversation centered in her areas of expertise.

In addition, there were a couple of gals from out of town whose names Alison had not caught. She thought they were acquaintances of Liz and their purpose seemed to be to provide two chairs' distance between Liz and Beth's girlfriend.

Also along with them was Mary Clare Echevarria a local friend of Liz's and also, unfortunately, the cousin of Marta Goicochea. In all the time that Alison had been adoring Stacy, Alison had fallen from grace only once, and the woman with whom she had made that fall was Marta Goicochea. Yes, it had been done while she and Stacy were fighting, yes there had been alcohol involved, but there it was and she had not only done it, but done it without telling Marta there was someone waiting at home. She had been a shit on all fronts, and Mary Clare was about the last person in the world with whom she wished to have dinner. In her opinion the more time she spent in the com-

69

pany with Mary Clare, the more time Mary Clare had to casually let Alison's infidelity with Marta drop, being to Marta as Liz was to Stacy.

So of course, Mary Clare ended up sitting on Alison's right and it was a measure of Alison's discomfort that she would have preferred even Beth's girlfriend.

Having extra people there meant Alison couldn't talk about Livia, which was irritating, though she tried to be a good sport while everyone else, all in high spirits, congratulated Liz on the SEPS confrontation. That led to discussions of the Michigan s/m wars, from which Alison was excluded because she hadn't been there and then to a lot of conversation about the last Powersurge, from which Alison was also excluded because she hadn't been there either. She had rather thought this might happen and had picked up a couple of queer publications while passing through the foyer, just in case Beth's girlfriend went on too long. Two papers were local, but the third was the previous month's *Lesbian Connection*.

The group gaiety settled down a bit when the food finally came. Everyone turned to her plate and then to her neighbor, except for Beth and her girlfriend who were rather obviously having foreplay if not actual sex beneath the table. Alison turned to her left, where Stacy was sitting.

"You know the woman you told me to stay away from, Scar?" Alison asked Stacy, blowing on a huge bite of burrito. She put it in her mouth and closed her eyes. Nirvana. She had not really planned on bringing up the Scar thing, but not being able to discuss Livia was making her impatient and unable to make small talk.

"Yeah," Stacy replied in kind of a duh voice—who doesn't and what a jerk she is—but preceded it with a split second pause only a girlfriend would notice. Alison, who was pretty good at the unspoken, high court gestures of Stacyese, figured immediately that Stacy had done something sexual with Scar at some point before Alison entered the picture. She herself did not think that she was prone to go mad dog with jealousy, but Stacy always seemed to think she was. Actually, it was probably more that Stacy enjoyed pretending she had a lover who went crazy with jealousy without actually having to deal with the reality of a lover who went crazy with jealousy. Either way, she didn't talk about her past sexual history a whole lot except when she was trying to stir things up. Which was fine with Alison—she didn't really want to find out if she had the mad dog potential.

"What's her story?" Alison asked. Down the table she could hear Beth's girlfriend going on about the Colorado Explosion in a bulldozer monologue. Alison knew from painful experience she could go for days without stopping for a breath.

"Story may be the operative word here," Stacy replied drolly. She had regained her composure quickly—flustered to droll in ten seconds. "Why, what did she tell you? Being chased by the FBI again, is she?"

"Well, no. She knows something terrible about someone here and wants to know if I think she should call the police."

Stacy burst into loud laughter and choked on a shrimp from her fettuccine. "Oh, Alison!" she said after she set her glass down, shaking her head fondly as if Alison were a favorite but not too bright child. "You didn't take anything that Scar said to heart, did you?" She twirled the straw in her girly drink. "Liz, listen for a minute." She leaned across the table and pulled Liz's sleeve. "Scar's been telling Alison that she saw something the police should be in on!"

Liz, who had been laughing over something with Mary Clare, turned in her chair. "Oops, better put out a 911! Better get your gun out!" She and Stacy and even Dana and Mary Clare laughed.

"Well, not all of us know what's funny!" Alison tried to keep the sulky tone from her voice, but a sharp look from Stacy told her she had not been completely successful. She tried again. "Okay, I've been had. What's the joke?" She didn't try to correct Stacy, that Scar had said she knew something, not that she'd seen something. It didn't sound as if it mattered.

"Oh, Alison," said Dana, leaning across the table and exposing a pin-up shot of her cleavage to Mary Clare and Liz. "Scar is such a joke. She's been driven out of practically every leather community in the U.S.! We drove her out of Seattle last year—nobody would have anything to do with her. If she doesn't make it in San Francisco she's going to have to go to Europe. Which I suppose could be an advantage," she said thoughtfully, giving her head an unconscious little toss to make her earrings dance. "She wouldn't know the language, so maybe they'd let her stay around for a while."

"What's her problem?" asked Alison, expecting nothing less than a decapitation scene. In her experience the leather community was amazingly accepting.

"She lies," said Liz in a disgusted tone.

"That's it?" Alison could not keep the surprise out of her voice. "She lies? She's been driven out of the community because of that? Who doesn't lie now and then?" She herself, who seldom lied to friends and family, had no qualms about occasionally calling in sick to work when really she just wanted to stay home and watch Ricki Lake, or telling her grandmother she loved the skirt and vest when they were already in the Goodwill box. In addition, of course, there was the thing with Marta, about which she was going to lie, bold-fucking-faced, if it ever came up.

"Not like Scar," said Dana, who was tossing pheromones right and left. Alison wondered whether she was doing the mating dance for Liz or Mary Clare. Probably either would do at this point. Dana was in Denver to party down. "She lies about… everything. Stupid things. Not to cover her ass, just stupid things she thinks are going to give her status or make people sorry for her or that kind of shit."

"Like, she did a scene with Kate Clinton at a play party," said Liz. "Really. I heard her say that."

"Or she has leukemia and is getting chemotherapy," said Dana.

Alison remembered the thinning hair. "Well," she protested, "she is losing her hair…"

"Oh, Alison!" broke in Stacy, "she's been losing her hair for years. She's been losing her hair ever since I've known her. That's all it is—losing her hair! She never had chemotherapy! My dad had chemotherapy and it makes you sick as a fucking dog! You can't go out and stay at a dungeon all night like Scar does! She just made that up because she didn't want to do her work shift! She's the reason I didn't want to have work exchange." Stacy paused for a moment to let everyone know she wasn't over not having her own way. "Or one of the main ones. She goes to every leather event in the country, and she always tries for work exchange and she never works her shift. I mean, she always manages to scrape together enough money to fly to Seattle or New York, but she can't come up with that eighty dollars to get in the door!" She gave an evil little smile. "But she didn't get work exchange here—at least I blocked that. And I blocked her from community housing, too." She gave a quick little glance down the table, which told Alison this had been a private rather than a collective decision.

"She has to go to every leather event," put in Dana. "Nobody local will play with her anymore—at least nobody in Seattle."

"Nobody in Atlanta, either," said Liz. "I was talking to one of the Atlanta girls at lunch and they told me that someone passed a 'Not-Wanted' poster of her around town and after that she couldn't pay her way into a party."

Alison was beginning to feel a bit sorry for poor Scar who sounded as if she needed good professional help.

"Oh, Alison, don't!" said Stacy, who could spot and reject compassion about a mile away. "She's not like that!"

"Well," protested Alison, "it does sound a lot like she's some unlikable little kid all of the big girls have decided not to play with."

"Actually," said Dana thoughtfully, "she's not really all that unlikable. She just tells a lot of lies."

"Yes," said Stacy shortly, "and that would be what makes her a sociopath, wouldn't it?" Stacy was obviously getting tired of Dana's tits being laid out on the table like a bundt cake, particularly on top of having sported higher heels all too recently. "I mean, that and the fact that she lies for no reason at all! Oh, honestly, you should hear some of the stuff she's spread around over the years!"

"Like, that she was on the road with Cris Williamson in the early days and got kicked off the tech staff because she was into the leather scene," said Dana.

"Or that she's getting disability because of the cancer. Except that this time it wasn't cancer, it was…" Liz screwed up her face with concentration. "This time it was…lupus?"

"The symptoms of which totally fail to manifest."

"Except when she's supposed to be doing a work shift," put in Stacy dryly.

"And then there's always the money situation," said Dana. "Always money problems, always trying to borrow money or get a free meal. Never her fault. She was shorted on her paycheck. Her disability check didn't come. Her parents closed her checking account."

"I did wonder about that," Alison admitted.

"You did right to wonder," said Liz.

"And wonder as you may, I'll bet you never came up with the solution," said Stacy, setting the coffeepot down with a thump in the vicinity of Dana's breasts. "Because it doesn't work that way! You can't just close another adult's account because you know the bank manager!"

"Which is how she explained it," inserted Dana in a sidebar.

"Because here in the real world we call that felony and fraud! You go to prison for it!"

"Well, she found somebody here to play with," Alison said, remembering the woman with the hood.

"Courtesy of your local Lavender Pages," said Dana, holding up her conference schedule. "This has got to be her— 'Out of town Bad Boy seeks local Bad Girl in need of serious discipline.' Ya-da, ya-da, clean and sober, she brags a little about how good she is and how all other tops are going to be a letdown after you've been with her. Okay—'I can come early and stay late and if you really, really beg, maybe I'll let you be my submissive all weekend.'"

"She has to come early," said Stacy. "That's the only way she can find someone who hasn't heard of her."

"Oh," broke in Liz, "she's not all bad. At least she plays safe and she doesn't try to fuck with your head." She turned to Alison. "Who knows? Maybe she does know something."

"Oh, Liz, she does not!" said Stacy scornfully. "She just likes making a fuss. Everything's always got to be about her. Remember that time at MSIL" —at which Alison had not been either— "when she tried to get everybody to leave the dungeon because she said there'd been a threat on her life and she was afraid there was a bomb in the building? Who was it that time—the FBI or the CIA?"

"All I'm saying," said Liz to Alison, ignoring Stacy, "is that even a compulsive liar can tell the truth sometimes. Like once I asked her if Stacy was upstairs and she said yes and Stacy was upstairs. And another time she told me the bathroom was empty and it was. So she is capable of occasionally passing along generic information intact and unaltered."

"I don't think what she 'heard,'" Alison made little quotation marks with her fingers, "fits into the generic information category. I am given to believe that there might be a life in the balance and there's been a lot of build up and leaving the room just before she's going to tell the secret."

"She's lying," said Dana bluntly. "Don't let her pull you into it."

"Oh, Alison," said Stacy fondly. Even though it was fond, Alison was getting a bit tired of 'Oh, Alison'. It made her feel like a slow child. "You want to see things like that. You want to find a body in the basement! That's why she targeted you! You give off a scent!"

Alison thought this rather insulting and since the choice was either confronting Stacy and creating a public scene or eating it, she remained silent. It so happened that the conversation at the other end of the table had come to a pause too, so there was a moment of awkward silence.

"How about them Pattys?" said Mary Clare finally.

Everyone at the table had a Patty story and no one wanted to get in the middle of a Stacy and Alison spat, so the table suddenly became alive with talk and laughter. Alison, even though she had a couple of Patty stories herself, remained silent, thinking about what Stacy had said. Was she really the kind of person who could not be happy except in a crisis? No, the accusation was totally unfair. She could hardly help it that dead bodies were always turning up in her path, nor could she help it that someone chose to confide in her or turned out to be a well-known fuck-up—at least well known to everyone but her.

The waitress came by with more water and the conversation drifted off toward food (the best in town!).

"What's new in *Lesbian Connection*?" asked Liz, picking up Alison's copy from the table.

"Let me guess," said Mary Clare. "Lots of letters complaining."

"About leather dykes," put in Stacy.

"And photos of fat women on the cover," said Beth's girlfriend from the other end of the table. This surprised Alison who had assumed Beth's girlfriend did not read. It seemed too outside herself.

"And keeping animals as slaves," said Dana.

"There was an interesting letter," said Alison obligingly. "It was from Denver, actually.

"Oh, Christ," said Liz. "Then it must have been from Jane Severance. She's got a letter in there every damn month. Doesn't she have a job?"

"No, it wasn't," said Alison, taking a tiny sip of coffee. "It was about a woman who'd had an affair with her therapist and it really fucked her up."

"I'd think that'd do it," said Beth. Either she or her girlfriend must have come, because all four hands were back on the table. Either that, or they'd just gotten hungry. "My therapist is about the last person in the world I'd want to have an affair with—not after telling her all the bad things I've done and crying in front of her and giving her every bit of information in the world about how to punch my buttons. You know that movie, *Prince of Tides?*—I couldn't understand that at all. I mean, telling somebody the very worst, secret thing that I'd had happen to me in my whole life—boy, that'd sure put me in the mood to fuck!"

"I saw that letter, too," said Dana. "Did you see the letter in the last issue that sparked it off? The one about the high school teacher and her student and what we need to do to police our own in the community?"

Liz gave a shudder. "Every time anybody starts talking about policing our community I get nervous," she said. "I'll bet those SEPS at the Meet and Beat thought they were policing their community."

"Yeah, well," responded Stacy who had pretty much managed to get through her whole cheesecake in the space it had taken Beth to speak. "At least we're all of age. That whole shit about a patient with a therapist or a teacher with a teenager—that's like the very worst kind of non-consensual s/m there is and I don't want to play. I mean, you know who's topping those scenes and there's no safeword. It is wrong and we should do something about it."

Alison remembered the conversation she had overheard from the bathroom. One of the women had talked about there being no balance of power between them. Should she have done something?

"You can't," said the waitress who had been listening intently and openly while she filled their water glasses. She had a shaved head that worked much better than Best Boy's and chains going from both sides of her nose to her earlobes. She was wearing a flowered, fifties style housedress over long underwear, and Doc Martens. The Merc encouraged fancy waitresses.

"Why?" asked Alison, who agreed with Stacy.

"Because they won't listen," said the waitress.

"Well, maybe we need to make them listen," retorted Stacy. "Maybe we need to stop being so afraid of what the straight community is going to think about lesbians and get the law involved. Revoke some licenses and do some firing if we have to."

"No," said the waitress, ignoring the waves from the other tables. "That's not…I mean, the kids won't listen. It's the kids who won't listen. They have to say it's wrong and they so won't. We won't."

"I sense a true story," said Stacy, lifting an eyebrow.

"Well, yeah," said the waitress. She thought for a moment and finally said. "I'm queer. I mean, she didn't make me queer. I so knew I was queer since I was little."

"Who?" asked Stacy. She had gone into a gentle mode that had nothing to do with the wisecracks and laughter, which had spilled across the table earlier.

"It was creepy," said the waitress. "I mean, I didn't think it was creepy then. I thought it was all romantic and beautiful. You know, I was just a kid, and I was all *Romeo and Juliet* and she was all 'oh, I'd marry you if I could, but I'd lose my job' and I just thought, okay."

"Teacher?" asked Alison in a wary tone.

"Yeah. Sophomore history."

Alison was horrified, but not surprised. More and more these days it seemed as if something bad had happened to almost everyone she knew. Stacy had been battered by her husband. Michelle had been raped twenty years before by someone she knew. Liz's mother had been murdered when Liz was in high school. Both Janka and Mary Clare had been sexually abused by family members when they were children, and some crazy had beaten the shit out of Marta the year before. And, sad as it was, it was not the first time that she had heard the story in *Lesbian Connection*. She knew of at least four other women personally who had been brought out by counselors, teachers, therapists and even a nun. Most of the stories she had heard were from the past, but there had been one in which she could have intervened. If she'd just known what to do. She'd looked the other way instead and regretted it still.

"So what could we have done to help you?" asked Stacy. The girl looked blank, so she rephrased. "What could older lesbians in the community have done to help you?"

"Nothing!" said the waitress. "Would have pissed me so off! I was all like 'I'm a grownup and I'm all in love and society's fucked and that's what the problem is.' Not like some dirty old man trying to grab your pussy—my Uncle Walter did that one time and I was all freaking out and told my mom and she was all 'I'm going to kill him if I ever see his bony butt around here again!' 'Cause I knew that was so not right—him trying to do that. 'Cause I was just a kid and I so knew grownups weren't supposed to do that with kids. But he was all grabby but she was all 'I love you and you're so beautiful and if anybody finds out they're going to put you in a foster home or maybe your folks won't pay for you go to college or I'll lose my job and then I won't be able to take care of you.'" She stopped a moment, as if it was painful to tell.

Up and down the table Alison could see the mirroring pain and shame in the eyes of the older women and she wondered how many of them had not stepped in.

"You so couldn't have told me," the waitress went on finally. "I would have tried to knock the shit out of you or, like, burned your house down or something. I would have so called you a liar. Like, the facilitators at the queer youth group were trying to say how skanky it was and I'm all 'well, you're just jealous because you're old ladies and you don't have anybody to do it with anymore." She shook her head. "I was so dumb," she said. "I mean, when I finally grew up I was all 'oh how could I be so dumb.'"

Alison looked at her fresh, unlined face beneath the piercings and the stubble. She could not be over twenty at the very most.

The young woman went on, "So, I'm like in this group now over at the queer center that's for kids who were perved on by people they trusted."

One of the other diners had become so agitated that he was actually up at the counter asking for salsa in a loud voice, so the waitress turned away. A few feet from the table, however, she stopped and turned back toward them. "And you know what?" she said. "This is the worst. She's still at that same high school, and she's still perving on girls in her classes. Because there's this girl I know at queer group and she's all 'oh I'm so in love but it's a secret until after I graduate' and I'm thinking I so know what's happening."

Liz, who had been fumbling in her wallet, stood up and leaned across the table, offering the young woman one of her cards. "I'm a criminal lawyer, but I have some really vicious friends who'd be happy to sue the shit out of her. Pro bono."

The girl took the card, looking perturbed. Alison could read her doubts as clearly as if they were flying across her forehead on ticker tape: Yeah, but hadn't she been to blame, too? Yeah, but what were other lesbians going to think if she exposed one of their own? Yeah, but...

Liz was reading her thoughts too. "Or they can just write her a really nasty letter threatening to expose her that will put her into a twist for months."

"Or I'd be willing to call and say I'm from the Ricki Lake show and say she's been recommended for a segment in which teenaged lesbians want to confront their abusers," said Alison. It had just popped out, and she was embarrassed as soon as she'd said it, fearing it would sound as if she were making light of an experience that had been both hateful and harmful.

The young waitress, however, laughed aloud. "Oh, I so want you to do that!" she said, pointing the card at Alison.

"Excuse me!" A woman from another table had approached, the tone of her voice making the apology sound like anything but. "What exactly do you have to do around here to get some service?" She gave the table of lesbians a cold eye. "Or is it who you have to fuck?"

The waitress turned to face her, putting her hand on her hip to show that she wasn't taking any of that crap. "Excuse me, but Marilyn told me that I so didn't have to wait on anyone who said anything homophobic." Not everyone knew that Marilyn who was the heart of the Mercury, had a lesbian sister as a silent partner and considered any gay slam not just wrong in general, but a direct insult to her family. "I'm going back into the kitchen to see if your order is ready and decide whether I think that was homophobic. If you don't get any food then you'll know I decided it so was."

She left as Beth's girlfriend stood up and put on her jacket, which started a general shuffle.

Stacy who had made a beautiful batik jacket for Marilyn a few months before, had food credit and insisted on paying the whole bill. Or, at least the bill for her end of the table. Beth's girlfriend got all butch and insinuated that no femme was ever going to pay for her, which embarrassed Beth and made Stacy give Alison a fond little look that made up for the 'Oh, Alisons!' Stacy never objected to a butch paying if she was being gallant, but she had to be allowed her own opportunities to be generous, and if you picked up the check there could never be a hint that it was because Stacy couldn't take care of herself.

It took a while to get out because once they stood up, they noticed several other parties of women from the conference sitting in the Jungle Room. Which was to be expected, since the Merc had been at the top of the list of restaurants mentioned in the conference packets, being both gay friendly and within walking distance of the mansion. Everyone except Alison knew at least one of the other diners, so of course they had to say hi and talk about how great the food was and how badly the Pattys had been acting and all that stuff. Alison stood patiently by the door, leafing through the alternative newspapers and reading the posters on the wall. Goddess Theater was putting on a new show and Monkey Siren was going to play a whole month of smoke free Friday concerts upstairs.

She glanced back into the Jungle Room to see if Stacy was anywhere near ready to go and realized that she did know one of the women sitting down to dinner. Stuck over in the back by the pool table was Scar and another woman Alison had seen at Tara that day. Scar saw her before she could pull her head back into the foyer and waved her over. Stacy was still deep in conversation with the femmes from Atlanta, so there was no excuse for Alison not to go, though she did so reluctantly, aware that both Mary Clare and Dana had noticed and were exchanging amused looks.

"Hi!" said Scar. The table was set for three, although there were only two of them. She introduced her companion as Crescent. An older woman, mid-forties, Alison would guess. She was handsome, with very short, dark hair that had just the barest hint of an odd sheen, as if she'd had a bad henna experience or something. Into it was shaved a crescent swath reaching from the nape of her neck to the upper tip of one ear. On her scalp were several elaborate tattoos—a star and a moon and the head of a dragon reaching from beneath her hair. Alison supposed that at one point in her life she'd had more of her head shaved. At least the tattoos didn't go down onto her face—Alison couldn't imagine it was easy for forty-five year old women with facial tattoos to get a job, and only so many could run leather shops. "I'm sorry I didn't get a chance to talk to you."

For a moment Alison was afraid Scar was going to try for a heart-to-heart right there, but she went on. "I think maybe things are going to be resolved. I'll talk to you tomorrow if I still need advice." She then looked across the table and smiled at the other woman.

Alison was relieved to see Stacy waving at her from across the room. She made a non-committal little sound of good-bye. Scar's companion who had not said a word, looked annoyed, and glared impatiently as though she had no desire to be with Scar at all, and wasn't going to wait for the third party much longer.

On the way out they passed their waitress who was deep in conversation with a woman Alison recognized as being from Wildfire but nothing more. Femme, pretty, long dark hair. They had their heads together, talking softly but with animation. Alison caught the tag end of the story as they passed. The waitress was saying, "And then she was all 'well I'll call Ricki Lake' and I'm all 'oh that would be so great!' Everybody at group is…"

The femme, whom the young waitress obviously knew, had an odd look on her face, like she thought the story was funny but was troubled by something else. She tipped her head as they walked by and Alison realized she was the woman who had been unmasked by the SEPS at Tara, the one who had perched herself on Scar's knee. Which probably made her the woman who had answered Scar's ad. She tried to poke Stacy and get her to look so that she'd have a name to put with the gossip, but by the time Stacy realized it was a message poke and not just a quick feel, they were out the door.

Liz and Beth had to go back to Tara to do something, but Stacy was free until the Fantasy Night performance which began that evening at nine. She and Alison had driven over to the Merc together since Stacy had taken the light rail down that morning. She had a nice car and she hadn't wanted to leave it parked on the street down by Tara in case the SEPS or somebody all hyped up with drugs or injustice decided to make a statement. Alison's car was not the type that would draw outrage.

"Don't forget your toy bag," Alison reminded her as she dropped her off at home. Stacy's bag, which she'd had with her earlier for demos at the novice workshop, was locked in the trunk.

"Oh, just leave it." Stacy leaned in through the window to give her a kiss. "I'll get it from you tonight." As Alison began to pull away from the curb she waved and called, "See you tonight, Hot Stuff!"

Chapter Seven

At home Alison had a nap followed by a good hot shower, in which she lustily sang every single Mary-Chapin Carpenter song (except the silly ones) she could remember. Singing, she had discovered, pumped up her endorphins almost as much as a workout.

Out of the shower she popped in a Tannahill Weavers tape and began putting herself together.

She was still in her robe, just finishing her hair, when there was a courtesy knock at her door and Janka walked in.

Janka Weaversong, a slightly built woman with strawberry blonde hair that she often wore pulled back into a ponytail, had been married to Alison's best friend, Michelle, for seven years. This was kind of a remarkable thing in itself and had happened only because of her amazing patience and ability to blow off about half of Michelle's hyperactive and paranoid behavior. Michelle, though a hard worker and as loyal as they come, was not an easy woman to love. She saw everything in the starkest shades of black and white, right and wrong and once she made her mind up, it was almost impossible to change it. After Alison had become involved in the leather scene, Michelle had struggled with her almost daily, vacillating between supporting her dearest and oldest friend and sticking to her guns about something she thought was just plain wrong. Because she couldn't bear to be on the outs with Alison, Michelle usually saved her attacks and spiels for Stacy and Liz, one of the many reasons Stacy was ticked about Alison buying in on a house with Janka and Michelle rather than herself.

"Hey," said Janka, dropping down onto the futon in the living room as if she had climbed not a flight of stairs but Mount Yale at the very least.

"Hey yourself," Alison replied. She tried making her voice sound welcoming, rather than dreading. Alison liked Janka, she really did. Janka was an ally when Michelle was on a tear, Janka had a sense of humor when Michelle had none, Janka was a nurturer with a kitchen always smelling of promise. Janka was also the mother of Sammy, Alison's eighteen-month-old godchild, whom she adored. Over the years Alison had built a friendship with Janka which stood independently of her friendship with Michelle.

Lately, though, Alison had been avoiding Janka. It was not just the depression into which Janka had slid after Sammy's birth, following a pregnancy which had been difficult both physically and emotionally. Alison could deal with depression. All her friends had their ups and downs and Janka had enough credits on the upside to see her through quite a long period on the downside. No, the reason Alison didn't want to talk to Janka was because she had suspected what Michelle was doing and was afraid that eventually Janka was going to ask her straight out, and then she'd be in a bind. Of course, now, with the information Liz had given her, she didn't just suspect, she knew and that was going to make things even harder.

"Where's Sammy?" Alison asked quickly. If she could keep Janka on approved topics, perhaps she could keep her from asking if she thought Michelle was having an affair. It had worked so far.

"Oh, Michelle took him over to see your dad." Janka sighed, as if this was just too depressing to contemplate, although she was actually great friends with Alison's father. Alison's father, who had known Michelle since she was ten years old and thought of her as an adopted daughter, had gotten a really bad case of grandpa-itis the moment Sammy was born. His own grandchildren lived far away and he was a man made to be a grandpa. His infatuation was compounded both by Alison's mother leaving him unexpectedly the year before and the fact that Michelle and Janka's families were lukewarm to downright hostile about having a turkey baster baby in the family. Sammy spent at least one evening a week at Grandpa Mike's, being bounced on his knee and pretty much allowed to destroy anything in sight, while Grandpa Mike looked on fondly and talked about how smart he was. Grandpa Mike had already started a college fund so that Sammy could go to Stanford if he didn't choose the police academy.

"Are you making anything pretty?" Alison asked, giving her hair one final little pat. Janka was an exceptionally talented weaver who traveled to a handful of women's festivals throughout the year as well as having clothing at chic stores in Cherry Creek.

"I'm trying," Janka replied with another deep sigh which made Alison realize that she'd inadvertently touched on a sore spot. Janka and Michelle, who was a stained glass artist also being able to do just about anything from raising bumper cucumbers to reroofing a house, had been going around about day care for months. Michelle thought that, particularly since they both worked at home, Sammy should stay out of the school system as long as possible. Which was fine, Janka said, except that Michelle ran off to her garage studio where Sammy wasn't allowed and stuck Janka with all the childcare. Not that she didn't love spending time with Sammy, but it was hard working on a loom with a toddler around. Alison had heard both sides of this argument quite a few times.

Alison hummed along with the *Boys Of the Lough*, pretending nothing was wrong. Damn that fucking Michelle, anyway! And why couldn't Persimmon have gone into Santa Fe if she needed wage work? Michelle hadn't said anything about Persimmon being in Colorado and she certainly must know. So add being secretive to long, unexplained afternoon errands and erratic behavior of late, testy one minute and almost euphoric the next and to Alison that spelled affair. And she didn't want to know about it. Because some day soon Janka was going to ask her about it and she wanted to be able to say she didn't know with conviction. If push came to shove, if Michelle and Janka split the sheets and the friends, she would have to go with Michelle. There was too much history between them to do anything else. However, she'd much rather remain ignorant and hope the situation would resolve itself if at all possible.

"What are you wearing?" asked Janka, still flat on her back. The whole situation was made worse by the fact that Janka knew good and well she'd been a drag lately and was trying to be a good sport. Alison wished she could give Michelle a good smack and then run Persimmon out of town on a rail. Perhaps she could blackmail Persimmon into leaving instead. She did know a rather horrible secret about her, so it was worth considering.

"I'm going military," Alison replied. "Stacy wanted me to go full leather, but she forgets about my budget when she thinks of these things. Oh, that reminds me!" She peeled off five hundred dollars from the wad in her pocket. "I've got my mortgage money."

Janka had wandered into the kitchen, where she was eating sugar straight out of the bowl. She gave a little nod when Alison put the money on the table.

Alison went back into her bedroom, where she spent quite a bit of time (though nothing compared to the time it took Stacy to get ready) pulling herself together and making sure her shirt was tucked in right and her pants didn't make her butt look too big and her boots were shiny and all that butch stuff. There was some extra primping necessary because she was packing and wanted that to look just right as well.

When she was finally done she rather hoped that Janka would be gone, but she was sitting on the sofa watching TV. Not a bad sign for Alison, who watched a lot of TV and rather indiscriminately, but a very bad sign for Janka, who wouldn't even allow a TV in their apartment for fear it would suck Sammy's vulnerable little brain dry.

"Well, I guess you gotta go," she said mournfully when Alison picked up her keys.

"Yeah," said Alison, knowing that what she should be saying was 'Do you want to come along', or 'Let's take a walk', or 'Have you taken your Prozac?' She knew she was not being a good friend to Janka and felt it was Michelle's fault. She needed to have a talk with that girl soon. She made a little mental note to cross-examine Salad too. Perhaps she actually would blackmail Persimmon. Or maybe she could just make her uncomfortable by showing up where she was staying and letting vague threats fall into the conversation. She thought seriously about both these choices as she got into her car and headed toward the Blue Rider Bar and Fantasy Night.

Chapter Eight

Some of the work exchange people hadn't shown, so they all found themselves with jobs when they got to the bar. Alison was working the door, Liz was video taping the fantasies, Flame was bouncing, Beth's girlfriend was topping the lights and Stacy was working herself up into a whole new tizzy about things she couldn't change.

Alison was glad to be working the door, a job she'd been assigned even before the current work exchange crisis. She always like working an event—selling beer at a dance, handing out flyers at a concert, being a marshal at Pridefest. Working gave her a reason to interact and it also justified her presence if she decided to step back and watch. Stepping back and watching was one of the little things she liked best in life, along with gossip. She liked to know about people, to ponder their little neuroses and habits. It detoured as well as aided her police work. She was good at noticing and putting things together, but she had a tendency toward over-involvement. She had to watch her own compassion. Compassion got you fucked.

The crowd, of course, was mostly the same crowd that had been at the Meet and Beat. Alison was starting to recognize a few. Two hundred women had seemed like a lot on paper. In reality and a small space, however, Alison had found herself distinguishing them from the herd almost immediately. There was the handsome Latina woman who had stared at Stacy the night before. Tonight she was dressed simply in tight jeans and a leather jacket, which she managed to make seem more put together than outfits on which hundreds had been spent. There were the two women with the identical tattoos, who were doing some kind of master/slave thing that involved a leash and spiked collar. Alison had brought them in from the airport on her first run. There was the handsome blonde women from Georgia, who gave her a big old smile before sauntering off to find a seat, dragging the heels of her cowboy boots against the hardwood floor. There were the Pattys, who were stalking one another between talking vibrantly to other women and Livia and her crew, who had snagged a front table.

There were also, of course, a big handful of Denver women in the audience. They ranged from Stacy's femme friend Beth (who was tonight dressed as Xena, Warrior Princess) to G-hey! and Salad, the Lesbian Avengers she knew to speak to without knowing much about their personal lives. She had met them the summer before on womyn's land in New Mexico. There was also a whole group of women wearing the standard leather jacket/chaps/skirt/pants whom she knew she had seen around town without being able to remember the place or their names.

"Woof!" Alison had not seen Liz coming up behind her and she gave a little start. Liz didn't notice. She had that same glazed look she'd worn the previous evening before disappearing forever into the crowd. In one hand she was carrying her camcorder. "Wow!" she said to Alison, surfacing just enough to make basic conversation, "don't you feel like you just opened a box of Whitman's samplers?"

"Oh, yeah," Alison agreed and then, "but if you tell Stacy I said that, I'll tell her you're lying."

"As if she'd believe that," Liz scoffed. She turned to watch a blonde woman in a form fitting black leather dress walk by on black spike heels studded with rhinestones. Liz swiveled her head to follow like an owl. "Oink, oink, oink!" she added, so softly that only Alison could hear her.

Alison thought for a minute. Liz, being Stacy's best friend and hence the ever watchful guardian of how Stacy's girlfriends treated her, was probably right about who would be believed if they told differing stories. "Okay," she said, "You're right. I'll just have to kill you if it looks as if it's going to come out. And what's the difference between woofing and oinking?"

"Woof means that she can fuck me in the parking lot," said Liz, still looking after the blonde. "Oink means that she can fuck me right here on the table and I'll squeal like a pig when she does it."

"Excuse me."

Alison turned back toward the ticket table. A woman who looked familiar was standing in front of her, tapping her clutch absently against the cash box; her beauty took Alison's breath away.

The femme asked, "I don't have to pay extra for this event, do I?"

She was much smaller than Alison, making her feel protective immediately. Like Stacy she had been done up pretty and she had been done up right. Her dark hair was pulled into a deceptively simple French twist, providing an alluring background for tiny gold and diamond earings. Her eyes which were dark and heavily fringed, had a tilt in the corners which suggested an Asian or possibly Native American grandparent, as did her skin, which was the color of heavily creamed coffee.

She was wearing a black lace dress that Alison, from Stacy's forays into the vintage clothing stores, knew was an antique. It looked great on her—simple and classy—she had resisted any urge to busy it up with accessories. The earrings were her only jewelry, her hose were a plain smoky black and her heels were only a bit higher and less chunky than office pumps. She had gone for the elegant look and had succeeded. The only bit of glitter she had allowed was her clutch bag, which was beaded in black and gold. Alison guessed her to be in her late twenties.

She spoke with a half smile, giving Alison a look so amused and knowing it made her flush. "So, do I have to pay extra, or is this part of the package?"

"Um, it's part of the package..." Alison wanted to say more, but she resisted the urge. She knew she babbled when she was flustered. Better to let the woman think she was the silent type than think she was an idiot. She wondered where this woman had been the evening before. Not at the Meet and Beat. She would have noticed. Wait a minute—wasn't she the woman in the hood that the SEPS 'rescued,' the one who had perched on Scar's knee? Right, and hadn't she been talking to the waitress at the Merc Cafe?

"Thanks." The femme moved away from the table, but not before giving Alison a long, knowing look that registered everything from her combat boots to her butch cut. She knew she was probably just having her tail twisted, but it still made her knees weak for a moment.

"Well, hose you down!" said Liz, looking after the woman as she moved toward the stage. "Pick your tongue up off the table—it's not pretty. What's your arrangement with Stacy, anyway?"

"I'm not looking to buy, I'm just looking to look," Alison protested. She tried to fight her way out of the cloud of pheromones which had suddenly engulfed her like a Welsh fog by shuffling the money. She and Stacy had discussed having other play partners during the conference, but the main part of the discussion had been about Stacy beating strangers, not Alison being carried off on a cloud of passion.

"You don't want her anyway," said Liz, turning back to the table. Another woman had come through the door. It was Mary Clare. "Alison's getting ready to chase Bad News," Liz told Mary Clare chattily.

Mary Clare, who was digging around in her pocket for her pass, looked past Liz's shoulder. Bad News, the woman in the lace dress, was still standing, looking out over the crowd for a vacant chair.

"Odd woman," she said, finally finding the pass in her wallet. "Brilliant musician, though."

"Bad News is a freaker," Liz told Alison, an eye on Mary Clare for confirmation. Mary Clare nodded. Alison had no idea what this meant and wasn't about to ask any questions while Mary Clare was standing there. She wished, in fact, that Liz would just shut the fuck up.

Liz, however, was on a roll. "She's one of those women who wants to do a scene and sets up a scene and gets into a scene and then freaks out in the middle of it. You know, she cries. 'This is sick and I hate myself and I'm warped so bad I can never be normal and it's all lesbians' fault.'"

"Well, gee," started Alison, preparing to be compassionate.

Liz saw it coming and cut her off at the pass. "No," she said. "Nononono. There is a place to work that kind of thing out. It is called therapy. It is not called playing with a stranger when the only thing that has been negotiated is a little beating." Again she looked to Mary Clare for confirmation.

"Damn straight," said Mary Clare. "I didn't play for two years when I was dealing with my incest survivor issues. You want to talk, you talk to a friend. You want to use s/m to let you lose control then you'd better make it real clear and you'd better make it with someone you know."

"Aren't you supposed to be taping?" Alison asked Liz. She was not interested in talking to Marta's cousin, Mary Clare.

"Oh, they wouldn't give us permission to tape this one. Afraid it would scare the folks back home," Liz answered in a distracted voice, still looking at Mary Clare.

It looked as if this conversation was going to go on quite a bit longer than Alison was comfortable talking to Mary Clare, so she opted to turn away. Bad News had found a chair and was talking to a great big butch girl who was flagging heavy on the left. The pretty ones could always find a chair and they were always bad news, thought Alison sourly. Sometimes she suspected Liz of making up stories just to keep the peace with Stacy.

The entertainment was basically a lesbian talent show. There weren't quite so many lesbians with three chords and a guitar as there would have been at the Lesbian Follies, but there had been a sizeable chunk of bad poetry and an erotic modern dance that had left the audience puzzled. The acts that were really being applauded were the fantasy skits. They were set up along the same line as the fantasies that were part of the Miss International Leather competition. This meant that each act was choreographed to a piece of music and could last no longer than three minutes.

"We've got to set a time limit," Alison remembered Stacy telling Liz over dinner. "Otherwise we're going to be there for hours watching somebody get whipped while she's holding a burning candle in her cunt. On and off again." She had picked thoughtfully at her burrito. "I wish it were possible to hold tryouts." As with all aspects of Mistress Anastasia's leather conference, she longed for complete control. "But we're going to have to just take the first ten entries and hope they're not dogs."

Well, thought Alison, lifting her eyes from Bad News to the stage, she hadn't seen any dogs yet. So far the women who had performed had done a pretty good job. They had obviously practiced and most had tried to be inventive. There had been a few which Alison thought old and dull as the hills, but even they had been greeted with applause. She supposed people liked seeing the old favorites. They were probably the same ones who had kept *I Love Lucy* in syndication for thirty years.

There had also been a number of inside jokes slipped onto the stage. At the moment, in fact, about half the women in the audience were roaring with laughter at something Alison had not understood, though she thought it had something to do with a large glass jar sitting on the corner of a prop desk, filled with water and something that looked uncomfortably like a shrunken head.

Since she wasn't getting the joke, Alison let her eyes wander over the crowd. The sunken dance floor, which had been set with chairs and tables, was packed. The waitresses were having a hell of a time getting in and out. Women without seats were lining the walkway which skirted the floor, leaning on the railing that stood about two feet above the heads of the sitting audience. It was a rowdy crowd. They were having a good time and no one was feeling the least bit shy about yelling or stomping their feet. There had even been some barking. Everyone was dressed to the nines. It was going to be a dressed to the nines kind of weekend, Stacy had warned her, though things would relax by Sunday. Alison was glad that she had given in to Stacy about the fatigues—she was pulling a number of come hither looks.

She noticed that Mary Clare was hanging over the edge of the railing between a woman dressed as a French maid and one who had gone the cowboy route. Safe to return to the door, then.

Liz was still standing by the table, looking peeved.

"This isn't my job," she complained, her eyes on the dance floor. Liz wanted to be where the action was.

"I needed to pee," Alison lied. "Thanks for filling in." This last was said to Liz's back, which for the first time Alison noticed was criss-crossed with long, thin welts. Liz must have been partying down the night before. Liz would never let herself be detoured by a little paint.

While she had been gone Liz had allowed someone to take the folding chair, so Alison settled herself on the corner of the table. She wondered if anyone else would be coming in. Probably not—they were almost to the end of the show, at which time everyone would adjourn either to private parties or the dungeon. She was going to have to go to Livia's party, which was not going to make Stacy happy.

As if mere thought had summoned her, Stacy suddenly appeared, carrying two beers by the neck. She handed one to Alison with a smile and then perched beside her on the table.

"What do you think?" she asked. "Do you think it's going well?" She did not wait for Alison to answer, but answered her own question. "I think it's going well—I really do. Oh, that time limit was such a good idea—otherwise we would have been here until next year! The poetry was awful, it always is." Stacy had a real thing against poetry. Emily Dickinson could have been on stage and she wouldn't have liked it. "But it gave everybody a chance to use the can and move around." She looked out across the floor. "It's crowded, but that's good. Something like this is better in a crowded space than in an open space. It's more sexy."

Alison looked at her. She didn't know if the event was sexy, but Stacy herself certainly looked sexy. Her face was flushed with excitement and her hair, as if it had caught the fever too, had broken out of its careful coiffure and was standing around her head like a great, dark mane, the way Alison liked it the best. The strap on her thin tank top had fallen down one shoulder. Another inch and she was going to have a bare breast showing. Alison thought that was a good idea. She put her arm around Stacy and pulled her close, pushing the strap down at the same time. She nuzzled her face into Stacy's hair, ending up with an earring in her mouth.

"Oh, yeah," said Stacy, in a voice that was not unpleased. "You don't want to do anything on stage, but you want to make out in front of two hundred people.

"You didn't tell me I could fuck you on stage," Alison whispered to her neck. "Would you like that? Would you like to be fucked on stage, with everyone watching?" She didn't know what the answer would be. Stacy was not a top and only top kind of gal, but she did prefer to top in public and had certainly been in bitch-on-wheels mode for most of the conference. "Would you like that?" she persisted, her mind scrambling for a way to make this happen from the bottom. "Tie me to the wall and grind your pussy up against my face? Make me lick you, fuck you with my tongue, beg to fuck you?"

Stacy's answer was to turn to her, throwing a leg across her lap, which Alison took as a yes. She was wearing patterned stockings with a garter belt— Alison found the top edge immediately with one hand. She pushed up above it, sliding her hand up Stacy's bare ass, letting her fingers trace up the crack and then back down again. She was wet. She was ready. Alison fingered her pussy for a moment, playing with the lips of her cunt, then, in response to her moans and whispers, thrust three fingers inside her. Stacy preferred her foreplay after she came—fucking and kissing should always be alphabetical.

Alison was aware that, though most of the women were turned to the stage, they would be in full view of anyone who turned around. That made it better. There was no one there who would disapprove or censure. The worst that could happen was that they would draw a crowd and at the moment that didn't seem awkward or embarrassing. She liked the idea of someone standing in front of her, watching as she fucked Stacy's cunt from behind as Stacy wrapped herself around her.

She pushed Stacy's skirt up higher, as if she truly did have an audience. Stacy, who had been thrusting down against her, turned so she was straddling Alison's lap. She reached down to her zipper and drew out the dildo she had asked Alison to pack. She lifted herself slightly to allow Alison to slip it inside her, moaning as she slowly took the full length.

"Do it," she said to her, her voice soft and excited but commanding. "I want you to fuck me and I want you to do a good job. That's what you're best at. That's why I keep you around—to fuck me whenever I want you to."

They had played this game before and Alison immediately clicked into submission, adding details from times before. In her real life, on her job, she was in control, spent her days telling people what to do and how to do it. In this fantasy she had no power. She was chained to the wall, waiting to service the woman for whom she lived and for whom she would die if it came to it. She had only one obligation and no other distractions. She was on call twenty-four hours a day and the time that she did not spend fucking she spent waiting.

She pushed up Stacy's skirt with both hands, settling them on her hips so that she could guide her movements. Stacy had pulled her legs up onto the table, resting with her knees on either side of Alison. She pushed herself up, so high the dildo almost slipped out of her cunt. This was the long one, the one made for fucking in a harness. Stacy could never have been content with a real dick—she liked it way too big and long and Alison was honored to oblige. That was her purpose in life, to thrust up deep in Stacy's cunt, fuck her hard and rough and tight when she demanded service. She pulled Stacy's ass down as she thrust up inside her, nuzzling against Stacy's breasts with her mouth at the same time. Stacy pushed her head away and she drew back immediately, not having to be told that Stacy had also slipped into the fantasy of the sex slave. They had acted this one out many times—the chains that had bound Alison to the wall did not exist solely in her mind. She knew the scenario from the way that Stacy denied her her nipples—in the scene she was not allowed to touch as one might touch a lover, for she was not a lover. She was something that had given its whole self over to service, whose very being hung on the asking. She felt, as she pulled Stacy down on her, that given the chance she could reach up inside Stacy and grasp her heart in her hand. Stacy looked down into her eyes and she returned the look, giving permission for whatever Stacy desired. She pulled her head away from Stacy's chest, knowing, without words, that Stacy wanted to slap her, closing her eyes and turning her face to take the blow. Other times, other performances flowed into her mind—Stacy with pretend anger at her incompetence, herself begging to please. Please let me fuck you, make you come the way you want. Beat me, slap me, tell me you love me while I push my fist inside your legs on my shoulders spread open wide, fuck you hard. Please let me fuck you the way you want it, let me be yours to serve.

The crack of Stacy's hand on her cheek sounded loud enough to drown out the sound of music and applause; she had lost herself totally in the interface of memories and the now. Had to fuck her hard now to avoid the displeasure of her Mistress. The blow to her face had freed her from restraint. A horse will run more swiftly when ridden by a jockey and Alison, too, performed best when urged with a crop—not through fear of pain but fear of displeasure, fear of inadequacy. She was the servant when Stacy mounted her like this—her life was bound in the service.

Far away she heard the sound of laughter which for a moment puzzled her, for she had forgotten everything but Stacy riding her like a goddess. Stacy's hands were tight as a vise on her shoulders as she drove herself to climax, taking the dildo so deep within her hot cunt that it could not be seen between them. Then Stacy's mouth down on her hair, muffling her cries. She folded completely into Alison's arms, trusting her completely to keep her from falling.

From the dance floor there was another roar of laughter. Almost immediately, so close behind it that some women were still laughing while others were making that universal 'What happened?' noise there was some kind of commotion in the audience. The sound was enough to make Alison to look up. While just a moment before, fucking Stacy in front of a crowd had seemed like a really great idea, she suddenly felt shy. It was different imagining an audience who was totally into what was happening than the reality of being caught in the act by a bunch of people who were pissed off.

Stacy had slid off her lap and was adjusting her skirt, so Alison adjusted her clothing and stood up to look at the stage area to see what the problem was. About twenty women were on their feet. They were all in a crooked line leading from the middle of the crowd to the dance floor exit. Most of the audience, some baffled, some sounding supportive and some clearly ticked off, were looking toward the exit where a woman was pushing her way through the group surrounding the floor. Even from the door Alison could see that there was no 'Please, excuse me,' going on—this was shoving and elbowing and complaining and it looked all the more impolite considering that the woman cutting the swath was none other than the impeccably dressed Bad News.

On stage the fantasy was still playing out—something that looked like a schoolroom scene, set to a piece of classical piano music. A woman wearing pigtails and dressed in a little girl outfit was strutting around showing her panties and from the stubborn look on her face, was determined to finish her act. Either she couldn't or her finale was hidden from Alison as some of the audience stood up to cheer, howl with laughter or boo and hiss. There was a lot of floor stomping. whistling and shouting too.

Alison caught only that glimpse before Bad News plowed through the tag end of the crowd and came roaring up to the door.

"That is shit!" she spat. She was actually shaking with either rage or indignation. Perhaps a combination of the two. Alison was not sure if she was addressing Alison personally or as a representative of the leather community. Or the world.

"You should have stopped it." Bad News said, panting as if she had run a race. Alison supposed it had taken a lot of energy to push her way out of the crowd like that. "Are you in charge? Are you the one putting all this on? Because I'm writing a letter to complain! Believe me, you're getting a letter and you're not going to be the only one! I've been silent way too long, but this just makes a mockery of the whole issue. I came tonight because she asked me to. I came to be supportive and nice and forgiving. Then she does this! And not only that—she used Mozart, too, my favorite piece, the one I played in the competition. And I'm not letting her get away with it. Not anymore. I'm going public with this. I'll write to Ricki Lake if I have to. I'll write to the university where she teaches, you'd better believe it!"

With that she swept out the door, catching one high heel on the edge of the door jamb for just a second, which made her stutter-step and somewhat spoiled the exit.

The crowd was applauding and whooping, unless they were booing. In any case it looked like things were breaking up. That must have been the last act.

Alison, coming down from the rush of adrenaline that had been fueled first by the sex and then by Bad News' outburst, suddenly felt bone weary and three-year-old cranky. Almost more than anything else she hated this aspect of her condition—that urgent need to go home and to bed right now, right now, right now! And she couldn't go home—she had to go to Livia's stupid party.

It seemed to take forever for everyone to stop milling around and finally leave. And where was Stacy? She forced herself to smile and be gracious to the women who were slowly making their way out, their voices loud with opinions and comments on the fantasies.

"Nice set up," said a lovely black woman close to Alison toting a big prop bag. "Good stage."

"Good sound, too," added the woman with her. Alison knew she had seen them both on stage. She couldn't recall what they had been doing, but the music had been salsa. She nodded, a forced smile on her face, because nodding was easier than keeping the snap out of her tone.

"Thanks for doing this," said the woman behind them who was carrying a bull whip coiled over her arm on one side and a purse to die for on the other side. Her platinum blonde hair had been cut to half an inch all over her head, but she was wearing full eye make-up and gold earrings that dangled down and touched the shoulders of her purple leather jacket.

Again Alison nodded and smiled and the woman moved on and out into the parking lot and that meant she was that much closer to finding some place she could sit down, and tomorrow she could sleep in because G-hey! was driving the early shift…

"You should have controlled the audience better."

For a moment Alison, who had followed Earrings out the door with her eyes, longing to be headed for her own car, did not even realize she was the one to whom the statement had been addressed.

"What?" she asked, realizing half a second too late that she didn't want to ask what, she just wanted to usher this woman out with a smile like the others.

"You should have controlled that audience better!" It was none other than Crescent, the woman Alison had seen with Scar at the Merc, her voice firm, her face belligerent. She had to be one of those people who described herself as assertive, a strong woman who didn't take shit, when she was really just obnoxious. "That…woman…totally disrupted my fantasy."

She must have been talking about the scene Bad News had objected to.

"You were the last act. Maybe everyone was just ready to go to the dungeon," Alison said. She was damned if she was going to get pulled into either mixing it up or defending herself this late at night.

It didn't work.

"There was no excuse for letting her create all that commotion in the audience," Crescent persisted. "That's your job—I don't expect to have to compete when I perform." She leaned over the table. Alison felt like popping her in the nose ring. She was a handsome woman, or probably would be, thought Alison ungraciously, when she kept her mouth shut. Since Alison was being ungracious anyway, she decided Crescent probably kept her vibrant head tattoo hidden the rest of the year and was too old to dress that way to boot.

"Whatever," Alison said dismissively, tired of the whole thing. She had always promised herself she was never going to be the kind of person who said 'Whatever,' but she had been watching sleaze TV when she couldn't sleep and it had kind of snuck up on her. Who did the stupid bitch think she was, talking to her like that? Alison, like everyone else on the committee, was volunteering her time. She didn't let anyone talk to her like that for less than twelve dollars an hour and even then only once in a great while.

Stacy suddenly appeared back at the table. "What's wrong?"

"We didn't control the audience during her scene," said Alison, making her voice bored.

"That last act?" Stacy raised a disapproving eyebrow as if this complaint was so stupid she just couldn't believe her ears. She shot a look at Alison—is this for real? Alison, still blasé, gave a bored little nod.

"We will be more than happy to refund your money." Stacy whipped a checkbook out of the pocket of her jacket. "Give me your name tag."

There was a short little pause while the two of them tried to stare one another down. This happened to be something which Stacy was really good at, so Alison was not at all surprised when the other woman spoke first.

"Look," she said, turning back toward Alison, whom she had rightly identified as being the more easily bullied. "I don't want to make a big stink, but it is your job to control the audience during performances. That's just part of the production agreement. It's like providing a stage and lights and a sound system. I don't expect to be competing with the audience when I'm performing."

Alison said, "Well, why don't you write a whole bunch of letters then. That's what she's going to do—"

She was stopped by a strange, unreadable look on Crescent's face. It gave Alison a chill.

"And I don't expect to have my hump busted over something we couldn't anticipate," said Stacy shortly. "So we can do one of two things. You can be an asshole and get your money back and go home, or you can not be an asshole and I'll keep your money and you can attend the rest of the conference. Which is it going to be?"

"Hmmph!" Crescent decided to cut her losses and run before she got eighty-sixed too. She picked up her cane tube and her prop bag, pigtail wig sticking out, and sailed through the door.

"Asshole," said Stacy looking after her. "A three minute fantasy and they suddenly think they're Cher. Hell, my cat could have put on a better show than some of them! Okay, the place is clear. Let's hit the dungeon!"

"I can't go to the dungeon," said Alison. Oh, dammit, this was going to be an issue and an issue was the last thing in the world she wanted to deal with right now. "Stacy, I have to go to that party Livia's having in her hotel room. I told you that already." Alison was not actually sure that she had told Stacy, but considering the state she had been in all day figured she could get away with it even if she hadn't.

Stacy turned, disappointment clear on her face. "You never said anything about that! You said you were going to the dungeon! You said we could do something together."

"Stacy, I told you this afternoon that I had to go to the party." Alison tried to speak in a matter-of-fact kind of voice.

"Fine!" snapped Stacy in a tight little voice that said it was anything but.

"Oh, come on," pleaded Alison. She hated it when her friends were mad at her, hated it the most when it was Stacy. She reached out and put a hand on her arm.

"Fine!" Stacy pulled away from her. "Fine! Do whatever you want, but don't try to manipulate me into saying that it's okay or that I like it! Do whatever you want, but don't expect to get my stamp of approval!"

Before Alison could reply, or indeed even think of a reply, Liz approached the table with her little work exchange crew in tow. "We're out of here," she said, her voice relieved. "Let's blow this popstand."

"Alison's not coming," said Stacy in a voice so hard and brittle it could have been used to scrape the dance floor. "She's going to Livia's."

Liz the leather lawyer was no fool. She knew when it was time to mix in and when it wasn't. "I'll wait in the car," she said.

"You do look awful," observed G-hey!, as usual just blurting everything out. "And your face is all puffy." She reached over and picked Alison's hand off the table. "Your hands are swollen, too. You know who she looks like?" she said, turning to Salad. "She looks like your mom when she has MS." She turned back to Alison, ready to get into a conversation. "Salad's mom has MS sometimes and it's really…"

"She has MS all the time," corrected Salad. "You can't have MS part of the time. She's just symptomatic part of the time."

"Let's go," interrupted Flame. "I'm supposed to meet someone and suck her blood." Flame was well known in the community for doing scenes with a vampire theme. Of course she wasn't really allowed to suck blood at an official dungeon—it was unsafe—but everyone knew that she liked to take girls who weren't fussy back to the warehouse where she lived and do the real thing there. Flame was the only leatherwoman Alison had met who seemed to have no fear whatsoever of AIDS. Maybe she thought she was just too strong for it.

"Salad's mom," said G-hey! who was now standing close looking thoughtfully at Alison's face as if she were going to poke it too, "does a lot of acupuncture and eats macrobiotically. She hardly has it at all anymore. You should try acupuncture."

"She's hardly symptomatic anymore," corrected Salad, speaking at the same moment as Stacy who said crossly, "Well, Alison doesn't have MS!"

"Okay," said G-hey! agreeably. She picked up her toy bag. "Do you want a cookie?" she asked Alison. "Salad's mom made a whole bunch of snicker-doodles for the refreshment table at the dungeon."

"Salad's mom made cookies for the dungeon?" asked Stacy incredulously. Her own parents had hardly spoken to her after she left her abusive husband and she got great enjoyment over imagining them turning over in their graves because of the things she was doing now.

"Oh, Salad's mom raised her to be sex positive," said G-hey! putting her things back on the table. She snapped open the bag and dug in for the cookies.

"Yeah," agreed Salad. "Her girlfriend lived with her and my dad the whole time we were growing up. They were members of Beyond Monogamy and—"

Let's go!" interrupted Flame. Alison, who was always a bit uneasy around Flame stood up obediently, but G-hey! ignored her, passing out cookies. Alison bit into hers right away, hoping it would push back the feeling she was about to burst into tears. She didn't want to cry in front of G-hey! who would want to talk about it and give her hugs, nor did she want to cry in front of Stacy who would think she was being manipulative. Most especially she didn't want to cry in front of Flame who might pick her up and crush her head for keeping her away from the dungeon.

"Did those women from New Mexico get housing finally?" G-hey! asked Flame. Alison had already noticed that G-hey! either didn't notice or tended to ignore social signals. She saw that Salad, who picked up a whole lot better, was trying to give her a private pinch. G-hey! squirmed out of reach and went on talking. "Because Marta Goicochea—you know her, she's Mary Clare's cousin—she and Mary Clare bought the building next door to us?" G-hey! also had the habit of occasionally lifting her voice at the end of statements, making them sound like questions. "And—this is so cool—they're keeping this one little place in the back open so it's available as an emergency space for battered women?"

"We put them up with Beth's girlfriend," said Flame, who obviously wanted to cut the whole thing short and get to the party.

"That's nice of them," said Alison, because something was obviously called for and neither Flame nor Stacy was going to say it. Hearing about Marta being nice made her feel like even more of a shit. She wished Marta would move back to Idaho.

They made it through the door in a clump, everyone nibbling on one of Salad's mom's cookies. They were really good. Stacy followed Alison to her car.

"I need my jacket," she said shortly. "And my toy bag. And I've had invitations to use it, too. So if you're not coming tonight then you'd better just tell me and I'll find somebody else to play with."

"Then fuck you," Alison replied. She jerked the trunk open and tossed Stacy's bag onto the pavement. She'd had no idea that she was going to say fuck you to Stacy, but it sounded so good that she said it again. "Fuck you, okay Stacy? You go ahead and be the center of attention like you always are. Hook up with some real butch woman who doesn't have to work and who can go all night without sleeping. And be sure and get her phone number, because you just might want to call her the next time I fail you in some way."

"Oh, that's right," Stacy answered heatedly. "I forgot that you were the big detective! The big detective hot on the scent! Kinsey Millhone, hot on the trail! You won't bottom for me, but all Livia had to do was flash a little green under your nose and you're dancing on your hind legs like a Chihuahua! You're probably the entertainment at that party and you don't even know it! Watch the big detective bottom for Livia! Well, hey, Kinsey, I've got a wad of cash, too! If I'd known you were for sale, I would have put it up next to Livia's! Is it too late to do that now? Can I buy your contract? Or should I just go straight to Livia and talk to her?"

"You don't know anything, Stacy!" Alison threw her door open. She couldn't remember ever being so instantly angry with Stacy and had no idea how they had gone from hot fucking to screaming at one another in the parking lot like a couple of drag queens on Ricki Lake. "You don't know one damn thing, so why don't you just shut up and look pretty, because that's what you're good at!"

Even as she heard the words coming out of her mouth she could not believe she had said them, would have given a paycheck to call them back. She opened her lips without being sure what she was going to say, hoping something comforting would fall out with the same ease that something ugly and on target had. But before she could even form one word Stacy's face changed from terrible pain to an equally terrible anger and she took a step forward as if what she had to say needed to be spit out at close range.

"Well, excuse me for asking, you goddamn hypochondriac! I'm so sorry I thought maybe my lover might want to play with me!" She took another step and Alison fought the impulse to throw up a hand. Even furious she did not really think that Stacy would hit her in anger. Did she?

"Or maybe lover's not the right word, is it! It's not like we ever have sex anymore! Because you're sick, or you're too tired! You think I'm too stupid to get somebody else? Well, guess what, there are women who would line up for the chance to lick my shoes! And then you can just stay home and moan because your hips hurt!"

She turned and pushed away from the air in front of Alison as if it were the side of a pool.

"Fuck you, Alison!" she called over her shoulder as she all but ran toward her car (the only other one in the lot). "Fuck you and everybody who looks like you!" Though Liz had already done the smart thing and retreated back by Stacy's car, Stacy did not open any door but the driver's. She snapped into reverse before she even turned her headlights on and backed up so quickly Alison feared a moment for the fence that lined the opposite side of the alley. Together she and Liz watched her tail lights as they sped down the alley and out into the street.

After a moment Liz walked over to Alison's car. She moved slowly and carefully, making no sudden moves as if Alison were a terrorist or a feral cat.

"All I want is to go to my car," she said. "I would call a cab, but there's nowhere to call from around here. Just take me to my house."

Alison gave a short, curt nod. It was not Liz's fault she had said something ugly and unforgivable, nor was it Liz's fault that Stacy had said something ugly and unforgivable in return. Yet for all her innocence, it would have been somehow satisfying to snap at Liz and Liz, with her careful moves, knew it.

Alison unlocked her door. She leaned across the front seat to unlock the passenger door, but Liz was already climbing in the passenger side.

"Goddamn it!" she said, in a voice both sour and fired with a passion much more suitable to great betrayal, "You'd think Stacy would know that if you don't lock all the doors it doesn't matter if you lock any of the doors! That's just what I need—my car ripped off on top of everything else."

Liz said nothing. She seemed to be surrounding herself with a thick and cold silence that blanketed her like a force field. They had not gone ten blocks before Alison turned to her and belligerently said, "What!"

"I don't want to get into this," Liz replied in a voice so distant a listener would have assumed that they had never met before.

"You're in it." Alison had no idea what was making her push against Liz—it was as if she had set off an explosion of such magnitude that the only move she could now make was to destroy anything that had miraculously survived the first blast.

"Fine," said Liz without looking at her. "I think that was about the meanest thing I've ever seen you do and I can hardly wait to get out of this car and away from you." Liz was Stacy's best friend, and it had been a given for the past three years that one of her jobs was to notice and object if Alison was acting out of line. Liz did it for Stacy and Alison did it for Michelle and Michelle did it for Alison and someday Stacy would do it for Liz again. That was one of the points of having a best friend. But, though they had often been allies in the face of Stacy's tizzies, never before had Liz spoken to Alison in this tone of complete disdain. There was not another word between them for the rest of the ride and Liz climbed out of the car without saying either thank you or goodbye.

Chapter Nine

Stacy's hateful words were still ringing in Alison's ears as she gave her car keys to a different but equally nice boy in uniform in front of Livia's hotel. Stacy was probably right about Livia using her as entertainment. She usually was about that kind of thing. Alison had half a mind to go up and give the money back. Except that she'd already given most of it to Janka. And she would be damned if Stacy was going to bully her.

She knocked tentatively on the door, wondering if Livia's love of drama had extended to guest lists and secret passwords. No—maybe other nights, but not tonight. That was the whole point of the party tonight—it was open to the little people and presumably the blackmailer was going to show, like it was an Agatha Christie story or something.

God, Alison thought, I just hate intrigue. I'd rather be run over by a truck than have someone jumping me through a hoop. Oh. Yeah. That was kind of the point, wasn't it? For a moment she had forgotten that this was something being done very nonconsensually.

The door opened a crack and then was pulled back by Best Boy.

"It isn't usually like this," she said to Alison, her tone a combination of befuddlement and outrage. "Usually Livia's parties are so…so exclusive. So A-list. I mean, it's hard to get an invite to Livia's parties and if you do you have to be holding it in your hand—you can't just say 'Jo sent me' or 'I left it back at the room.'" Her mouth shut with a little snap of disapproval as she looked out over the crowd.

It was a pretty big group, and even Alison could tell it wasn't the A-list. For one thing, the Pattys were both there, engaged on opposite sides of the room in the absolutely rapt conversation Alison had already learned preceded fur flying. Nobody, she thought, would have invited them on purpose. Through the open door of the first room she also saw Scar, delivering some kind of monologue to a very large woman who looked quite desperate to escape. Even a room away Alison heard the word 'FBI' float out over the other conversation. Poor Best Boy—she had been sucking up for the right to run this party for years and look how common it had become.

"It looks great," Alison lied. Actually, it looked like an outer ring of hell.

No one was pretty when you felt like shit and your girlfriend had stomped off to party all night with women butcher than you.

The two doors between the rooms were open again. Obviously each space had been given a purpose. The far room was the dungeon and from the sounds it was already in heavy use. Again most of the chairs had been pulled into the middle room, where there was also food and booze. The first room was probably supposed to be the chill out room, but it was now absorbing the spill over from the food room.

Just the fact that there was alcohol made Alison uncomfortable. She had been taught booze and beating never mixed. Okay, okay, she wasn't here to lecture on tolerance or dungeon safety. She was here to find out who was harassing Livia. Forgetting for a moment how angry she was with her, Alison wished Stacy had come. Stacy was a marvel at chatting up everyone in record time and reporting back with inconsistencies. She had never been to a play party without Stacy before. Come to think of it, she had never been to a play party without Liz, either. They had always been there to give her the social cue, as one might watch the hostess pick up her silverware. She knew she didn't want to go into the far room. Livia's crowd creeped her out—she was afraid to see what head games might be taking place. Besides, she was not likely to find out anything in the dungeon room. Small talk among the audience was discouraged. It was hard to get the endorphins going if someone was going on about having their carpets cleaned during a beating. Probably her best bet was to hang out with the food—eventually even the hardiest players were going to have to pause for a little refreshment. Maybe then she could cut one or two from the crowd. Although she had looked at the bar with disapproval it might actually work in her favor—nothing like some heavy beating and a drink or two to make people start sharing their secrets.

She strolled over to the buffet, looking around with interest that was largely manufactured. Gotta pump up and get in role or she might as well carry a sign saying, 'Notice Me!'

There was quite a crowd around the party trays, which featured Swiss cheese and roast beef. Not to mention the two boxes of chocolate flanking the trays. Livia would hate to hear it, but she bottomed well. Everybody was chowing down—the food was good and it was free and the Fantasy show, like any amateur night, had gone on way, way too long.

Alison filled a plate and then glanced around the room. Okay, where and with whom did she start? Over by the windows she saw the woman who had given her the once over the night before, the mystery femme whose name Dana had not known. She was obviously being hit on by a compact butch who, though attractive, looked to be trying too hard even from this distance. Just as obviously the mystery femme was attempting a blow off of the nodding and murmuring 'mmm-hmm' kind.

Alison was just considering cutting in on the action when the femme looked up and caught her eye. She brightened and gave Alison one of the most beautiful across-the-room smiles that she had ever seen—the kind that is accompanied by violins in movies. Alison found herself about twenty feet closer without conscious plan.

"There you are, my darling," said the woman, reaching a hand out to Alison across the butch's shoulder. Alison responded without hesitation, pulling her close with a twirl as if they were going to two-step. "So nice to meet you," she said to the crestfallen butch as she rested her head against Alison's shoulder. "We must talk again."

The butch gal adjusted her face, girded her loins and marched away with a pretty good air about her—no one who had not overheard the exchange could have told that she'd just been blown off.

"Thank you ever so much," said the femme, giving Alison's hand a little squeeze before she dropped it. "I just don't go for the earnest type and they're all too earnest to realize it. I would have been trapped for hours and they follow you if you walk away by yourself."

"Any time," Alison replied, feeling gallant. She was all ready to talk about how hard it must be for really pretty women, a speech Stacy very much enjoyed, but the femme spoke first.

"Where's the girlfriend tonight?" she asked brightly. "And incidentally, my name is Erin. Erin Oleander. "

"Burning in hell," Alison replied. The response had been startled out of her—she'd had no idea anyone had been watching her that closely—and she'd meant for it to be much funnier than it actually came out.

"Oh, so you're here alone?" Erin said in a sexy voice, not asking for the details. Obviously the 'alone' part was the only thing she was interested in.

Alison felt a flush that seemed to rise from her rapidly beating heart. She adored Stacy and sex with her was still hot after three years. But she had forgotten that quick stirring which came when someone new and lovely looked your way—the way your nipples hardened automatically even if all you were discussing was the weather. She glanced again at the three delicate bracelets, studded with tiny stars and spikes, which Erin was wearing on her left wrist, and in the space of that glance had stripped off her shirt for this woman, knelt before her, her cunt open like a flower, and...

"I've got to talk to you. I really mean it. This is way serious now."

Alison was ripped out of her fantasy by a jog on the elbow and a voice which had become just a bit too familiar in the past few days. Tonight Scar wore leather and a black beret, which actually wouldn't have looked bad if she'd been standing anywhere except right up in Alison's face.

"Later," she said, hoping that would be enough. Of course, it wasn't. With her instinctive grasp of the dramatic this was, of course, the one time that Scar would be insistent.

"I've thought about this. I thought there would be room for reconciliation, but there isn't. Not after tonight. A person has to be sorry to be forgiven. She has to show she feels she was wrong."

She made another one of her mysterious little pauses, into which Alison inserted, "Fuck off!"

She was a bit taken aback by the vehemence of her own reply. But, damn it, what business did this woman have demanding anything from her? She had tried to listen and take her seriously, only to be teased and toyed with. She didn't like being a nonconsensual prop. "If you really had something to tell me, you would have told me at the Tara. I don't want to play head games with you! And you're standing too close to me!" She took a step forward, all but stepping on Scar's toes as she tried to force her back. Alison needed about two more feet of personal space than most Americans.

"No, you don't understand… Scar, attempting for penitent, sounded only petulant. "It was just that I wasn't sure if I should interfere. I mean, ten years and she never did anything about it herself. And who knows if everything that comes out in a playdate is true? I got them together to talk…a mistake. I didn't realize how really bad it still was. It fact it's really bad now, out of control and there's no safeword out for this. It's freaking me out big time…"

Erin smiled at someone across the room and shuffled her feet a little as if getting ready to move on to where the grass was greener, which made Alison's words come out even more harshly. "No," she said, "you don't understand. Just stay away from me. I've been warned about you and now I'm warning you—just stay away!" She put her hand beneath Erin's elbow and turned her again, this time so that they were standing with their backs to Scar, facing the bar.

"Sorry," she said in an undertone, bending her head close to Erin's as if they were talking about something very, very private. "She has been stalking me all day."

Erin laughed conspiratorially. "Oh, I know Scar," she said. "I'm happy to help however I can." She gave Alison a soulful look just in case she had missed the emphasis.

Annoying as the interruption had been, it had served a worthwhile purpose. It had jolted Alison back to reality. Reality was a fight with Stacy from which they would probably recover the next day if she didn't mess with Erin at Livia's party and probably never if she did mess with Erin at Livia's party.

"Where are you from?" she asked, thinking that if Erin were local it might be worth a go. She wasn't about to risk what she had with Stacy for a one time fuck and a long distance relationship, but she was just pissed enough to consider a local gal. That would show her—fuck you and I got a new girlfriend before your vibrator even cooled off! She knew this was really quite odious to even be thinking and was glad that people's thoughts were monitored only in the world of fiction.

"Oh, far away," Erin replied, placing a forefinger on Alison's wrist. Alison could almost see the steam rising. She'd better stop this while she still was able.

"Look, " she said. "I don't mean to be an asshole, but you are absolutely hot and my girlfriend would put my head on a stake if I did anything at all with you. Probably even talking to you is too much."

"Would she have to know?" Erin asked, stroking the back of her hand. "She must not be too concerned if she let you come by yourself. My room is on this floor."

Once again Alison almost lost herself to the seductive eyes. Why would Stacy have to know? She'd been an absolute shit to her, pushing until Alison had blurted ugly words she couldn't take back. Stacy was probably whaling on some big butch gal who knew how to reshingle a house and could stay out 'til all hours even now. So what would it hurt—?

"Never mind," Erin said with a sad little smile. "Forget I said that. You love her—I can see it in your face. I don't want to be an ugly part of that."

Alison felt a huge rush of relief. "Thanks for understanding," she said. "You really are hot—if I wasn't—" She pulled her hand away and used it to shade her eyes as she looked down at the floor. "Maybe it would just be better for both of us if I didn't look at you."

Erin laughed, but not really heartily. She was being a good sport, but it was obvious it was an effort that was not up to including raucous laughter. "Why are you here?" she asked bluntly. "I mean, if you're not allowed to play with strangers and your girlfriend is somewhere else? Why isn't she here?"

"She hates Livia," said Alison, a second before realizing Erin might well be a friend of Livia's and if so, this was the wrong approach for a chat up. And chatted up Erin was going to be. If she couldn't play with her, then she goddamn sure was going to pick her brain. She wondered for a moment if Stacy would accept her being beaten and fucked by a beautiful blonde on the chance of gathering information through pillow talk. Nope, she could still see her head on a pike.

"Everyone hates Livia," Erin replied in an almost ghoulish tone. Loyalty was not going to be a problem here. "I certainly do. That's why there're so many people here. Nobody wants to miss a chance to get in Livia's face. She's been having closed parties for years and everything has been played her way. She's the top top with a lot of bleed-through. No femme tops at all. But why are you here, then?"

Alison extracted the photo from the pocket of her jacket. She showed it to Erin. "I'm doing a favor for a friend. She's writing a book about leatherwomen—kind of a history, biography thing. She wants to interview this woman—somebody told her she really had a story to tell or something. I don't know what—she just gave me the picture and asked me to show it around the party."

Erin took the photograph from her hand. "Let me get this straight," she said. "You are here without your girlfriend, who is, I take it, pissed about the whole thing, just so you can show a picture to women who are going to be majorly focused on other things and irritated about disruption. That story sucks. You need a much better one."

Alison pursed her lips and regarded her thoughtfully. Busted immediately. Bet that never happened to Kinsey. "How about if I add the fact that it's really an ex-lover and she has cancer, so she can't get out and do it herself? And she thinks the woman was connected with Livia's court one year, so that would be why I had to come to this particular party?"

"Better," Erin conceded. "But you should get all that in the first sentence. I have a better idea, though. Actually, two. Have you told that lame story to anybody else yet?" Alison shook her head, smarting a bit from the 'lame' part. Okay, so she was new at this. "Well, what about this? She," Erin tapped the photo, "is either someone who did your girlfriend way wrong and you're looking to kick the shit out of her, or you think there's a chance that one of you gave her a real nasty venereal disease and you want to get hold of her so she can get treated before her cunt rots and falls out."

"Why wouldn't I know her name if I'd been intimate enough with her to give her VD?" asked Alison, testing the idea.

"It was a festie fling. D.O.F.O.—Duration of festival only. You didn't exchange much information and you're just trying to be honorable now."

"I think I like the other one better."

"Yeah, well, they both have their pluses and minuses. There's a whole class of butch who's going to sympathize with the 'she done the girlfriend wrong' story. But, if you come across anybody who actually knows her and likes her, she's liable not to tell you the truth. If you go with the syphilis one, nobody's going to try to hide anything from you. On the other hand, no one is ever going to want to play with you or your girlfriend for the rest of your lives and she might not appreciate having that kind of rumor floating around." She spread her hands. "Good luck. I don't mean to be rude, but I'm here to party and you're married and something delicious just walked in the door."

"Wait a minute," Alison protested. "So which one do you think is better?"

Erin turned away and then turned back. "It doesn't matter," she said. "I've seen that woman and I know that she dropped out of sight three or four years ago. You'll never find her."

"Wait," started Alison.

"That's all I know," Erin said, turning again. "You never find them once they disappear. She's probably married to some young thing, living happily in the suburbs and raising Basenjis. You can't find people after they've dropped out of the scene. This is a whole other world here. If this photo was taken at Michigan the woman who took it might not even know her last name. Hell, she might not even know her first name! She might go by 'Hellraiser' or 'Wolfsbane'. And if she dropped out, she's not going to welcome anyone from that past with open arms. There was probably a reason. You know, only a small percentage of this group is going to stay in the scene for longer than a couple of years. The others are going to go in and out and finally leave for good and get really different girlfriends. Girlfriends who might not appreciate a photo like this."

"But, do you—?" Alison said, grasping at the only straws that had come within range.

Erin shook her head. "I saw her around, just like everybody else. That's all. I can't tell you more." Her voice was firm. Alison could tell from her tone that it would be a mistake to try and push it.

Erin's smile had pulled her away from the food, so she decided to go back to the buffet and start all over again. She let her eyes roam over the crowd as she filled her plate. Okay, there was someone who looked familiar. She gave her a big, old Colorado smile and went to stand beside her before belatedly realizing that it was the butch gal from whom she had helped Erin escape.

"Femmes," Alison said with a weak laugh. "You can't live with 'em and the world would be so dull without 'em." She was willing to pretend to be a fellow loser for a little information.

The woman looked at her for a moment and then raised her hand for a high five. Alison was a little slow and almost dropped her plate, but it came out okay in the end.

"And there's never enough to go around," the other woman said in a sad voice. "Not of the real ones, anyway. Permanent femme shortage. You'd think nature would create a better balance. My god there's—what? Ninety million kinds of insects? Forty-five different kinds of house cats? But there's never enough femmes."

"What do you mean, the real ones?" Alison asked, holding her plate out to share the grapes. "And I'm Alison." She needed to get names over right away, otherwise she was going to tag this woman 'Loser' in her head and wouldn't that be ugly if it slipped out?

"Ramona. Well, haven't you ever heard of dykes of convenience?" She took a few grapes.

"You mean like straight women who hook up with someone in prison?" Alison asked.

"That, and like some of the straight feminists in the seventies—the ones who lived lesbian lives because it was the right thing to do politically. And some of those women in Jane Addam's time—when was that? The eighteen hundreds?"

"She was a lesbian," Alison protested. "I've read some of the poetry she wrote to her lover."

"Oh, sure, she was. But a lot of those women who were reformers around that time weren't. They were just part of that very first wave of educated American women. They were the first ones who had gone to college and knew that anything they tried to do was going to be fucked by a husband and ten kids, so they lived with each other. Dykes of convenience. Boston marriages."

"And femmes of convenience?" Alison asked. This was kind of interesting—she had almost forgotten that chatting tonight had a goal. Okay, that was fine, there was nothing wrong with a few minutes of foreplay first.

"Your first conference?" Ramona asked her pityingly.

"My first anything." Alison was, as well, willing to appear stupid for a good cause.

"Okay, see that gal over there in the long skirt?" She pointed with a jerk of the head. "The one whose boots aren't quite right?"

"Yeah." Actually, from being around Stacy, Alison knew exactly why the boots weren't right, but she didn't volunteer to clarify. She and Ramona were still in the hand squeezing stage and she didn't want to lose points by coming out with femme fashion tips.

"Well, she's not a real femme. She's one of those androgynous types who plays both ways. She looks around when she goes someplace and if there's more femmes she plays butch and if there's more butches she plays femme."

"Oh, that's just plain wrong!" blurted Alison, horrified by the very thought of meeting a past playdate in chaps and a harness. God, for all her temptations maybe being monogamous with Stacy was indeed for the best. Didn't matter whether she was sewing or camping or playing soccer, Stacy was always a femme's femme. No unpleasant surprises there.

"Amen." They stood quietly for a moment in solidarity. Alison decided to try plan A with the photo—I want to kick this woman's butt. It was interesting how Erin had seen through her first story so immediately, as well as identifying the photo as being from Michigan.

"Do you know who this woman is?" she asked, pulling the photo from her pocket.

Ramona took it from her hand. "God," she said, "is she out yet? Or is this an old photo?"

"What do you mean, out?" asked Alison.

"This woman," Ramona tapped the photo the same way that Erin had, "was in prison the last I heard."

"What! For what?" Damn, her best and only clue locked up! Or maybe not. After all, Livia had never been contacted in person. Conceivably everything could have been manipulated from the inside. Up until this moment Alison had been looking for the woman as a witness, someone who could tell her who had been on the other side of the camera. However, a con sounded like a pretty good suspect.

Someone brushed past them and Alison looked up to see Crescent hurrying by. She was supporting another woman and it looked to Alison as if she was afraid if she didn't get her to the bathroom soon there was going to be an accident of mammoth proportions. Considering that, thought Alison, watching them go into the other room, it was kind of strange that Crescent didn't just use Livia's bathroom, but went for the suite door instead. Oh, well, she probably had a room on the same floor. Wisely, the hotel had put all the Wildfire woman together. Alison assumed this was a way to keep the horrifying of straight guests to a minimum.

Just as Crescent opened the door the other woman pulled away for a moment and did a half turn, her hands up to her face. She looked dreadful. With a start Alison recognized Bad News. For a moment Alison worried, wondering if she should interfere, then remembered how futile that had been with the Pattys.

Well, it was really rather cozy, wasn't it? The woman who had fussed about the commotion and the woman who had caused the commotion— and now there they were together. So maybe Scar had succeeded getting them to resolve their differences after all. Maybe Bad News wouldn't be sending off all those letters.

"…beat the fuck out of this woman and…" Ramona had been going happily along, not realizing that Alison wasn't listening.

"Wait, wait," said Alison, holding up her hands. Dammit, now here came Scar again, looking a little ill herself. Alison looked at her roast beef sandwich, wondering if Livia had decided to get back at the mystery stalker by poisoning the food. Scar focused in on her and she hastily turned her back. "Start again," she demanded. A quick peek over her shoulder—okay, Scar had read the rebuff and staggered out the still open suite door into the hall.

"She killed somebody," said Ramona. "At Michigan a couple of years ago. Beat the shit out of her—beat her black and blue and damaged her kidneys so badly it killed her. She was playing without a safeword and the bottom begged her to stop and she just went right on." She exchanged a horrified look with Alison. "Yeah—pretty awful, huh? You've got to be careful—there's crazies out there and they look just like we do."

Alison took the photo back. "Do you know what her name is?" she asked.

"Yeah, her name is Falcon. I never really knew her. I mean, I never played with her or anything. She was just a part of a big group. I wasn't there the year it happened, that she killed this woman. Somebody who was there told me about it. Dragonslayer, maybe? But I was there the year before and I met her then. She was with Livia's group—you ought to ask her. Why are you looking for her, anyway?"

"I don't know," Alison replied, putting the photo back in her pocket. "I thought that she was the person who was stalking my girlfriend, but if she's in the pen I guess she's not."

"She could be out," Ramona offered. "I don't think she was actually tried on a murder charge, even though I know the woman died. I heard it was assault and she only got a couple of years. She could be out by now."

"There's a frightening thought," said Alison with a shudder.

Something had happened in the other room and suddenly there was a big wave of women picking up their coats and leaving the suite.

"What's going on?" asked Alison. Within the space of a few minutes over half the crowd had disappeared.

"Oh, Livia must be getting ready to give communion." Ramona walked across to the door of the dungeon, beckoning Alison to follow her. She was enjoying being In The Know. Alison peeked over her shoulder.

Livia, wearing the miter of a Bishop and a purple robe, was sitting stately in a chair draped with one of the bedspreads. Alison could not help but wonder where one bought a miter. Surely you couldn't just mail order them. Someone must have made it, she decided. Lined up across the room was a row of women on their knees. Livia beckoned and the first approached her, shuffling forward. Livia made a gesture of beneficence as the woman bent her head for a moment and then, still on her knees, shuffled to the side so that the next woman could approach.

Alison pulled Ramona back into the other room by a handful of shirt.

"If you tell me those are real communion wafers, then I swear I am going to leave myself. God, that woman is nasty!" She herself had been raised with a healthy disregard for the church, but still.

"Isn't she?" Ramona asked in a pleased voice. "She's totally twisted. That year they had the s/m wars at Michigan I felt like going to some of those women and demanding that we be paid for keeping her in the leather camp. I mean, what if she was loose in the general population? There's no telling what she'd do! I personally think she was the one who contaminated all that food that gave everybody shigella. Wouldn't that be a kick in the head? Ten thousand women topped nonconsensually and from afar! That'd be right up her alley. I heard she was a psychiatrist and that woman she leads around on a chain is one of her patients. I don't think the wafers are real, though. I mean, they haven't been blessed and I think it would be hard to steal them from a church. But that's not why everybody was leaving. See, this is one of the things she does at all her parties. It's her trademark. Except for one, everybody gets a placebo. A plain wafer or a cracker or something."

"And what does that one get?" asked Alison. "I'm afraid to ask."

"You know that date rape drug?" asked Ramona. "I can't think of what the name of it is. But guys put it in their dates' drinks and then they fuck them while they're under?"

Thanks to Ricki Lake, Alison did know about the date rape drug. She couldn't remember what it was called either.

"She's drugging one of those women?" Alison asked in a horrified tone.

"Well, totally consensually. I mean, everybody who wants to take communion knows what's happening. I guess it's kind of like handling snakes—kind of a test of faith. You know—it won't happen to me. Or maybe they're hoping it will happen to them—kind of the ultimate submission. Because that's the deal—whoever gets doped then Livia does whatever she wants with her while she's out. Or orders done. She doesn't ever do much but supervise herself."

Alison felt sick to her stomach. "That is so dangerous!" she sputtered, barely able to make a coherent sentence through her outrage. "That's crazy! You can't play with somebody who can't safeword! My god—who the hell knows what somebody like Livia might do?! The woman could wake up and find she'd had her nipples sewn together."

"Oh, nah, they never do anything too bad. Some of them are sane. The last time I was here all they did was shave this woman's pussy. But they told her they'd done a bunch of other stuff. You're right, though, it's not safe play. That's why all those women left—they're the ones who think it's a really bad idea and don't want to be part of it. That's probably also why Livia did it so early in the evening—she knew it would drive the crowd away. Livia usually has closed parties. Do you have any idea why this one was open? I heard she had to do it because of a bet—you known, some kind of bottoming thing."

Alison ignored that. "So, why are you still here?" she asked. "Do you think that," she jerked a thumb toward the other room, "is okay?"

"No. I don't. I think it's dangerous and way too twisted. I saw her do it at Michigan first and it was a real turn-off. But if everybody who's not crazy leaves, then who does that leave in charge? I figure if they decide to kill her and eat her raw liver that maybe I can suggest shaving her pussy instead." She looked at Alison, who was still wearing the same mask of horror she had put on at the beginning of the explanation and added hastily, "Just kidding! No death scenes! I'm not really afraid of that happening! But it is a good idea to have a few outsiders who haven't been drinking stay, don't you think?"

Alison did not have any idea what she thought. She did not know where to begin feeling horrified—the booze, the scene without a safeword, the mock communion. She would not have been the least bit surprised if Livia's next performance was a Black Mass. She wanted to be anywhere but here. Fighting with Stacy was preferable. Watching a foreign movie was preferable. Riding on a roller coaster was preferable. Hell, fighting with Stacy while watching a foreign movie on a roller coaster was preferable.

"I'm freaking out," she told Ramona, momentarily forgetting that she was there to watch the crowd. "I gotta go take a break."

In the bathroom she splashed cold water on her face and tried to put her exhausted thoughts in order. Was Ramona's story about the woman in the photograph true and if it was, did that mean she had found her blackmailer?

Or, was the blackmailer still in the other room? If she had come to the party, would she have left when the 'communion' started, or would she have stayed, possibly using the ritual as an excuse for the blackmail to continue? Hell, Alison was ready to blackmail Livia herself at this point. Once again she wished Stacy was here to tell her who was who and what their history was like. She felt like Bunch, the Victorian policeman in those Anne Perry books that Stacy read and insisted on recounting in great detail over dinner. He was always being sent to parties where he didn't fit in, not being a gentleman himself. She did not fit in here and she was almost frightened to think of what might happen if the wrong person discovered this. Livia, it was true, was her patron, but would Livia be able to control a crowd? Would she even try, or would she consider her money lost and well spent?

She went back into the chill-out room, wanting nothing more than to be alone for a few minutes. Sitting on the bed she picked up the remote and wondered if it would be uncool to turn-on the TV. It was time for the late night reruns of *The X-Files* and even though she had already seen the show listed in the TV Guide, it was a favorite. It was, in fact, the one she thought of as the most twisted episode of all, where the mutant sons kept their mother under the bed. Surely this gang would get into that. Although that might be a reason to leave it off—nobody here needed any new ideas.

There was a jangling noise across the room and she looked up to see the woman Livia referred to as fuckbaby walking through the adjoining door, still naked and still carrying her own leash between her teeth. Now it was going to be *The X-Files* for sure, because she just did not have a clue how to make conversation with anyone who called herself Livia's pet.

"You have to help me."

"Huh?" Alison started. She had been pretty sure one of Livia's rules was that fuckbaby did not speak first. In fact, this was the first time she had heard her speak at all.

"I want to get out of this. I want to leave Livia, but she won't let me. Please, you have to help me."

Now, Alison Kaine was capable of a great deal of dithering. She was a person who had trouble with grey areas. In her perfect world everything would have been a clear-cut black and white, except she'd find another term for it because that sounded racist. Her father, who had been raised as a Catholic, was just the same and he had deliberately raised his children outside the church, convinced the worrying which had given him an ulcer was a result of too much time in confession and thinking about limbo. It had done no good. Both Alison and her brothers were all fusspots who worried routinely about hurt feelings and what was right and wrong and noble.

Alison, however, drawing a salary or not, was also a really good cop, and part of being a really good cop was being able to tell immediately an emergency situation from a dithering situation. She was off the bed before fuckbaby had finished her second plea, options and rejections rushing through her head at the speed of light. Had to get clothes, no, couldn't risk going in the other room while this one was so perfectly empty, Livia was going to know it was her if fuckbaby just disappeared; couldn't take her to her own house because that was the first place anyone would look and she'd given Livia that stupid deposit slip with her address on it. She strode quickly around the room, rifling the closet and a few drawers. There was no sign anyone was staying there. No clothes, no out. Fuckbaby—oh Jesus, Alison thought, I gotta find out her name right away. She couldn't go on thinking of her as that; it made a little shiver run right up her spine.

She crossed the room to the double bed, stripped back the thin hotel bedspread and pulled off the top sheet, tossing it over to fuckbaby who stood blankly, as if the four sentences had taken all her energy and initiative.

"Put it on!" Alison hissed, making a wrapping motion above her head. From the hall came the noise of both laughter and angry words. Alison pushed fuckbaby, still clutching the sheet in one hand and staring blankly, into the small closet, which was really just an antechamber for the bathroom and opened directly perpendicular to the hall door. "Be ready to go when I tell you!" she said, shutting the door.

Immediately, she pulled the hall door open, praying that the noise she heard in the hall was other women from Wildfire. Luck was with her in the strongest way. Level with the door were the dueling Pattys who had both left when the communion scene had started. They appeared to be returning—at least they were moving the right way, both moving rapidly and both talking angrily at the same time, neither giving any indication that she was listening or had in fact ever listened to the other.

Behind them was a slightly larger group of four or five, all of them carrying toy bags. Going to or coming from the Wildfire dungeon.

"Hey!" Alison called, putting on a persona far more outgoing than came to her naturally. "Private party! Food and pretty women! Come on in!"

It worked with such beautiful precision that for a moment Alison was tempted to stand back and admire it. The two Pattys turned through the door without breaking stride or accusation and the other women followed like a river diverted from its path. Everyone moved immediately into the central room and clustered around the party trays with cries of gratification— dungeon work was hard work. No one even looked Alison in the face.

She opened the closet door, hooked a hand through fuckbaby's arm and pulled her into the empty hall in one smooth motion, leaving the door ajar. The more commotion, the less likely Livia was to target her for the jailbreak.

The elevator pinged and Alison pushed fuckbaby through the door that led to the stairs. She followed close behind, but not close enough. Before she could shut the door she heard, like a voice from a recurring nightmare, "Hey! I want to talk to you!"

She hissed to fuckbaby, "Go down to the first floor and wait for me." Alison stepped back into the hall and shut the door behind her with a firm little click. Once again Scar was standing way too close. This time, just to make things a little harder to deal with, she appeared to be drunk. She must have knocked back a few in short order since she had accosted Alison at the party.

"Help me," she said in a slurred voice, staggering forward and all but crashing into Alison. Apparently, she forgot her lovely manners while she drank. Alison held out a stiff arm to hold her off, to which Scar reacted as if it were a lifeline. Clinging to Alison's hand with both of her own she said again, even more urgently, "Help me. You gotta get me out of this place."

Alison glanced down the hall. Beside the door to Livia's room which was still wide open and now teeming with traffic, only one other door was ajar. Using her arm as a level she tried to turn Scar toward it.

"Get your playdate to call a cab," she said brusquely. She was already in the middle of one rescue—she didn't need to get involved in another. Besides, she hated drunks—couldn't stand to have them around her. The needy, weeping drunk was the worst. She would rather face a belligerent head-basher any day.

"Not…going…back," Scar muttered, giving each word such a separate space that they seemed unrelated. She staggered over to the elevator and began punching buttons wildly. She had lost the beret.

The elevator gave a little ping and Alison moved quickly right up to the point where the door would open, ready to hop on immediately. Scar was not her problem. Her problem, she hoped, was waiting for her in the stairwell.

The door slid open and suddenly Alison was standing face to face with a whole crowd of women trying to push past her. She recognized a couple as she was being buffeted—the big butch gal who had flirted with Stacy and the woman she remembered as Earrings.

"For Christ's sake," said someone in an irritable voice, "At least let us get off the elevator first!" Alison was not the only one who had stayed up past her bedtime and gotten cranky.

Before the last woman was out, she made her move. Glancing over her shoulder she saw that Scar had been pushed back also and was now clutching the shirt of the big butch gal while she pleaded and slobbered. Alison found a karmic justice in this and hit the 'Close Door' button as quickly as she could. As the doors slid shut she caught sight of Crescent pulling Scar off the big butch gal, saying, "Oh, I'll take care of her."

And that was all.

Chapter Ten

"I can't believe this," said Marta. She looked at Alison and she looked at fuckbaby and then she looked back at Alison again. "I gotta tell you—you've got a lot of nerve. I can't believe you're over here waking me up in the middle of the night and asking me to do you a favor."

Alison couldn't believe it herself. But where else was she going to take the waiflike young woman whose only contribution to conversation in the drive over had been to say that her name was Janet? She thought. She couldn't take her to her own house, because she had given Livia the stupid deposit slip with her address. Livia might be twisted, but Alison did not think she was stupid and she was bound to suspect Alison of the breakout sooner or later. Regretfully, Alison thought of the second thousand dollars, which she had suspected had gone out of her life the very moment that fuckbaby had come into it. She couldn't take her to Stacy's house because Stacy was mad and this would make her madder and she couldn't take her to Liz's because Liz was way too smart to take the wrong side when Stacy was mad. She couldn't take her to her dad's because explaining would require putting out much more information than she wanted to share and she couldn't take her to a motel dressed in a toga even if she could find one that would take a personal check. Which kind of ran through all the possibilities and people she could wake at three in the morning, except for the room that G-hey! had mentioned. And she couldn't wake G-hey!, because she didn't want it on the grapevine and she couldn't wake Mary Clare because even though she knew the area where she lived she didn't know the exact house. For better or worse, that left Marta.

"I know," Alison said humbly. "I'm sorry. I really am. But I'm not asking for myself." With a nod, she indicated Janet, standing beside her wrapped in the sheet, Alison's jacket slung over her shoulders. She stood barefoot in the thin layer of ice that glazed the mud. She looked pitiful and cold and Alison was glad, because pitiful was all she had to play.

Marta looked at fuckbaby and then back at Alison. She was a good-hearted woman. Alison would have known it just from the look, even if G-hey! hadn't told her about the apartment.

Marta looked back at Alison. "Don't you think it's kind of your responsibility to take care of them after you've taken their clothes off?"

"I didn't take her clothes off." Alison stepped a little closer, speaking in an undertone, although fuckbaby seemed oblivious. She simply stood where Alison had placed her, looking blankly ahead. Alison guessed she was probably really good at following directions. "This is a rescue, okay? I know you think I'm a piece of shit, but this is a rescue and I don't have anywhere else to go! Okay? I don't! Because if I take her home with me, her…" She struggled to find a word that would express Livia's relationship to Janet and settled for an imperfect shorthand. "…lover is going to be there in a couple of hours. That's the first place she'll look! If she's not there, then maybe I can convince her I didn't have anything to do with it! And maybe I can get this one on a bus and out of town."

Marta looked at them both again. Compassion was winning—Alison could tell. Compassion tended to be her downfall too.

"Oh, for Christ's sake!" Marta said finally. She stepped out on the grass and pulled the door shut behind her. For the first time Alison noticed what she was wearing—a pair of grey sweatpants, too old and stained for anything but sleeping and a Virago T-shirt Alison knew for a fact was an antique, since Virago had dissolved almost twenty years before. Her feet were shoved into a pair of flip-flops, the kind with the thick, striped soles and she was clutching a really ratty terrycloth robe around her shoulders. Either Marta didn't care much about her clothes or didn't make a lot of money. "For Christ's sake," she said again, looking pointedly at Alison as if she wanted to make sure that Alison knew she knew this was just emotional blackmail. She stood for a moment, shrugging her arms into the sleeves of the robe. She turned, picked out one key from the ring she was carrying and locked the deadbolt behind her. "This way," she said ungraciously, jerking her head toward the side of the house.

The empty apartment was in the building next door, up a flight of outside stairs that you wouldn't look forward to climbing in the winter. Inside it looked to Alison like an afterthought—as if whoever had divided the original house had planned poorly and ended up with this little dab of a place that hadn't fit well into either of the other upstairs apartments. There was only one real room, which was furnished with a single bed, a dresser with a small microwave sitting on top of it and two wooden chairs. Inside a tiny, doorless closet hung perhaps ten second-hand shirts, sweaters and jackets in a variety of sizes. The closet floor was littered with shoes, also in a wide range of sizes and also second-hand, except for a couple of pairs of flip-flops the same style as Marta's. One side of the closet was lined with narrow shelves on which were stacked a few dishes, some silverware, three mugs, five paperback books and some food of the Ramen Noodle and cracker variety. Nothing that needed refrigeration. There was an extra blanket folded at the foot of the bed and a single pillow that had seen better days.

"The bathroom is down the hall," said Marta, pointing to an inner door. "There's soap and shampoo and towels and all that stuff in it. Help yourself. There's some sweats or a nightgown or something in the top drawer of the dresser. I'm not sure what's in there right now—I've got some stuff in the wash. There should be some pants. There's food in the closet."

It was pretty bare bones. There was nothing in it, from the furniture to the books, which had not seen at least one previous incarnation. The blankets on the bed, though clean, were second-hand and patched. But it was warm and there were clothes and a door with a deadbolt between them and the street and how much more could you ask for if you'd run naked from a hotel room at two in the morning? Marta turned to go and Alison followed her, leaving fuckbaby standing blankly in the middle of the floor as if she'd just walked through a door to another dimension. Look, she'd gotten the woman out and had found her a safe place to stay. That was as far as it was going, at least for tonight.

"Thank you," Alison said to the back of Marta's head as they went down the stairs.

"Don't bother," Marta answered. "I didn't do it for you, I did it for her." Obviously now that they were out of Janet's earshot she no longer felt she had to keep her hostility under control.

"Look," said Alison, "I'm doing a decent thing. I know you think I'm just the great Satan, but I'm doing a decent thing right now when I'd rather be home alone in my own bed."

"Well, that makes two of us who wish you were home alone in your own bed," shot back Marta over her shoulder without slowing her pace. "Sorry if I can't get it up to tell you what a great person you are. I'll practice, okay? If you're doing such a good deed then why didn't you take her over to your froufie little girlfriend's house? Surely she would have understood."

Okay, then, so Marta wasn't even going to pretend to be buddies. The effort was just too much for Alison to make alone. She thought fiercely about her own bed and sleeping until noon and to hell with Stacy and any obligations with the conference. She couldn't even remember if she was supposed to do anything this morning, let alone what it might be.

"Thanks again, sorry I'm alive and just to warn you, I'll probably have to come back to deal with her. I'll try to stay out of your way."

Marta turned toward her door without answering. They were done talking. With a huge sigh of relief, Alison started toward her car, which was parked in one of the tenant spaces lining the alley.

"Goddammit all to fucking son-of-a-bitching hell!" Marta didn't scream the curse, but rather pushed it out from between clenched teeth like it had an air hammer behind it. Same effect. Real pissed.

Alison stopped. Oh, dammit and she had been so close to her car! Ten more feet and she could have legitimately pretended not to hear.

She turned. Marta was shoving and kicking the door with angry and ineffectual blows that made it look more as if she was trying to hurt it than open it.

Alison took a couple of careful steps in her direction, praying to God that she would be rebuffed. No one in the world could blame her for leaving if she was sent.

Marta spun to face her. "Well, you're a goddamn cop!" she said, teeth still clenched. "So why don't you just kick the damn thing in like they do on TV! Come on, just show me the cop kick!"

From the house next door there was the sound of a window flying up and a woman's voice called from the ground floor, "Come on! Please! There're people trying to sleep over here!"

"To hell with you!" Marta shouted back. "I'm your goddamn landlord and I know you've got more than one cat in there! If you don't shut up right now I'm going to evict all three of you and you're going to be out on your butts in the snow!" There was no snow, but you kind of got the idea Marta could conjure some up for the occasion. Catching Alison's eye she mumbled, her teeth clamped together once again. "I will apologize tomorrow. I will give her a free month's rent. Now just help me open the damn door!"

"Is it locked?" Alison asked cautiously, pretty sure that whatever she said was going to be the wrong thing.

"Of course it's not locked! Why would I be kicking the door if it were locked? Do you think I'm an idiot?"

Alison decided to react to this situation as if Marta were Stacy. "No, I think you're a beautiful woman doing someone else a favor in the middle of the night out of the goodness of her heart."

Marta turned and gave her such an evil glare she could almost feel it burning a hole through her forehead as if it were a laser. "Oh," she said scathingly, "and does that work with Fifi? Do you just say 'Pretty girl' and give her a little dog treat and then she dances around on her back legs in her little high heels?" She slammed her shoulder into the door with such force Alison winced. The cheap wood—the original had probably been sold off years ago—reverberated, but did not move an inch.

Alison did not think it fair of Marta to be ugly about Stacy, who after all had not done anything at all to wrong her other than existing. However, defending Stacy's honor was currently way down on the totem pole, right there with cleaning her refrigerator or getting a mammogram. She looked at her watch.

"I'm going to leave in three minutes," she said. "So you have three minutes to tell me if there is anything that I can do to help you open your door. If you want to call me and my girlfriend names instead, that's fine, but I'm still leaving in three minutes."

She could see that Marta was torn, but practicality won.

"Stay there," she said. She walked over to the garage, used another of the keys on the padlock, opened the door and reached inside. Alison tentatively tested the doorknob, just in case Marta had been mistaken about it being locked.

"I told you it wasn't locked," said Marta from behind her. In her right hand she was carrying the biggest rubber mallet Alison had ever seen in her whole life. She had stuffed her keys into the pocket of her robe. They looked dangerously close to falling out, but Alison wasn't going to say a word. Not one single word. "You get down here and push with the knob. Just a steady push."

Alison did as she was told. Marta reached above her and with a curious delicacy that was completely at odds with the size of the hammer began a series of taps up along the top. Somebody else threw up a window and complained, but this time Marta ignored it. She was concentrating too fiercely. Tap. Tap-tap-tap. Tap-tap. Obviously she'd done this before.

Suddenly the door gave, jerking Alison off her feet. She sprawled foreword, a windmilling arm catching Marta on the way down so that they both ended up in a tangle of arms and legs inside the door. Alison tried to disentangle herself, but that only seemed to make things worse, so she lay perfectly still, letting Marta pick herself free as if from a blackberry bush. Only when Marta was standing did she gingerly rise to her feet.

"Good night," she said, because she could just not bring herself to say thank you again. She had never realized before just how essential it was to hear 'you're welcome.'

Marta had turned away from her, pointing herself up the stairs. As Alison tried to brush by her without pushing she noticed, in the harsh light of the sixty watt bulb which lit the stairwell, that there was a huge, dark stain on the back shoulder of Marta's bathrobe. It hadn't been there before. Huge and spreading and now that she was looking both the robe and the antique T-shirt had a long and jagged tear in them which hadn't been there before, either.

"You've hurt yourself," she said with a heavy heart, wondering what it was she had done that had made God cast her into hell. "You must have caught a nail or something on the way down."

"Fine. Go. I can deal with it." Marta reached up over her shoulder. She couldn't even touch it, so you knew she couldn't bandage it. Besides which, at the rate it was pumping Alison thought she might need stitches.

She opened her mouth with a sigh, remembering a couple of years back when she and Stacy and Michelle and Janka had rented *The Fugitive* and Stacy hadn't been able to stop laughing over Harrison Ford.

"Look, look!" she had hooted, elbowing Michelle when Harrison had blown his cover in the hospital because he simply had not been able to mind his own business and refrain from being a compassionate and caring doctor.

"Isn't that just like Alison? Isn't it?" Michelle had laughed, too.

"Let me come upstairs and at least look at it," she said with a heavy heart. She was never going to get a chance to go to sleep again in her whole life. That was what hell was really all about—never sleeping and the coffee was always cold.

So they went up the stairs, Marta so pissed that she had stopped cursing altogether and Alison bumping up behind as if she were being pulled. Once inside Marta's door they were immediately surrounded by an army of black and white tuxedo cats, all of whom looked with concern upon Marta and then censure upon Alison, as if they, too, recognized her as the great Satan.

Marta shrugged off the robe and pulled the T-shirt over her head, holding it bunched across her breasts with her arms still in the sleeves. There was blood everywhere. It took Alison half a roll of toilet paper to get a good look.

"Yeah," she said finally, "it must have been a nail. I think you might need stitches." She had forgotten how lovely Marta's back was. She had a long torso. Even though she was several inches taller than Alison their legs were roughly the same length. Her height was all through her waist. Her olive skin—both Marta and Mary Clare's grandparents were Basque immigrants—held none of the winter pallor which Alison despised in her own. She felt something like a faint echo of that passionate night she had spent with Marta over a year before and beat it down with the same horror with which she would have squelched an urge for serial killing. Not here, not now, not anywhere, not ever.

"No," said Marta, as if she could barter the wound down, "I don't need stitches. Just put some Super Glue on it. It will be fine."

Alison opened her mouth to protest and Marta turned on her fiercely. "I don't need stitches! Where do you think I would get the money to pay for stitches? Do you know how much it would cost to get stitches in the middle of the night? I don't have a rich girlfriend like you do! I don't have a job that comes with perks and insurance! Every single bit of money that we've taken in from rent next door has gone right back into the house for repairs and remodeling and it's going to be that way for another three years at least! I only make six dollars an hour on the phones—if I have to pay out two hundred for three stitches what are the cats and I going to eat this month?"

"Super Glue it is," said Alison, who knew when an argument was futile. She could not, however, keep from adding, "You know, she doesn't pay my way. I pay for myself."

"But she could," Marta said. "And that's all that matters, that in an emergency she could."

It took Alison a good fifteen minutes to hold the two sides of the wound together and apply Super Glue and she glued her own fingers together twice in the process. But it did stop the bleeding. Alison went into the bathroom to wash her hands, wondering if she should mention AIDS tests to Marta.

Nope, she was willing to take her chances.

In the other room, Marta had finally shed the bloody, nasty T-shirt and was pulling another over her head. Like the Virago shirt, it too looked as if it belonged either in the trash or the archives. Alison had forgotten how pretty Marta's breasts were, just as she had put her back out of her mind. Or had she even seen them? They had come together with a savage passion that had not allowed time to remove their clothes and Marta had left the house while Alison was sleeping. Not now, not ever, she thought, trying to fill her head so completely with the mantra that there would be no room for an echo of anything else to sneak in around the edges.

"Good night, I'm sorry, thank you," she said as if she were really heading for the door instead of watching her hand come up to cup Marta's breast, her thumb sweeping across the large, dark nipple. She fully expected Marta to rebuff her and possibly throw her down the stairs as well. Instead there was a jolt between them that made Alison jerk as if she had been hit with an electric shock. She had forgotten the look of Marta's back, but she had not forgotten this feeling, which had come to her only one other time in her life, the first time she had taken Marta to her bed. With Stacy she felt there were times she held her heart cupped in her hands, times when the passion was so intense that the only words she could think to describe it were words usually reserved for religious ecstasy. With Marta, it was something altogether different. She and Stacy were in perfect tune, a couple who had ice danced together since they were young, never missing a beat or throwing a partner accidentally into the rail. With Marta it was as if they were inside one another's thoughts—no, that there was one mind between them and playing on it, the size of the IMAX, was a movie in which they starred together. With just that one touch, Marta's nipple hardening immediately beneath her thumb, Alison was taken back to the more-than-fantasy which had filled her mind and driven her to a frantic fever once before.

They were back together as if they had never been apart, as if no time lay between the meetings, no chase, no cold, no wet nights of waiting and stalking. No calls to the office of the Lieutenant, demanding to know how just one woman had managed to slip through the woman cop's grip time and again. No escape made because she had given in to her animal urges and fucked the beautiful master criminal who wore Marta's face before cuffing her. No attempt made on her life. And now, here they were again. Only this time it was the handsome butch cop who lay on the ground and the woman she knew only as Jezzabella standing above her with a gun. On her shoulder she could feel the wound where Jezzabella's bullet had grazed her, feel the blood dripping down warm on her arm.

Jezzabella's heavy dark hair was pinned up in a French twist. She wore the same jewelry with her long, backless gown that she had worn the time before, when it was black jeans and jacket, torn at the knees and elbows from the chase. Gold on her hands and in her ears.

"Do you remember me, My Lovely Destiny?" Jezzabella asked first in Basque and then in English. "Remember fucking me with that big stick of yours?"

The cop did remember. She remembered forcing her to her knees and the way that she had used her hands to spread her cunt to take her nightstick. She remembered the way she had seemed to exist inside the other woman's mind as she thrust inside her, so that fucking the criminal's throbbing cunt was like fucking her own, so that she seemed to be bucking back to meet the thrusts, to meet the whole length just as Jezzabella was. She had lived on that image for over a year, holding it close and private, only to lose her prey at the last moment to a broken arm. She ran it through her head, a single looped clip, the few times she had taken women home from the bar during that long year. They had been a disappointment, all of them. They had been passive or gentle or eager to please while she had thought back on this woman who had never given in though she had held her completely within her power.

"Missed me, didn't you?" Jezzabella purred from above her. In one hand she was still holding the gun that had appeared from her little black clutch when the cop had surprised her. The cop had made a mistake. She knew that now. She had not seen the clutch, just the form fitting dress that could not possibly disguise a weapon. She had stalked Jezzabella with all the obsession of a wronged lover, waited for her to leave the dance floor and head for the bathroom and thought that she would have her then. But she had not seen that little black clutch, which must have been lying out of sight beneath her chair or on the table and she had paid for her oversight. They would give her a cop's funeral with a draped coffin and though the men at the station would call her foolish and obsessive they would hunt Jezzabella as a cop killer. They would pursue her into all her dens, using the notes the cop had left behind her, until they caught her or killed her. Even lying there on her back, blood puddling on the floor, the cop felt a rush of sadness at the thought of Jezzabella caged. It was like imagining a tiger, savage and magnificent, pacing forever in a ten by ten cell. She would much rather have seen them—beast and woman both—dispatched with one clean blow to the heart. That was how she had planned on taking out Jezzabella—one clean blow to the heart for which Jezzabella would thank her with her last breath. A woman like that in a cell would die and the death would be long, painful and ugly.

But she had failed to shoot when it mattered, superstitious like an old woman at the last moment, remembering the way fucking Jezzabella had seemed like fucking herself, afraid that a bullet entering the heart of Jezzabella would at the same moment enter her own. She was like a big game hunter who had refused to take aim at the rushing tiger, mesmerized by the sight of its beauty to the point where she could not raise a gun.

Jezzabella had lifted her heavy skirt a few inches and with a long and lan-

guid step had moved so she stood with a foot either side of the cop's head. One of her spiked red heels grazed the cop's ear as it came down on the floor with a sharp little click. Jezzabella dropped the skirt, engulfing the cop again in the dark, hot tent which trapped her smell, heavy like incense. the cop knew that smell. A year before she had tracked Jezzabella to her lair, and though she had openly turned it over to the boys who did the crime scenes, she had first pocketed two things. One was a pair of panties, black, cut high like a thong. She had slept with them under her pillow many nights, letting the smell of the woman enter her dreams. The other was a gold ring, a smaller version of the ones Jezzabella wore in her ears. It now rested between the cop's legs, threaded through a hole pierced above her clit with fire and steel.

She heard the voice of the woman who had referred to her as her Destiny, but it seemed as far away as another dimension. This was her world, where reality combined with obsessive fantasy, when in the end it did not matter if years of hunting ended with her the hunter or the hunted. She was engulfed in the smell of Jezzabella's open, wet cunt, a smell she had smelled half a dozen times in the lairs she had entered a day, an hour too late.

She arched her back, longing to feel the taste of the smell on her tongue and was rewarded by a lowering, a bending of the knees as graceful as that of a ballet dancer. She had not had a lover who pleased her in a long while and she had never had one to whom she had submitted in this way. She had always been the one who was in control—she was the one who knelt above the other's face and made her beg to use her tongue. Only this woman, who had tried to kill her twice, had been powerful enough for this. She had not even allowed Jezzabella to touch her the last time, had fucked her from behind with her nightstick through a hole she had slashed in her pants, making her take it on her hands and knees. But even then she had known she was priming a pump, that the power she had seized would spring back and engulf her if the chance were given. She had lost the distinction between the other woman and herself—just as she had felt as if she were fucking herself the time before she now was not sure who was the dominant and who the submissive, who held the gun in her hand and who did not—

Alison did not know how much time had passed before she woke ·in Marta's bed. The sun was well up. She had slept from pure exhaustion but she could tell from the muddled feeling and headache that without her medication she had never gotten past REM sleep, down into the state below dreams where the body rejuvenated. She could get by today and possibly even one more day, but she knew from the past that she would be horribly ill, would have at least a week where she slept seventeen or eighteen hours out of twenty-four, where dragging herself to the acupuncturist was a chore that seemed insurmountable. And all for Marta, who had not said one nice thing to her in over a year, who had snubbed her when they attended the same concerts or ran into one another at the Merc!

Alison had stood firm against Erin Oleander, who had been willing to flatter and take time and yet had fucked Marta in her nasty old robe and flip-flops with the same intensity and lack of shame as an alley cat. She couldn't have done even a quickie with any other woman—not tired as she was and she suspected the same was true of Marta, woken at two and injured besides. What the hell was it between them, anyway? Alison sat up cautiously in bed and looked at the woman lying beside her, the woman who referred to Stacy with derision and would probably laugh in Alison's face if she suggested a short skirt and high heels. With Stacy she had everything she had ever dreamed of, yet that spark of oneness she shared with Marta when they came together had drawn her back again.

She winced at the clock on the bed table, which said it was past noon. She couldn't remember her work schedule, but she'd no doubt let a whole horde of women down. Oh, well. She was still half-dressed and she tried to pick up her shoes and her keys quietly so as not to wake Marta. Being considerate, yes, but also because it would be so much easier that way—a note on the table, a short goodbye with no recriminations. What could she say to Marta—that it was hot and exciting and maybe she could have loved her had it not been for Stacy, who took up such space in her heart there was room for no other? That despite the passion which had flowed between them she had not wanted this to happen again and would have sold her soul to change it?

She almost made it. She was actually on her way to the door when the biggest of the black-and-white cats leapt from the dresser to Marta's side of the bed. He must have weighed at least twenty pounds—Marta's eyes flew open with a panicked start.

"Oh," she said, looking at Alison dressed, her shoes in one hand. Her eyes said that she knew Alison had thought it better to walk barefoot through the puddles ringing the back steps than to have to talk to her. "Why didn't you just chew your arm off?" she asked.

"I…" began Alison, trying to think of something trite and cheerful to say, something that didn't make her look like a shit.

"Don't," said Marta, holding up a hand without lifting her head. "I know you're going back to her. I can just bear it if you don't lie to me about it."

Chapter Eleven

Alison stood beneath her shower until the water began to grow chilly, washing her hair twice, using half a bottle of shower gel as she tried to wash away Marta. What had she been thinking? How was last night with Marta going to make anything in her life better or easier? Did she want to leave Stacy? She didn't think she did. Even if she did want to break up with Stacy without yet being conscious of it, where was she going to go from there? Not straight into the arms of Marta, who probably wouldn't take her even if she was that sleazy.

Michelle walked in as she was toweling her hair and sat down without being invited. She was carrying Sammy in her arms and, after a quick look around the room to see what could be destroyed or eaten, set him down on the floor. She helped herself to a banana from a bowl in the center of the kitchen table and picked up Alison's newspaper. It was actually everyone's newspaper, but lived at Alison's house because it was safer from Sammy.

"How's Grandpa?" Alison asked, because she sure as hell wasn't going to get into the Persimmon thing—not this weekend. Her own plate was full.

"Adoring," Michelle replied, her head already buried in the Lively Arts section. "First he read Sammy every single Dr. Suess book that was ever written. I'd never heard that one about the pale green pants before. Then he showed him a trick about multiplying by nines. I think next week is Euclidean geometry. He didn't talk to me at all. I'm not sure he knew I was there. Oh, and he took pictures. Lots of pictures." She put the paper down, went into Alison's kitchen and pulled the refrigerator door open. This, thought Alison, was a bad sign. In times of peace Michelle much preferred to eat in her own house, which usually smelled of something delicious. It was only under siege that she retreated to Alison's kitchen.

Sammy, who had been pulling himself along the edge of the coffee table, came upon the newspaper. The rustle and texture caught his attention immediately. He let himself down onto the floor with a thud, pulling a page of the paper after him. Very seriously he set to crumpling and ripping it, his face a study of concentration as if he was on the verge of achieving perpetual motion.

Michelle came back into the living room, eating an old burrito that she was viewing with some disdain even while stuffing it into her mouth. Ew, ick, chomp. Ew, ick, chomp. She sat and picked up the *Lesbian Connection* that Alison had tossed down on the table the night before when she had returned from the restaurant. By now Sammy had the entire five sections, including the Spotlight, down beside him.

"Out of town bad girl seeks local bad boy," Michelle read aloud, her voice laced with the same disdain with which she had viewed the burrito. Too late, Alison saw that what she had picked up was not *LC* at all, but the Wildfire program.

"Oh, just put it down," she said. "I already know I'm a horrible, sick person who hangs out with horrible, sick people. All it's going to do is make us have a fight." To Sammy she added, "If you put that in your mouth you're going to have newsprint all over your face."

Their responses were identical. Sammy went right on stuffing and Michelle went right on reading.

"'I want to fuck with your head while my girlfriend fucks with your ass. Get on your knees and spread it for us, baby. Fats and femmes absolutely encouraged.'" She looked up at Alison with a pained expression on her face. "Oh, Alison, I can't believe—"

"Leave me alone," Alison warned. "I don't want to fight with you right now. I've had it with drama this weekend. If you can't leave me alone then I want you to go downstairs."

Michelle threw herself down on the couch with ill grace, her mouth drawn up in an ugly little line. Alison went into the bedroom, looking for a clean pair of jeans. When she came back into the living room, her clean shirt untucked and carrying her boots in one hand, Michelle was still reading the program. Michelle rarely missed a chance to torture herself with the misbehavior of others, particularly the misbehavior of Alison.

"That's only going to piss you off," Alison warned again.

Michelle did not listen. Not listening was one of Michelle's strong points.

"Oh, Alison," she began, standing as if to show her strength of commitment. "This is so gross. Ass-fisting workshops. Please."

Alison glanced at her watch before answering. She was a little ahead of schedule. She could afford a small scene.

"Michelle," she said, as she bent over to tie her boots. "I told you that program was going to upset you, but you had to keep on reading it so you could remind yourself of what a bad person I am. I have only one word for you and that word is 'Persimmon.'" She straightened and watched Michelle get the crafty look on her face she got whenever she was thinking of lying to her.

"Oh, right," Michelle said, obviously trying to work up a bluster. "You and your girlfriend devote your entire lives to violence against women, but I make one slip that hurts no one and you're going to bring it up and hold it against me for the rest of my life. You—"

"Michelle," said Alison. She bent to take a pen away from Sammy. He had abandoned the newspaper and was mining beneath the couch. "Don't piss in my ear and tell me it's raining." She had heard that almost six months before on *NYPD Blue* and had been waiting for a chance to use it. "I may not have gone to Cornell or Harvard, but I'm pretty damn smart anyway. I know Persimmon is living in Boulder and I know you've been having an affair with her." Actually she had only surmised the last part, but the look on Michelle's face told her she was right on the money. "So don't lie to me, okay? It makes me pissed and it makes you look stupid, plus when it all comes out in the end you're going to have to apologize to me for lying on top of everything else and you don't want to go there."

"Okay, okay!" Michelle threw up her hands, simultaneously sullen and relieved. "I have been seeing Persimmon. I can't help it."

Alison gave her a full look, one eyebrow lifted, even while she swallowed hard.

"Okay, I don't want to help it! I don't! Persimmon is like…Persimmon is like Janka used to be when we first met. She encourages me. She thinks I'm talented. She thinks I'm funny. She thinks I'm smart. But Janka either thinks I'm an errand boy or that I'm in the way. I don't want to live my life like that! I have nothing with Janka anymore!"

"Actually," said Alison, checking her watch again, "you have a lot with Janka. You have a marriage and a son and a house." She could already see a million ways for her to get screwed on the house if Michelle and Janka split up. "Those are kind of important things, Michelle! Don't you think they're worth trying to save? And don't you think you would have a better chance of working on them if you weren't fucking Persimmon?"

Michelle got a pained look on her face. "I don't 'fuck' Persimmon," she said in the voice of Queen Victoria. "We—"

"I don't care how many angels are dancing on the head of your pin, Michelle! Cheating is cheating, no matter what you call it! If you agreed to be monogamous with Janka—and I was there when you promised, Michelle!—and you're fucking someone else behind her back then you're cheating on her and it doesn't matter what fancy names you give it!"

"Oh, and I suppose you never did anything like that!" Cornered, Michelle decided the best defense was attack. "What about Marta? What about that?"

Alison winced. And Michelle didn't even know about last night. And wasn't going to know, either, if she had her way. "I was wrong, okay? I was wrong to do that to Stacy and I was wrong to do that to Marta and how come all of a sudden you want to use anything I do to justify what you're doing to

Persimmon? You spend most of your time telling me what a horrible person I am—how come all of a sudden I'm your role model?"

"I don't think you're a horrible person, Alison," Michelle replied. "I think you've made some bad choices. I don't think you're bad—I think what you do is bad." Michelle obviously thought she could get off the conversation at this stop, as if she were alighting from a runaway train.

"I gotta go," Alison said. "But I'm going to tell you this—I am not going to lie and cover up for you. Only if you come to your senses and stop seeing Persimmon right now." She figured that she owed Michelle that much. "Then maybe. But if you keep it up and Janka asks me, then I'm not lying." Please, she thought, oh pleasepleaseplease let Janka not ask me.

"I didn't ask you to lie," replied Michelle all in a huff, like it was Alison who was behaving badly. "I didn't ask you to stick your nose in my business at all!"

"You didn't have to ask," said Alison. "That's my job! And incidentally, I know it was you in that pickup truck!" Jostled loose by the conversation she suddenly realized where she had seen the truck before. Not at their house, but from their trip to Mariposa. That would be why Michelle had been wearing the bandanna. Not so much to hide her identity, which would have been unlike Michelle, but to keep from being identified with Persimmon until she decided to what degree she was going to fuck over Janka. "And Stacy almost had to go to the hospital because you got paint in her ears."

"Somehow," said Michelle, "I am not concerned about sending a woman who regularly lights herself on fire to the hospital. If the doctor spoke harshly to her she could just call it a scene."

Alison held up a hand. "You know that's bullshit! You know it is! And I paid for that paint and I sure didn't do it so you could ruin my girlfriend's leather jacket. You were supposed to save that so we'd have it when the shingles needed touching up. You could have at least used something you found in the alley instead of something I paid for!"

For the first time Michelle, who was a black belt tightwadder, looked truly regretful. "Well, I tried," she said. "But all I could find in the alley was black and white and everybody was worried about whether they'd make enough of a statement."

"Well, you made a statement, alright," said Alison, opening the door. "You made a couple. One was, 'Fuck you, Alison' and the other was that violence against women sucks unless your elite little brown shirts are the ones doing it. Let me tell you, there's a bunch of women who would have liked to have safeworded out of your little scene. And if you have to repaint the entire front of the house in a couple of years because we don't have any touch-up paint, then you're paying for it! Not me!"

She left Michelle to lock up and clattered down the stairs away from rebuttal. Anything Michelle had to say at this moment was just going to piss her off anyway. It was bad enough that Michelle was fucking around behind Janka's back, but worse that it was with Persimmon. She knew something about Persimmon that Michelle did not know, a weighty secret she had discovered during their dreadful trip to Mariposa. Exposing Persimmon would have hurt a lot of innocent people and unless it was the only way to stop Michelle from being an asshole she intended to carry it to her grave. But it didn't stop her from wishing she could blackmail Persimmon into going back to New Mexico. Or anywhere else.

As she walked across the front lawn the downstairs door was suddenly pulled open and Janka popped her head out. She looked cross. "There were people looking for you last night." Her tone matched her expression. Alison had never before heard the word 'looking' said in quite that way, as if it meant something altogether different and disgusting. "At four in the fucking morning! And they made so much noise that they woke up Sammy, and I'd just been up with him two hours before!"

It was on the tip of Alison's tongue to say, You wanted a baby, now you have a baby and being up all night is what having a baby is all about, but it was ugly, so she refrained. Partly because she knew Janka was probably going to get shafted soon and partly just because it was good practice—it sure seemed as if she had been blurting out every other thing that had come into her head lately.

"I'm sorry," she said meekly instead.

"There must have been ten people out there." Janka was not mollified. "Knocking on your door and calling your name. One of them knocked on my door! I almost called the police. Four in the morning!"

Alison didn't really think it was fair to blame her for what other people did, but again she held her tongue. Or, maybe it was fair. Get involved with somebody like Livia and she was bound to come knocking on your door sooner or later.

"I'm sorry," she said again. "I can't get up with Sammy tonight, but after this whole thing is over why don't I sleep downstairs with him and you can go up to my place and get a real night's sleep?"

At least Janka's expression softened just a little before she slammed the door.

***

Alison scouted Tara carefully before getting out of her car, hoping, she realized, to see Stacy in a compromising situation which she could blow up to cover her own guilt. Stacy, luckily for the state of Alison's soul, was nowhere to be seen, although everybody else in the whole world seemed to be out. There was Erin Oleander sharing a cigarette with Stacy's big butch friend, side by side with that obnoxious woman with the dragon head tattoo, Crescent, who had been with Bad News and Scar at Livia's, neither of whom was anywhere near her now. Crescent was chatting up Salad who seemed to be half-listening to her and half-listening to Flame. Flame, though talking a mile a minute, was looking not at Salad but at the Pattys who were over on the side of the porch winding up to go for it again. And all around them women were drinking coffee, eating bagels, reading the newspaper and making playdates. Another perfect day in leatherland. Caught up in the scene, Alison did not realize until it was too late that she was walking right into Liz and Mary Clare who were standing just inside the front door with their heads together.

"Oh!" said Alison, bouncing off Liz like she was a cartoon character and going into the spiel she had rehearsed on the way over "I'm sorry I was ugly to you and made you get caught up with me and Stacy when you tried to stay out." She pulled a bag of M&Ms out of her jacket pocket and handed them over. Like Stacy, Liz believed that all civilized apologies involved gifts. Gifts involving chocolate were preferable.

"Oh, well, Stacy was a bitch, too." Although obliged to be on Stacy's side in all altercations, Liz was actually pretty fair in discussion. This meant that, though she mostly wouldn't do anything about it, she would admit to Alison when she thought Stacy was wrong. "She's not over it, either. She's still stalking around here getting ready to nail your hide to the wall. You should have waited a couple more hours."

Mary Clare, without saying anything to either of them, walked away.

"I thought I was supposed to drive the shuttle or something," Alison said. "I just came back to check."

"Well, you were. Two hours ago. G-hey!'s doing it. Stacy's pissed about that, too."

"I think I'll go have breakfast at the Merc," said Alison hastily.

"Good idea. I'll walk you to your car."

"How was the dungeon last night?" Alison asked, casting a wary eye down the path and around the porch for Livia. That would make things perfect. Best Boy was guarding an empty table and a plate of pastries, so she must be around.

"Not bad. Some competition from Livia's party, but that made more room to swing your whip."

"Did anyone tell you about that freaky communion thing she did?" asked Alison.

"Yeah. A lot of people, actually. In fact, there're a lot of people who thought that was just the last straw. They want her banned from everywhere—MSIL, Powersurge, here, the Atlanta conference."

"What do you think?"

"Well, I'd like to see her banned for almost any reason. But I don't think it would stop her from doing it. She parties mostly privately, anyway. I mean, sure she's here because of the conference but she could have gotten a party together just as well if she wasn't registered. And I've seen her do that scene before—nobody's forcing anyone to take the drug. Of course, if you're willing to do that, the argument is that you're probably not smart enough to make your own play decisions anyway."

"I need your advice," said Alison, thinking about fuckbaby back at Marta's.

"Actually," said Liz, "I need to talk to you about something first."

"What?" asked Alison, immediately wary. No good had ever come from any conversation starting, 'I need to talk to you.'

"You know, about that head thing," said Liz. "If you don't want yours to end up on a spear on the courthouse lawn, then you'd better be a little less blatant."

Alison's mouth went suddenly so dry that she had trouble peeling her tongue down from the roof to answer. She tried for an innocent, I don't know what you mean, but all that came out was "What?" And it sounded so guilty that if she'd been the judge she would have convicted on the spot.

"Let's not pretend," said Liz. "Mary Clare told me you spent last night with Marta."

"Dammit!" Alison looked hastily around, as if this might be a set up and Stacy was ready to jump out from behind a door at any second. She really had to stop watching Ricki Lake—it was affecting the way she saw the world. "That goddamn Marta!" She knew this was being unfair, but it was always easier to blame someone else than it was to blame oneself. She wondered for a moment if this was true the world over, something anthropologists studied.

"Goddamn Marta?" Liz replied, lifting an eyebrow. "Marta doesn't have a girlfriend—she can do whatever she wants to do. What'd she do—tackle you and pull down your pants?"

"No. Dammit! I know it's not her fault. I'm just a bad person, right? Is that what you want to tell me? I already know it. I don't know what I was thinking. I wasn't thinking. It happened when Stacy was mad at me and it just happened and I felt bad afterwards and tried not to see Marta again." Even in her state of truly abject shame she was careful with her words. If Marta, via Mary Clare, had not told Liz it had happened twice, then she certainly wasn't going to tell her.

"Twice?" Liz raised the other eyebrow. Alison was pretty sure she was not aiming for the expression she got, which was two parts astonishment and one part horror. It came out looking kind of like Beaker from the Muppets. "It doesn't happen twice unless you want it to, Alison. Once can be forgiven—twice is something else."

"Well, Stacy was mad at me then, too!" Alison could not help whining. "You don't know what that's like!"

"Please," said Liz, raising a hand to indicate they were not going there. "I am the wrong person to say that to. Stacy's mad at me all the time. I know exactly what it's like."

Alison tried playing the other side of the street. "Then you should understand!"

"Alison, it is exactly because I do understand that I'm talking to you instead of Stacy."

"Well, why aren't you telling Stacy?" Alison asked. She was willing to grovel and promise to change her ways to either Stacy or Liz, but not both. If Liz was going to spill the beans then she might as well just save it up.

"I'm not telling Stacy for the same reason that you're not telling Janka about Michelle. Because you're hoping it will blow over and three lives don't have to be destroyed in the process. You know, Alison, Stacy's kind of like a cocker spaniel."

It was Alison's turn to lift an eyebrow.

"They're nice little dogs. They like kids and they're cute and if they jump on your grandma they don't knock her down and break her hip. But they're kind of high maintenance. You've got to watch their ears. You can't have them on a farm—they've always got bear grass in their ears." She paused and looked expectantly at Alison as if this analogy made things perfectly clear.

Alison thought for a moment. Liz had grown up on a farm and occasionally came out with little parables about fertile eggs and butchering hogs that made no sense at all to a city girl. Finally she asked, "And your point would be?"

"My point would be that not everybody wants or is able to take care of Stacy's ears. She had some pretty awful girlfriends before you came along—I did think somebody's head was going to end up on a stake. I wish it had—instead she just got all beaten down and desperate and it was just ugly. There's a lot of butch girls out there who want to fuck a femme like Stacy, but that's all. They don't really appreciate her—they think that because she wears lipstick and high heels she's dumb or they're kind of embarrassed about wanting a femme and they don't want to bring her around their friends. You've been really good to Stacy—she doesn't have to feel apologetic for what kind of lesbian she is. You're proud to have a pretty, femme girlfriend. You know she's smart, you know she's creative and you don't mind picking a few cockleburs out of her ears now and then. You're good for her and she's good for you. So stop fucking Marta!"

"I have, I have!" Alison turned her head away, embarrassed. Everything Liz had said had been true. It was Stacy she loved and it was shameful the way she had used Marta to wipe a bad scene out of her head.

"And that fucking crazy-ass crew of Livia's has been going around telling everybody they came to your house last night looking for Livia's slave and you weren't there, so you'd better come up with something good to tell Stacy before it gets back to her."

With a start, Alison snapped back to fuckbaby. No phone—she was going to have to go over there to check on her, which meant another errand in an already chaotic day. And it wasn't going to be like picking up eggs, either—there was going to have to be serious talk, needs met. Dammit, she hated rescuing. It reminded her of the seventies, when hardly a week went by without some down-and-out dyke sleeping on the couch in the apartment she shared with Michelle and three other women. It was no problem handling that back in those days when they had lived on the passion of one crisis after another, when someone else's problems were almost as good as your own. Now she liked things peaceful about her. One blow up from Stacy was all the excitement she needed for six months.

Checking on Janet would also mean taking the chance of running into Marta again and she didn't know if she could bear to do that. Maybe she could persuade Liz to come along with her.

Alison had not been the only one embarrassed by the Marta talk. Liz, too, wanted to move quickly to other things. "I wish I could remember where I saw that woman in the photo," she said, shaking her head slowly in the same way that you might try to start a car with a sluggish battery.

"Me, too," said Alison, "because I don't have a thing to tell Livia. As far as I can tell, it could have been just about anybody here."

Liz brightened. "Tell her it was everybody! You know—kind of a *Murder on the Orient Express* kind of thing. I'd certainly strike the first blow if someone organized it. Do you suppose it's too late to pull something like that together for the weekend?"

Alison looked at her watch. "Do you have a half hour?" she asked.

* * *

Dressed in an old blue flannel shirt that swam on her, Janet was easier to talk to than she had been the night before, wrapped in a jacket and sheet. Alison had not thought of food until they knocked on the door, so she was relieved to see crackers and tea out on the counter. She wondered for a moment how many women had spent a night or two here, running. Liz also looked around curiously and Alison wondered if she was remembering her own time on the run when, almost twenty years before she had been liberated from the mental ward of Denver General by two lesbians she hadn't even known.

"How long have you been bottoming for Livia?" Alison asked bluntly, sitting in one of the two rickety chairs. She'd have to see if her dad didn't have something better in his basement. No, dammit, she needed to stay away from this place! Find your own charity, she told herself sternly. Better to hand out sandwiches down by Tara than be involved in anything further around Marta.

"Oh." Janet put the back of her hand up to her forehead and sighed. "I hardly remember. It's as if my life began and ended with her." She pushed up

130

the sleeves of the shirt in a sad, slow gesture, which told even the audience in the last row she was devastated. She was sitting on the neatly made bed with her feet curled up beneath her. She had not washed off her eye make-up. The overnight smears added to the waiflike look.

Alison gave Liz, who had taken up a post leaning on the dresser, a look. Liz gave her a look back. More clearly than words it said, 'What did you expect?' You couldn't just blast your way into Jonestown and expect the people you rescued to come out with a 'thank you' and 'now it's time to take my place in society.' Kinky sex was one thing, weekend scenes were another, but you had to wonder what was going on with anyone who willingly entered into a life contract of not wearing clothes.

As if she had read Alison's mind, Janet plucked at the collar of the shirt. "It feels funny," she said with an apologetic little smile. "I haven't worn clothes in—oh, I'd guess a year. Since the last time Livia took me out. I don't really know how long it was. Livia didn't let me have a calendar. She said there was no point. The only things I had to do were things she told me to do and since I was hers forever it didn't matter what day or year it was. But it's springtime, isn't it? It's hard to tell through the window in Portland."

This was starting to sound like something out of a sleazy dyke pulp novel. Alison thought for a moment. There were two avenues to take. One was simply practical. Where did Janet want to go from here and how did she plan to get there? She was not, Alison suspected, a woman with a great vocation or a fat bank account. She wasn't secretly a dentist or a trust fund baby.

The other was purely selfish. What did Janet know that could help Alison discover who was blackmailing Livia? Perhaps it was using her a bit, but it seemed only a fair trade for getting her out of that hotel room, particularly since Livia was probably going to shut her wallet with a very final snap if she found out Alison was involved.

"So what do you want to do?" Liz asked, saving Alison the trouble of choosing between selfishness and using. "You all are from Portland, right? Is that where your family lives? Is there someone there you could call for money for a bus ticket? I mean, if you want to go back. If you don't want to go somewhere else instead." Alison noticed Liz was doing her best not to make staying in Denver a choice. "I don't suppose you had your plane ticket with you when you ran, did you?" she asked doubtfully. "Because if you did you could exchange it for someplace else with a fifty dollar reissue fee." Liz always knew these things.

"Plane ticket? Oh, no." Janet laughed shortly, deprecatingly. "I didn't have a plane ticket."

"Yeah, Livia's holding it, right?" said Alison, trying to think of a hand signal she could give Liz to remind her Janet had been stark naked.

"Oh, no," said Janet, shaking her head in a kind of wondering, little girl way that Livia must have liked. It made Alison want to hit her with a rolled up newspaper. Of course, that could have been the attraction. "I never had a ticket."

"Huh?" Alison thought back to the airport. She was sure she had picked up Janet with the rest of Livia's court. She had been thinking back on this since she had met Livia at her hotel room. The whole court had come from the airport together. She remembered from conversation that though some of their planes had come in earlier, they had all been instructed to wait for Livia's flight. She suspected no one had been allowed to take a flight that came in later.

"No, Livia never allowed me to fly in the cabin if we flew. She always made me curl up under her fur coat in one of those big dog kennels and shipped me through with the baggage." She smiled a wistful little smile that someone else might have given recalling a happy summer evening a lifetime ago.

This was too much for Liz. "Come out on the porch with me, Alison," she said. "Let's have a smoke." Janet opened her mouth as if to invite herself, but Liz squelched her firmly. "You're not allowed to smoke," she said. Submissive training could come in handy, Alison could see.

"Do you really have cigarettes?" she asked, hopefully as they stepped out the door and onto the deck, which ran along the side of the house. It seemed like a good time for that first last cigarette.

"Of course not," said Liz, leaning both forearms on the wooden rail. "That was a bad, bad thing to start again, remember? If I have to go through quitting again I'm going to have to kill myself. I do, however, have chocolate." She reached into the pocket of her jacket and drew out the package of M&Ms, which she shook into both their hands. "What you have in there, Alison my friend," she said after a moment of crunching, "is a crazy person. Take it from someone who has spent a weekend or two chained to a radiator herself."

"Yeah, I suppose there's something funny," admitted Alison. "I mean, I know I picked her up in the van. She was pretty obvious."

"Naked?" Liz asked in a tone that made it clear she really was hoping this was a no.

"Close. Long fur coat—I remember that. She probably was naked in it. But the thing is, I didn't pick up any dog kennel. I guess…well I suppose they could have rented one or stored it at the airport."

"Alison. Stop." Liz held up a hand. "It doesn't matter. Either she's lying about flying in a dog kennel, which makes her a crazy person, or she really let Livia do that to her, which also makes her a crazy person. Only the details are different."

Alison sighed. She hadn't rescued anyone in a long time except as a cop using social services. Yeah, sure, she had lent friends twenty dollars against payday which she sometimes got back and sometimes didn't, but it wasn't the same as taking somebody in off the street. It wasn't anywhere near the same and she was glad. She didn't want runaways on her couch anymore. She preferred her good deeds once removed.

"I suppose I'm going to be footing the bill for this bus ticket." Liz broke into her thoughts.

"Yeah, I thought so," agreed Alison. "I'll kick in twenty bucks. That'll get her to Colorado Springs at least. Fifty if you help me find out who's blackmailing Livia."

"I already helped you with that chart," Liz protested. "I would have charged a client a hundred and fifty dollars for that."

"Dream on," said Alison, turning her back to the rail and her face up to the sun. It felt good and besides that way she had a much better chance of not meeting Marta's eye if she walked by.

The door opened and Janet hesitantly walked out, carrying two steaming mugs before her.

"I made you some tea," she said, handing one to each. Alison thought it was a good sign that she had figured out a way to do something she had been told not to do. Maybe there was hope yet.

"You got that photo?" Liz asked, startling Alison, who had been thinking that maybe they could stick fuckbaby—Janet, Janet, Janet!—on a bus after all. Maybe she did have a nice family somewhere.

"What?"

"The photo, the photo!" Liz snapped her fingers. Alison gave her a look. "Sorry," Liz apologized. "I forgot where I was."

"You forgot who you were," said Alison. "For a minute there you thought you were a really big asshole." She looked at Janet. "Do you know why Livia hired me?" she asked tentatively, wondering what the ethics were here. Okay, she had done something that Livia would probably call stealing from her, but that was totally separate from her agreement of discretion.

"Humph." Liz made a little sound in her throat and then pulled her to one side by her sleeve. "Excuse us a moment," she said over her shoulder. "Alison!" she hissed into her ear, "That woman was the dog! She was there all the time! She knows everything! You do not have to fear giving anything away!"

Alison thought about this, remembering Livia sending fuckbaby—Janet!—to her corner while they talked.

"Okay," she said, taking the photo from the envelope while she turned. "You know that Livia is being blackmailed, right?"

Janet nodded. It was going to be a lot easier to think of her as Janet, thought Alison, after she washed her face. Here in the sun for the first time, Alison was surprised to see that Janet was not, as she'd first supposed, in her early twenties, but closer to her own age. Maybe even older. She had one of those thin, wiry little bodies with small breasts, which made it hard to tell.

Somehow, that made the whole thing a little creepier. It seemed easier to understand a twenty-year-old getting herself into this kind of situation. Someone her own age, she thought, should really know better. The age thing again.

"Do you know the woman in this picture?" Alison asked, holding it up.

"She's here," Janet said. "I don't think any of the rest of them know it. Livia doesn't. But she's here. I've seen her. I've seen her walk right by Livia."

"Why didn't you say something to Livia?" Alison asked, stunned. How could the big butch in the photo be here without either her or Stacy or Liz having seen her?

"She didn't ask me." Janet turned her face up to the sun as Alison had done, smiling a very small and secret smile. She had been bad and she knew it and was happy about it.

"Hey!" A voice called up.

Alison's first thought was that Marta had, unheard, climbed the stairs behind her. And just what was she going to say?

But it was Mary Clare, carrying a toolbox, a bag from Einstein's and a rolled up newspaper beneath one arm.

"Hey!" she said to Liz, making it sound like 'How are you doing?' and then "Hey," to Alison, making it sound like 'What the fuck are you doing here? You asshole.' Whatever Mary Clare's excuse, Alison knew the real point of her being there was to get in her face. Very like Michelle in her strategy, except that Michelle was really in a class of her own. Nobody could get in your face like Michelle.

Alison stepped back and sat on the metal glider against the wall, then stood again. The sun was great, but it wasn't strong enough to have warmed the metal. Liz's face was turned away, so she gave a look to the back of her head. Let Liz deal with Mary Clare. Take her downstairs, fuck her in her car, she didn't care what it took.

"I'm Mary Clare," Mary Clare said to Janet, laying on the charm like Janet was wearing a ball gown instead of a tatty second-hand shirt and they were meeting at a cotillion. "My cousin, Marta, and I own this building. She left me a note you were here. I didn't know you knew Liz and Alison. Marta said there was a problem with her door jamming, and I came by to fix it." Oh, great, Mary Clare was handy, too. Now in addition to feeling as if she should be wearing a scarlet letter, Alison could feel like an inferior butch, too.

"Fuckbaby," said Janet, bowing her head as if giving Mary Clare permission to smack her on the back of it.

"Look," Alison said curtly to Janet, regretting her tone immediately when she saw the look Mary Clare gave her. "Put some clothes on and we'll take you out to lunch."

"But I'm not allowed to wear clothes," said Janet, eyes still cast down. "I shouldn't even...Livia has forbidden...oh—" Something about the pretty way she colored in confusion made Alison not only sure she was playing to the audience of three, but that she had assigned Mary Clare a front row seat.

Liz must have caught it too, for she stepped in firmly. "I'll bet there are clothes in here that will fit you," she said to Janet and "Can you help?" to Mary Clare. All three disappeared into the apartment.

Alison braved the glider again, this time staying down. It wasn't too bad. Made her ass a little numb, was all. She picked up the morning newspaper Mary Clare had set beside her toolbox. She knew Liz was going to have to tell her at least part of the Livia story and hoped she would give out as little information as possible.

She glanced at the front page. The Broncos, to the astonishment of the sports world and the manic delight of Denver fans, had taken the Super Bowl this year and were trying in the aftermath to push through a bill for a new stadium, the estimated cost of which was going to be more money than Alison could make in ten lifetimes. Alison, feeling crabby, skipped that. She hadn't voted for the new airport, either, but somebody had and used her taxes to pay for it, and doubtless the same thing was going to happen with the stadium.

Somebody across the way was playing KYGO, the country oldies station Alison listened to in her car. The singer was talking about the year Franklin Delany died and Alison, as she always did, wondered if Franklin Delany was a real person.

The song went into a news break. The d.j. sounded new and nervous. Somebody had been crunched and killed by the light rail again and, worse for Marilyn, it had happened right by the Merc. There had been a period, right after the light rail had been installed, when light rail casualties had been an almost weekly occurrence, and if you called the Merc to find out the concert schedule it was issued along with a light rail warning. But that had ended once drivers started paying more attention and now the only people who got hit regularly and fatally were the winos and druggies who hung out down by the Merc because the Denver Rescue Mission was only five blocks over. Cars hit them regularly and sometimes fatally as well. It was a problem and no one, least of all Alison, knew what to do about it. This accident, Alison noted, was slightly different in that the victim had been a woman. However, like all the recent victims, she had been drunk.

She looked up just as Janet came back onto the porch, dressed in a pair of faded jeans which had obviously once been Marta's, for she'd had to roll them up three our four times at the bottom and probably cinch them in at the waist with a belt, also. Because she was wearing an oversized and untucked shirt Alison could not be sure about this. She looked very waiflike and Alison wondered if this was intentional. She could not imagine that Marta and Mary Clare had put only their own cast-offs in the drawers of the dresser—they must surely be aware that the majority of women who would stay in the apartment would be between their two sizes. Janet, she was beginning to see, rather enjoyed the part of waif and victim. In one hand she was holding a bagel sandwich with a tiny bite already taken from it, in the other a cup of coffee.

"Do you know who's been blackmailing Livia?" Alison asked bluntly.

Janet shook her head and took another nibble of the bagel. There went the out-for-lunch idea. Mary Clare must have brought it for her—another point for Mary Clare being a better butch than Alison. Perhaps she could arrange to have Mary Clare hit by the light rail. With Persimmon.

"No." Janet swallowed three drops of coffee and shook her head. Another nibble. Alison wondered if this was the way Livia had wanted her to eat or if she just had an eating disorder.

Janet caught the glance. "Livia doesn't like it if I gain weight," she said in a conversational tone, like they were just talking about the weather or *The X-Files*. "I'm only allowed to consume two thousand calories a day. Eighteen hundred on weekends."

Below them, Alison had caught sight of a woman with dark, thick hair tied back with a purple scarf. Oh, damn it all to hell. Marta. Alison could not tell if she was coming or going or maybe planning on sprucing the place up a bit. At the moment she was talking to her huge black and white cat, which was sitting on the railing of the porch next door.

Janet still had her mind on Livia and food. She looked at the bagel and sighed. "I guess I'll have to call Einstein's and find out how many calories are in this. I'll probably only be able to have vegetables the whole rest of the day and I really wanted a glass of milk."

This, on top of being caught between Mary Clare inside and Marta at the foot of the stairs, was too much for Alison.

"Hey," she said rudely, forgetting for a moment that if you're going to play good cop/bad cop you have to have a good cop, "Guess what? Livia's not here! She's not in charge of you anymore. Eat whatever you want! Eat like a pig! I'll take you down to Lick's if you want and buy you a banana split!" She stood and moved back against the brick wall, where it was warmer and Marta couldn't look up and see her.

"Oh, ice cream," said Janet in that wondering way, like she'd been raised in the desert by wolves and was just getting used to civilization. "Ice cream? Oh, I remember ice cream, and don't you sometimes get chocolate on it? Do you think I could do that?"

"Oh, for fuck sake!" snapped Alison, totally at the end of her tether now. Janet had to be putting it on and she just wasn't in the mood for a show. She had risked a lot of money taking Janet with her out of the hotel and further risked her relationship with Stacy by sleeping with Marta again and that never would have happened if she hadn't come around seeking sanctuary for Janet in the middle of the night. "Livia's not here, okay? She doesn't own you anymore—she never did own you! What the hell were you thinking to let someone treat you like that? You're a grown woman—why would you agree to something so stupid?"

She knew the instant the words were out of her mouth she had been wrong to say them. A stony look came over Janet's face as if a curtain had passed before it. "I need to take a shower," she said, not looking at Alison's face. She began to drift back across the porch, still clutching the bagel.

"Oh, come on, I didn't mean—" Alison's attempt at an apology was cut short as she turned and walked smack into Mary Clare. Janet slipped around her and was gone.

"Boy, you sure got her to come clean," said Mary Clare, with grim satisfaction. "Liz was telling me what a great detective you were, but I'm really glad I got a chance to see for myself."

Alison could not think of anything to say that would not make things worse. The last thing in the world that she wanted to do was give Mary Clare a chance to hang around long enough for Marta to head this way.

"Jesus, Alison, what did you say that to her for?" asked Liz in a disgusted voice. She must have used up today's quota of tact in not telling Stacy about Marta, Alison thought.

"We can talk about it in the car," she said to Liz, trying to give her a high sign without actually pointing at Mary Clare.

"I mean, my god, you couldn't have said anything worse if you'd tried! What were you doing, blaming her? That's about the last thing she needs—to have somebody be judgmental!" Liz rolled right over the top of her. "How many times have you been in a destructive relationship, huh? Did you need to have somebody blame you afterwards? Did that help you get out of it and feel good again?"

"Well, I never let anybody ship me in a dog kennel, if that's what you mean!" This was just way too much. Liz was an asshole and Mary Clare was an asshole and Livia was an asshole and stupid fuckbaby, who deserved to be called fuckbaby, was an asshole too. She hated everyone.

"I'm going downstairs," she said to Liz. "And then I'm going to start my car. If you want a ride you should come with me or you're going to have to get your little friend to take you home." She pulled herself up to her full height and looked condescendingly down at Mary Clare. It was a cheap shot, but it was the only shot that she had.

"Oh, hurt my feelings," said Mary Clare scornfully. "I lie awake at night and cry because I'm not as tall as Alison Kaine, the hot shot detective and liar. Not!"

Alison turned and clattered down the stairs. Just as Alison was popping into reverse, Liz grabbed hold of the passenger door. She would have rather liked to shift into drive and drag Liz across Marta's lawn, hopefully running over Mary Clare on the way, but realized it would be one of those things that was only really fun for a second or two, before the police got involved.

"You have got the biggest bug up your ass!" Wisely, Liz waited until the door was closed and her seatbelt buckled before starting on Alison. "Can't you be a little bit tactful? Didn't your mama ever tell you that you catch more flies with honey than with vinegar?"

"Oh, yeah!" Alison whipped down the alley way too fast. Okay, slow down, get a grip. "Let's talk about tact, okay? Let's talk about reaming me out in front of Mary Clare! Did you think that was helpful? Did you think, 'Oh, this will really be constructive and help Alison get motivated?' I don't think so! Why didn't you just lean over the railing and call up Marta?"

"Oh." Liz snapped her mouth shut. After a moment, during which Alison passed three side streets and ran a stop sign she said, "Well, maybe you should talk to Marta about this. She's a psychic, after all."

"She's a phone psychic, for Godsake," snapped Alison. "She's one of those people you see advertising during Ricki Lake! She's not any more psychic than you or I!"

"All I know," said Liz, obviously happy the topic had been turned away from her tact, "is that last year when I was working on that incest case—"

"Stop it!" said Alison. She pulled to the curb and put her hands over her ears. "I don't want to hear about Marta! I don't care if she found JonBenet's killer! Do you hear me? I don't care! It doesn't matter! How could I possibly ask her to help me, even if I thought she could, which I don't?"

They sat quietly for a moment, looking out opposite windows. Alison opened her door and went around to the back, where she had a twelve pack of Diet Pepsi. She popped a can for herself and brought one back to Liz, who accepted it in silence.

"Are you getting your period?" she asked finally.

"Don't start with me," said Alison in a voice of relative calm. "I already hate you."

Liz thought about this for a couple more sips and decided to backpedal. "Well, I didn't mean to embarrass you in front of Mary Clare. But—"

Alison held up a warning finger. "My daddy told me that any apology with 'but' on the end isn't really an apology."

Liz thought again. Apparently she could not figure out how to apologize without 'but,' because she didn't try it again. "Well," she said, "at least we found out that woman's here."

"What woman?" asked Alison. Her head was still too close to exploding to remember much.

"Falcon—the woman in the photo—the one Livia gave you. You know...what's-her-name, back there told you about her being here."

"I intend to spend the rest of my life not referring to what's-her-name," said Alison with feeling. "As far as I'm concerned, she is now Mary Clare's problem. I hope she moves in with her and eats her out of house and home.

I hope she runs up a five hundred-dollar phone bill! To Circle of Friends Psychic Vision!"

"Okay." Liz decided to sail right on over this. "The woman formerly known as fuckbaby. She said that big butch girl you've been looking for is here."

"Liz, how could Falcon be here without one of us knowing? How? We've seen every big butch here a hundred times at least. I've never been more than fifteen feet away from most of these women! Hell, you worked registration—did you talk to anybody then who looked like that?"

"Well, I didn't ask to see tattoos," said Liz defensively. "You don't have to bite my head off. I'm just reminding you what she said."

"She said she doesn't know her own name, Liz! How could she remember someone from three years ago?"

"Oh, she remembered her own name," Liz scoffed. "That was all just a show for us. Livia hasn't kept her locked up for five years. I'll bet she's got a copy of all the keys and Livia's credit cards hidden somewhere. I'll bet they play a little game where Livia finds her stash when they're both bored and beats her black and blue. She probably doesn't even live with Livia. Stacy's probably right—she's probably a high-price doctor or a judge or something and this is just a little thing they do at Michigan and conventions. I'd love to know who else has rescued Janet."

Alison held up a hand. "Stop. I feel like enough of an idiot if she's legitimate—if I'm a prop then I just can't bear it."

Even Liz, the leather lawyer, did not have an answer for this and since Alison could not think of a single thing to say that wasn't bitchy, they drove to Tara in silence.

Chapter Twelve

Salad was still out with the van and Alison didn't want to talk to Stacy while Stacy was pissed at the world, particularly when explaining almost anything would involve Marta. So she stayed outside Tara, leaning against the brick wall bordering the front lawn. There were quite a few women lounging in the sun. After a moment Erin Oleander, who was standing further down the wall, detached herself to come stand next to Alison. She nudged her gently with her elbow and offered a cigarette. She probably would be in a lot less trouble right now, thought Alison, if she'd just given in to Erin and followed her to her room. That's what happened when you tried to do the right thing.

"Thanks." Alison took it and the lighter. She had been off for five years, then on again during the fatal trip to womyn's land when they had all binged on cigarettes as if they were seventeen and unable to imagine their own deaths. Then off again for almost a year. Pissed at the world seemed to be the perfect time to restart the vicious cycle.

"You're upset," Erin observed after a few puffs. "Did you go to a workshop that upset you?" She didn't look at Alison, but straight out ahead, and that made it easier.

"No, I'm upset because my girlfriend is being a great big asshole!" Wow, she hadn't expected that. She had thought she had forgiven the fight and moved on. Apparently not. It felt quite empowering to say it aloud.

"You weren't feeling very well last night, either?" Erin French inhaled her smoke. She really was a very striking woman. She was wearing tight jeans and black high tops decorated with studs. A tightly cinched belt echoed the chrome on her shoes. She was obviously the kind of woman who knew enough not to overdress for the occasion.

"No, I wasn't." It was as if the sympathetic sentence had opened a floodgate. Suddenly Alison found herself telling this stranger everything—all the things she had never told Stacy or even Michelle. "Sleep disorder...numb...aches...medication...support group..." Quickly she stumbled over her own words, outlining the visits to her doctor, to the chiropractor, to the orthopedic surgeon, and finally to the rheumatologist. She told this women she didn't know about her fear of losing her job, of becoming so disabled she could not care for herself, of the horrible fatigue that lay in ambush for her at unpredictable moments, of Stacy's anger and accusations.

"Wow!" said Erin, when she finally ran to a stop. "That sounds awful. Your girlfriend does sound like an asshole."

It was one thing for Alison to say it herself—it was quite another for someone else to say it. Before she could protest, Erin went on. "If you've told her all this, and she still isn't cutting you any slack, then you ought to confront her on her able-bodied attitude."

If. Oh. Alison felt an uncomfortable blush beginning to creep up her neck. She crushed her butt savagely.

"Oh," said Erin, after a moment or two of silence. "Being butch, were we?"

No, not exactly that. Alison shook her head, trying to think of how she could explain. It was more that, faced with pretty grim literature, faced with a diagnosis where the word 'chronic' came up way more often than she wanted to hear it, she had clamped herself shut, unwilling to explain or ask for help until she desperately needed it. What if she needed her friends to take care of her for two days in an emergency, and they had used up all their sympathy on swollen hands and muscle cramps? What if she became her mother, always complaining of aches and pains no one else could see, the tyrannical invalid upon whom all plans hinged?

"You know what I'd do?" said Erin, gesturing in that campy way only queenie boys and leather femmes can pull off. "I'd tell her what was going on. Right now." She paused for a moment, looking around them. "Or, would you have to peel someone off her rack?"

Alison looked around also, aware for the first time they were standing in a little leather community that was kind of the toned down, daytime version of the opening scene of Meet and Beat at the Detour bar. Everybody had already done the first greeting scene, so there was not nearly so much squealing and hugging. Also, there were more women this afternoon who were doing basic maintenance things—eating, smoking, buffing their shoes or brushing their hair. Still, you would not have mistaken it for a church picnic. Just the outfits assured that. There was a lot of gender bending going on. Dykes dressed like guys trying to attract baby butches who liked Daddy play. Femmes who had gone the mini skirt and boots route. Two or three gals in uniform and a dozen more in full leather, as well as the handful, like Alison, who were just doing the jeans and T-shirt thing. Some groups were chatting about the weather while they shared a Marlboro moment, but there were others who were obviously on the edge of a scene right out there in the open. Real good thing the wall was there.

"I don't know what she's doing," Alison admitted. "I just got here."

Erin offered Alison a program, presumably as an aid to tracking Stacy.

More workshops. Fisting. Piercing. Mind fucking.

"I didn't know dykes needed a workshop in that," Alison said, pointing. "I thought we mind fucked naturally."

She had expected a laugh, but there was only a pause. Finally Erin gave a stiff little, "Ha-ha" and said, just as stiffly, "I think they're talking consensual. Within the boundaries of a scene."

"Oh, well," said Alison, feeling foolish because the joke had so obviously failed, "that would be different." She gazed across the lawn. She had no idea where Stacy might be, and, further, had no idea if she even wanted to hunt her down and talk to her. It didn't matter, she thought stubbornly, that she had been less than forthcoming about the doctor's diagnosis. Stacy should have been there for her, regardless, and if she hadn't been able to be there, she should at least have not been such a bitch!

"What are you doing now?" she asked Erin, fully aware she was about to move into that hazy area of non-consensual mind fuck.

"I'm just going to stand out here in the sun."

"Do you want to go over to the Merc? Can I buy you a cup of coffee?" asked Alison.

"You better think on that one while I'm in the bathroom," said Erin. "I don't know if that sounds like such a good idea. You might not be able to just say no again."

Alison was still standing against the wall, watching Erin, when she felt someone come up on her other side. She didn't need to turn to know it was Stacy. Stacy always wore Shalimar. The scent of it usually was a turn-on, but Alison was still feeling crabby and poorly treated. She turned slowly. Stacy nuzzled up next to her as if she were a kitten looking to be petted and looked up at her with big round eyes and a little pout. This, Alison knew, was her way of indicating she wanted to be forgiven without apology. Sometimes Alison just wanted to smack Stacy a good one—and not in an erotic way, either.

"I brought you something," Stacy said. Presents always figured in her I-was-a-bad-girl act. She held out a Dove ice cream bar, still in its wrapper. She had her own bar, chocolate covered, with nuts. She stuck it into her mouth as Alison took the other, looking at her with bedroom eyes as she sucked the end. Stacy could be more suggestive with an ice cream bar in broad daylight in a crowd than most women could be with their clothes off in the bedroom.

"Are you my little love-bunny?" she asked Alison. Baby talk was another habit of Stacy's which grated on Alison, but she was willing to overlook it in the name of peace.

"Yeah," she said, hoping none of the other butches had heard. "Look, I have something I need to talk to you about…"

It was unfortunate that Erin chose to reappear at this moment. She either didn't see Stacy or didn't care—she walked straight up to Alison and plunked her purse down on the wall beside her, giving her a smile, which under other circumstances might have made her toes curl. With Stacy standing there beside her, all it did was make her stomach turn over.

Stacy had not just fallen off the turnip truck. She needed neither a diagram nor a single word spoken to figure out exactly what was going on. And, being Stacy, she saw no need to mince words. "Are you coming on to my girlfriend?" she asked, in a voice which should have warned Erin to run like a bunny. Alison herself would have run if she hadn't been blocked in.

But it seemed Erin was not a woman to be pushed around any more than Stacy was. "Yes," she drawled, raising one eyebrow as if in amusement. "I guess I am. Actually, though, it was kind of a mutual thing." She gave Alison a quick glance as if to apologize for giving her up. It didn't matter. Alison was dog meat either way.

But, though she had seen a fair number of Stacy's rages—Hurricane Stacy, Liz called her in this mode; she destroys everything in her path—she was not prepared for Stacy's next move. Which was to lash out with her Dove Bar as if it were a tennis racket and smack Erin so hard on the side of the face that her head reeled back.

Alison could only stare in amazement. Erin, with a sheet of chocolate adhered to her temple, was apparently in the same state. Her jaw had dropped open and she made no move whatsoever to protect herself from the backhand for which Stacy was obviously winding up.

It was Liz, appearing from out of the crowd with that radar best friends sometimes have, who literally caught Stacy by the arm and dragged her four feet backward before she could deliver the next blow.

"Excuse me," Alison said in a daze, turning her back to Erin as she jumped in to help Liz. Pound for pound, Liz had the staying power of a shrew, but Stacy had been known to channel the family Soricidae herself, and she outweighed Liz by a good thirty. Liz was maintaining dubious control only because she had one hand buried in Stacy's hair and the other twisting the collar of her shirt. She gave a desperate look to Alison, who jumped back and grabbed Stacy under the arms. Together, they managed to drag her back off onto the grass, out of ice cream range. The leathergirls who were lounging in the sun watched with interest.

"What the hell is wrong with you?" sputtered Liz, giving Stacy's head one final shake so severe Alison expect a clump of hair to come out in her hand.

"Yeah!" agreed Alison. "What's wrong with you? You're going to get us all kicked out of here if you don't watch it!" Too late she remembered they were the ones in charge of the kicking. Unceremoniously she dropped Stacy on her ass.

She expected some Stacy remark— fuck 'em if they can't take a joke, or I've been thrown out of better places or it's my party or some other blow off. What she didn't expect was for Stacy to start to cry.

A couple of butch girls who had drifted over in the hopes of catching a scene hastily retreated. Everybody there had made her own girlfriend cry at one time or another, and it was not something you were eager to see again, even vicariously. Both Liz and Alison were dumbstruck. Liz started to drift away, but Alison caught her by the elbow. Whatever this music was, she was not going to face it alone.

Stacy crying was just like Stacy doing anything else—there was nothing halfhearted about it. Alison had no idea what was wrong or how to comfort her. She might have taken her in her arms, but she had a bad feeling that something she had done was behind the outburst of tears, and she didn't want to get in close. Stacy had dropped the Dove bar on the bricks—even now a stray cat that thought he had died and gone to heaven was making short work of it—but Stacy didn't need a frozen dairy product to cause havoc. Alison knew.

"What's wrong?" she finally asked, squatting on the grass at arm's length.

"What do you suppose is wrong?" Stacy managed to say between sobs. She was starting to wind down now. Stacy gave it her all when she cried, but she didn't have any staying power. She jabbed angrily at her eyes. "What do you suppose is wrong? You don't want to touch me anymore, you don't want to fuck me anymore, you're just too tired! Fine! If you want somebody else, then you just have somebody else! But you tell me the truth! Don't dick me around anymore!" She gave a long snuffle.

"I'll go get you a Kleenex," said Liz. Relief was plain on her face—thank God it's Alison and not me!

"Oh, Stacy, oh, Baby, it's not that, I haven't been feeling well…" Alison was horrified. It had never crossed her mind that Stacy would see her lack of energy as rejection. She had never allowed it to cross her mind. She had been too busy covering, too busy trying to avoid saying the word 'chronic.'

"Oh, don't give me any bullshit!" Stacy cut her off, so mad she was spraying spit. Added to the tears, it made her a pretty soggy little cookie. "I might have been born in the dark, but it wasn't last night! I can tell when someone doesn't want me anymore!"

"No, baby." Hastily Alison moved in and caught Stacy up in her arms. This was important, this was worth risking a black eye. "I have something to tell you—that's what I wanted to say. It's not you. I think you're the most beautiful woman on the face of the earth. I think you're Helen of Troy. " She could tell by the set of Stacy's shoulders that she hadn't yet said the right words. "I think you're the sexiest woman to ever walk the earth with mortals. I can't even look at other women, let alone think of fucking them." A little shudder of relief passed through Stacy's body. Okay, she was on the right track now. She hastened to sweeten the pot. "I wasn't flirting with that woman—I was just talking to her because I felt sorry for her, because no one else will have anything to do with her." No reaction—she wasn't quite getting it. "I had to feel sorry for her—you know, she doesn't even hold a candle to you." Another sigh—she was on target again. She mentally apologized to poor Erin, but she'd give up the president if it meant getting back in Stacy's good graces. "Look," she said, holding Stacy away from her so that she could look into her face. "It's not what you think. It's not that I don't want you. It really is that I haven't been feeling well. Really."

"Then why don't you go to the doctor! Then why don't you…" Stacy, though no longer in high attack mode, was far from mollified.

Alison broke in hastily before she could wind herself up again. "I have gone to the doctor, Stacy. I just didn't want to tell you about it."

Silence. Stacy's eyes flashed 'cancer!' Alison went on quickly. It wasn't good news, but it wasn't anywhere as near as bad as that. "No," she said. "I've been seeing a rheumatologist. He thinks I have a condition called fibromyalgia syndrome. Have you ever heard of it?"

"Isn't it like chronic fatigue?" Stacy asked, surprising her.

"They think it's related. But it feels more like—oh, like about every other week I have the flu. You know—not the puking, but that kind of fever where everything aches and you can't imagine getting out of bed." Except she had been getting out of bed, and going to work and trying to stay on top of her life and keep up with Stacy too, instead of treating herself gently, as the doctor had suggested.

"How long have you known this?" asked Stacy, and she didn't have to add that Alison wasn't allowed to have secrets—you could hear it in her voice. "Why didn't you tell me?"

Suddenly Alison was angry. "Because I've heard you talk about women with chronic illnesses! 'Oh, Beth thinks she has chronic fatigue. Must be nice to draw a disability check. Gee, I'm tired. I must have chronic fatigue.' Do you think I want you to talk like that about me? 'Oh, Alison's got a backache, so she thinks she has FMS. Oh, Alison has a selective illness—it just acts up whenever I want to do something that she doesn't.'"

Stacy was silent. She had stopped crying, but her outburst had ravaged her make-up. When Covergirl said their mascara was waterproof, they meant it would stand up to a normal act of God, not an outbreak of Hurricane Stacy.

"You need to fix your face," said Liz from behind Alison. Alison didn't know how much she had overheard. From the look on her face, everything.

Liz handed Stacy a wad of toilet paper and a can of Diet Pepsi.

Stacy blew her nose heartily three times and then took a hit of the Pepsi. She stood. "I need to compose myself. I'll be back in a minute."

"I hope she doesn't run into Erin," said Alison, looking at her back. "Do you suppose she got that out of her system?"

"With Stacy," answered Liz, "one never knows. But one can't keep her on a choke chain all the time."

They were both silent for a moment. Then Liz said, "Did you ever have a dog when you were a kid, Alison?"

"I have heard the dog comparison already, Liz. Let it go. And I don't wish to be compared to a grain of mustard seed, either."

"You obviously haven't heard it enough," said Liz. "She needs her girl-friend to pay attention to her. I don't mean that she needs a butch around the house to change her light bulbs or fix her plumbing or anything like that. She's a very capable woman. She can either do that kind of stuff herself or pay to have it done. That doesn't matter to her. But she needs to have her girl-friend compliment her and pay attention. She needs to be told that she's pretty and sexy and hot."

"Liz," said Alison, wishing she had one of Erin's cigarettes. "I'm feeling a bit insecure myself here. It's not easy to tell your lover you have a chronic illness. It's so fucking boring! Who in the world wants to hang around some-one who feels like shit all the time?"

"Stacy would," said Liz. "That's what I'm trying to tell you. All you have to do is make Stacy feel like she's Aphrodite, and she'll stick by you through anything. Do you think she hasn't noticed there was something wrong? She thought you had cancer, and she was prepared to stick with you through that. This is nothing compared to that."

Again there was silence, and again Liz was the one who broke it. "And incidentally, it wasn't just Stacy who you weren't giving much credit by keep-ing this a secret. You weren't giving me much credit, either. Have you told Michelle and Janka?" she asked.

"No," said Alison, sullen as a thirteen-year-old.

"Well, much as I hate to say it, you're not giving Michelle much credit, either."

Alison said nothing. Liz could not possibly imagine her panic, her fear at becoming her mother. She looked across the brick patio. "Do you think I should go look for Stacy?" she asked.

"I think those femme gals are going to eat you alive if you try it," said Liz. Alison followed her gaze. Sure enough, every woman in lipstick or a dress was glaring darkly at her. Stacy had gone away crying—that automatically made Alison in the wrong. They stood there for awhile, pinned to the wall by the accusing eyes. After about ten minutes Liz spoke out of the side of her mouth.

"I'm going to make a break for it. I don't think they're hostile to me. You stay still until I'm about ten feet away—I don't want you to draw their atten-tion to me."

"If you even move, I'm going to start yelling," said Alison. She gave the women watching them a cheerful smile. "We go together or we don't go at all."

"You really are a horrible human being, Alison," Liz replied with her own

146

false smile. "I should have just let you deal with the femme squad by your-self."

"Together or not at all," Alison repeated.

Liz took a deep breath and then nodded her head. Big everybody-loves-me-smiles pasted on their faces they marched briskly across the lawn, look-ing neither to the right or the left. The French doors on the side of the house stuck a bit, which gave them both an anxious moment, but no one moved in to give them a good piece of her mind, although Alison suspected her chances of making a playdate with any of the femmes at the conference was now about as good as her chance of waking up beside Uma Thurman. Seeing that she hated everyone, this was fine.

She had wondered if perhaps the reason that neither Stacy nor Erin had returned was because Stacy was busy putting Erin's head on a stake and so was quite relieved to find no sign of carnage in the kitchen. Rather, women were standing about chatting in small groups, nibbling on the cheese and fruit that had replaced the bagels. She glanced carefully around the room with only a small, slow movement of her head, still suspecting enemy recon-naissance.

Dana came strolling across the room, all but arm in arm with Mary Clare. Mary Clare was still carrying a newspaper under her arm.

"What'd you say to Stacy?" Dana asked as she drew even with Alison. "She went tearing out the front like a bat out of hell—I think she might have clipped the van's bumper."

Alison, who had been opening her mouth to ask why Dana would auto-matically assume she had said anything at all to Stacy, why she would assume she was in the wrong was cut short by Mary Clare who said, "Boy, you're really batting a hundred today, aren't you?"

"Fuck you! Nobody asked your opinion on anything! Fuck you and everybody who looks like you!"

"Well, you already kind of did that, didn't you?" Mary Clare asked nas-tily. Despite her anger, Alison had spoken in an undertone. Mary Clare, how-ever, was using that public, shaming voice dykes tend to use when they're indignant, that I-have-nothing-to-hide voice. Another minute and she was going to be throwing names around.

"And another thing," Mary Clare went on, just as if she'd read Alison's mind, "I don't want you to think that you've dumped your little problem on me and Marta. Don't even think that! Because you haven't and you're not going to! I want to know when you're going to come over and—"

"Where the hell were you last night?" Never before had Alison thought she would be glad to hear Livia's voice, stern and commanding as if she were talking to a really bad dog. "I practically had a riot at my place and—"

"We're talking," broke in Mary Clare. "Wait your turn." In that part of her mind not busy thinking of a quick answer for Livia, Alison noticed with a purely academic interest that Mary Clare seemed to have the ability, like certain frogs and lizards, to puff herself up to almost twice her normal size when attacked. Liz might channel a shrew, but Mary Clare channeled a wolverine.

"This is business," said Livia without even looking at Mary Clare, like that took care of it because she was royalty and Mary Clare a serf she could have beheaded any time if she chose. "I'm paying you," she went on, giving Alison the alpha dog look. Alison, who to be truthful, had seen enough of the alpha dog look this weekend to last a lifetime, glared back. "And there's practically a riot in my suite and people from the hotel are knocking on the door and talking about the cops and then when the smoke clears I find you're gone and my slave gone! What the hell were you doing? You must have been doing something because you sure as hell weren't doing your job!"

"Number one," said Alison. She wanted to get up in Livia's face, but couldn't because of Mary Clare and Dana, neither of whom was making any sign of moving. Mary Clare was obviously not done reaming her out and Dana was just having a good time watching the show. Alison had to settle for shaking her finger a couple of feet away from Livia's face. "Number one—you didn't hire me as a bodyguard or a bouncer or a babysitter! If you wanted to police your party then you should have told me that and then I would have very politely told you no because I hate leathergirls!" She was still trying to keep things quiet and the last bit came out in such a horrible whisper that everyone backed away a little. "Number two—I was only there because I was trying to do the job that you hired me to do and I left because I was still trying to do the job you hired me to do." She could make something up later—she followed somebody or something. If she thought quickly enough it could also cover why she hadn't been home when Livia's hired guns had come by. "And number three—I don't know anything about your slave missing, but somebody lifted my leather jacket and it was expensive and if it was your slave then I'm expecting you to pay for it." She glanced quickly down at herself, hoping that she wasn't wearing the leather jacket. Thank goodness—she must have taken it off in the car when it started getting so warm.

"Just what—" started Livia.

Alison broke in. "And for somebody who wanted things to be confidential, you sure aren't choosing a very secure place to talk." She suspected that Livia had just not been able to resist a public scene. She gave a quick glance over her shoulder—sure enough, the gang was all there, just waiting for the high sign. She gave Best Boy a little wave that so horrified her she looked close to fainting. "And if you want to do a public scene, then I charge extra for that and it also voids all confidentiality agreements."

Livia silenced, she turned and glared at Mary Clare. "And did you want to say anything else to me?" Mary Clare glared back but said nothing. She had obviously gotten the runaway slave bit and wasn't about to give fuckbaby up to Livia. Which was what Alison had figured and it had probably been crummy of her to use it to silence Mary Clare, but, oh well.

"Are you ever going to drive that van again?" Oblivious to the glares and bad vibes, G-hey! barged right past Livia and up to Alison, keys in hand.

Alison had never thought she would be so grateful to see G-hey! in her life. She vowed to start being nicer to her and quit being so judgmental. G-hey! was obviously just passing through the kitchen. Alison put a hand out for the keys and held on for dear life. There was a confused moment of faces rushing past her, a door opening and closing and suddenly they were both inside a room off the kitchen that Alison had never seen before, behind a door she had always assumed led to a closet. She looked around in wonder as if she'd just fallen through a rabbit hole. The space was small and two walls were lined with shelves. On one side they seemed to hold mostly toilet paper and light bulbs. The other looked as if it had been used for somebody's junk drawer starting about the first day Tara was finished. There was a small table at the far end and on it sat a computer. A long, orange extension cord snaked beneath the door.

"Where the hell are we?"

"It's the pantry," said G-hey!, who had tossed the keys on the table and was taking down a couple of rolls of toilet paper. "Haven't you been in here before? I guess not. We have to keep it locked because of the boys' computer." She nodded. "I mean, they let us use it for registration, but not until Stacy promised to pretend to be a leather boy and have cyber sex with them. And it's only their spare, anyway. Can you believe that? It's just an extra! It's better than Salad's and it's just their extra! They bought something new last month."

"What?" Alison was dumbfounded. She must have been tuning out more of Stacy's preconference tizzy than she had been aware. "Why are you using this computer?"

"For registration. You know. Salad did most of it on her computer at home. But this one was here and it was easier to bring a disk in than the whole thing. She doesn't have a laptop—she wants one, but she doesn't have one. They're really expensive and…" G-hey! chatted along happily as if she hadn't just pulled Alison from in front of a firing squad and it was totally normal to be locked into a pantry with a computer.

"Do you mean to tell me that the registration list is right there?" Alison asked, pointing at the dark screen.

"What? Oh, yeah, sure. We had to have it here because we were afraid there would be people who'd lost their nametags and they'd try to kick up a big stink and that way we could check. What a bunch of buttheads," G-hey! went on cheerfully. "Salad and I don't think we want to be in the leather scene at all. Mary Clare said that maybe we'd like it, but we've worked our butts off because none of the work exchange people showed up and you should have seen the dungeon last night after everybody left—you'd think people would have the decency to pick up their own condoms. And not just condoms, either! You should have seen the stuff that got left behind!"

"Real names?" Alison interrupted. "Are there real names on the registration list?"

"Oh, sure, we had to have real names so we could check I.D. because we couldn't risk having anyone underage." G-hey! shook her head. "That's so dumb—I'm twenty-one now and last year I was twenty and so what happened on my birthday? I didn't suddenly become wiser or anything like that…"

"G-hey!" said Alison humbly, "could you show me that list?" She was not sure, exactly, what she expected to learn from a list of real names. Maybe nothing. But the fact that half the women at the conference where using aliases had troubled her a great deal. Besides, she knew that Kinsey would want not just to see the list, but a printout as well.

"Oh, sure." G-hey! stopped rummaging and dropped into the chair. "It'll take a minute to boot up." She flipped a switch and then swiveled to face Alison. "How are you feeling this morning?" she asked. "Do you take amiltriptalin?" She turned back to the computer and punched a couple of keys.

"What?" Alison was completely taken aback.

"Well, you've got chronic fatigue syndrome, don't you? Or something like it? Maybe fibromyalgia syndrome? Because of the way you swell up? And they treat that with amiltriptalin, don't they? Because it's a sleep disorder problem?"

"Well, as a matter of fact, yes," Alison admitted, promising the goddess silently that she would not only be nicer to G-hey! and become less judgmental, but work on her age issues too.

"That's a drag," said G-hey! "Stacy should be nicer to you about it than she is."

Alison had already gone there with Erin and didn't want to go there again. "Do you know who this is?" she asked, pulling the photo out of her wallet. It was beginning to look a little dinged up. She needed to put it in a notebook or something, except that she hated carrying anything that she couldn't shove in her pocket. It was a butch thing.

G-hey! took the photo. "Oh, yeah," she said. "I mean, I don't know her name, but I saw her on the web site."

"What?" Alison was lost again.

"On our web site?" G-hey! said, making it a question. "You know, the Wildfire web site, where it told about the conference?"

Alison shook her head. She was not completely computer illiterate—she could make the computers at work do a couple of things if no one else was around to do it for her. But that was it. She had never seen the Wildfire web site, though she knew from conversation between Stacy and Liz that there was one and Salad had put it together. Or whatever you did. Salad had made it happen.

"Okay, so you haven't seen the web site?" G-hey! asked.

Alison shook her head. G-hey! thought for a moment, her brow furrowed as if she were trying to fit a completely alien bit of information into a primitive culture.

"Have you ever been on the internet?" she asked in a cautious voice, as if she were afraid this was going to be offensive.

"Only at the library." Alison did not add that it had been only once and she had to be rescued from a frozen screen by a twelve-year-old who was using the computer next to hers to research the China Silk Road in the 1400s.

G-hey! thought a moment longer and then began in that same cautious tone. "Well, there was a page where we had all the information first."

"Can you show it to me?" asked Alison, pointing to the screen, which now had a list of names and addresses showing. "After you print the registration list for me?"

"No. Not here. Not on this computer. Because it's not hooked up to the net. You have to have a phone line for that." G-hey! looked doubtfully at Alison, as if not quite sure that she would understand this. Alison nodded. "And I can't give you a hard copy of the list, either. Because there's no printer here."

Damn. Okay, so when blocked, maneuver. "So this photo was on the web site?" she asked, still unsure of exactly what this meant. "Did Salad put in there?"

"No." G-hey! shook her head. She had started to root through a cardboard box that was sitting on the floor of the pantry. "Can you believe some of the stuff people left last night?" she asked. "Look, here's a really decent whip." She held it up. It had a handle of braided black and red leather. "And somebody left their purse!" She held up a black and gold beaded clutch. "No, we had a bulletin board that was attached to the web site, so that people could leave messages. So you could ask if someone was coming or you could arrange for a playdate or whatever. Look for a ride. Whatever. And somebody scanned that photo in."

"Just the photo," asked Alison, still trying to picture what G-hey! was describing. "Did it say anything?"

"It did say something—something stupid like 'Danger!' or something like that. I can look again the next time I'm over at Salad's." G-hey! was still rooting around in the lost and found. "I hope nobody claims any of this," she said. "If they don't I'm going to save it and give it to Salad for solstice." She had the black and gold purse in her hand again. "But you'd think that someone would notice her purse was missing. Doesn't Stacy notice if her purse is missing?" she asked Alison. "Do you want to look at this list or do you want me to ask Salad to print it up?

"Mountains move if Stacy has misplaced her purse," Alison replied with feeling. "Is there an I.D. in it?" Stacy had a similar clutch—actually four or five similar clutches—and the one lucky enough to accompany her on a night on the town usually contained keys, mad money, a driver's license and nothing else.

G-hey! popped the clasp. "Bingo!" she said. She pulled out a driver's license and read, "Kathy Corbeit. Oh, I know her! She lives in the apartment next door!" She looked up at Alison to see if the name had rung a bell. It hadn't, so she handed the license across. Bad News' face smiled up at her from a better-than-average I.D. photo. She looked as if she weighed about thirty pounds more than she actually did, but at least she didn't appeared to have her face plastered against a window with her nose turned up like a piggy's, the way Alison did in her driver's license photo.

"Oh, god, I almost forgot! How could I! Did you hear what happened?" G-hey! spun around to face Alison. Her voice was horrified, but Alison was focused on the clutch. Money all right, but no keys. A folded up paper on which it looked as if she had been writing a letter. Alison refolded it without reading. She might have read it if G-hey! hadn't been there, but G-hey! was giving her a look.

"Did all this stuff come from the dungeon?" Alison now remembered that Bad News had had the clutch at Fantasy Night. She couldn't imagine that Bad News had gone from Livia's party to the dungeon—she had looked dreadful. She tried to remember if she had been carrying her clutch when Crescent had helped her from the room at Livia's.

"I don't think that it all did," G-hey! replied. "I think some of it came from the workshop rooms and stuff like that. Even from private parties. I think I saw one of those creepy Portland women bring that in this morning."

One of Livia's. Alison had a bad feeling about that.

"But listen to this! This is so bad! Somebody was hit by the light rail last night!"

"Yeah," said Alison, still not looking up. She didn't say 'so what' out loud, but So what? It happened all the time.

G-hey! read the unspoken so what. "No, I mean, not just somebody. One of us! A woman from the conference!"

"What?" Alison froze for a moment, the clutch still in her hand. "What!? Who—how did…?" She faltered, feeling as if she'd been hit in the face with a bucket of cold water.

G-hey!, luckily, did not need prompting. "Flame told Salad this morning. She practically saw it happen. She was on her bike and there was an ambulance and the whole thing and she stopped to look and when she saw the woman she was one of the out-of-townies." There was a note of honest horror in her voice.

If it had been anyone else in the world, Alison would have asked what she had been doing out at three in the morning—and on her bike no less. Being Flame, she said nothing. Flame was well known for wandering all over town in the wee hours of the morning on her bike and the area by the Melbourne was where it was rumored she lived.

"Who was it?" Alison asked, putting down the clutch altogether. "Did Flame know? Do you know? Does Stacy know?"

"Yeah, Flame did know," said G-hey! "I mean, she'd seen the woman who was killed and when Flame described her then I knew. She was the one trying to hit on Salad when Liz kind of pulled me off and warned me. Except that she told me her name and now I can't remember it." She tapped herself rapidly in the middle of the forehead with her index finger like it was going to shake something loose. "This is such a bummer. I'm totally blanking. Okay, she was the woman who's been playing with my neighbor." She pointed at Bad News' clutch, which confused Alison for a moment. "So, do you know who the dead woman is? The only reason I really noticed her was because she was playing with Kathy. Kathy's kind of fucked up. She was in that book that came out a couple of years ago on gay youth? And they made it sound like she was so together because she was this musician and came from this really troubled background but she'd risen above it. But she's fucked up. I think the editors were going for a class mix, so they hooked onto her even though she's got a lot of problems. The article didn't say anything about her problems."

Alison was silent, trying to pull from the jumbled bits of information G-hey! had just given her the name of the woman Flame had seen hit by the light rail. "The woman who was killed was a musician?" she asked cautiously.

"No! My neighbor, Kathy, is a musician! It was the other woman, an out-of-townie!" Alison was still drawing a blank, so G-hey! elaborated. "Thin hair," she said, sketching in the air above her own head, which at this moment was sporting a kind of purple double mohawk. "Nobody likes her." She made her hands into little puppets with snipping mouths, talking behind the woman's back.

"Scar?" Alison asked, barely moving her lips. Oh, god, and she'd seen her drunk. Scar had begged her to take her home and she'd blown her off and walked away, even though it had been obvious she was three sheets to the wind.

"Oh, yeah, that's it! And you know what? I'll bet she was staying at the Melbourne Youth Hostel. You know, it's that really cheesy motel that's just up the street there from the Merc? It's right by the light rail and some of the women who couldn't afford the conference hotel booked rooms there and then they were all pissy at us because it's so sleazy. Like that was our fault! We didn't recommend it! They could have asked for community housing and we would have placed them." She shook her head and then looked at her watch. "I've got to go. Do you want me to get a hard copy of this?"

"Yeah. Thanks." Alison could hardly answer. Alison felt almost faint with horror. My god, what had she done? What had Scar done? Had she decided to walk from the conference hotel to the Melbourne? She could have easily.

It was a reasonable distance. If you were sober. But hadn't Scar said she was staying with her playdate because she couldn't afford a hotel and no one was willing to put her in community housing?

"Well, Kathy's sure going to freak out," said G-hey! She clicked the mouse and pressed a couple of keys. "Too bad! It looked like she was getting close to her—to Scar, I mean. Kathy didn't have a lot of close friends—not from what I've seen. She was kind of fucked up, like I said. I never see her bringing anybody home much. A couple of times. Women who are older. Butches. Tops. I guess I should take her purse to her, huh? And tell her what happened. That would be the right thing to do, wouldn't it?" She sounded quite resigned—willing to do the right thing but not prepared to like it.

"Let me do that," offered Alison. Somewhere, around the great cloud of guilt, new thoughts were pushing in. She needed to make sure Bad News-Kathy was all right. Scar had told her over and over that she had something to tell, something that was getting worse and freaking her out. Something the police should be involved in. Could it have been, for all her posturing and play-acting, that Scar actually had known something? Something Alison had the feeling might involve Kathy? She thought back to Liz's comment in the Merc. Just because Scar was compulsive liar doesn't mean she didn't tell the truth now and then.

"Great!" said G-hey! "Hey, and you know what? I really reamed out Salad for telling that woman you were a cop. Sometimes she acts like she doesn't even know what confidentiality is."

There was a quick tap on the door and Stacy stepped inside. It was getting pretty crowded. It was a good-sized little room for a pantry, but it had not been intended for a three-way. "Dana thought you were in here," she said to Alison. It was obvious to Alison's trained eye that she had retreated somewhere and completely redone her make-up. "I have to tell you something. I mean, we need to sit down and talk a lot, but there's some kind of crisis with the catering and I have to deal with it. But I have to tell you something right now." She looked at G-hey! who was sitting with her arms crossed, a pleased smile on her face, totally oblivious to the fact that Stacy was attempting to bad vibe her out of the room.

"Alone," Stacy finally said pointedly. Even that took a minute to sink in.

"Oh!" said G-hey! "Okay! I've got to go anyway!" She squeezed past Stacy, taking her daypack and three rolls of toilet paper with her.

"I'm so sorry—" Alison began.

Stacy stopped her with a hand. "It's okay," she said. "We need to talk, but it's going to be okay. But I need to tell you this right now, before she leaves."

"Before who—"

"This woman," said Stacy, pointing to the photograph that was still sitting beside the keyboard. "I know who that is. That's the woman I hit with the ice cream bar."

Chapter Thirteen

"What?" Alison was starting to feel like she'd been a day late and a dollar short all weekend. "What are you talking about? She doesn't look anything at all like this woman." Even at the height of surprise she was able to keep herself from referring to Erin by her first name. It was just better that way. Privately she wondered if Stacy wasn't just trying to create a situation in which she had been justified in smacking Erin alongside the head. Making her into a killer would certainly do it.

"Yes! Yes! Look at her! Not what she's wearing or how much she weighs. Different clothes, different orientation, different weight, different hair, but same eyes, same mouth, same tattoo as in your picture! She's got a dragon claw tattoo on her right shoulder, Alison! I saw it when we were in the bathroom together!"

"You were in the bathroom together?" Alison asked, raising an eyebrow.

"Well, what did you think, that we were going to get into a big old cat fight and claw each other to death?"

Actually, that was exactly what Alison had been thinking, but again prudence won out and she just said, "Oh."

"Well, I had to apologize, didn't I?" Stacy demanded. "And I had to tell her what a big butthead you'd been so that she understood why I'd done that and didn't think I was just some crazy person like the Pattys." She looked at Alison's face and added, "I'm sorry, honey. It's a femme thing. We have a hard time admitting we're wrong—we're much better at understanding and being forgiving. So we were in the bathroom because I looked like a clown and she had chocolate on her face. And in her hair. Everywhere." Stacy paused for a moment with a little smile on her face. Perhaps she had apologized and even admitted she was wrong, but that did not mean she did not savor that moment of first contact. She came back to herself with a little start when Alison cleared her throat. "Oh! And on her shirt. So you know how chocolate sets in your clothes and you never get it out…"

Alison did not know. She had very poor laundry habits, the cornerstone of which was immediately consigning anything on which she dripped food or oil to the second-hand pile. If it didn't come out in a regular wash cycle, then it was stained for life.

"…so we were trying to rinse it and it was all over the back so I pulled it up…"

"Okay, okay." It had been a mistake to question Stacy's conviction—this was the kind of thing at which she excelled. "So why would she be here all femmed out?"

Stacy gave her a big, old 'duh' look, which she deserved. Who was going to want to play with a killer and what better disguise than femme drag? "She's here now, but she might not be for long. She might decide to go back to the hotel and change. I think she's just waiting for the shuttle."

"Well, that would be me," said Alison, looking at the keys in her hand.

"Then go for it, Tiger!" Obviously a part of Stacy's femme forgiveness was attempting to be supportive. Alison had the feeling a high five might be just around the corner.

"I have something I need to tell you, though," Alison said as Stacy opened the door to the kitchen. "And you're not going to like it." Sometimes it was just better to preface bad news with a blanket warning. "Scar was killed last night."

"What!" Stacy's head almost flew off and hit the ceiling. Now it was her turn to say, "What are you talking about?! I saw her last night!" She gripped Alison's wrist tightly. One wrong move here and they were going to be talking compound fracture. "You promised me, Alison! You promised me no dead bodies!"

"Don't be ridiculous!" Alison interrupted. "This had nothing to do with me! She was killed in an accident—she walked in front of the light rail! I wasn't even there!" Stacy wasn't keeping her voice down, so Alison didn't bother with hers, either. Everybody was going to know about Scar within about the next fifteen minutes anyway.

"Oh, of course it had to do with you! It always has to do with you when someone is killed! You're always there or you're the one who finds the body or the family wants you to look into things or you knew her twenty years ago! It always has to do with you!" Stacy was shaking with emotion. Alison suspected this was more a result of the stress she had created for herself the past three weeks than feeling for Scar. Still, it was always a shock when someone you were acquainted with was killed suddenly. As a cop, the most common reaction she had seen to sudden death was of the But I Was Just Talking to Him variety.

"Hello! It has to do with me because I'm a cop and my friends keep sending crazy people my way! What do you think—I'm some kind of death magnet? The first death I was ever involved in was because—" At the last minute she choked back her words. The first murder in which she was involved had to do with Stacy and that was a demon Stacy must exorcise herself. In the same way that Jean-Luc Picard did not need to be reminded that his capture by the Borg had resulted in the destruction of thirteen Federation ships, so Stacy did not need to be reminded of her slain clients. "She walked in front of the light rail," she repeated. "I had nothing to do with it. No one had anything to do with it. She was shit-faced drunk."

"Oh, Alison!" Stacy's hand flew up to her cheek and her eyes grew round with apprehension. "Do you think this is going to be a police thing? Oh, shit! Do you think they're going to trace her back here? Oh, shit! We're going to be on the fucking six o'clock news, aren't we? Do you think that's what's going to happen? 'Cause if it is, maybe I ought to make an announcement. There might be some women who'll want to get the hell out of Dodge."

Alison had thought of this too. "I don't think so," she said carefully. "I think it would be jumping the gun. Accidents aren't quite like murders and she was drunk. What they're probably doing now is going through her wallet and trying to make a connection with her family. Maybe waiting to see if anyone will come forward. But it was only an accident—nobody's thrown up any crime scene tapes. I don't think. You could ask Flame. She was the one who was there."

Around them the leatherwomen ebbed and flowed, going to workshops or playdates, picking at the food or heading outside for a smoke or a little meditation in the sun. Nobody was paying much attention to them. They had all been jaded by the Pattys. If you weren't exchanging blows then it wasn't worth paying attention.

"Oh, shit!" said Stacy again. "I knew I should have thrown out that woman's registration when I got it! But, oh, no, I had to be all collective and ask what everybody thought and then they had to be all open and liberal and say they didn't think that would be fair. I should have just thrown it out! I knew she was going to do something like this!"

Alison gave her a look. She did not like to hear the love of her life going on like an ugly American.

"Oh, don't even give me that look," Stacy snapped. "Scar has never had an accident in her whole life. Everything's planned! I wouldn't be surprised to hear she walked in front of that light rail on purpose just to get one more shot at being center of attention! In fact, I wouldn't be surprised if there was foul play! God, she'd love that! What a way to go! Story in the newspaper and on TV and everybody at the conference fucked! Oh, god, she wasn't staying at the Melbourne, was she? That's going to be the first place the cops are going to look—it's right on that corner and I'll bet she has all of her conference information in her room! Oh, we are so fucked! I gotta go find Liz."

"I don't think it's that bad," Alison soothed. She thought back over all the little bits and pieces of information Scar had fed her, bit by bit. "I don't think she was staying at a hotel. I think maybe she was staying with Kathy Corbeit. And I haven't seen Corbeit today, so maybe she doesn't know what happened. Maybe she thinks she was just stood up."

Stacy didn't know who Kathy Corbeit was by name so they had to spend a couple of minutes on that. Alison finally remembered the clutch and pulled the driver's license out again.

"Oh!" said Stacy, looking at the photo. "So maybe we're not screwed after all. Is that what you're saying?"

"Actually," Alison replied in a rather rueful tone, "I'm battling with my conscience. We should call the police ourselves."

"Oh, Alison, let it go for once! What does it matter if they know who she is today or tomorrow after everyone's gone home? It's not like a crime scene, like they've got to get in on the first twenty-four hours!" Stacy liked cop shows as well as *Star Trek*. "Give Kathy a chance to do it herself—if you go in she's going to be even more fucked than the rest of us. Let her wait and then tell them Scar was a pickup. Or better yet..." she choked this one back, but it didn't take a Betazoid to predict. "Better yet, don't tell them at all. Let Kathy throw her stuff in the alley and if it ever, ever came up let her tell the cops Scar had just been a pickup and she had never connected her disappearance to the article in the newspaper."

"I sometimes question your morals," Alison said to Stacy.

"And I sometimes wonder how it is that you've been able to survive in the real world," Stacy shot back. "Are you looking forward to being on the evening news? The Denver PD is going to love that!—and I didn't even think that was kinky! Boy, they're going to love us!"

Alison had thought of all this with much the same conclusions, so she said nothing.

"And speaking of getting fucked," said Stacy, "you should go and talk with Ms. Tres Femme before she disappears." This was a double whammy as a distraction—it both set Alison's guilty conscience all aquiver and reminded her of the task at hand. A task that, unlike Scar's accident, was very much her business.

Beth walked up, speaking on a cell phone. "Uh huh," she was saying, "uh-huh, uh-huh." She put her hand over the receiver and said to Stacy, "It's the caterers. They're trying to fuck us."

"Well, tell them to get in line," Stacy replied. She took a deep breath and squared her shoulders. Suddenly she was Barbara Stanwyck and they were going to run sheep into the Big Valley only over her dead body. Alison knew she was on her own. Finding out who was blackmailing Livia was one thing—no food tonight was in a whole other and much more important class.

"Let me talk to them," Stacy said to Beth. A vile aura was starting to seep out of her mouth and Alison thought she could smell brimstone. Stacy took the phone but held it to her chest a moment as she looked around the room. Over near the sink Liz was deep in conversation with a large femme.

"Here," Stacy said, reaching over and plucking Liz away from her tete-a-tete by her collar. "Take her with you. Keep her out of trouble," she said to Liz. "Be a lawyer."

Liz was irritated at being plucked from her negotiation and Alison was irritated Stacy thought she needed help keeping out of trouble, but since either one was better than watching Stacy summon the devil and push him through the phone wires they both agreed, with a bit of eye contact and a little nod, to just let it shine. "You know, I was just about to come on to that woman," Liz could not help grumbling a bit to Alison. It was like bitching in the army—it was the only privilege you had.

"Liz," said Alison, ushering her out the door, "you have been about to come on to someone for the whole entire weekend. And, besides, that woman is three times your size. She'd kill you if she rolled over."

"You know," said Liz back, "you really have some issues about size. First you were trying to bully Mary Clare because she's smaller than you. How do you think that makes me feel? I'm smaller than you, too. Am I supposed to roll over every time you say woof or am I just supposed to feel bad about my size? And now this. What is your problem?"

"I don't have size issues, I have age issues," replied Alison sullenly, as if the one automatically canceled the other.

"Either way, you've been watching too many Calvin Klein ads and I like fat girls. And I have no idea what we're doing out here or how I'm supposed to be keeping you out of trouble."

"Want to guess?" asked Alison, steering her over toward the foyer, where Erin was sitting on a bench. From the corner of her eye she could see Stacy's big butch friend approaching in a predatory manner, so she double-timed them. "Here's a clue—nobody will like it and everybody will be unhappy when it's over!" They cut the big butch gal off with a couple feet to spare, though it meant Alison had to plop down in a manner she suspected was unattractive.

"You certainly have all the pretty women sewed up this weekend," said the butch gal, which Alison thought was a rather sporting thing to say.

"I'm going to keep the other one," she told her, "but I'm going to throw this one back. Come by again in a half an hour."

"Half an hour?" said Erin with a lifted eyebrow. "I thought you said you weren't free. What, your girlfriend cut the leash and sent you out here with a little help in case you couldn't take me down yourself? This isn't a three-way thing, is it? Because there is no way I am going into a scene with that woman." She pointed back toward the house and Stacy inside. "I'm sure she's very hot but it would just turn into a battle of the tops and you'd probably be cut to ribbons in the commotion."

"Better," said Alison, who had decided the only way to play through this one was as kind of a smart-ass. She whipped the photo out of her pocket once again. "Still don't remember?" she asked. "Looking for her because she done my girlfriend wrong and I want to kick her butt?"

"Dammit!" said Erin, throwing her cigarette down and crushing it with far more force than necessary. "It was the tattoo, wasn't it? I knew she'd seen that damn tattoo." She looked at Alison with a little smile on her face. "You wouldn't have made me otherwise, would you? The girlfriend is pretty sharp."

"She is that," said Alison wryly. "And no, I never would have made you otherwise." Liz, in fact, was still looking from the photo to the woman with a puzzled expression.

"What?" she asked.

Alison held the photo up beside Erin's face. "Look," she said to Liz, "Dr. Erin and Mr. Falcon. Two sides of the same tarnished penny."

"What?" asked Liz again.

"We don't need a lawyer yet," said Alison. "I'll clue you." She looked at Erin, who had settled back down on the bench with another cigarette. She didn't look upset or nervous. In fact, she looked quite pleased with herself. "So, Livia hired me to find out who was blackmailing her," Alison said. "And that would be you, I assume?"

"Nope," said Erin. "When you blackmail someone you ask for something. I didn't ask for a thing. All I was doing was twisting that horrible woman's tail and she fell for it because she's so paranoid. You want to tell her? I'll tell her myself. I'll tell her at the banquet tonight, because I want to make sure there's a big audience. Maybe I'll go on national TV and tell her—I'll call Jerry Springer—I'll bet he'd be interested."

In spite of herself, Alison was curious. She had thought she would confront Erin/Falcon and then drive over to Livia's and collect her thousand dollars. Erin could do what she wanted—she could leave the conference or brazen it out and what-the-hell-ever. But now she found herself reluctant to just walk away.

"What the hell did she do to you?" Alison asked.

"Oh!" said Liz suddenly, making the connection a few beats behind.

"Okay," said Erin, drawing in a breath so deep that it changed the pattern of the smoke hanging above her. "Tell me what you've heard about Falcon."

"Well…I…nothing really," Alison blustered. She could feel herself flushing and was glad she was wearing her sunglasses.

"Don't lie to me, okay?" Erin put one hand down on the bench in a gesture that was not quite a slap, but just as authoritative. Her rings made a little clanking sound. "If you want me to be straight with you, then, goddammit, don't you lie to me."

"Okay," said Alison in a chagrined voice. That was fair, that was reasonable. She was ashamed that she had tried to evade Erin's questions. But it was hard to repeat the words Ramona had said to Erin's face. "I heard that you killed someone in a scene." She bit her lower lip, hoping that Erin would let out a small shriek of anger and say, 'That's a fucking lie!'

What she did instead was turn her head to the side and light another cigarette. She smoked it half way down before she spoke. "Okay," she said finally. "Do you want to hear what really happened?"

Alison nodded. Liz, who was still a half step behind, just looked at her.

"It was at Michigan," Erin said slowly, as if this were a story she had not told often. "Have you ever been there?"

Alison nodded. The big women's festival was almost a coming-of-age ritual—all of her friends had been there at least once and she herself had been four or five times.

"Camped with the leathergirls?"

"Once, but it rained a lot and I got the flu. I didn't get out a lot."

Erin put down her cigarette and played with her drink. "It was the year they had the big s/m wars. Have you heard anything about that?"

"A little."

"Well. It was the pits. There was a group of women there who had come with the agenda of driving the s/m dykes off the land, or at least underground. They harassed us constantly. They had brought thousands of anti-s/m leaflets—they were everywhere. They tried to break up our workshops. They came to the dungeons—they thought if they were there singing and blessing us then everyone would be too ashamed to play in front of them."

"They didn't know this bunch," Alison guessed.

Erin cracked a very small smile. "You're right," she agreed. "They didn't know this bunch. All it did was make everybody mad. Make everybody more determined they were going to do exactly what they wanted to do. Made women who were usually pretty private get right up in everybody's face." She paused and took a small sip from a Diet Coke that was sitting on the bench beside her. "Then they got the festival girls in on it. We were running really tight security. We were using a workshop tent—you know, one of those big circus tents that you can close off completely—for dungeons, and we had security people on all the roads, you know, telling anybody who was likely to wander in what was going on, take a different route if it upsets you, so nobody could be unpleasantly surprised. I worked a security shift myself—there was no way anyone could have walked in on us by chance." She paused again, and then said in an angry voice, "I mean—what do those women think? That it's a turn-on to do a scene in front of someone who is repulsed by you? Please." She made a negating gesture with her right hand, and then grabbed up her cigarette and sucked down two angry puffs.

"So." Her voice was calmer. "They made up this story. They went to the Womb—you know, the healing tent. One of them pretended to be hysterical. Her friends told the women there she had just been walking by herself, taking in the night air, and she had accidentally strolled into the middle of this really violent scene, and now she was freaking out. Couldn't have happened, no one could have stumbled in accidentally! But they managed to convince the women in the Womb, and they got on the horn to the security people, and before we knew it, the festival was trying to shut us down. It was a nightmare."

It was an interesting bit of history, but Alison was beginning to wonder what exactly it had to do with Livia. As if she had read her mind, Erin began to speak again. "If you haven't camped with the s/m dykes, you don't know what it's like. It's a constant battle of the tops. You know—that whole I can top you and everybody else shit. Livia," she gestured out toward Tara, "had pretty much held the title for as long as I'd been going. Money," she said, rubbing her fingers together as if over a sheaf of bills. "The girl had money to burn. She would rent a suite at a motel before the festival—if you were invited to the party, you were part of the in crowd—if you weren't..." she flipped her wrist as if she were throwing out a piece of trash. "She had all the best camping equipment—all the stuff the rest of us look at in the REI catalog and want but can't afford. Lanterns, coolers, fold up carts to pack your stuff in. For Michigan only—she isn't an outdoorsy kind of gal. She went on a big shopping spree before the festival—brought in beer and cookies and steak and all the things you don't get in the food line and let anybody who camped with her eat out of it. Arranged the workshops. Ran the last night auction, and controlled the fuck-bucks—you could only get them through her. The whole s/m camp was her scene, and she topped it big time."

"Were you invited to the party?" Alison asked.

"Yeah," answered Erin shortly. "Yeah, I was part of the hip crowd that year." She was silent again, lighting another cigarette. "So we were all pretty stressed out," she went on. "We were hassling with the festival crowd—they were telling us we couldn't use the tents at night, telling us that if we didn't shut it down right now they were going to eighty-six us. Of course, they were upset, too—they had these other girls chewing on their tails, convincing them we were performing Satanic rituals and eating our own dead, and they knew damn well that shutting us down was going to take the police, and nobody wanted that. The dungeons were liked armed camps—Livia was really in her element—she had brought walkie talkies and I don't know what all—she likes high tech. Infrared goggles and flame throwers for all I know. She was really getting off on the whole trauma-drama, but she was stressed out, too." Erin took a couple of long hits of her cigarette. "So the last day, the festival staff dropped all the workshop tents."

Alison was not able to keep from grinning, and Erin caught it. "Yeah," she said, "pretty good non-aggressive confrontation. So we picked a new place to party—out by the Twilight Zone and the parking lot. All the party girls camp in the Twilight Zone and they don't care what other people do. Everybody was really high—I don't mean drugs, not that. But it was the last night of the festival, and we had been bucking the SEPS all week long—most of the dungeons were more like protests than parties—and we were ready to party. A lot of leatherwomen from small towns—Michigan is the only place they play all year." She pushed her hair back from her face, remembering something she didn't want to remember.

"There was an auction," she said finally. "Services and goods. Everything, tons of variety. Femmes selling their stockings and a chance to take them off. Women who wanted to be spanked, or fisted or caned or anything you can think of."

"Like the one they were going to have here that first night," said Alison.

"Yeah, except that for this one you didn't use real money. Livia had printed stacks of phony money—fuck-bucks—that she and her crowd handed out. More power—you had to be close to her, hang out in her campground to get any money."

"Were you giving it out?" asked Alison.

"Yeah."

"For what?"

"Oh, different shit. Livia wasn't much of a camper—she'd pay for other women to clean up the place, or put up her tent, that kind of stuff. I went for cute accents, outfits I liked, women who had come to the workshops for the first time. It doesn't really matter. What mattered was that there was an auction, and I offered a flogging.

"It went for a fairly high price. I have—or, rather, Falcon had—a very good reputation. There were several women who were bidding. Finally, though, this whole group of women from Kansas pooled their money and bought me for a friend. It was her birthday, and that was what she wanted." She sighed deeply and rolled her head back on her neck so that when she continued she was speaking to the roof of the gazebo.

"You have to understand, it was quite late at night by this time. There had been a very theatrical opening scene that had gone on for-fucking-ever, and there had been a lot of services for bid." She sighed again. "It would have been a lot better if everyone had just gone home and slept and collected the next night. But there wasn't a next night. It was the last night—everybody was pulling out the next day. And this woman was going back to Kansas. This was going to have to last her six months or so. She told me that. We chatted a little before we got started. Of course! I wasn't a novice—I asked her about health problems, about what she liked—I didn't want to hurt her!" She paused. "Well, I did want to hurt her. But I didn't want to harm her."

"So did you…" Alison started and then trailed off. How could she ask, did you beat this woman to death? Besides the ugliness of it all, it sounded more and more unlikely given the rest of the story. If Erin had been the kind of woman given to using excessive violence, would she have had a good reputation as a top? Would she have taken the time to ask about the other woman's health issues?

"What was her name?" she asked, instead, unconsciously using the past tense. The story was far from over, but she could already tell that it did not end well.

"Judy," answered Erin. "Judy Di Nardi. Like I could ever forget it. I must have heard that name a thousand times, even though I only spent an hour with the woman."

"What happened?" urged Alison.

"What happened was that right in the middle of this very intense flogging scene, Livia decided it was time to pack up and go. And she did. And she took all the light with her."

"What?" asked Alison incredulously.

Erin spread her hands. "She wanted to go back to camp. Who could blame her? It was late, she was tired, she was stressed out. But we had all walked over together. We'd brought several lanterns—her lanterns. I'd carried one in—it hadn't even occurred to me to bring a flashlight. And when Livia left, she took all the lanterns with her."

"Why didn't she just leave one and let you bring it back?"

Again Erin rubbed her thumb against the tips of her first two fingers. "Power," she said. "Livia likes to top the whole scene—she did not like it if anybody played outside her boundaries. She wanted to call the shots—where the parties were, when they started, when they ended. She was like the little kid who'll only play if you use his ball and bat, and the game is over when he wants to go home. She was over it, we should be done. She was ticked off, too—she'd offered some kind of humiliation scene and nobody had bid on it."

She sighed deeply again. "But we weren't done. Or rather, Judy wasn't done. I was tired, I was sorry that I'd offered a service, I would have been glad to have said, Sorry, how about a rain check. But Judy was not done at all. She had been looking forward to this for a year. She was totally hyped up, and of course I couldn't finish in the dark.

"So she started to cry. Not just sniffling, hysterically. All that emotion that was going to come out in the scene—there was nowhere for it to go but into crying. So I'm thinking, great, now I've got to go into this nurturing role with someone I don't even know, this sure wasn't what I signed up for. So I'm trying to release her—she was in standing bondage—in the dark, and she starts to choke."

"You didn't have anything around her neck, did you?" Alison gasped.

"Of course not! She was choking herself. The fucking fool—she had told me she had a bad back, be careful of it, had told me all kinds of stupid ass details that didn't matter, but she didn't tell me she had asthma! She's crying like she can't stop, and then she starts gasping and choking and I don't know what to do!"

"Was there anybody else there?" asked Alison.

"Yeah. Judy's friends. You remember them—the ones who bought her the birthday present. Some present that turned out to be! But a couple of them were still there, and one of them knew what was happening. Judy had an inhaler—this woman was shouting at me, trying to calm Judy down, trying to find the damn inhaler. But it was pitch black, Alison, and none of us had a light. It wasn't just that we had come in with the lantern—there was a full moon, you hadn't needed a light for the past couple of nights. But it had clouded over—you know how it gets there."

Alison nodded. She had suffered Michigan downpours at more than one festival, had awakened damp and slogged through days in wet clothes that would not dry in the after-rain humidity. When it rained in Michigan, it really rained.

"We're all freaking. Can't see a thing. And then it starts to rain." She threw up her hands. "It would have been funny if it had been a comedy. What do they call that, when one thing after another goes wrong?"

"A comedy of errors," said Alison quietly.

"Yeah—it would have been another story. You know, like the time you set your props on fire, or split your good leather pants right down the back in the middle of a scene. But it wasn't funny, because she died. She died, Alison."

They all three were silent for several moments.

"Did you try to get any help?" Alison asked finally, even while cursing the cop's mind, the way of thinking that always sought details before offering comfort.

"Not from the festival," said Erin, shaking her head. "We were out in the sticks—we were as far away from the main camp as you can possibly get. We went back under the fence and into the parking lot. We threw her into my car—by that time the lightning had started, so we could see that much. It was like a strobe light," she said in a voice that was almost dreamy. "You ever dance in a strobe?"

"Yeah, I grew up in the seventies, too," said Alison dryly.

"It's so unreal. That was the only way I could deal with it—pretend it was a dream. An important dream, a dream where I knew it was important to do my very best, to take charge and handle things the right way. But just a dream."

Alison said nothing. She knew all about slipping into that state where you were operating from behind a sheet of glass, remote from anything that might get in the way of efficiency. Every cop did. Or, every cop who stayed on the force long did, because the ones who didn't, who got too caught up, who wept over the daily tragedies they were forced to witness while at the scene did not last. Unless you wanted to turn in your badge the first year, you learned to weep at home, after your shift. And then, gradually, you learned not to weep at all.

"You had your car keys with you?" was what she finally asked.

Erin started, as if from a sleep. "No," she answered. "They were in the ignition. I lost them one year—I thought that was the safest place for them. I figured no one was going to steal my car at Michigan."

"Didn't you have to pass through the gate? Those women had radio contact, didn't they?"

"Judy didn't need first aid, Alison. She needed to be in a hospital. It probably took us less time to get into town than it would have taken to get a doctor from main camp to the gates on those roads. I knew where the hospital was—I had gone there myself the year they had shigella. I still think it was the best choice. But the rain was pouring down—we had a hard time just staying on the road. It wasn't quick enough. She died anyway."

There was another long silence. Alison broke it with a question. "Why have you been blamed?" she asked. "I mean, it looks to me like an accident. You surely weren't charged with murder, were you?"

"No," replied Erin. "I wasn't charged with murder. But I was charged with assault. The woman had marks from the flogging on her. She wasn't in any shape to tell them it was consensual. It might not have made a difference anyway—in a lot of states it doesn't."

"Did you get a lawyer?" asked Alison. "Did you…"

"Alison, I ate it. What else could I do? The more fuss on my part, the more chance that the festival or the other s/m dykes were going to be dragged into it. I didn't want that to happen. I behaved in the way I thought was the most honorable—I took the rap, I did not implicate anybody in any way, I did the time. Not a lot of time—if I had really killed Judy I would have been sadly under-punished. But I didn't kill her, and I didn't assault her. I kept quiet to protect everyone else. The women who were there, her friends—one of them was a school teacher. The other one was a small town lawyer—it would have ruined either of them if they'd had to testify on my behalf. And Livia," she gave a bitter laugh, "even at that point I knew Livia wouldn't stand up for me. I knew how she operated—she wouldn't take any of the blame, that's for sure. As far as she was concerned, I had brought the whole thing on myself by playing past her bedtime. Besides, she had a vulnerable job as well—she was always very paranoid about being outed."

"So how…? Alison opened her hands to indicate the whole situation, the rumors, the warning on the Internet. How had that happened if Erin had really behaved with the honor she described?

"Livia." Another short, bitter laugh. "She wanted to make darn good and sure that she wasn't blamed in any way. I was arrested at the hospital—the only reason my stuff didn't just rot in the rain at the festival was because the Kansas girls went back and broke camp for me. They were the ones who posted bail too. They had been there—they had seen me try to save their friend. By the time I got out of jail, Livia had passed around her own version of the story, and believe me, it did not include her pulling the light in the middle of a heavy beating scene."

Alison thought back to the story Ramona had told her—choking, unsafe bondage, playing without a safeword.

"Yeah," she said. "I think I've heard it."

Erin snorted. "I'll bet you have. With all the trimmings. So you see why Falcon had to die. She was a leper."

"What about the Kansas girls?" asked Alison. "They were there, they saw what really happened."

"The Kansas girls are in Kansas," said Erin simply. "They're great if you want to go to Kansas. But the rest of us are right here. That's who Livia networks with—the big town girls. And she put out the word on Falcon. There were probably some people who didn't believe it but nobody wanted to tangle with her. Not Miss Moneybags, not Miss I'm-the-Only-Game-in-Town."

"Come on," protested Alison. "I've seen these women—I can't believe that all of them are just going to follow Livia. I mean, they're just not the conventional type."

Erin held up a hand. "In certain areas. Yeah, you're right, some of them wear their full leather to work and have no qualms about doing a scene in the parking lot at Seven-Eleven. But this is different. The word is that I killed a woman, Alison! I only top—would you want to bottom for me if you'd heard that story?"

"Hell, it would attract some women," Alison joked weakly. Weakly, because of course she wouldn't bottom for anyone with that rep. She wasn't even sure she would bottom for Erin at this point, when she was fairly sure she was telling the truth and had been blameless in the death. That was the point of scandal, she supposed—it tainted you even if you were innocent.

"Crazies," said Erin. "Women to stay away from. I don't want to be part of anybody's death scene."

Liz spoke for the first time. "There really isn't a reason for me to be here, is there? That was just Stacy being Stacy, wasn't it?"

"It was Stacy being Stacy," Alison told her.

Liz looked around the yard, which at this point seemed full of couples. She sighed and stayed where she was. "Okay," she said. "So you've told us why you hated this woman. Hell, I hate her now, too."

"Yeah," said Erin. "And it wasn't an isolated incident at all. It's no good having power unless you use it, you know. Livia was well-known for dicking women around. Nothing this bad, of course, but she acted a lot like the popular girl in the big clique in junior high. Let's be best friends today, but tomorrow I'm not going to speak to you, and none of my friends are going to speak to you, and I'm not going to tell you why. She likes to surround herself with women who don't have a lot of money—you know, women who might not be able to come to this kind of event if she didn't put them up and pay for their food. You get a lot of devotion if you're what's standing between someone and the street."

"Yeah," said Liz. "So you decided you'd get back at her by threatening to out her at work? I gotta say, that's not pretty. I mean, you threatening to tell about something you are yourself?"

"Have you ever been in prison?" Erin asked.

Both Liz and Alison looked so horrified that a no was not even necessary.

"Okay, then. It's dreadful. I mean, I know it's supposed to be dreadful. That's the whole point of it. But I think people forget that. You tell other dykes that you spent time in jail, and the whole reaction is 'Ho, ho, ho, lock me up with a bunch of other women, that's really going to punish me.' But it's not like that at all. I'm thirty-seven years old. I've lived by myself for ten years. I'm an insomniac. I'm a vegetarian. It wasn't like what you see on TV—nobody tried to rape me with a coke bottle or beat me up or buy me with cigarettes. It wasn't that. It was being shoved right into the middle of a very communal style of living with a community that was not my choice. It was trying to sleep in a room with six other women snoring and talking in their sleep. I was exhausted all the time—I never slept more than four hours a night. It was trying to eat what they called vegetarian meals—which mainly meant a whole plate full of iceberg lettuce. I lost fifty pounds while I was locked up. It was spending whole days, whole fucking days, doing nothing but playing cards. It was having everything, every little nuance of your day, controlled. What you ate, when you ate it, who you sat next to when you ate it. What you read. When you could use the phone. Do you know that they take people on tours of the prison? You're sitting there doing nothing, because there is nothing to do, and you look up, and there are people looking at you through the bars as if you were on exhibit at the zoo."

"Jail sucks," agreed Liz.

"Oh, yeah," said Erin. "And that's not even counting trying to deal with what's happening to your life on the outside. Trying to find someone to sublet your house, so you don't lose it while you're not working, and hoping they don't rip you off because, after all, you only interviewed them over the phone. Arranging to have your mail picked up because you just don't have it in you to explain to your seventy-year-old mother why you are in jail. Hoping your friends don't get tired of taking care of your old dog, that they remember to give him his medicine. Waiting for hours for the one pay phone to be free so you can check on any of these things. And if the line is busy or they're not home, well, that's the end of your turn anyway and you've got to go to the end of the line and stand behind some woman who's been in and out at least five times while you've been there and she wants your phone number on the outside so you can date when you're sprung."

"Let me guess what happened next," said Alison. "But you thought at least there would be some dignity when you got out—that everyone in the leather community would acknowledge you covered their asses."

"Bingo," agreed Erin. "Some kind of hero. I had no idea, at this point, what Livia was saying. The first leather event I went to after I got out, I couldn't understand what the fuck was going on. They practically wouldn't let me in the door, and then no one would even talk to me. It took awhile to find out what was being said, and then another while to trace it back to Livia. I probably never would have found out—none of my personal friends were in the leather camp that year—except for those gals from Kansas. They were out of the loop, you see, it didn't matter what they knew or believed. They saw the whole thing start—they came back to the campsite to get their stuff, and the first person they ran into was Livia. She was horrified when they told her what had happened. She was so apologetic and so solicitous— she helped them pack herself and got a special shuttle in to cart their gear. Because she didn't want them to talk to anybody else. By the time that shuttle was pulling out she was doing her thing. They were the ones who told me about the rumors and they were the ones who traced them to Livia. They had kept in touch with me even while I was locked up—they knew I had gone to jail for them."

"I'll bet you really wanted to even up the score," guessed Alison.

"Oh, yeah, you're right," said Erin. "I really wanted to kill the stupid bitch. But I didn't. I had been in jail. Jail sucked. There was no way I was going back just to get even with a power-tripping liar. But I had her box number. She didn't give out her home address, she was paranoid about that, but she had a box number. And if you have a box number—well, all you have to do is pay somebody to watch the box. Eventually she's going to pick up the mail and then drive home. And, if she drives home, she can be followed. All you have to do is look in her hometown Yellow Pages under detective agency."

They all three stood there for a moment thinking about this. Alison was thinking that it certainly sounded as if Livia got what she deserved and Liz, as her next comment made obvious, was thinking about money. Who knows what Erin was thinking. "How in the world did you ever switch from butch to femme?" Alison asked.

At the same moment Liz said, "What about if we offered her a settlement?"

"What?" For the first time since they had started the conversation, Erin seemed flustered. "What do you mean, a settlement?"

"Well, let's just ask her to pay money. Not for blackmail or extortion, because we're not going to admit to that." She was getting into it—Alison could tell by the way she had started to use 'we.' "But we could bring a libel case against her totally legitimately. Do you have any friends who've heard her say that you killed someone?"

"Oh, yeah," said Erin.

"Okay, so we tell her we're going to bring suit and offer a really reasonable amount to settle. Not fifty million or anything like that. Say ask for fifty thousand and settle for ten thousand. Something she could get together this weekend. Do you think you could get over having your feelings hurt for ten thousand dollars?"

"I don't know," replied Erin thoughtfully. "They were hurt pretty bad. And I've really been enjoying stretching her rack." To Alison she said, "It wasn't that hard. Not for me. I mean, you think of the whole butch/femme bell curve and down here at one end," she spread her hands to indicate this was a honking big bell, "are the really butch girls who pack all the time and would commit hari-kiri before wearing a dress even in grade school and then over here," the other hand, "are the really femme girls who are always in full make-up even at home and never questioned that was the way it was going to be, thank you very much. But there's a lot of us in the middle. I never felt hugely butch identified. But in the leather scene you get more action if you go with one or the other and it's hard to be a femme. It's a lot of work if you want to keep up the image and besides, a lot of dykes don't like femmes. Inside the scene, yeah, but not in the regular community. They're just dykes and they either don't identify cause they're in the middle of the curve, too, or they see femme dykes as women who are doing things they really fought against doing and it pisses them off. Plus, I weighed so much and it just seemed that would be able to work better in the butch framework."

Liz gave Alison a look and then passed it on to Erin, who caught and interpreted it. "Yeah, I know," she said. "Body weight issues."

Alison stuck out her hand as if she were introducing herself. "Age issues."

"Body size issues," said Liz, jerking a thumb sideways toward Alison.

"I've-fucked-more-women-than-you-and-am-in-MENSA issues," said Alison, pointing to Liz.

"My-butch-friend-is-talking-to-a-pretty-woman-and-it-isn't-me issues," said Erin, pointing back toward the house. They all knew she was talking about Stacy. "Do you really think I could get some money?" she asked Liz.

"Actually," said Liz, "I think there's a very good chance you could get some money. That's how Livia thinks." She looked over at Alison for confirmation. Alison nodded, remembering how pissed Livia had seemed that there were no demands with the photos. Remembering, also, how important it had been to Livia to prove that she had a price. "People who think in terms of buy-off are usually really open to settling out of court."

"Could you put a gag order on her too?" Erin asked, her face all screwed up in concentration. "So she had to stop with the lies and the bullshit?"

"You're never going to be able to be Falcon again," Liz said bluntly. "Even if I could gag her. Gag orders work best when you're trying to keep someone from talking to the media. She's going to keep right on trashing Falcon in private. But we don't have to let her—or anyone—know that you've created a new persona. Have you been using your real name here?" Erin shook her head. "Do you need money?"

"Oh, yeah," said Erin with a heartfelt sign. "Oh, yeah. It's really expensive going to jail. I was part owner in a house cleaning business before I went in, and my partner bought me out to help me keep my house. So now I'm working for her, which was nice of her and everything, but it's not the same money as it was before. And I don't want to be cleaning houses the rest of my life."

"Ten thousand dollars," said Liz again. "Go back to school or seed money for a new business. And you make a great femme. Just go with it." She rubbed her hands together with some relish, as if it was already a done deal. "I gotta go," she said. "I gotta go make some phone calls."

"I have a question," said Alison. "If Livia is so paranoid about being outed, what the hell is she doing here? Why isn't she staying at home trying to keep her nose clean?"

"She's a power junkie," said Liz. "And this is the kind of place where she gets the biggest thrill."

"No," said Erin, looking at them both a little pityingly. "She's here because I told her to be here."

Alison and Liz looked at one another.

"What do you mean?" asked Alison.

"I sent her a little note with the original flier telling her to pack up her old kit bag."

"Well, she certainly didn't tell me that," said Alison. "It might have been helpful to know."

"I'm sure she didn't," said Erin, getting a smug cat-who-just-ate-the-left-over-pizza look. "She didn't want anybody to know she'd actually given in to a demand. Spoil her reputation. Let me guess—it was more like some kind of weird scene where she was willing to pay a lot of money to get you into a no-win situation."

"Kinda like that," Alison admitted.

"There you go!" said Erin. "She really loves setting up shit like that. She should have been a stockbroker or one of those guys who goes in and does hostile takeovers."

"Maybe she is," said Liz. "Nobody seems to know."

"I know!" sang Erin, waving her hand in the air. "That was one of the things my little private eye told me!"

"And?" asked Alison, lifting an eyebrow.

"Guess!" said Erin. "You saw the pictures."

Liz and Alison looked at one another again.

"Is she a nurse?" asked Alison tentatively, remembering her thoughts at Livia's hotel.

"Cold!"

They thought some more.

"I'll bet," said Liz, "that it really is something to do with serial killers. That genre at least. Because it just keeps coming up. And Livia has always given me the impression that she would have a hard time lying about anything personal if she thought it might impress people. I mean, me, if I wanted to lie about what I did, I'd say I was in insurance sales. But I can't see Livia doing that."

"Ou," said Erin, giving her a look that had nothing at all to do with what they were discussing, "You are in MENSA, aren't you? Okay, here's what it is. She actually is a psychologist—or a psychiatrist? I can never remember which one is which. Anyway, she actually does interview criminals associated with violent crimes and then testify as to their sanity at the time they committed the crimes."

There was a long silence.

"I find this frightening," said Alison finally. "Fuck the cash—I think you should out her. She's crazy herself! She shouldn't be in a position to make the call on anybody else! My god, who knows who she's turning back out on the streets?"

"Well, I agree," said Erin. "I mean, I don't know if she's really crazy or just twisted. Doctor Demento. But I can't out her. It's like," she turned to Liz and asked, "Who are you?"

"Liz Smith, twisted lawyer of great prowess," said Liz.

"MENSA issues," said Alison.

"It's like Liz says, I can't out her for being something I am myself. I mean, you know and I know there's a whole world of difference between her and us, but the straight world doesn't know that and we're all going to come out tarred with the same brush."

"I never did understand what that meant," said Alison thoughtfully. The big butch gal was circling and she tapped her watch and flashed twenty more minutes with her fingers behind Erin's back.

"I'm not sure either," Erin admitted. "It didn't come out quite right anyway. Okay, put it this way. I was willing to risk a little bad karma by yanking Livia's chain. She deserved it. But as a leather dyke myself I think it would be really hypocritical to try and get her fired because she's a leather dyke. You see what I mean? I was pretty much done with her anyway."

"The party was a good idea," said Alison, who was rather sorry to hear that Erin was done twisting Livia's tail. She could see her point, though, and could also see in Erin the person who decided to go to jail rather than screwing everybody else. "Did your guy get anything else on her? Is there some way we could out her without it coming back to being in the leather scene?"

"No," said Erin regretfully. "I thought of that, too. Expect for being a liar and an unsafe player she's actually pretty boring."

"Do you have this investigator's name and number?" asked Liz, who was obviously tired of talking and wanting to put the screws on someone.

"Yeah, at my hotel room. Although she's actually a gal. Got her e-mail, too, if you've got a computer."

"Want to help confront Livia tonight?" Liz asked Alison.

"Oh, I so do."

"Then don't fill up your dance card. Just head her my way."

Chapter Fourteen

Bad News' apartment, as Alison already knew from G-hey!, was in the house next door to Marta's. G-hey! and Bad News each lived in one of the apartment in the same building where they had stashed Janet-fuckbaby. Bad News lived in the apartment from which a woman had called the night before complaining about the noise. Both houses were divided Victorians. Alison had had neither the time nor the inclination to compare the two the night—well, the early morning—before, but as she pulled up in front with Bad News' clutch in a bag on the seat beside her the contrast was all too evident. The square, brick building in which Marta lived had been chunky and ugly from the moment it had been completed and it had been made uglier by a cheap add-on laundry room and a rickety set of outside stairs. The only landscaping was two of those weedy-looking trees that grew for free along the highway and a couple of clumps of juniper bushes, which appeared, from their placement, to have been volunteers as well. There were strips of paint peeling from the frames of the downstairs windows.

It contrasted almost comically with the house where Bad News' driver's license said she lived. That house, which Marta and Mary Clare and the bank owned, had managed to retain a taste of its original lovely flavor. One would never think of leveling it with a wrecking ball, which was what popped into Alison's head every time she happened to drive by Marta's house. It had been painted recently. The colors of the trim and the shingles that wrapped around the second story balcony looked as if they had been chosen by a faggot with a good eye. Nothing Alison—who mistrusted teal—would have put together, but they worked. For a moment, Alison stood lost in thought, wondering what the world was going to be like after AIDS was through with it. Like the South after the Civil War, she supposed—a whole generation of young men lost. Who was going to choreograph their dance, run their art galleries, make their music and act on their stages? Who was going to paint cute little Victorians and fill the yards with lupine and columbine? Capitol Hill without faggots was too sad to think of.

Alison stepped out of the car and looked up and down the street. She wished she knew what kind of car Marta drove. Even more she wished Bad

News lived on Gaylord or Vine or even up by Platt Park. No, scratch that. Stacy would not appreciate Alison having a femme neighbor as beautiful as Bad News. Okay, just any fucking other place in the whole city than next to the woman Alison had slept with less than twenty-four hours before.

There were a couple of skinheads mooching along the sidewalk, smoking and shooting a 'Dirty Queer' look her way. There had been some kind of big altercation on the street involving the skinheads last winter, just after she and Robert had arrested the one who had assaulted Mary Clare. Alison tried to remember just what it had been and who it had involved, but could not, even though she was fairly sure it had made the queer papers. But that was just stalling. It was the middle of the day—Marta was probably at work and even if she wasn't, they were going to run into one another sooner or later and better alone when Alison could attempt an apology than with Stacy, who sniffed out fishy situations like radar.

She went up the wide stairs to the porch, which flanked two sides of the house and was flanked itself by a waist high wooden wall. Obviously there had been some renovation when the house had been divided—four mailboxes meant four apartments meant four bathrooms—but much of its original grace had been allowed to remain. The ornamental doorknobs, for example, had not been replaced with the cheap black ones Alison had noticed on Marta's building. Through the heavy leaded glass that made up the top half of the front door she could see a foyer and grand staircase, which both still looked as if they were tended with love. Two of the spindles near the top of the stairs had obviously been replaced. They didn't quite match, but still, care had been taken. Marta and Mary Clare had done the best possible job within their budget.

The apartment she was looking for was on the first floor, around to the side in what might have once been a dining room. The door was shut and locked—Alison tried automatically after a volley of knocks went unanswered. Like the front door, it had a window. This window, however, was a lovely pane of stained and leaded glass. It was divided by the wooden frames into a pattern of leaded triangles framing a center diamond. In the diamond, upon a sea of blue, floated a white water lily. Michelle's passion and sometimes main job was working with stained glass, which meant Alison had seen a lot of stained glass over the years—enough to know this was a beautifully executed piece. It's only flaw was the bottom right triangle, which matched neither the style nor the other pieces, but was a pane of plain glass. Alison guessed that, like the banister, it had been damaged and replaced with what the owner had been able to afford. Stained glass, she knew from her long association with Michelle, was not cheap.

Alison bent down and looked through the glass pane. One glance was enough to answer a question that had been puzzling her—why didn't Marta and/or Mary Clare live in their own building? Obviously Marta did not live in her own building for the same reason that the lobsterman's children didn't eat lobster—it was way too expensive. Alison could only see the one room, but it was quite nice—spacious with a recently finished hardwood floor and new paint on the walls. It was furnished in the type of style that always made Alison feel a little apologetic about her own place—an antique side table on which rested a stack of mail and a newspaper, chairs and a sofa which obviously had not been passed down, throw rugs which matched one another and artwork that had been done by real artists and framed by real framers, as opposed to Alison's collection of old lesbian posters stuck in snap-em-together frames from Hobby Lobby. The unclutteredness spoke of other rooms just as big beyond—a kitchen, certainly, and perhaps more than one bedroom. Alison suspected the apartment took up most, if not all, of the first floor.

Alison rattled the door again, this time calling, "Helloooo?" Two lovely grey cats—one a very fat tabby, the other a long-haired, white-faced beauty not much more than a kitten—sauntered through the door leading to the rest of the apartment. They both looked at her through the window for a moment, but not as if they thought her very interesting. The longhaired cat gave one of those head to toe stretches which make yoga masters blind with envy.

Just beyond the tasteful couch was a music stand holding a sheaf of sheet music so fat that a couple of pages had fallen to the floor. Around it were several stringed instruments, most in their cases. There was a banjo and a guitar, both in cases, and a bass fiddle lying on its side. That bass must be an expensive instrument—seemed strange not to keep it in a case.

The longhaired cat walked over to the open banjo case and stepped into it. There was a towel in the bottom, which made Alison suspect this might be a regular habit. The tabby hurried over as if they had a date and they curled together as perfectly as two almonds in one shell. Neither of them even looked at the huge bass case, which was lying on the floor behind the bass itself. Too big, Alison supposed. Not cozy enough. In truth it was the biggest instrument case she had ever seen. It was all hard plastic and wheels and if you'd seen it on *Star Trek* you'd know someone was about to be jettisoned from the ship in a survival pod any second.

Well, so. Alison went back around the house and looked at the mailboxes. Nothing in the one marked K. Corbeit. No papers piled up, either. Until she had seen the happy cats, Alison hadn't realized she had been holding her breath. She had seen Bad News at Tara that day. The last she had seen of her was when she was being helped out of Livia's party and one of the last people with whom she had seen her had been Scar, who was now dead. Had it been such a stretch to wonder if Bad News had been injured or killed in the same accident? Alison had Kathy's I.D. in her hand—if she had been involved in Scar's accident the hospital wouldn't even have had a name to release to the papers. But, from the look and feel of the apartment—happy cats who were obviously not hungry—it seemed as if Alison had once again been fishing for red herrings. There was an old English folksong (for which she had a proclivity, collecting Steeleye Span, Silly Sisters and the Pentangle alongside Mary Chapin Carpenter and Trisha Yearwood) which always popped into her head whenever this kind of thing happened and she thought of it now.

And the men in the forest they asked it of me,
Saying, "How many strawberries grow in the salt sea?"
I answered them weel wi' a tear in my eey,
Saying, "How many ships sail in the forest?"

It seemed that once again she had tried to find a ship in the forest and she was not unhappy she had failed. Bad News' upset the night before had probably been nothing more serious than a tiff with an ex-lover or something of the same ilk and because of it she had just decided to do her own private little boycott today. Alison wondered if she should write a little note, telling her about Scar, but decided against it. No, she would let fate decide. If Bad News heard about Scar and went to the police, then that was what was meant to happen. If not, then that was meant to be as well. After all, it wouldn't be as if Alison had not tried to find her, or had asked her to suppress information or lie.

Lost in thought Alison walked down the wide wooden steps (also in good repair and recently painted) and ran smack into Marta.

"Oh!" she said, scrambling for words as well as a foothold. The steps, which a moment before had seemed so nicely done, were suddenly way too slippery. "Excuse me! I was just…I mean…I didn't mean to run into you!"

Marta said nothing. In one hand she was carrying a square, shallow plastic bucket which looked as if it might have been made out of one of the bottles in which they sold clumping kitty litter over at Sixth Avenue, the dyke pet store. Out of the top poked a bottle of Lysol and a scrub brush.

Marta herself looked better than Alison had ever seen her look before. Just as she had not noticed the details of the building, she had not noticed the details of Marta. Marta had been depressed the first time they had slept together. Now her long, dark hair had been trimmed and shaped and she was obviously using something beside dish soap to wash it. She had it pinned up on one side with a barrette of quilled silver which matched her earrings. She was wearing a pair of jeans, which looked fairly new. They fit well and the extra length had been taken up in a hem, not just turned up or left to drag in the dirt. Her T-shirt, which advertised the Mercury Cafe, purple on black, had been a freebie. Alison knew this because she had one like it—the Merc had been handing them out at Pridefest the summer before. But it was clean and the right size and tucked into her jeans so you could see that she had a waist and a butt, instead of hanging halfway down her thighs as if she wished she could disappear. All in all she had what Stacy called that Prozac glow. Or would have, if she hadn't been staring at Alison with kind of a hopeless expression, as if she couldn't quite make-up her mind whether she should talk civilly, snub snub or take the brush out of the bucket and rap her a good one on the head.

Alison stepped onto the top step, hoping that would establish a little dominance and eliminate choice three. She had no reason to think that Marta would do anything physical, but, then, she hadn't seen that ice cream bar coming, either. Fighting with a femme was a no-win situation. You could fight back, which would mean all the other butches would sneer at you, or you could allow yourself to be beaten, which also meant that all the other butches would sneer at you.

"The place looks great," said Alison, blurting out the first nonpersonal comment that came to mind.

Marta said nothing for a long moment. Then she sighed. "Look," she said. "Okay, last night. Okay—I guess I'm just as much at fault as you are. I guess I should have said no. But the thing is, I don't think I can say no to you. I mean…okay…obviously whatever is happening to me isn't happening to you. Because if it was—"

She let the thought trail away and Alison filled in the blank. Because if it was, then you wouldn't just walk away. She opened her mouth and then shut it. What good would it be to tell Marta that, yes, it was happening and, yes, she was just walking away?

"I'm sorry," Alison said instead and again, because at least that was true. "I really am. I didn't mean to jerk you around. I really didn't."

"Okay," said Marta with a little negating movement of the hand, like they weren't going there. "But what I need you to do is stay away from me. Really. I need you to not be in my space." She was talking in a voice that was firmly reasonable and had set her face to match it, but Alison suspected that both things were only temporary. Alison remembered the first time she had met Marta, at a wake where Marta had said to her, tears streaming down her face, "I cry all the time." Obviously she had gotten past that, but Alison sensed both that tears were not far away and that Marta would be humiliated if she could not hold them back.

"I'm sorry," Alison said again.

Marta, however, had obviously thought about what she was going to say and she plowed ahead without response. "You've got to stay away," she said. "Please. Please. I know we're going to run into one another—you always do. Don't worry about being rude. I don't care. But you've got to stay away from me. Just pretend you don't know me if you see me, 'cause it's fucking me up to sleep with you and, like, have this intense mind trip that you're not having and then to have you jump out of bed and take off in the morning like nothing happened."

"I am just so sorry," Alison said again, more as a token than anything else, since she didn't yet think that Marta was in listening mode. "I really am. I didn't mean to fuck with your head."

As she had suspected, Marta rolled right on down the line. "I feel things," she said.

Alison tried very hard not to get a look on her face, but it must not have worked.

"Yeah, yeah, I know, 'Marta's just a phone psychic, ha-ha, if she knows so much why doesn't she pick the lottery numbers?'" In a bitter tone Marta recited the words just as if she'd plucked them right out of Alison's head. "I don't care what you think. I don't care if you think it's all a big fake. I don't care! You're one to talk—you're so afraid people won't believe that you're sensitive that you can't even tell your girlfriend you've got…" she paused and did a little hand thing like she had forgotten a word and was trying to pull it out of the air. "…whatever it is you've got. Or whatever it is that's bothering you. The medical thing. The flu thing."

"How did you…?" Alison began.

Marta smiled a great big old Cheshire cat grin and wrinkled her nose. It was the first smile she'd flashed Alison's way in a long time and it made her so cute that, even though she thought she'd crushed it down like a cigarette butt, Alison felt a little surge of lust. Jesus, no!

"I'm sensitive," Marta said. Either she hadn't felt the lust or, like Alison, thought maybe if she ignored it that it would go away. "So stay away from me. Leave me alone. Don't bring your straysover in the middle of the night. Don't ask me to two-step. Don't get buddy-buddy with my cousin. Please." She turned abruptly and walked through the door. "Incidentally," she said over her shoulder, "you have sleep apnea, too. You ought to get it checked."

"Is this a little psychic insight?" asked Alison, a bit taken aback.

"No," said Marta, ignoring the tone of the question. "That one I guessed." She made a guttural and quite horrible choking noise in the back of her throat, followed by several seconds of no breathing and then another choke. It took a moment for Alison to realize that the dreadful sound was supposed to be her sleeping.

"Good thing the girlfriend sleeps like the dead, huh?" Marta asked. She didn't wait for Alison to ask the obvious question. "That one," she said, pulling the door shut, "I knew."

Oh, dammit. Alison felt the paper bag crackle beneath her arm. She should have given the clutch to Marta. She wasn't about to leave Bad News' wallet in her mailbox—not in this part of town. She noticed there was a big Victorian mailslot in the front door. Inspired, she folded the bag over twice and wrote 'Kathy Corbeit' on it. She pushed it through the mail slot, standing well back from it so she did not have to meet the eyes of Marta, who was down on her hands and knees wiping down something at the back of the foyer. Then she hastily took her leave. She had planned on checking on Janet, again, but she just couldn't deal with her weirdness after the whole Marta thing, which had left her feeling like a shit. She would have felt better, she thought as she hustled back to her car, if Marta had just been hostile or mean—then she could have copped an attitude and told herself Marta was an adult and had jumped into bed with her of her own free will and with her eyes wide open. Marta being brave and mature made her feel as if she had taken advantage of someone she'd known to be vulnerable. She'd send Liz over to do the fuckbaby thing later.

Alison was actually in her car and pulling away from the curb before Marta appeared on the porch again. She put a look of fierce concentration on her face like the street was filled with traffic, instead of just a different set of skinheads giving her the same look. She was not about to stop for any more psychic insights from Marta. She was sorry, but she just wasn't.

"Fucking butt-ugly dyke," said one of the skinheads conversationally through the window. Which distracted Alison even more and made it almost impossible to catch the words that Marta was calling after her.

"And you're looking for the wrong woman!"

Chapter Fifteen

Everyone was meeting at Stacy's apartment before the dinner. This was part of Alison's penance. She and Stacy had talked for a good hour and a half after she'd come back from delivering Bad News' purse. Apologies had been made, reassurances given, promises promised. Alison felt better than she had felt since she started secret visits to the doctor. Feeling better made her once again want to do the special little things for Stacy she had done automatically before she had become ill. Stacy didn't like to go places separately—she liked to arrive on the arm of her girlfriend, who was the setting to her jewel. Okay, Alison could do that. She brought a corsage, too.

Liz was already there when she arrived, reading the cartoons in the *New Yorker* with a look of resignation on her face. Stacy was not a woman who could be hurried. Liz was wearing a black cowboy hat, black cowboy boots with spurs that clinked on the floor when she uncrossed her legs, black leather chaps over a black thong and a pair of black bandoleers, complete with what looked like two real pistols and real ammunition. But for Mistress Anastasia, Liz was the queen of costume. Since she had been dating Stacy, Alison had seen a twisted version of a doctor, a service man, a construction worker and a dozen versions of deprived leather girl on Liz. Unfortunately, because of her fair skin and freckles, black was not really Liz's color, particularly if she was baring skin that hadn't seen the sun in years. It gave her kind of a fluorescent tinge. Alison thought Stacy should tell her this—it seemed like a best friend kind of duty—but Stacy refused, saying Liz had a mirror.

"What tribe are you from?" Alison asked Liz.

Liz was amiable. "I'm a Zapatista," she told her. "A kinky Zapatista." She looked Alison up and down. "Love the headdress," she said. "What the hell are you?"

"I'm doing kind of a Braveheart thing," Alison replied. The issue of costume for the banquet—tribal theme—had actually been quite a big deal. Originally Alison had just planned on wearing her tightest jeans and black tank top and saying she was with the Butch Tribe. But Stacy had called her a party pooper and nagged until she promised to come up with something. The problem was not being tribal, but being tribal and sexy. She wasn't willing to just throw on a hide and feathers. Finally she had decided to be a Celt, a decision inspired by running into Flame's friend, Cleo Du Bois, at the midnight showing of *Interview with the Vampire*, accompanied by one of the sexiest old men she had ever met. (Calm down, she didn't want to fuck him, but she could still tell het sex appeal when she saw it.) The old man, whom she'd had the impression was Cleo's grandfather, had been wearing a kilt with all the trappings. He had been easily six feet six and upon his leonine grey hair had been wearing a headdress he claimed to be not only truly Celtic but made from the skull of an enemy he had killed in hand-to-hand battle on the fields of Killiecrankie. He was either two hundred years old or was wandering in the mind, but the headdress had impressed the hell out of Alison. The nineteen-year-olds he was trying to hit on had liked it too. Since Alison hadn't been able to use a human skull, hers was not quite so impressive, but she had done a pretty credible job, working around the skull of a coyote that Linda Lane had picked up for her in the mountains and embellishing it with bits and pieces from the flea market. She had thought about doing the kilt thing, but instead had gone with leather leggings and a sporran and a quiver of arrows over the shoulder of a tight brown tank top draped with fur.

She looked great, there was no denying it. She had admired herself in the mirror at every stage of dressing, thinking, God, she was a sexy woman and she ought to date herself!

"Did you hear about Scar?" asked Liz, bursting her little bubble. "Wasn't that awful? I mean, she was pretty awful herself, but still. And what a way to go! It's worse than being crushed to death at a Who concert! Thank god she wasn't carrying her Wildfire information with her!"

They talked about the Pattys and a couple of women whom they both thought were playing way to close to the edge and Flame's blood thing and then the scene Bad News had caused at the entertainment the night before.

"That girl is going to be lucky if she can find anyone to play with, now that Scar is dead," said Liz darkly and rather, Alison thought, callously. "She's pretty, but nobody wants to deal with that crap."

"Was she embarrassed about it today?" Alison wanted to know. "Isn't she a friend of Mary Clare's?"

"Yeah," said Liz, glancing at her watch in a reflex gesture, for there was certainly no other point in it. "She plays music with that same group that Mary Clare plays with."

Although until that weekend Alison's only face to face contact with Mary Clare had been official, she still knew a few things about her. It was the lesbian thing. In Denver, at least the Capitol Hill area, if you had been around the lesbian community for fifteen or twenty years then you were bound to have crossed paths with any other woman who had been around for the same amount of time. Liz had played soccer with Mary Clare on an over- thirties team several years before. She had, also, hired Marta to do some psychic legwork for her the previous winter in connection with a murder case and Mary Clare had come along for the ride. G-hey! was Marta's tenant and Beth's girl-friend was a neighbor of Mary Clare, who lived over in the Broadway Terrace area. Marta had been in a therapy group with Tam, Dana's ex-girlfriend who had been electrocuted in her bathtub, and both Marta and Mary Clare had come to the now famous wake where Stacy and Michelle had mixed it up after Stacy'd had a few too many wine coolers.

The point was that Alison already knew Mary Clare, who had been raised by parents with slightly less nurturing instinct than a sea turtle, had somehow in her erratic childhood managed to latch onto a cello and never completely let go. Alison believed, from half listening to a really long story Liz had been telling earlier in the weekend, that it had been one of those touching instances where one caring teacher had made all the difference. Alison had even seen Mary Clare perform once, when her quartet had opened locally for some bigger name, which Alison could not now recall. Cris Williamson or something. She remembered Mary Clare mostly because she had looked so handsome in her black tuxedo. Now that Liz had pointed it out, Alison thought she could also recall Bad News, playing the bass and wearing a beautiful black gown with a high collar, her hair piled up on her head and secured with rhinestone clips. If it hadn't been her it had been another woman pretty enough to remember.

Liz had been chatting right along, not realizing her audience was not with her. She was also eating pistachios from a big bowl Stacy had sitting on the coffee table and several of the half shells had adhered themselves to various bits of bare skin, which she must not have realized because they looked really dorky and Liz hated to look dorky even more than most. Alison thought looking dorky came with the territory now and then, but Liz was the kind of woman who, faced with an unattractive hat, would opt for frostbit-ten ears. She was going on about Bad News buying a new bass that had to be shipped from Europe, for god's sake, and how Mary Clare said the shipping crate had cost more than her car, cost so much that part of the deal was that Bad News had to send it back to Europe. Or something. Liz, like the lovely Stacy, had a tendency to go on and on, particularly if she was high, which from the smell of the living room Alison guessed she was.

"Is that her gig?" Alison asked when Liz paused for air. "I mean, all she does is music? She doesn't have a day job?"

"Nah, she does something with computers," said Liz, who had discov-ered the pistachio shells and been, as Alison had suspected, absolutely horri-fied. She was picking them off with such distaste that, even though Alison had been sitting right there watching, it was hard to imagine they had any-thing at all to do with something she had actually ingested. "Something where she makes money. And I guess she's got a couple of music jobs. The main one is with the Philharmonic, but she plays with a dance band, too.

Bluegrass or country-western or something like that."

To Alison there was a huge distinction between these types of music, but she held her tongue. Liz liked jazz, music that lowered Alison's attention span to about thirty seconds. Liz was now looking over her shoulder like an owl, trying to make sure there weren't any shells stuck to her back side. Alison took pity on her and brushed her off.

"I think Mary Clare said she even played with Monkey Siren a couple of years ago."

"That's a lot of different kinds of music," said Alison

"Well," said Liz, "Mary Clare says she was some kind of child prodigy. You know, Mary Clare had a rough childhood and one day she was reading *Bastard Out of Carolina* while she was sitting over there in her truck and Kathy," (it took a moment for Alison to remember this was Bad News' real name), "came over to say hi and they started talking about the book and it turned out they kind of bonded on the bad family issue. Except that Mary Clare says her life was cake compared to Kathy's. I guess her family was living with relatives and in cars half the time—it sounded really gruesome. Her dad drank and her mom left them."

"How'd she ever go from that to playing in the Philharmonic?" Alison asked. "I mean, it doesn't sound like her dad was paying for music lessons."

"Mary Clare says that she had a grandma who played the banjo and she taught her that and then I guess when she was a little older she had a teacher who took an interest in her." Trust Liz to have gotten all the details. "Practically adopted her, I guess. Took her under her wing—more or less bought her from her dad. There were a bunch of kids—I guess he was just as glad there was one less mouth to feed. It happens sometimes. Look at Tonya Harding. Who would have thought a kid with her background would make it to the Olympics?"

"Well, I guess being gifted doesn't have to do with money."

"No, but having the leisure to practice six hours a day sure does. Being able to afford coaches and teachers and tutors and instruments and ice time sure does." The pistachio shells had made Liz nervous about her outfit—she had to go stand in front of the full length mirror Stacy had set up in her work room to reassure herself. Alison simply could not understand why anyone as concerned about her appearance as Liz had not yet realized black was not her color. "God," she said, having done two or three full turns, "are they ever going to be ready? I'm going to die if I don't eat soon."

"Where's Dana?" asked Alison.

"They're dressing together," said Liz. "I think it's kind of like a mutual disarmament—you know, that way nobody can wear higher heels or bigger earrings." Liz stretched.

"Hey," said Alison, "I didn't know you had a tattoo. Who's Cynthia?"

"Oh, god," said Liz, "someone from a long time ago. When I was still stupid enough to do something like that. Eighteen or nineteen I think. I hardly even remember what she looked like. You could be her for all I know."

"Well, at least it still looks good," said Alison. "If I'd had a butterfly tattooed on my ass when I was eighteen there'd be an eagle there now."

"Well," said Liz, "it did used to just say Cindy."

They laughed about that and then Liz picked up one of Stacy's three or four remotes and clicked on the VCR. Alison, no matter the amount of tutoring given, had never been able to figure out which remote controlled which function. This bothered her a little, kind of the way it bothered her that she had never been good at softball and was never truly successful at changing a tire. She didn't want to actually do any of these things—she just wanted to be able to do them all splendidly. It was hard being a butch.

"What's this?" she asked, squinting at the screen. Poor lighting and an amateur cameraman. She hoped Liz wasn't trying to share some erotic little experience she'd had at MSIL or something. Alison found porno flicks kind of embarrassing even when the stars were strangers and she certainly didn't want to watch anyone she knew in an awkward position, any more than she wanted a mirror on her ceiling. Some things, she felt, were best done without too much thought about how they looked.

"It's the fantasies from last night," Liz told her. "Remember, I was taping? We're going to sell copies for a fundraiser for Project Angel Heart."

"Oh, okay." Now that she'd been told Alison recognized the stage. "How could you make a video? I mean, surely people objected. I thought nobody was even supposed to take photos."

"Well, nobody but the official photographer," Liz replied absently, looking at the screen. "Who would be me. Plus, we asked everybody who was doing a scene for written permission to tape them and if they didn't give it, then I didn't film their scene. Did you see this one? It was really funny. If it had been a real competition I would have given it first prize."

Alison had seen a little of the fantasy, but it had been funny, so she was willing to see it again. The background music was light and Lawrence Welkish. To complete the ambiance someone offstage sent a bunch of bubbles across the footlights every few seconds. The two women on stage were dressed as a magician—tall silk hat, mustache, cape over a white silk shirt and leather pants—and her lovely assistant. The assistant was made up to look like Betty Boop. She had big round eyes with lashes mascaraed like a sunburst and a pouty little mouth drawn up like a kiss. She was wearing the shortest little black skirt Alison had ever seen on an actual woman—as opposed to a model or an actress—along with fishnet hose, garters which couldn't help but show and black heels so high they made her feet look rather like little hooves.

The two had practiced and they were very good. The magician flourished her wand and the assistant went trip, trip, trip around the stage like the littlest Billy Goat Gruff, fetching props, which she offered with Vanna White gestures.

The joke was that whenever she turned her back to the magician and bent to pick up a stack of cards or a pitcher of milk the magician would wave her wand with a leer and do a variation of a standard trick behind her so that birds, scarves and flowers all seemed to pop or fly out of her cunt. It really was funny, especially since the assistant played the whole thing dumb and unaware—she had no idea doves were flying out of her ass.

There was a lot of applause and laughter when the skit was done. Liz didn't show the audience—it would have been too difficult to get a release from every single woman who wandered in. Alison, for example, would not have been real thrilled about having a tape of herself in a leather audience floating around.

Liz had cut the tape after one curtain call. There was a brief moment of static. Then the picture came back, once again focused on the stage. The music had not yet started and it was possible to hear bits and pieces of conversation from the audience. In the middle of the stage sat an old upright piano. This must have been when Stacy had decided to take Alison and Mr. Winkie for a ride. It had to be the act Bad News wanted to write letters about.

A woman in the plaid jumper of a Catholic schoolgirl skipped out onto the stage. She wore saddle shoes on her feet and pigtails with ribbons in her hair. Beneath her arm she carried a sheaf of music, which she placed on the piano. She pulled the bench out, sat with a little flounce, which showed the audience her white cotton panties and began to practice. Classical music began flowing over the sound system as soon as she touched the keys. Then the girl gasped suddenly as someone else came onstage, off-camera.

"We don't have permission on this one," a voice obviously right next to Liz said over the music. Just as obviously Liz had been surprised. The camera jerked and swung to the right, catching a brief and blurry shot of a woman brandishing a cane, then coming to rest for a moment on a pierced nose which probably belonged to the speaker before going dead.

"I'm going to have to cut that part," said Liz in a thoughtful tone, as if it were a really artistic decision instead of just stating the obvious. "Just as well. That fantasy creeped me out."

There was a sudden burst of laughter from the kitchen and Stacy and Dana burst through the door. They were dressed similarly—long flowing skirts made of scarves and shawls, lots of jewelry and nothing else. Alison was glad she'd gotten a wrist corsage. They both looked great and it was pleasantly obvious they both knew it.

"And what tribe are you?" asked Liz, hitting the pause button on the remote.

"We're Amazon fireflies," said Stacy, rattling an arm full of bracelets. "We flash the message, we mate and then we kill. We're planning on a large body count by the end of the night."

The Amazon fireflies weren't quite ready even yet. First there was fussing about what to wear as a top in the car. No one was sure whether it was actually illegal for women to be topless in public in Denver. Legal, however, was not the issue. Though they were quite willing to expose themselves to an appreciative audience of women, neither Stacy nor Dana wished to be leered at by passers-by. Once that was dealt with (leather jackets—there was a cloakroom which locked) there was dealing with purses (again the cloakroom) and shoes (both women were barefoot, but thought it wise for shoes to be available). So it was another fifteen minutes before they were out the door.

"What creeped you out?" Alison asked Liz, turning from the driver's side of the front seat to speak. As a trade-off for arriving together, Alison had insisted on driving. She wanted to be able to leave the moment she felt the first twitch. Stacy and Liz had agreed to take the shuttle or a cab if she had to bail early and Dana was obviously planning not to return to her own bed.

It took Liz a moment or two to remember what Stacy was referring to.

"The piano fantasy," Alison prompted. Stacy was like a computer with a print job—once she was set on a task she'd pick it up automatically, no matter how long she'd been turned off.

"Oh!" said Liz. She sounded curiously distracted. Alison wondered if Dana was getting ready to make her first kill for the night. Alison hoped that whatever happened, Liz would remember that it was just sex and not love. Liz, for all her I-fuck-whoever-I-want attitude, had been sending out girlfriend vibes for a while. Alison didn't want to see Liz's head fucked with. "That piano teacher fantasy. It gave me the creeps. I don't think we should allow fantasies with kids in them."

"Pardon me?" Stacy was incredulous. "You, of all people, think that we should be censoring people's fantasies?"

"Well, jeez," replied Liz, with a little hint of pout in her voice, "you make me sound like the world's biggest pervert!"

"You are the world's biggest pervert!" Stacy said. She had unfastened her seat belt so she could hang right over the seat. "They're fantasies! That's it! Half of those women up there would never want anything in those fantasies to actually come true! It's like the things you think in your head when you're about to come—I sure as hell don't really want them to happen! I don't even want anyone else to know that I'm thinking them!"

This gave the conversation pause as everyone wondered what the hell Stacy, who was not at all shy about sharing some really twisted stuff, could possibly be thinking that she didn't want others to know.

"Well," said Alison, after deciding that it had to involve either necrophilia or cannibalism, in which case she hoped Stacy continued not to share, "I don't like kid fantasies either. I think Liz is right." She stopped the car and carefully looked both ways for the light rail. Alison did not wish to join poor, stupid Scar.

"No," put in Dana, "Stacy's right. Those fantasies aren't about children. They're about fantasy. There are a lot of women who are into playing Daddy's girl. Or even just cross-gender playing. I mean, just because you strap it on doesn't mean you want to be a man. Just because you have rape fantasies doesn't mean you want to actually be raped. I was raped, so I know. It wasn't anything like my fantasies had been. For one thing, I didn't really want to be frightened! I had never imagined being so scared that I wet my pants. I mean, that just wasn't attractive. Also, everybody in the fantasy was pretty and smelled better."

She was obviously trying to put a funny spin on the story, but they all fell silent anyway. Going right back into the fantasy conversation seemed to negate Dana's experience, which must have been frightening and horrible, while following up with questions or commiseration seemed to Alison a form of invasion, insisting on playing serious a story which Dana obviously wanted to play light and funny. Alison was glad the Masons' hall they had rented for the banquet was only a block further. It was always hard to know what to say when a friend told about a past abuse. She had hoped it would become easier as she got older and it had. Sometimes. When she had a warning, when she had already suspected. But she was still tongue-tied over a casual admission such as Dana's.

Of course they were the very last ones to get there and of course there had been some kind of work exchange crisis into which Liz and Stacy were immediately absorbed the moment they stepped through the door.

"Run like the wind, little bunny," Alison murmured to Dana, taking her by the arm and plowing into the crowd, "or you'll end up washing dishes in the kitchen."

The invitation had said, 'Amazon Feast—Tribal Dress Encouraged,' but the tribal part had been translated pretty loosely. There was a huge contingent in furs and beads and necklaces made of plastic bears' teeth—the cultural appropriation girls wouldn't have known where to begin being offended—but there were also women from outer space, cowgirls who had forgotten to wear anything under their chaps, gladiators and women in evening wear, too as the gals who had just worn their dress leather. There was food happening at the packed tables—as far as Alison could see there was not an empty chair in the room—but there were other things happening also. No, not those kind of things, although they probably were going on in the bathrooms and back corners as they had been all weekend. There were organized activities. There was a place where you could throw knives and a pit made of mats for wrestling. Dana was swirled away by a great herd of femmes running wild and Alison squirmed through the crowd to stand beside the wrestling pit.

Crouching on the edge of the mat was a blonde woman with a knife. She was certainly not the only one in the hall with a knife—there was a ton of hardware being toted on costumes. If the party had been busted, half of the women there could have been arrested immediately for having concealed weapons. The other half would have been arrested for being too near naked. This woman was both.

The woman with the knife had gone the beads and leather route—she had on a wooden necklace and a kind of skirt made of slashed black and purple suede and, as far as Alison could tell, nothing else. It was hot in the hall and there was a fine sheen of sweat across her shoulders and breasts, which were femme pretty with pink nipples. She stood by the mats where the women were wrestling, with her dagger in one hand, screaming "Fuck her! Fuck her!" whenever anyone went down. Just as she was not the only one with a knife, she was not the only one thinking this. She was just, as yet, the only one screaming it out loud.

Another woman, also blonde, though her hair was cut short and spiked up, came and stood behind the first, rubbing the bodice of her black gown against the other's bare back. There was music—some kind of New Age Nubian slave stuff—and in a moment they were dancing. From Stacy gossip Alison knew the woman with the knife—she could not remember her name—only played with butches, and rough trade butches at that. But there was a lot of femme on femme energy in the place, women in dresses and heels dancing and flirting with other women in dresses and heels for the appreciation of the butches surrounding them.

The dancing became so hot a little circle of the wrestling fans broke off to form a ring around them. Then the woman in the gown was swirled off by a crowd of serving wenches carrying platters of whole chickens over their heads. The woman with the dagger went back to her place at the very edge of the mat.

"Fuck her!" she screamed, when one of the women went down, and then, because it was someone she knew, she added, "Just lay down and let her fuck you, Josie! She's going to kill you otherwise!" This elicited a laugh from the crowd, and there was another laugh a minute later when the ref, who had been getting more and more nervous about the enthusiastic way in which the woman was wielding her dagger, as if at any moment she might decide to leap out onto the floor and gut one of the downed wrestlers, attempted to take it from her. The blonde broke into a big smile and, without warning, slammed the blade into the base of her neck as if she were Juliet. The plastic blade retracted as prop daggers had been doing for stage Juliets for years.

There had only been butches wrestling thus far, but now Alison saw a small woman draped mostly in jewelry and scarves stepping up to the edge of the mat. She kicked off her high heels and turned to face the woman following her. The second woman was young-boy butch, and had forty pounds on the first. Everyone was silent for a moment, wondering how this was going to work out. Then, when the ref brought her hand down, the femme leapt at least three feet into the air, throwing herself at the other woman, who caught her at chest height. She was big enough so she didn't go down under the femme's weight, but neither could she pin her, nor even get her off her shoulders. The women in the crowd began to laugh and stamp their feet, cheering for the pluck with which the femme clung—even upside down, for the butch woman had managed to turn her—and the way she was attempting to topple the butch using her hanging weight alone. "Fuck her!" screamed the blonde, even though the other woman was not technically down, and for the first time the other women around her joined in the chant. Everyone wanted to see the pretty femme get her cunt pumped while she was hanging upside down with her legs around the waist of the boy butch.

But the femme was not giving up that easily. She managed to swing herself upright and it was this movement which sent the butch-boy careening off the mat and into the startled crowd. The blonde with the dagger was caught squarely in the chest and she dominoed into someone behind her, who caught her head and kept it from crashing into the floor.

"Fuck her!" yelled someone in the crowd, because even though she had gone down with a crash you could tell that she hadn't been hurt, and it was too funny to have the tables turned. Especially since her ragged leather skirt had been pushed up and, as everyone suspected, she was wearing nothing underneath. Her cunt, like her tits, was as pink and femmie as if it had been made to order to match her outfit. Her public hair had been trimmed short, and she had a ring through her labia. She was wet.

She looked up at the crowd around her, and a look with a mix of fear and excitement crossed her face. She made a move as if to push herself up with her hands, in one of which she still held the dagger. After that one call the crowd had gotten almost silent, so it was easy to hear the next sound—the snap of someone pulling a latex glove tight over her hand.

"Don't."

Obviously the blonde had not noticed the woman who had saved her head from striking the floor. At the sound of her voice the blonde froze, and then looked up slowly, an unreadable expression on her face, an expression that could have been passion or horror or excitement or fear, or any of a number of feelings. Again from Stacy gossip, Alison knew the woman who had spoken was the blonde's ex. The blonde had told perfect strangers she hadn't known the ex was coming, she was having trouble with it, that, after all this time, she still hated seeing her with other women. Her friends knew beyond this that the blonde still, though the two had not spoken for almost a year, loved this woman with a doomed passion and that, despite the dancing and flirting, no one had touched her—not to play with, not to make love to, since they had broken up the previous autumn. All this Alison knew because Stacy had told her, and Stacy knew because the blonde had spilled it in the femme empowerment workshop. A woman in a gladiator costume, a friend of the blonde's who had driven up to the conference with her (Stacy had gotten all the details), made a move as if to help her to her feet, but she was stopped by the woman who had snapped the glove over her hand.

The ex-lover was a beautiful butch with dark hair that was long in the back and spiked on the top. Her translation of tribal was a long black duster and a black cowboy hat, and she looked sexier fully clothed than many of the women who were wearing next to nothing. She looked down at the blonde and then up at the crowd, and her look said there was not going to be a gang scene, consensual or no, that she would have to be killed first for that to happen. There was a discernable movement in the crowd—everyone stepped back half a step. Then the dark haired woman leaned down and put her hands on the waistband of the blonde's skirt. She lifted slowly, until her ass was almost a foot off the floor, and then she bent closer to her face and said softly, "I'll wrestle you, baby." She swung her back and forth between her legs, and then let go, so that the blonde was thrown backward onto the mat, landing on her back with a little "Oof!"

There was no heckling as the blonde scrambled to her bare feet. The dark-haired butch began to disrobe as if the match had been agreed on, as if the two previous women didn't have the right to two more rounds. She was wearing a heavy harness under her coat. The blonde, obviously, was topless to show off her tits. The butch was topless because she had a beautiful back. She was the kind of woman you would like to watch chop wood, bare to the waist, and then afterwards dig your nails into as she fucked you standing against the house.

A woman wearing only a collar helped her remove her black cowboy boots. The blonde had backed up to the edge of the mat, crouched down as if she were going to fight, yet looking anxiously over her shoulder as if she wanted to make sure the option to run was still open. The ring was packed solid with women who wanted to see her thrown down and it was obvious she was pinpointing her friends in the crowd, women she could count on to back her up if she decided to safeword out. Once again the woman in the gladiator's costume made a move toward her, bending down to put a hand on the blonde's shoulder. "Don't do this," she said, in a voice that was audible to the crowd, "You got away from her once. Stay away!"

The blonde squeezed her hand, but made no move to back out of the ring. And then it began. They had wrestled before—that was obvious from the stances they took. They had played together, and played hard. This was obvious from the way they came together without any regard to pain when their bodies met. The butch was bigger and heavier. And she was the top. The blonde had submitted to her body and soul, and she had replayed those submissions over and over in her fantasies during the year they had been apart. It gave the butch a tremendous psychological advantage. But the blonde was strong, too. And though there was a part of her that wanted to lie down for this woman, she was pissed. You could see that in her eyes as she went for the butch's legs—could see the anger of betrayal and abandonment. They both went down, and the femme scrambled away from the other, knowing she would never be able to flip her once she got on top.

The dark-haired woman looked at her almost lazily, as if she had not fallen, but had somehow ended up full length on the mat as part of a plan. At the last possible moment she reached out one large hand and wrapped it around the blonde's ankle. And that was the end. The blonde might have been able to fight back if she'd kept her head. And she might have kept her head if the crowd hadn't taken up her chant, if every woman surrounding the mat hadn't started to yell, "Fuck her! Fuck her!"

That was what finally threw her off, made her lose every little bit of strategy and disintegrate into tossing herself futilely from side to side and cursing as the dark butch proceeded to reel her in hand over hand. The blonde flipped herself onto her front and began to push herself up with her arms. The butch reached up beneath her skirt with the gloved hand and shoved three fingers into her cunt. The blonde cried out as if she had been struck, and struggled to pull away, but by now the butch had her by the hip, and she slowly pulled her down on her hand. The blonde kicked back, hitting her shoulder, and with a roar of anger the butch pulled out of her and used both hands to slam her onto her back. She snapped her left arm down between her breasts, her elbow on her sternum, her hand around her throat. Everyone there who had ever watched them play had seen her use this hold before.

"Safeword out, Tina!" The blonde's friend had stepped out onto the mat, which of course should have meant the match was no good and would have to be restarted. Except, of course, everyone, including the ref, had forgotten how it had started, or the fact that there were once rules. The blonde turned her head toward her friend. But friends are always so much wiser than we are and their eyes could not really meet, because the blonde's had shrunken to pinpoints and it was obvious not only was she not going to use her safeword, but that she probably had forgotten what it was. The dark-haired woman slapped her sharply across the face, as if she didn't like her attention wandering when she was topping. The blonde cried out, a cry barely audible over the chanting, which had renewed itself to a fever pitch. The butch moved her hand directly from the blonde's face to her cunt. With one brutal shove her fist was in. "Fuck her! Fuck her!" the crowd was shouting. But the woman with the dark hair was not listening. She was looking into the eyes of the blonde as she reached deep inside her, as if she were reaching up to grasp her soul.

And the blonde was not listening, either. She was gazing back into the eyes of the other woman, and with one hand she was stabbing the dagger over and over into her back.

Alison reeled backward, feeling dizzy from the combination of heat, the heavy smell of sex and the imagery of the butch with the dagger in her back. She either needed to find Stacy and fuck her right on one of the tables or find a bathroom and splash some cold water on her face.

She turned, meaning to wriggle her way out of the crowd, and ran smack into Livia. Livia hadn't even tried to dress tribal. Again she was wearing complete black with her hair loose down the back of her leather jacket. With a flash of insight Alison suddenly knew Livia did not have the imagination for costume—that in her mind there was only one leading role and she played it daily without the ability to change. She could bring in a prop, the way that she had bought Alison, or she could change the setting by going to Wildfire or Michigan, but the basic plot-line was always the same.

It was the first time Alison had ever seen her when she was not surrounded by a full court. Both Yesman and Best Boy were close and struggling to be closer, but it looked to Alison as if even the iron will of Livia had not been able to keep the current of the carnival from sweeping the rest of her handmaidens to all corners of the room.

"Did you even try to find out anything?" Livia demanded seizing Alison's arm. She had to bend close to her ear to speak. She smelled like Dr. Bronner's peppermint soap, a smell Alison so associated with wholesome normalcy—her dad used Dr. Bronner's, for god's sake!—that she had to pull back for a moment and make sure it really was Livia who was talking to her. "I paid a lot of money for your services, and so far I've gotten nothing."

It was nice, thought Alison, that she'd chosen this moment to be a great big asshole. Any hesitancy she'd had about the ethics of Liz's suggestion was totally extinguished by Livia's tone.

"Actually," she said, "I've been looking for you. I know just who's been contacting you and we need to talk." She enjoyed the startled look on Livia's face. Just as she'd thought all along, Livia had never actually expected her to find anything.

Luckily, they had been jostled toward the back of the room, near the doors to the kitchen. Alison ducked through the tail end of the crowd, beckoning Livia to follow. Amazingly, she did. Without comment. She must really be in shock, thought Alison. All the better for Liz to crunch her up.

In the kitchen, Liz and G-hey! were standing over at one of the big metal sinks. Alison caught only a few words of their conversation, but it was enough to tell her that they had been talking about Scar's accident. She had caught similar snippets all over the banquet room. Whatever the work crisis had been, it seemed to have resolved itself. Stacy was nowhere to be seen.

Alison caught Liz's eye and beckoned. Liz detached herself and went into the hall with Alison and Livia. There were several doors opening off the short hall and Alison wordlessly tried them until one opened. She waved Livia and Liz inside. Obviously the room was used for daycare.

"Who the hell are you?" Livia said to Liz. They both ignored her.

"Okay," said Alison. "I know who's been doing it. Now give me my money."

Livia looked incredulous. She had recovered from the shock and returned to her old arrogance. "Our agreement was that you would stop this harassment," she said. "I haven't seen any proof you even know who it is, let alone have made any move to stop it."

"I didn't agree to stop it, I agreed to find out. I have found out and just as a bonus I've arranged for you to stop it yourself. Ms. Smith here," she gestured toward Liz as if she were wearing a pin-striped suit instead of her tits hanging out on the table, "is willing to discuss an out of court settlement on behalf of Erin Oleander."

Liz sat down in one of the little, child-sized chairs and whipped out a document consisting of several pages and a pen. Alison had no idea where she had been carrying them.

"A what! Who?" Livia sputtered.

"Erin Oleander," said Alison. "You used to know her as Falcon. The woman in the photograph who went to prison for two years because of you."

There was a long silence. Livia looked around the room, moving only her eyes, several times.

"I don't even know—" she began.

"Oh, okay then," broke in Liz. "Guess we made a mistake and you'd rather go to court. I've got some papers here for you—you'll probably have to come to Denver for the trial. At least that's what I'm asking."

"What are you talking about?" Livia's face had closed down completely—only her mouth moved as she spoke and it only a little.

"Well, my client, Erin, is planning on suing you for slander. And for telling people verbally, in writing, and on the Internet to stay away from her because she killed someone. In fact, she was never tried for either murder or manslaughter. She feels as if it really caused her a lot of grief and anxiety— we're going to ask for fifty-thousand dollars. Because of the nature of the case, I'm willing to work pro bono and—"

"This is extortion!" snapped Livia. "All this is is extortion! I know extortion when I see it and that's all this is!"

"Actually," said Liz in her courtroom voice, "When there's a lawyer involved, it's not called extortion. It's called settling out of court. I imagine she might be convinced to settle. We could talk about an amount you could pay right away and that way you both can be done with one another. Otherwise we can all go before a judge." She smiled at Livia like they were friends and said conversationally, "The press is going to have a field day with this one! 'Kinky Leather Doctor Denies—'"

"And what about the fact that she's been blackmailing me!" broke in Livia. She was really flustered. Alison couldn't tell if it was because of the

shock or if she just didn't do well without her chorus. Either way, it was satisfying to watch.

"Well, if I were a judge I wouldn't call it blackmail," said Liz in a regret-
ful tone, as if she really cared about Livia's tail being caught in a wringer.
"Because she never asked for anything and she never threatened anything.
But you're right—you have every right to countersue. Let's see—what would
The Enquirer have to say on that one? —Leather Doctors Says, 'I Only Beat
Them, I Never—'"

"Oh, and what are your other clients going to say when they see your
name in the paper!" spat Livia, grasping at straws with both hands. "You and
that idiot woman who wouldn't stop a scene when I told her to! Then none
of this ever would have happened! If any of this comes out, then we're all
going down!"

"Yeah," said Liz, still acting like she gave a shit, "we are. However, I'm
already out. Everybody and their judge knows I'm a pervert. I'm the perverts'
pervert." She pulled a piece of paper from the bottom of the file. It was a
Xerox of a newspaper clipping that showed Liz standing in front of a judge's
bench with her hand on the rail. Although Alison was too far away to read
the fine print of the article, the caption did indeed refer to Liz as the
'Perverts' Pervert.' It was not an article she had ever seen or heard mentioned
and she had to refrain from giving Liz a look.

Liz charged on. She was way into it. "And Erin—well, she just spent two
years in the pen and is working at Taco Bell. Employers aren't exactly knocking on her door with jobs anyway. Fifty thou would be a great grubstake—
she could learn a new skill, move someplace new and start over. Or she could
sell her story—I'll bet inquiring minds would love to know."

"Fine. Fine! Just stop it! And you call it whatever you want, but you
know and I know that all this is is extortion!"

"And I want the rest of my money right now," said Alison, figuring she'd
better deal with it while Liz was there to pull the strings. "Plus, I want an
extra hundred and fifty dollars to cover my jacket which your slave stole."
Might as well keep pushing the idea she'd had nothing to do with that. Livia
gave Alison a look of absolute hatred and Alison could not resist twitting her.
"Was it worth it?" she asked. "Finding out what my price was?" She suspected
that if Livia had not reacted to the letters, Erin would have dropped the matter without further action. She had told them she had wanted to risk neither
parole problems nor bad energy. Well, maybe a little bad energy.

"And does everybody down at the police station know about your pro-
clivities?" Livia asked Alison coldly. "This is the Hate State, right? The city
that voted in Amendment Two? How are the good people of Denver going to
feel about not just a lesbian cop but a—"

"That's two thousand extra dollars just for saying that to her," Liz interrupted. She slashed at the unsigned papers with her pen, crossing out and

initialing. "Plus, you're behind the times. Alison isn't with the cops anymore; she's doing investigative work for me. She's the Perverts' Pervert's Pervert. And the Perverts' Pervert does not care what she does either in the privacy of her own home or on the statehouse lawn. Drop it, Livia. Just as a hint, extortion doesn't work unless someone has secrets. Say if they're, oh, a doctor." She paused for a moment and then added," with big a trust fund from a daddy who's still alive and head of surgery." Alison could tell from the very pleased look on Liz's face that she'd done a little phone calling.

That was it. The last straw. Livia had been beaten. She sat back in her chair with such a look of surrender on her face Alison almost felt sorry for her. Almost.

The door opened and Mary Clare stuck her head into the room. Her only concession to the tribal theme was a red beret.

"I need to talk to you," she said to Liz.

"Doing private business," Liz replied. "Not going to be done for awhile."

"You'll do." Mary Clare nodded curtly at Alison.

Alison, who was afraid Mary Clare was going to start blurting out information about fuckbaby, leapt to her feet, forgetting the chair in which she was sitting was only about a foot off the ground and shooting out of it like a rocket.

"I want my money in cash," she said to Liz.

"Don't worry," said Liz, "It's all going to be in cash. We'll be gone for a little while. Have fun without us."

"What tribe are you from?" Alison asked politely of Mary Clare outside the door.

"What? Oh, I'm Basque. The rest of the outfit is dorky." Mary Clare obviously was still wanting to send Alison a message of disdain. She had decided to do this by talking to a spot over her shoulder rather than to her face. "Your little playmate took off this afternoon."

"Look," said Alison. She felt buoyed and brave by the thought of cold, hard cash. "I am sorry I hurt your cousin. Your friend. I really am. I behaved badly and I admit it. If there was a way I could make it so it hadn't happened, I would. I really would. But no matter what you think of me personally, Janet was not my 'playmate' and I was trying to do a good thing by getting her out of that hotel. So either talk to me like you're talking to an actual person or wait and talk to Liz, because I just don't need this grief in my life."

Mary Clare thought for quite a while on this one. "I'll wait and talk to Liz," she said finally. "I don't think there's anything to be done anyway."

"Fine," replied Alison. She walked down the hall and stepped back into the party.

She was buffeted from one end of the banquet hall to the other for about an hour, enjoying every second of it. Women were howling at the moon. She danced a little, flirted, narrowly avoided wrestling, snatched a bite here and there from a table and watched a whole lot. Eventually, as all roads do, hers led back to her own door and the lovely Stacy who had retreated into a corner to gnaw a chicken leg.

She tried giving her the short version of the Livia scene, but Stacy insisted on hearing every single detail and making comments too.

"Have you seen Kathy Corbeit?" Alison asked finally. "You know, that pretty girl who was playing with Scar?" They were both silent a moment, thinking of Scar. Neither of them could claim either to be fond of her or even to know her well. Still, it was strange knowing someone you had spoken to less than twenty-four hours before was dead.

"I read that story in the newspaper," Stacy said. "Scar was drunk? That was so weird. Didn't you say she was at Livia's dungeon? How could she get drunk there?"

"Oh, there was booze there. Didn't I tell you that? There was a whole bar happening."

"Christ," said Stacy, disgusted. Salad, wearing nothing but a gauzy scarf, floated by carrying a tray full of eclairs. Stacy snagged two. "So, in other words, Livia is now responsible for two deaths. And she'll never take responsibility for either one and she'll continue to buy women who don't know what's going on. I am almost sorry Liz arranged for her to pay that woman off." Stacy, of course, had been filled in on the whole scheme. "It would have been better if we'd just let Scar get up on the stage and tell everybody her story."

Alison had been thinking that she, and not Livia was responsible for Scar's death. If only she'd given her a ride! If only Janet had not been waiting in the stairwell! Despite her trip to Bad News' apartment, she was still worried about the woman.

"Do you know where Kathy Corbeit is?" she asked again. "Where Bad News is?" She had been the single person with whom Scar had spent time—logically, therefore, she was the one from whom Scar had heard something 'really bad.' If she had really heard something and hadn't just been trying to draw Alison into a non-consensual scene.

"Isn't that her over there?" Stacy nodded across the room. It took Alison a moment to figure out where she was pointing and then another to realize Stacy was indicating a woman dressed in full leather with a hood over her head. Oh right, Alison remembered. Bad News had been the woman in the hood at Tara when the SEPS had done their thing. Because of the crowd she couldn't tell for whom Bad News was bottoming now.

Liz appeared, still wearing the pleased look. "Here's your check, Bubba," she said to Alison, handing it across.

"I wanted cash," Alison whined.

"Don't worry, it's good. I took her down to Rick's—you know, my friend who's the bail bondsman—and made her take out a loan against her bank account at home." She snapped Erin's check in the air. Alison looked down at hers.

"Three thousand dollars?" she gasped. "Where'd that come from? She couldn't have decided to give me a bonus!"

"Nah, but I made her pay that extra two thousand for trying to threaten you and I tacked it on to your check instead of Erin's. I figured you could use it. Consider it your first paying job for the Perverts' Pervert."

Alison wanted to kiss Liz. Or rather, she wanted to show Liz some affection of the type one might show a brother to whom you are deeply indebted. "You are a genius," she said, giving her a little punch in the shoulder. "And where the hell did that clipping about the 'Perverts' Pervert' come from?"

"Oh, I just whipped that up on my computer and scanned in a photo I had from my first case," said Liz. "Just in case she decided to go there. I read her pretty good, didn't I?"

"Frankly," said Alison, "I am frightened by how well you got inside that crazy woman's head. I hope this is a gift which does not return to haunt you later."

"Nah," said Liz, whose attention was straying to someone in the crowd across the room, "it's all compartmentalized. I can pop it out and get rid of it like a big zit."

"And there you see," said Stacy to Alison, "why this woman seldom loses a case. It is because of her ability to place images like that into the minds of the judge and the jury."

G-hey! came pushing by, holding Salad by the hand. "We're going home to fuck," she told them. "We can't take it anymore." Salad, who was still wearing nothing but a scarf, looked pleased. Alison hoped that she had a coat in the lobby. Or at least a bathrobe.

"Come on out to the cloakroom with us," G-hey! told Alison. "I've got the key and I've got that stuff you wanted out there."

Alison, who had said 'What?' a whole hell of a lot over the weekend and didn't want to say it again, followed obediently, trying to figure out what the hell G-hey! was talking about. Oh, okay, the printout of the conference list. She didn't need it anymore, but felt it would be ungracious to say this after G-hey! had gone to all the trouble. She was beginning to like G-hey!

Inside the cloakroom G-hey! thrust a plastic bag with the logo 'Twist and Shout' into Alison's hands. There was such steam rising off G-hey! and Salad that it was obvious to Alison they were probably going to fuck right there on the floor of the cloakroom, so she let herself out politely.

Outside the door she opened the bag and looked inside. There was the list, which was five pages long and had all kinds of information, such as names and phone numbers, that no one would appreciate being in her hands. Good thing she wasn't planning on using it for the advancement of evil.

She had just finished thinking this when Erin herself came out into the foyer, her hand hooked beneath the collar of Stacy's big butch friend. How sweet. A happy ending for everyone.

Erin planted the big butch girl by the door and told her to stay. She crossed the room and spoke to Alison in an undertone. "Liz just gave me the check. Thanks."

"Sure," said Alison. "I've been meaning to tell you, I really thought the party idea was great. It really pissed her off. I don't think you heard me when I said it before."

"What?" asked Erin.

"Putting the ad in the program? 'I like Swiss cheese and roast beef?'"

"You mean she didn't do that herself?" Erin asked in a surprised tone. "I wondered why she was throwing an open party. Great idea! Wasn't me, though." The big butch girl was looking at her with such longing Alison could feel Erin being sucked away and out the door.

"Have fun!" she called after them.

Alison again looked into the bag, which was still really bulky even with the list out. There were a bunch of printed pages, which after glancing through them, Alison decided were probably pages from the Internet. As near as she could tell from her one experience, Salad had done a search on all the names—both legal and play—and then downloaded anything that had come up in the search. First there was the Wildfire page, including the personals and the photo of Falcon, which read beneath it. 'Unsafe player! Stay away unless you're into a death scene! Warn your friends!' Alison detected the fine hand of Livia behind this and was delighted all over again that Liz had stepped in. A couple of the women had personal web sites and someone was an expert on Marine wildlife and one of the craftswomen was trying to sell her whips. Then there was a book review about a book on young lesbians that left Alison puzzled. Somebody had talked to her recently about a book on young lesbians, but who had it been? She felt as if she had been absolutely deluged with information over the weekend and unfortunately the moment she had solved Livia's problem she had lost most of it. That's why they called it short term memory. Oh, well, it didn't matter any more.

Liz came into the foyer, humming and smiling. "I got a date!" she sang. "I'm the best shark in town and I've got a date with a hot woman who is going to let me buff her boots before she beats me black and blue and fucks me in the ass with a night stick. God, life is good!"

"I truly am envious," said Alison, still looking in the bag. She truly was envious, although at this moment she was so tired that the thought of staying up for more than another forty-five minutes made her sick to her stomach.

"Who's got the key to the cloakroom?" Liz asked.

"Actually, I do," said Alison, putting down the bag to take it from her pocket. "But G-hey! and Salad are fucking in there."

Liz waved this off. "Oh, they won't mind. I was in a three way with them once—I've seen them buck naked before."

"Everybody in this building has now seen Salad buck naked," observed Alison, picking up the bag again. The last thing in it was a book, which turned out to be the same book mentioned in the review. *Movers and Shakers* it was called. *Fifty Young Lesbians Who Will Change the World* said the subtitle.

"Hey," said Liz, "what did Mary Clare want to tell you?"

"I told Mary Clare I didn't want her to talk to me if she couldn't give me the respect I deserve," said Alison stiffly. What she really thought was that Liz should not have anything to do with Mary Clare if she was going to say nasty things about her, but that was probably asking a little too much.

"Oh!" said Liz. "Well, you just let me know how getting Mary Clare to treat you with the respect you deserve turns out. I'll be really interested."

With this pronouncement she opened the door to the cloakroom. The air that escaped smelled so heavily of sex that it hit Alison like a wave and she staggered back on her feet.

The hall was beginning to empty more rapidly. Luckily only a few people had known about the locking cloakroom—the rest had either worn their jackets or hung them on the rolling rack which was pushed over by the wall at the end of the lobby. Alison saw Bernie whiz through the lobby, her oxygen tank being pulled by one of Liz's friends, who was looking at her with eyes jittering with excitement.

"Hey!" Alison said to Ramona, who came out wearing a really big I-got-lucky grin on her face, "who got the communion last night?"

"Nobody!" said Ramona in a supremely satisfied voice. It was unclear as to whether she was just matching her tone to suit her face or if the outcome of the communion had pleased her mightily. "Nobody at all! Livia was so fucking pissed off that she actually accused everybody there of messing with her drugs and then threw us all out! Even her own court! She had those three big rooms all to herself and Yesman had to sleep on my floor without a pillow and her coat on!" She looked over her shoulder and then swirled away into the crowd toward a woman with red hair, whom Alison recognized only belatedly and from the back was Dana.

There was a bit of a lull and Alison looked at the book again. It was a series of interviews with and stories about the fifty young lesbians who were going to change the world. Duh. It had photographs, which was a good thing, since Alison was unable to retrieve any part of her conversation with G-hey! At least, she thought it had been G-hey! The photos showed women black and brown and tan in dresses and jeans and dresses over jeans, working at their own queer publications and lobbying their congresspeople and saving the whales. The only thing the photos had in common was that the women were so, so young, all of them teenagers and some no more than twelve or thirteen. It was really a lovely book. Alison leafed past the photo of a young woman who had convinced first her high school and then all the schools in her hometown to go from styrofoam to reusable lunch trays, past another who had arranged a statewide protest over the ridiculous and revealing uniform shorts for the girls' track and field teams and came to rest on a photo which showed a lovely young woman with short, punk hair standing in front of a grand piano and holding a large gold loving cup. She was half turned toward an older woman who also had a hand on the trophy, smiling her biggest for the crowd.

The door to the cloakroom burst open and Liz came out.

"Oh!" she said, looking over Alison's shoulder. "I knew it. I just knew it! I knew that woman dressed straight at home! You can always tell the ones who grow their hair out to go back to work!"

Alison turned to her, but at that moment the big femme in the black corset walked out of the double doors into the lobby, snapped her fingers at Liz and pointed. That was all she wrote. Out the door they went, Liz shouldering a huge toy bag.

Alison looked down at the photo. What in the world had Liz meant?

Stacy came through the door. She had that radiant glow one tends to get when one's tits have been complimented all evening long, but it was overlaid with a heavy coat of exhaustion.

"You better go, babe," she said. "The work exchange people didn't show up and I've got to stay here and help clean up the kitchen. Has that wretched Liz escaped?"

Alison looked at her in dismay. It seemed so callous to just say 'Okay' and then walk away, yet she knew she could not stay. It was going to take a couple of hours at least to pick up the mess and she could already feel tears just around the corner. She compromised. "I'll stay for half an hour and help," she said.

"Fabulous," Stacy replied. "Could you start picking up trash in the banquet room?"

Picking up trash, thought Alison, as she took the bag Stacy brought her from the kitchen, was the perfect job. No sorting, no brainwork, no decisions. It was trash or it wasn't, it went into the bag or it didn't.

There were still some women who were lingering, among them Bad News in the skintight leather suit with the hood still over her face. Tonight it was not Scar who held the leash, but another butch woman Alison didn't remember seeing at any point earlier in the weekend. She was laughing with friends while Bad News crouched contentedly at her feet in a position Alison wouldn't have been able to hold for more than two minutes. Aging was hell on submissives.

She dumped a platter of chicken bones into the garbage bag and then looked over her shoulder at Bad News. Even though she could not see the face of the woman in the hood, just being near her had jogged her memory and suddenly she remembered the whole conversation with G-hey! in the pantry of the mansion. She put the bag down for a moment and pulled out the book, which she had stuck into the back of her pants. She flipped through the photos, holding the book beneath the table in an attempt to be unobtrusive, and turned to the picture of the young musician. Of course—femme her up and add ten years and it was Bad News. She ran her finger down the page, reading just enough to see if the story was the same one related to her by G-hey and Liz! Pretty much. Terrible poverty and neglect in childhood, salvaged by a caring teacher who had all but adopted her and, after nurturing her talents for a couple of years, taken her on a very successful young musicians tour, where Bad News—the book, of course, called her Kathy—had finished each recital by coming out to the audience. Because it was a dyke book it mentioned that the teacher, a Veronica Simons, was also a dyke and she and Kathy both talked a little about mentoring and how important that was.

Alison closed the book and stuck it into her quiver, which she then placed on one of the tables. She took her headdress off as well—the hall was awfully hot and she had the bad feeling it might be starting to smell. She would have liked to read more, but already she was beginning to flag and it wasn't fair to Stacy to promise only half an hour and then spend ten minutes reading. Chicken bones, paper plates and napkins into one bag; pop cans into the other.

The unfamiliar butch must have thought it was hot too, or perhaps she just didn't want to go out in public in scene, for she was loosening the hood pulled down over Bad News' head. Alison glanced up from a pile of bread crust just in time to see her pull it off.

And it wasn't Bad News at all. It was a completely different woman. Different in every way it was possible to be different. Different hair, different eyes, different build. It was, in fact, the woman who had been the magician in the talent show—all she was missing was the mustache. And that recognition jump-started another—the woman holding her leash was her lovely assistant butched out.

Oh, man. Alison felt fucked with. First Erin and now this woman. She wasn't sure she could get along in a world where butches cross-dressed. It seemed so wrong, so wrong! She felt as if she could just put her head down and wail.

The crying part clued her in. Oh, okay, it wasn't about the woman holding the leash or Erin. It was about being tired. It was about her FMS, an entity even more narcissistic than Livia and never content unless it was center stage. She had vowed to herself that she was no longer going to push herself to the point of illness, so she was going to have to tell Stacy she'd just overshot and promised something she couldn't carry through. Swallow the denial, swallow the pride and just fucking admit it before she broke down and bawled over the breakdown of traditional butch/femme roles.

Unless… She looked at the four women standing and talking. Removing the hood must have been the signal for the magician to come out of role, because she was right in there. Alison had never really done anything like this, so she had to think about it for a moment.

"Hey," she said finally, coming up close beside them. "I feel just awful and the work exchange people blew and I don't want to leave this whole job for my girlfriend. Could you all help me for a minute?"

They turned to her with pleasant faces and almost before the sound of the words had died out the magician had gone to the kitchen for more trash bags.

"You know," said the woman who had been holding the leash, "you do look just awful. We can finish up here. Why don't you go home?"

And Alison did.

Chapter Sixteen

Alison was not scheduled to drive the van until eleven o'clock the next morning, which meant that she got to sleep about ten hours. Fourteen would have been better. She was still going to have to call her acupuncturist and ask for double appointments this week. God bless Liz for making Livia pay that extra money!

The first thing she did after Beth passed her the keys from the early shift was to drive over to the building which Marta and Mary Clare owned. Holding her breath and hoping Marta was out having breakfast at the Merc, she darted up the outside stairs and knocked on the door of the one room apartment in which they had secreted fuckbaby. Face it, she was never going to be able to think of her as anything else. She felt badly about stashing her away and not checking back and hoped that perhaps Marta and Mary Clare had acted a little better toward her, for all Mary Clare's blustering.

No one answered her first tentative and then demanding knock and she had just put her face up to the window when someone behind her said, "She's gone."

Alison jumped and then lost her balance and came down with a thud on her butt. She was quite relieved to see that it was not Marta who had come quietly up behind her and equally displeased to discover it was Mary Clare, once again carrying a newspaper and tool box and obviously pleased as punch to have Alison at a disadvantage.

"She's gone," she said again and then, "Which I tried to tell you last night."

"Oh, would that have been when you were being so rude and ugly to me?" snapped Alison, who felt that she had not gotten one iota of credit for the rescue of fuckbaby.

"Be reasonable, Alison," said Mary Clare in a voice that itself bespoke reason. "How can I be anything but ugly and rude to you? You hurt my best friend. You made her cry. How would you act toward someone who did that to your best friend?"

Approached thus Alison was knocked right out of counterattack mode. She gave a big sigh. Of course if someone hurt Michelle she would have to do the same thing and had done the same thing. She in fact still held grudges against women whom Michelle herself had forgiven years before.

"All right," she said, knowing she was beaten. "All right. But could we just have a few minutes of truce to exchange information? Kind of like Christmas in the trenches?"

Mary Clare did not come right out and say yes, but she did not come right out and say no either, which Alison figured was probably the best that she could do without compromising Marta's honor.

"She was gone when I came by yesterday afternoon," Mary Clare said. "She left a note."

"What did it say?" asked Alison.

"It said, thanks. Literally. That was all it said. One word."

"Do you think she left or Livia found her?" Where would fuckbaby go on her own, in a strange city with no money? On the other hand, how could Livia have found her here?

Mary Clare shrugged. "You know," she said, "there's a lot of dykes living in these two buildings." Alison nodded. In this area of Capitol Hill dykes did tend to take over if at all possible. They were kind of like kudzu. "G-hey! lives over there and Kathy lives downstairs and they both provided community housing. Anybody could have seen her sitting on the balcony drinking coffee and passed it back to Livia's crew without even knowing what she was doing."

"But she did leave a note."

Mary Clare shrugged again. Obviously the truce was nearing its end. Alison decided to leave before it disintegrated entirely. 'You can't save everybody, Alison', she told herself as she clattered back down the stairs. It was cold comfort. She wanted to save everyone and so far she had saved no one.

Evil Stacy, the control freak, had surfaced once again that morning and had forced all the van drivers to carry her cell phone to make sure they were always within nag range. The phone began to ring as Alison climbed back into the van. It took her a moment to answer. Stacy was given to switching her phone's mode of transportation quite regularly and it was currently housed in a red plastic lunchbox with a picture of *One-Hundred-and-One Dalmatians* on the side. Don't ask why. At least it was better than the girly pink triangle purse into which Good Stacy sometimes put it.

"You're late," Stacy said, "People are waiting."

"On my way," said Alison, starting the engine so it wouldn't be a lie.

In front of the guest hotel she picked up the woman with the short hair and earrings who had complimented Wildfire at Fantasy Night, dressed in straight clothes and disinclined to talk. It was the end of a pretty intense vacation and Alison could see she was depressurizing—starting to think of cats and chores and lovers left at home and work tomorrow. She stared out the window as Alison drove in silence. A conference, Alison knew from experience, was not usually a time to sightsee. The drive to DIA and back was probably about as much of the town as any of these women would see.

To the intense annoyance of driver and passenger, the two people waiting at the next community housing stop were the two Pattys. Now why couldn't the light rail have hit them? Alison wondered.

"Don't stop," suggested Earrings, who was sitting in the front seat.

"I don't want them to be stranded in Denver," protested Alison, pulling to the curb. "They'll drive down the price of real estate."

"Strap them to the top of the van, then," Earrings said, a suggestion which Alison actually considered.

Tempting as it was, especially considering there was equipment in the van to do this quickly and properly, Alison instead parked the van and walked around to the passenger side to meet the two women.

"You," she said, pointing to the first Patty, "are sitting in the back. And you…" pointing to the second Patty, "are sitting up here by me." She glanced over at Earrings, who gracefully relinquished her seat for a good cause.

"I don't…" said both women together, but Alison shouted them down in her very best cop voice.

"There's not a choice! Did I say there was a choice? Because there isn't a choice! This is the way it's going to be! You either sit where I tell you or you can take a sixty-dollar cab ride! And if you start any, any of this shit you've been pulling all weekend then we're going to throw you out by the side of the road!" She turned to Earrings, who nodded her head eagerly, as if really looking forward to the possibility of this happening.

"And I have a gun in my purse and if we have to stop I'm going to shoot you both before we throw you out," Earings said, which obviously made everybody, including Alison, a little nervous. She didn't really think Earrings had a gun in her purse—how would she get in through the metal detectors?—but still, if anyone had a gun in their purse it would be one of these women. Alison was only about ten minutes away from wishing the whole leather community, including Stacy and Liz, would disappear from the face of the earth.

They rode in silence to the next stop. The front seat Patty mumbled, "Nazi!" once, but she was not brave enough to either repeat it or say it aloud, especially with Earrings riding behind her, her hand in her purse.

The phone rang again.

"House pickup," said Stacy, who sounded as if she had chosen terse over crabby. She gave Alison an address on Milwaukee.

Not until they turned onto Milwaukee did Alison realize it was G-hey!'s—and hence Marta's—address. She bit back a groan. Was she to be plagued forever by one night of selfishness and passion?

She pulled up in front of the building and honked, but there was no response.

"Well, are you just going to sit there?" snapped the back seat Patty. "Some of us have planes to catch!"

"You know that threat about throwing you out of the van?" Alison said, half turning in her seat. "It's kind of a blanket clause. Piss me off in any way whatsoever down to and including not being a Rockies fan or liking raisins and you're out on your butt."

Everyone nodded, except for the front seat Patty who said, "Don't you talk to her like that!"

Tempted as she was to mix it up with the Pattys, Alison knew this was only an excuse for not knocking on G-hey!'s door. Resigned, she turned her back on the possible ruckus and climbed down from her seat.

Just before she and Robert had taken the skinhead off to booking last winter Alison had asked to borrow a bathroom, and she was pretty sure the one to which she had been led belonged to G-hey!—around back and upstairs, directly across from Marta's.

There was a button on the bottom door that led to the stairs and thank god, thank god G-hey! was the one who answered her persistent buzzing.

"What do you want?" asked G-hey! ungraciously. "We worked our butts off this weekend! We're done! We hardly had time to fuck ourselves!" She was wrapped in a sheet that smelled so strongly of sex Alison's nipples hardened automatically. Still, even G-hey! pissed off was better than Marta under any circumstances.

"I'm picking up your guest," said Alison, showing her the clipboard on which she had written the address Stacy had given her.

G-hey! took the clipboard, letting the sheet slip down over her breasts as if they were on womyn's land or something, instead of twenty feet from an alley that was not only very well traveled but through which two guys with a shopping cart full of cans were now passing. It made Alison feel very anxious and she was glad when G-hey! passed the clipboard back to her and adjusted her sheet.

"They've made a mistake with the address," she said in an irritated voice. "My community housing guest went home last night. Thank god! That was the only smart thing we did all weekend! There wasn't enough help—all that crap about those work exchange people! We should have only used people we knew and Salad and I should get a full pass to the next Wildfire without working at all!"

If Alison had anything at all to say about it, there wasn't going to be a next Wildfire, but this wasn't the time to share that little hope. Instead she said, "I'll talk to Stacy"—a promise easily kept because she talked to Stacy everyday and hadn't been so silly as to promise the topic.

Immediately mollified, which made Alison feel guilty, G-hey! said, "Try next door. Kathy Corbeit had somebody staying with her." Bad News' name falling so easily from the lips of G-hey! was for some reason still rather startling, but of course, they were neighbors.

"I only saw her at the beginning of the conference, "Alison could not help saying. "Did you see her after Fantasy Night? She had a full pass."

"She's moody," said G-hey! shortly. "You know? I told you she was kind of fucked up. She gets pissed about things. Maybe she got insulted and stayed home writing letters to *Weird Sisters* and *Lesbian Connection*. She's a big letter writer." She glanced pointedly over her shoulder and up the stairs.

Making an inner vow that she actually would talk to Stacy about G-hey! and Salad, who really had worked their butts off, Alison walked back around the house. She was saved from knocking on Bad News' door, however. Coming slowly down the steps was Bernie, the frail butch woman from Arizona. She had her oxygen tank strapped to a rolling suitcase, which she was trundling slowly behind her.

"Hi!" she said, her face lighting up with a smile when she saw Alison. "Bernie. Remember?"

"Can I help you?" asked Alison.

"No, I can do this part. I might need some help putting my suitcase in." She paused for a moment at the bottom of the steps. "Do you know what I should do with the keys?"

"What?" asked Alison, wishing Bernie would keep on going so that maybe they could get out of there before Marta or Mary Clare appeared and she had to humble herself again.

"Her keys," said Bernie, holding a ring up before Alison's face as if this was going explain everything. On the ring were two new looking keys and a soft plastic square advertising *Curve* magazine, which Alison knew, for the same reason that she had known about the Mercury T-shirt, had been a freebie. The *Curve* girls had come through town on a promotional tour the summer before—she had a couple of key rings and a visor herself.

"Didn't she tell you what to do with them when you left?" she asked.

"Well, if she'd done that I would know, wouldn't I?" said Bernie and then, as if that had come out in a tarter tone than she had meant, "Actually, I only met the woman once—when she showed up for some clothes and took the case for the bass. Why do you suppose she did that? The bass fiddle was still there. It was late Saturday—she woke me up and I didn't think to ask about the keys. It was funny," she went on, "I'd seen her in one of the fantasies, but I never would have guessed she was my hostess. Too Butch. Never have guessed! Not from the stuff in her closet."

"When was that?" asked Alison, her heart starting to pound a little faster. If Bernie had only seen Bad News once… "Then you were feeding the cats?"

"Oh, yeah," said Bernie. "I figured it was the least I could do—it was nice of her to put me up. I couldn't have come if I'd had to pay for a hotel. And I had the whole place to myself—I thought I'd be sharing, but she must have met somebody really cute at the conference." She smiled. "I did that once. I met this fantastic, hot femme right at the start of Leather Together a couple of years ago—I mean, practically stepping off the plane—and we went to her hotel room and fucked the whole time. Didn't go to a single event, sent out for room service, never even picked up our registration packets." She smiled again. "But I don't know what to do with the keys. It's a deadbolt, so I can't leave them inside. And I don't want to leave the door unlocked, or put them in the mailbox. That's just like putting a sign out saying, 'Rob this house.' I took the mail in, too."

"When did you see her?" asked Alison again. "How did you get the keys in the first place?"

"Oh, she'd left them at the registration table. Left a note to tell me where the clean towels were and asking me to make sure the cats didn't get out. I only saw her that once—late, late Saturday night. We didn't even talk—I was so fucking tired! I could hardly even open my eyes! But she was in and out other times when I wasn't here—stuff was moved around. She took her dobro one time and then brought it back and got her bass case and some other music stuff and didn't bring them back. I guess maybe she had a gig over the weekend. And she was here fucking the first night—I mean, they had the bedroom door closed, but they were pretty loud."

"What's a dobro? asked Alison, momentarily distracted.

"Oh, it's that thing that looks like a guitar but isn't. So have you got any idea about these keys?" Without warning she thrust the ring into Alison's hand. Alison's fingers closed around it automatically. She could see by the look on Bernie's face that the keys had just become her problem. Where could Bad News have been all weekend?

"Well, I'm just going to push them through the mail slot." Alison made an executive decision. Bad News' mail slot was a way for things to be both put out of sight and mind. Thank goodness they were just keys and not a cat.

"And the funny thing was," Bernie repeated herself, "that I'd seen her around, tattoos and all—you know, at the Meet and Beat and the workshops and stuff—and I never realized she was my hostess. I never would have guessed from her clothes and shoes and stuff in the closet—so femme and small."

Alison hadn't seen any tattoos on Bad News. She had certainly kept them well covered. Alison looked back over her shoulder. "I'm going to run up and put these through the door," she said. "I'll help you with your suitcase. Don't try to lift it yourself."

"There's another one back there by the door," said Bernie agreeably.

Alison climbed the three steps and opened the mail slot. No problem. She pushed the ring through and heard it land on the wooden floor with a loud clunk. Okay, then, that was the last bit of business with Bad News—it was all wrapped up and she hoped she never saw the woman again, which was kind of funny, considering that she had been hoping that she would see her all weekend long.

She turned and saw that Earrings had climbed out of the van to help Bernie with her suitcase. Okay, then, she'd get the other one.

This thought had barely passed through her mind when suddenly the big front door flew open with such vigor that it seemed to pull at Alison as if it had created a little vacuum.

"Oh, Jesus," said Marta. Her hair was tied up in a scarf as if she'd been cleaning again. In one hand she was holding the keys and the bag from Clothworld in which Alison had returned the clutch. "I thought you heard what I said to you. I don't need you to be here! I need you to not be here! If you have something to give someone who lives here, then give it to her! Don't try to lay it on me! I don't see her! Nobody comes through here—they all have their own doors."

"I'm sorry I was a shit, I didn't mean to be, but I was and I'm sorry," said Alison automatically. Maybe if she said it enough times when she saw Marta alone Marta wouldn't get in her face the first time she saw her with Stacy. For the first time, Alison was glad that Stacy didn't like to two-step.

"Don't do that, okay?" said Marta. "Because then what it turns into is me feeling like I have to make you feel better about yourself and I am not up to it. Please! Just stay away and quit trying to suck me into being your delivery girl!" She shoved her hand over toward Alison with a little grimace, as if she wanted to make sure there was no physical contact during the exchange. Alison was a little slow. Before her fingers could close all the way the bag with the purse inside tumbled to the floor.

"Oh, for god's sake!" Marta, who had started the exchange in that same reasonable tone with which she had laid down the rules the day before, was starting to sound a little as if she suspected Alison had just bitten one of her cats' heads off. Alison didn't blame her. It was hard to be reasonable. "Here, let me get it!" She pushed in front of Alison and bent down. The clutch had fallen out of the bag. She picked up the bag first and then grabbed the purse as if she were thinking of throwing it. "I really wish—" she started and then went white as a sheet. Alison had pulled people out of wrecked cars and fights and fires and had even been down to the morgue, but it was the first time that she had ever seen anyone turn quite that color quite that way and quite so quickly.

"What?" she asked, automatically reaching for Marta with the intent of pushing her head down between her knees. It was another indication of shock that Marta neither threw a punch nor shrugged her off.

"Where'd you get this? Where the hell is Kathy? I haven't seen her all weekend." Marta asked, gasping each word as if she were speaking underwater. "This is bad, something's gone really wrong. Where's Kathy?"

Alison remembered the article she had read in *Circles* about the skinhead incident Marta and Mary Clare had been involved in the previous winter. There had been two photos accompanying the article. One, Alison seemed to remember, had been of G-hey! standing next to a dome tent. The other had been of Marta, looking tired and ill-cared-for, holding a telephone up to her mouth. Marta had assisted the police in some way, Alison thought. Some sort of psychic thing.

"It's… can I get you something to drink? Maybe you should lie down." Oh, jeez, what if Marta had a heart attack right there on the spot? Alison felt bad enough about the one night stand—she'd feel guilty the rest of her life if she killed Marta. Hardly aware of what she was doing, she pulled the clutch from Marta's hand and stuffed it back in the bag. "I'm going to go to the car for a minute—just hold on!" She had a cold Big Gulp sitting on the floor beside her seat. It wasn't in any of the Red Cross pamphlets, but she knew from personal experience that nothing brought you back from the verge quite like caffeine and sugar.

She was halfway to the car when she heard a horrible sound, worse than the squalling of a walrus fight. She put her hands up to her face so she could peek through her fingers. News like this was always better in small doses. In the van she could see a flurry of activity roiling around in the back seat like the cloud of dust Mort Walker was always drawing to represent the Sarge tangling with Beetle Bailey—only an occasional hand or foot clear in the fray. The Pattys had taken advantage of her absence to stir the fire yet again.

Beside the van stood Bernie and Earrings, looking more annoyed than anything else. They both looked as if they wanted a cigarette.

"I told you to make them ride on top," said Earrings crossly, looking at her watch.

"Watch this," said Alison. "Wait a minute, though, I want to take this to the woman on the porch." She went through the passenger door and grabbed the Big Gulp, handing it back to Earrings. "Take that back over there, will you?" she said to Earrings. "While I take care of these two."

"Are you going to hack them into little bitty pieces?" asked Earrings, hopefully. "Because if you are, I want to help."

"And I want to piss on them afterwards," said Bernie, in a hopeful tone of her own.

"Just take it!" snapped Alison, who would have blown up the entire block had she the means even if it had meant taking herself along for the ride. Without waiting to see if Earrings would take exception to her tone and want to confront her about non-consensual topping, Alison crawled over Bernie's suitcase to the back of the van. Femme Patty had Butch Patty backed into a corner and was whaling on her like she was playing a snare drum. She had a black eye and Butch Patty had a split lip.

Trying, not altogether successfully, to avoid getting hit herself, Alison quickly reached to either side and grabbed the dog wall. A twist and a click and it went together as easily as Beth had shown her. Let the two idiots beat or fuck one another to death. She didn't care which.

Earrings was already climbing in the front door, a huge smile on her face.

"I took her the coke," she said, "and then that—oh, what's her name? That little butch gal with the tight pants and the cute jacket? Anyway, she came along and said she'd deal with it if we'd just get these two out of town."

The description did not narrow the Wildfire field much, but Alison suspected Earrings was talking about Mary Clare. She looked up at the porch, which was empty, though the door was open and then glanced around the street. Sure enough, she saw the little red pickup truck with the 'I saw you naked at Michigan' bumper sticker she knew belonged to Mary Clare.

Thank god, thank god in heaven, she thought. She must have behaved particularly poorly in another life to have deserved this weekend.

The remainder of the trip was like nothing she had ever experienced or desired to experience. The Pattys rolled on the floor behind the dog wall, going from fighting to fucking several times, while the rest of them looked straight ahead and gritted their teeth with anger. Alison cursed Federico Peña aloud—if they had just stuck with good old, reliable Stapleton they could have been there and back already.

Finally, the surreal, white-tented roof of DIA could be seen on the horizon. "I'm going to need some help," said Bernie.

"Don't you dare drop me off with those two!" said Earrings. The two to whom she referred were now down on the floor, Butch Patty's leather pants down around her ankles and Femme Patty's fist shoved up her cunt as far as it would go. She was moaning and Alison reflected for a moment on what a total turn-off it was. She was so very sick of these two women by now that she would rather watch her grandparents do the nasty than the two of them.

She pulled up beneath the United sign—she didn't know where the Pattys were going or on what airline and she didn't care. United was just the first. She jumped down from her seat, followed by Earrings, who had turned out to be a really good ally. Alison was sorry she hadn't met her sooner. As if they had done this before, Alison inserted her key in the lock, mimed One, Two, Three and swung the door open. The luggage was out on the curb before the Pattys knew what was happening and they themselves followed in such close order there was not even a moment for protest. Luckily the fisting had stopped, though Alison would not have cared if they were stuck together like dogs. Let the porters deal with it; let the airport cops deal with it. Hell, let Peña come back from Washington and deal with it his goddamn self! But she wasn't going to deal with it for one more minute.

They were back in the van with the doors locked tight in a trice. Alison almost took the fender off a Yellow Cab in her haste to pull back into the driving lane.

"I don't see my airline," said Bernie in a tone of mild worry.

"You know, I don't see mine, either." Earrings was craning her head out the window, looking down the long line of signs which hung above the crowded sidewalk. "I'm going out on Florida Sun."

"Oh, we're at the wrong terminal!" Alison was beginning to feel a bit nervous about all the time they had wasted. Not only did it take longer to get to DIA than it had taken to get to Stapleton, it took longer to get from the main terminal to the gates and the trip involved a train ride and a couple of trips up and down the escalators. Gone were the days of arriving at the airport with only fifteen minutes to spare.

"Your phone is ringing," Bernie told Alison as she looped back past terminal A.

"Fuck 'em," said Alison shortly. Either it was Stacy, who had decided that she wanted to deal with things right this instant as she was wont to do, or it was somebody bitching about shuttle service. Either way, she didn't need it right now. She'd call back in after she got these two to their airlines, which in Bernie's case was obviously going to mean a wheelchair.

Earrings was humming a happy little tune under her breath.

"Why are you so happy?" asked Alison, her mind on logistics. "Glad to be going home?"

"Oh, I was just thinking how wonderful it would be if someone opened the emergency door on the Pattys' flight and they were sucked out of the plane."

That made all three of them laugh.

"What was it with those two, anyway?" asked Bernie, wiping her eyes with the back of her hand.

"Well," said Alison, "from what I gathered one of them had been the other one's—I don't know, her teacher or something. Somebody in power. And she seduced the other one, the student…"

"No, no, no," corrected Earrings, shaking her head with a jangle. "One of them went to Powersurge last year and the other stayed home. And the one who went was in a monogamous contract with the other, but she bottomed for the other one's ex-girlfriend."

"Are you sure?" asked Alison, remembering the conversation she had overheard from the bathroom. "I thought it was the teacher thing."

"Believe me, I'm sure," Earrings replied. "I heard the whole story from both Pattys. Accidentally sat next to one of them in an AA meeting and the other one at dinner. I can quote names and times. Besides, how could one of them be the other's teacher? They're about the same age." She snorted. "That was a hell of an AA meeting, let me tell you. Me and that crazy Patty and then that woman who got killed."

Alison was still thinking about the Pattys' story. "So there wasn't a teacher? Are you sure?"

"Actually, I heard the teacher story as well," Bernie chimed in nodding toward Earrings. "Except that I heard it from," she stopped a moment to consider and then went on, "The ex-lover, I guess she would be."

Alison had another question. "Scar was at an AA meeting?" she asked, trying to fit that into the newspaper story.

Earrings shrugged. "Yeah. I was surprised, too. She sure didn't talk about wanting to drink at the meeting. And she said she'd been sober for almost ten years."

They dropped off Earrings, who had been anxiously looking at her watch and her ticket at the curbside check-in and then circled back to park. Bernie's flight, luckily, was not going to leave for almost another hour. It was going to be a little tight, but if Alison hustled Bernie to her gate and then turned right around and drove fast she would be pretty much on schedule for the next run.

The phone started ringing again as she was struggling with the luggage. Naturally. She called up to Bernie to answer it.

"Where is it?" asked Bernie, obligingly moving slowly toward the front.

Well, that was a good question and she wasn't able to think of the answer quick enough, uncertain as to whether she'd left it in the lunch box or tossed it down between the seats. After she got Bernie settled in the chair, briefcase on her lap because she couldn't think of any other way to deal with it, Alison rooted around in the mess on the floor and finally came up with the lunch box. Beside the phone was half of yesterday's sandwich, carefully wrapped. Well, that was going to make the second run much better. For everyone. She stuffed the phone into the pocket of her jacket.

They checked the bag at the curb and tipped the porter a dollar, then went into the terminal. Going in on wheels was a whole lot different than walking, Alison found and the elevators and special lines and all of it took extra time. Hell, just finding out what to do and where to go took extra time. Bernie had never flown out of DIA before, so she didn't know a lot more than Alison did. At least, thought Alison, she was good-natured about everything. She chatted a little bit more about the conference and then, sensing Alison's anxiety, was silent, going through some papers from her briefcase. Alison tried phoning in, but according to the canned voice of the operator, Beth's phone was not turned on. Which probably meant, knowing Beth, that she'd forgotten to recharge it the night before. Either way, it must not have been Stacy trying to reach Alison.

They boarded the train along with a crush of other people, all of whom had that anxious, I-know-I've-forgotten-something look on their faces. Several of them were speaking softly in French. Alison looked at the advertisements mounted on the wall above the seats. It had been years since she had actually seen anyone off inside an airport. She disliked it enough so that she stood firm even to Stacy, who wanted her to be there gazing sadly out the window watching the plane taxi whenever she left town. It just seemed so stupid and artificial—the things that were important had already been said.

All that was left was guessing whether the flight would be on time or not. Saying goodbye at the gate, thought Alison, was like the final chase scene in *Con Air*—the mark of someone who just didn't know when the story was over.

The pleasant voice of the train, which reminded Alison of the computer on *Star Trek:Next Generation*, told them they were at their terminal. Alison was jostled away from the door by a French family.

"Oh, hello," said Bernie. Alison turned to look. The car had two doors and getting out of the next one over was Crescent, the butch who had complained to Alison on Fantasy Night—the woman who had helped Bad News from Livia's party. She was dressed in nice jeans and a blazer with leather patches on the elbows, button earrings, make-up applied with the hand of long practice, loafers and socks which matched her forest green L.L. Bean turtleneck. Alison had been right about the henna thing—her hair was much lighter than it had been on Friday night and she was wearing a forest green beret that covered the shaved patch. She looked respectable enough to run for congress. Strangely enough, this change of character made her seem very familiar to Alison. Where had she seen her like that?

The three of them were being swept along in the tide of French tourists, all of whom appeared to be trying to catch a flight for which they were terribly, terribly late. It took Alison a moment to extract Bernie from the crowd, a frighteningly long moment when she thought they were going to be forced any-which-way onto the escalator and then shoved over sideways at the top. She let out a sigh of relief when they finally reached the elevator.

"Yeah," said Bernie looking up at her. "Weird, huh? People don't seem to see you in a chair." She looked again at the papers she was holding and then said, "Damn it all! How could I have done that?"

"What?" asked Alison, punching the up button again as if it were going to make it come faster.

"Look." She held up a small handful of mail—what looked like a couple of 'To Occupant' pieces and a couple more that could have been personal or at least from the bank. "I must have picked them up when I picked my own stuff up." She handed the bundle to Alison, who took it with some reluctance. Every single time anyone had handed her anything over the last four days it had meant trouble. "I'm glad I realized it before I got on the plane. You can give them back to her," she added blithely.

"Oh, god, I'd rather die than go back to that house again," Alison whined. "I think I gave one of the women there a heart attack."

"You don't have to go to her house," said Bernie. "Just give it to her on your way out." She slung her briefcase across her chest by the long strap and then stood, carefully smoothing out the kinks in her air tube. "Just hand them to her on your way out."

"Huh?"

"Just hand it to her," Bernie said again, starting to inch her way toward the gate. "Didn't you see her on the train? She must be seeing somebody off." She laughed. "I'll bet it's whoever she was with all weekend."

The attendant called for pre-boarding. Bernie surrendered her oxygen and said thanks and goodbye and great conference. Alison stood by the chair a moment, sorting through the short stack of mail. Maybe there was nothing important and she could toss the whole pile without feeling guilty. Two 'occupant' post cards that could go right in the trash. Something from the motor vehicle department. Dammit, that was going to have to be returned. She started back up the corridor, swiveling her head from side to side, looking for Bad News. She didn't see her, but she saw several other dykes from the conference. Not everybody had taken the shuttle.

She looked from the right to the left, trying to spot that pretty, troubled face, wondering if she would recognize the woman from the back. Left to right, Air Alaska and a candy stand, then up the corridor toward the moving sidewalks…

She stopped dead in her tracks. Coming down the corridor, voices raised in anger, each dragging a suitcase behind her, were the Dueling Pattys. Alison looked around hastily for a place to hide. If there had been an open door she would have jumped right out it and hoped that fate would hold the damage down. She would have been perfectly willing to sprain an ankle or break an arm.

But the best she could do was to rush over to the window at Horizon Air and pray the Pattys weren't going to Boise, Idaho or Pullman, Washington.

She sat hastily in the chair and then pulled herself up to the window with an air of intensity which would have done Penelope proud. "No Pattys, no Pattys, no Pattys," she chanted to herself, not daring to look around. She didn't care if the next run was an hour late as long as she didn't become embroiled in yet another Patty-a-thon.

As if a gift from an evil goddess her phone began to ring. "Shut up, shut up, shut up!" she begged beneath her breath as she fumbled in her pocket.

"What!" she hissed into it. "I'll be there as fast as I can!"

But it was not the voice of Stacy or even Beth.

"This is Mary Clare Echevarria." Alison could barely hear her above the background static. "I got your number from Liz. Marta wants to talk to you. It's important!"

Alison put a hand to her head, still careful to keep her face turned to the window. She had been taught very nice phone manners by her mother, or she would have hung up.

"Where did you find Kathy's purse?" Marta's voice was, if anything more broken up than Mary Clare's had been.

"What?" Horizon Air had begun to load the Pullman flight. The smaller airlines didn't use the tunnel which attached to the planes. Alison supposed they were too expensive. Their passengers walked directly across the tarmac and up a pull-away flight of stairs.

"That clutch you pushed through the mail slot!" Marta did not tack 'You asshole!' onto the end of the sentence, but Alison could still hear it. Better than the rest of what she was saying, as a matter of fact. Down on the tarmac Alison once again spotted Crescent, walking toward the Horizon Air plane. "I only hope it's not too late—!" Marta's voice was lost in a sea of static.

The phone went dead. Saved by the bell. Alison put the phone back in her pocket and then took it out again. She meant to cut the power, but before she could hit the button something outside caught her eye. A luggage cart had pulled up to the belly of the plane and two men in brown coveralls were transferring suitcases and boxes. And one other thing. The biggest damn bass case Alison had ever seen, the kind that was worth a couple of thousand dollars all by itself, according to Mary Clare. Well, that was odd. She'd never seen anything like that before in her life and now, within a couple of days, had she seen two, or was it really Kathy going someplace. Maybe Bernie had seen her here at the airport.

The phone rang again and, still looking out the window, she answered it.

"Where's Kathy?" demanded Marta, without identifying herself. The connection was a lot better this time.

"Well, I think she's out here at the airport, the same as me," replied Alison slowly, looking around. What was it that Bernie had said? That she had only seen Kathy one time and that was early one morning when she had come by for some clothes and music stuff. "I never would have guessed it was her apartment," she'd said and also, "I'd seen her in one of the fantasies." But Bad News had not performed in any of the fantasies. During the last one she had caused a fuss and then left, upset by the little girl and piano fantasy while Alison and Stacy were still fucking. Marta's voice was threatening to peter out again. Alison looked at the phone as if it allowed her to look at the woman.

"Do you see her?" Marta was asking in a voice that carried a curious mixture of apprehension and relief. Like she really wanted to believe what Alison said, but couldn't quite.

"No," Alison admitted. She stood and looked all around. The Pattys were gone, as were most of the people who had been sitting near her. They had boarded the plane into which the two men were trying to wrestle the bass. Odd, a bass fiddle even in a fancy case shouldn't be that heavy, should it? The only dyke, in fact, whom she had seen while in the airport with Bernie had been that woman in the beret, Crescent. Could it be that Bernie thought Crescent was Kathy all this time, having only seen her hostess once at home, early Saturday morning?

She watched as the passengers got on the plane, looking for Kathy. She saw Crescent get on board with the others but no Kathy. Why would Crescent be taking the bass?

Marta was still talking, but Alison could not grasp what she was saying. She was thinking of that argument she had overheard coming from the bathroom the first day. And she was also thinking of the way Marta had doubled over when she had picked up the clutch, Marta who had helped the police catch a killer and find a body buried twenty years because she was what *Circles* had termed 'reluctantly psychic.'

The metal staircase had been pulled away from the plane and the luggage door was shut and sealed. Alison was the last one left at the window—even loyal lovers and wives had decided there was no sense hanging on any longer. Marta was still talking—Alison could hear her voice, tinny and insistent, explaining.

"I think I get it," she said, breaking in. "I've got to check something."

"Hurry!" said Marta, as Alison snapped the phone shut and stuck it back in her pocket, trying to remember what she had done with the book that G-hey! had given her. It had been in her quiver at one point, but she thought she had transferred it to her daypack to show to Stacy. Her daypack was back in the van. Had she actually put it in, or had she just thought about putting it in? In spite of the fact that the Horizon Air flight was going to take at least three hours to get to Pullman, she began to trot.

There was some kind of big jam up at the metal detectors. It wasn't unusual for there to be a line on the way in, but usually you could walk right through on the way out. But there was some kind of altercation involving the airport police and five or six people dressed in the orange robes of the Hare Krishnas and the crowd leaving was almost as slow as the crowd going in. Alison shifted her weight from side to side impatiently. She thought she knew what Marta had wanted to tell her.

She looked across the short wall that separated the incoming passengers from the outgoing passengers and recoiled with a start. Standing almost directly opposite were the women of Livia's court. Most of them were turned away from her, their attention on the people going through the metal detector ahead of them. However, right in the middle of the group, two paces behind Livia, was fuckbaby. She was dressed nicely in clothes that fit her, carrying the fur coat over her arm. And she was looking directly at Alison. As the crowd ahead of her shifted she was able to move directly up to the wall.

"Nice party," she said to Alison. "That was a good idea, don't you think?" She got a pleased look on her face Alison had seen once before. She had been bad and she knew it and was happy about it.

The outgoing crowd began to move, sweeping Alison along with it, but for a moment she struggled to stay in place. Fuckbaby had set up the party? Alison remembered Liz's comments about Livia's credit cards, the way she had wondered aloud just how many women had rescued fuckbaby. So just what was she seeing? A battered woman who had gone happily back to her abuser or a mindfucker who had drawn Alison into her scene as a prop? She would probably never know. And what about the drugs that had gone missing from Livia's room? Was that just another tail twist from fuckbaby as she was walking out the door, or was it something much, much worse?

Out at the van, Alison threw the door open and began to root around for her pack. She was still carrying Bad News' mail, which she dropped onto the seat. Her daypack was in the mess on the floor and she zipped it open and dumped the contents on top of the mail. She had put the book in—in fact she had put in the whole envelope G-hey! had given her. She pulled out the book and fanned the pages, searching for the photo of Bad News. There it was. This time, though, she was not looking at Bad News. This time she was looking at the woman who was her mentor. Alison covered her hair with her hand. Okay, add ten years, forget the tattoos and the shaved head and she became Crescent. 'Veronica Simons' it said beneath the photo. Alison put the book down and stuck her hand into the envelope again. She looked at the registration list, the one with the real names and addresses. And there it was, about three-fourths of the way down.

She stood for a moment and then picked up Bad News' purse. Inside was the folded letter. She picked it up and smoothed it out. It was a letter, scrawled in handwriting so furious it was difficult to read. Alison skimmed the text, her eyes coming to rest on the last sentences.

"…and I believe there are monsters among us, lesbians who abuse and commit incest with the very children whom they should be protecting. I know, because I was the prey of such a woman…"

Carefully, Alison put the letter between the pages of the book. She closed the door of the van and walked around to the driver's side. She didn't need to hurry. Veronica Simons was in the air and there was no way to bring the plane down. As Alison pulled out of the parking garage, fumbling in her pocket for change for the tollbooth, she wondered just how one asked for the number of Security at the Pullman airport.

Chapter Seventeen

The story was in the Pullman paper the next day and it was weird enough that the *Rocky Mountain News* had noticed the Denver connection, snatched it off the wires and shoved it in the 'A' section. The *Post* had missed it somehow—their front-page story was a rehashing of the JonBenet Ramsey case. Stacy brought her own copy of the *News* to the Merc. There were papers there—the Merc was reader-friendly—but people were always walking out with them and this story was something they both wanted to see. Stacy, of course, had been filled in on everything the moment Alison had returned from the last run to the airport.

"You're a genius," Stacy said, looking up from the article.

Alison smiled, savoring once again the approval of the woman she loved. She would have run right out on the tarmac and shot out the plane's tire if that had been what it took to change her status from World's Biggest Butthead to Hero. Luckily, all it had taken was one anonymous phone call.

Their waitress, an incredibly thin teenager who seemed to be wearing her underclothing on the outside, came by and politely took their order. She commented on the weather and they all agreed that spring was good. The Mercury Cafe did not serve Diet Pepsi, which everybody knew. Alison had two cold cans in her daypack. Marilyn didn't mind if you did artificial sweeteners to yourself, she just didn't want to be part of it.

"She's sure as hell never going to spill the beans," said Stacy, popping the top on her can and then holding a page of the paper up to her face to look at the photograph. "It's bad enough to be exposed as a pedophile—if she mentions Wildfire the press is going to have a fucking field day."

Alison nodded, hoping Stacy was right. Any good lawyer, she supposed, would advise Veronica Simons to keep quiet about the s/m part of her life. If she even told her lawyer about it.

"Hey, look!" Stacy waved.

Alison's heart dropped. Mary Clare had just walked through the door. Oh, dammit, she didn't want to see Marta again like this!

But instead of Marta, Liz was following close on Mary Clare's heels. They saw the wave and came over to the table. Liz had her own copy of the paper tucked under her arm. "Damn!" she said, pulling up a chair without being asked. "What do you think of that! I told you…" she started to say to Alison, but then stopped with a pained look on her face as Stacy pinched her under the table. Alison assumed she knew everything Stacy knew and it looked like Mary Clare had been OK'd for top priority clearance too. "I mean, who would have thought? The paper said she had that body packed in there for quite a while! And she just kept on coming to workshops like nothing was wrong!"

"Christmas in the trenches—" said Mary Clare to Alison and then "—she didn't want to draw attention to herself by changing her reservation or leaving early, I'll bet. Or maybe she had the kind of ticket you can't change. God, what a nightmare—trying to get rid of a body in a town you don't know! Is that them?" she asked, looking at Stacy's paper and pointing to the old photo of Bad News and her teacher in front of the piano, holding the loving cup between them.

"Yeah," said Alison. "That's the one that was in the book." She looked at Mary Clare questioningly and she nodded. She knew about the book. "I don't know how they got a copy."

Stacy put the paper on the table and ran her finger down the column. "It says she taught in the music department at the University of Washington."

"And I'll bet the board of trustees would have loved hearing Kathy's side of that story," said Liz. "I'll bet that photo was right up on Veronica's office wall and she talked about it like she was a hero. Must have been quite a little jolt for her to have run into her old student here!"

"And you know what's sad?" asked Mary Clare.

"It's all sad," said Alison. "That an older woman preyed on a child and no one stepped in, that ten years later Veronica still thought she was right in what she'd done. Can you imagine that! Can you imagine being confronted by someone you'd sexually abused as a child and then going ahead with that fantasy like nothing had happened?"

"It was like Livia hiring you and paying you all that money," said Stacy unexpectedly.

Everyone looked at her.

"No, really," she insisted. "If Livia had felt bad or remorseful for anything she had done, then she wouldn't have hired Alison. She suspected the person she said was blackmailing her was…" She paused, looking around for help as to which name she should use.

"Falcon," said Liz and Alison together.

"She would have suspected it was connected with Falcon and just blown it off. But she was so convinced she was right that she had to hire Alison. Or somebody. It was like a show of faith. It was something an innocent person couldn't have failed to do. Not doing anything would have meant she was doubting her own conviction."

"So," said Alison slowly, trying to get it all clear in her mind. She thought back to the exchange she had witnessed between Bad News and their waitress on Friday night. It seemed safe—particularly remembering the snippet of conversation she had heard between the two young women—to assume Bad News had been having dinner with Scar and Veronica in order to confront her old teacher about the terrible harm she had done. "So if Veronica had backed out of the fantasy…"

"It would have been just like saying she had been wrong. And once you take responsibility…" Stacy shrugged, "then there's all kinds of shit that can happen. Saying sorry usually isn't enough."

"I wish Kathy hadn't dicked around confiding in Scar," said Liz with a frown. "Maybe I could have gotten her a cash settlement, too."

"Kathy wouldn't have taken it," said Mary Clare, shaking her head. "That's what I was trying to say. She told me about the whole thing. Not using names or specifics. I mean, we were kind of friends, but she was really closed-mouthed and private. Just that she had been betrayed by a woman she trusted. I thought it was probably incest and didn't push to hear more—you can only tell that when you're ready to tell that. But she was very bitter and she was very angry. She wouldn't have backed off for money. Even from the little bit we talked about—she couldn't have been paid off. She would have wanted to expose Veronica and bring her down."

"Then why didn't she?" said Liz. "If she was that angry, why didn't she do it before?"

"Maybe she didn't know where Veronica was," guessed Alison. "Because Veronica ran. Some time after she'd been interviewed for that book I'll bet she broke away and disappeared. Even if Veronica didn't want to admit it was wrong, she knew it was wrong and she got away as soon as she could. That interview could have been done as long as ten years ago. It's hard to put together a book like that—the author could have written that part and then put it in a drawer while she went back to school or had a baby. And by the time Kathy had figured out she wasn't the one who would be blamed for what had happened between her and Veronica, Veronica could have dropped out of sight herself. She could have just gotten a new job and moved. That's happened to me—I've lost touch with old friends and never knew where they'd gone or why, and all that took was six months of not writing."

"The authorities found the body because they'd had a tip someone was smuggling drugs in the bass case," said Liz, looking at the article. "Hmm. Wonder how that happened." She looked at Alison, who smiled.

"If I had a body, I'd make Liz dig up the floor of her basement and put it there," said Stacy. "That's the whole point of having a basement."

Liz looked resigned and Alison made a mental note, just in case Stacy ever did go off the deep end. She looked again at the photo—a young, beautiful teenager and her older teacher, both beaming from behind a huge gold trophy with a piano on top. 'There are monsters among us,' Bad News had written in the letter in her purse and for her the monster was the woman who had not only nurtured her musical talent but had also seduced her at age fourteen. The imbalance of power, the paranoia and fear which had been carefully instilled in the teenager had, she had written to the Wildfire committee, damaged her for life. Only through the s/m community had she been able to find occasional sexual pleasure and even that was sullied by a past she could not confront. Or not, at least, until fate had brought Veronica Simons to Denver and a kind of arrogance, a conviction that she had not been wrong had made her go ahead with her fantasy. Liz had been right and Dana wrong. It had not been about fantasy. It had been about something true and terrible and seeing her story on stage billed as erotic entertainment had enraged Bad News. Filled with a righteous fury and backed by Scar she had gone to Livia's party to confront the woman who used to be her teacher. And she must have told her she was going to tell the world."

"That must have been what Scar was trying to tell you," said Liz, still looking at the story.

"Thank you," said Alison. "Please make me feel bad. And I had a chance to rescue Scar as well. Don't forget to put that in." She thought with resentment of the choice she had made, to turn her back on Scar so she could take fuckbaby to Marta's, rescuing a woman who had one way or another chosen to go right back to where she had been before.

"How could you know?" asked Stacy. "How could any of us know?" She pointed to the story again. "It says that she drugged Kathy."

"Livia's drug," said Alison. "That must have been why no one got it at the party. Everybody who'd ever been around her knew Livia had drugs. It probably wasn't hard to lift them. Crescent must have drugged Scar too—that's why I thought she was drunk, even though she'd been sober for ten years. The light rail accident certainly was inspired—when I saw her she was barely walking. I'll bet all Crescent had to do was escort her, then point her in the right direction when she saw the light rail coming. Hell, she probably thought Scar was staying at the Melbourne like everyone else seems to have thought."

"Oh, Scar didn't have a drinking problem," said Liz scornfully. "She just went to AA so she'd have a new audience."

Everyone looked at her.

"Oh, I know she's dead," said Liz. "And I'm sorry. But she's a liar! Even dead she's a liar! She could have told you at any time what was going on! She could have come to any of us! But she decided to orchestrate peace talks and confrontations. She knew too much for her own good. Veronica had no choice but to silence her too."

"You gonna call the police and get them to do an autopsy on Scar?" Mary Clare finally asked Alison.

"Nope—what evidence do we have? All we have is what we think happened. But the police have concrete evidence with regard to Kathy—they caught Veronica Simons with a body in her luggage—she's not going to walk. If we tried to explain our theory all we'd do is get Wildfire involved in a lot of bad publicity for nothing. And that would hurt the rest of us."

Stacy raised her glass and they all clinked. "To never doing this again," she said.

"To never doing anything again," said Alison. She was beginning to think that Stacy was right about attracting bodies, in which case the city should pay her a salary just to stay in her own little house.

"To policing our own community," said Liz.

"To Kathy Corbeit," said Mary Clare. "One of the young dykes who was going to change the world."

There was nothing anyone could think to say after that. They divided the papers and ordered breakfast and more coffee and settled in to read about the Rockies and JonBenet and what the weather was going to be like the next couple of days. Alison looked up only one time and then she quickly looked back down again, because Mary Clare was very butch and did not think she would want her to see the tears trickling down her cheeks.